T0196490

THE SAINT JAMES CONSPIRACY

JESSICA MURPHY

THE SAINT JAMES CONSPIRACY

iUniverse books may be ordered through booksellers or by contacting:

iUniverse
1663 Liberty Drive
Bloomington, IN 47403
www.iuniverse.com
1-800-Authors (1-800-288-4677)

ISBN: 978-1-5320-1760-5 (sc)
ISBN: 978-1-5320-1762-9 (hc)
ISBN: 978-1-5320-1761-2 (e)

Library of Congress Control Number: 2017904182

Print information available on the last page.

iUniverse rev. date: 05/09/2017

PROLOGUE

JUDAEA 36 A.D.

Over time they had learned that meetings of thirteen men and a few women were not conducive to consensus on any plan of action. So now only seven of them met. They sprawled casually on various divans, a tray of food and carafes of water and wine set amongst them on a rug-draped stool. Lady Mary oiled the feet of their leader, gently rubbing the aromatic balm into the callouses caused by many hours of tramping dry and dusty roads, in roughly-made sandals. Camel leather wore well but was stiff, biting into heels and toes alike. She had offered to buy him finer calfskin shoes, but he, of course, with a smile, had refused.

"The scriptures predict that the Messiah will be put to death in Judaea," their leader said. "We know the time is close."

"But is it so close that we must ensure that it occurs on the day of the eclipse? "Peter asked, and looked amongst them all, his eyes showing concern. "That is predicted to be in only a few days. Can we not wait for another?"

The leader shook his head. "If only such events were less rare. Then perhaps we could wait." He extended his hand to offer the food to his friends. He himself ate a few dried grapes. "And do not bruit about the day of the eclipse in the streets or taverns. We are lucky the priests here have lost the knowledge of prediction of such events. Our friends in the east have managed to keep the date secret; so must we."

The men nodded sadly; the woman bent her head to better hide the first glint of tears.

Having eaten only lightly, and drunk of the water deeply, their leader said "I would sleep now." He rose and Lady Mary draped his red woollen cloak over his shoulders and the two of them went into their private sleeping chamber, leaving the others in the large main room. They could see how thin his body had become, how almost ethereal his skin; the last few months had depleted him, body and soul.

"We will be quiet," said Judas. "You need your sleep." As one, the men shifted inward, bending their heads towards each other in a confidential way.

James scratched at his chin; until recently he had been clean shaven, and was not yet used to his now luxuriant dark beard. It made him look more like his brother than ever he had before. "You know I am ready to play my part."

"My God. Why does anyone of us have to do that?" moaned Peter.

The oldest man amongst them, James the Elder, so nicknamed to differentiate him from the brother, was white haired, tall, and usually bestaffed; every inch the image of a raging patriarch. He growled "We have gone over this. Over and over. The Master wants to fulfill the scriptures."

Peter snorted. "Heaven knows there are enough other scriptures to choose from. Why choose that one?"

"Because he believes."

"But if we carry out our plan, then the scripture is proven false, and if we know it to be false, why would we allow him to follow it to destruction?"

The older James leaned back, drank some wine, and exhaled deeply. "Perhaps what we are planning is exactly as written. The scripture says that: 'The man the Jews believe to be the Son of God will be put to death by the governor of Judaea.' And that will be what happens. They will all believe. Good thing the Word is silent on whether or not we all believe." He chuckled. James was famous—or infamous—for his joking, which was often in bad taste. How could he make fun tonight, about this?

"To work, gentlemen," said Judas. "None of us wants to do this, but we have gone over and over the plan. I particularly hate my part." He paused to look at the younger James. "But it is not as bad as some. Speaking of parts, is Caius ready? He has his men selected?"

Simon spoke up. "He is. And he has." Simon was particularly short spoken. If four words would suffice, he would find a way to use two. But his friendship with the centurion of the local Roman patrol made him a crucial player in the drama. "His son, a cadet in the patrol, will be with Caius. The other soldier can be depended upon to pass out over a flagon of wine, and never know what happened."

"But he will of course swear he was sober and alert all night?" sneered Peter.

"Of course. Why would Caius choose him, otherwise?" replied Simon softly. He personally did not like Peter. Never had. Those blond good looks, that sense of entitlement to a special place in the heart of the leader, his presumption that he would be the one to lead them, later.

They continued to eat and drink sparingly, and mostly in silence.

Then young James said "Well, as we are all expected at the temple tomorrow, and at our best for tomorrow night's supper, and we still have some plans to put into place, I suggest we get our rest. The next week is going to be difficult."

And so the conspiracy continued.

CHAPTER 1

One year ago. Innescarrig, Ireland

"Yes, that is it. Of course. It was here all the time." He leaned back, away from the computer screen. "It was here all the time, and no one could see it." He got up, walked across to the window of his office, and looked out at his garden, its stone wall, and the view of Kinsale Bay far below. He never tired of his view over the village of Innescarrig, on the southern shores of the bay, and never ever looked out from his office without a grateful thought. He mused aloud "No one could see it, and no one will ever believe it."

Mackellan Kirby watched the garden shadows lengthen, then returned to his desk, and methodically timed out of the program and shut down his computer. The Committee had generously allowed him unrestricted access to the hundreds of documents, and fragments of documents, that it had been entrusted with, and he respectfully adhered to the Committee's required access protocol. Including the members of the Committee there were less than a hundred people around the globe—scholars of various disciplines—who had been granted access to the computer images of the Quhram hoard, the so called Dead Sea Scrolls. And he was not about to lose that privilege.

His eyes ached. Even with glasses with lenses coloured to lessen the strain of staring at a computer screen, reading the faded and cramped script of Aremaic—technically Jewish Palestinian

Aremaic—and simultaneously translating into modern English, was, he thought for perhaps the thousandth time, not a job for a senior citizen. "Only barely a senior citizen," he harrumphed to himself. And wandered off to his kitchen to see what he could find for dinner.

CHAPTER 2

SEATTLE, WASHINGTON

The tall red haired woman ran, elegantly in spite of her five inch heels, up to a fellow carrot-top, and kissed him energetically. The faces of a few of the prospective travellers in the gate fell noticeably; the hope that she might have been travelling alone, and perhaps seated in an adjacent seat for the eight hour flight, falling with a thud.

She did not notice the effect she had on her public—she never did.

"Joe," she grinned. "It has been way too long. I thought we might not recognize each other," she teased.

The man she was embracing smiled back and gently removed her hands from behind his neck. Public displays of affection embarrassed him, especially when he was involved.

"Fiona," he said. "Sure, I'll always recognize you, even when that mop of yours turns to the purest white." He held her hands in front of him, and realized how happy it made him just to see her.

In one smooth motion she turned to walk with him, her hand at his elbow, her shoulder slightly stooped to coordinate their heights. "That won't happen, not as long as there is Clairol in the world." She continued gaily "And I have invested heavily, just to be sure."

Fiona guided her cousin—for that is their relationship—through to the miniscule bar located near their flight gate. Over a beer for him and a *pinot grigio* for her, they started the inevitable 'catch up' that fond, but too often distant, relatives indulge in.

"How is work?" Joe asked his cousin. "Whatever it is that you do?" The rise in his voice made the statement into a question. But she easily evaded it.

"Oh, same old same old. I am more interested in how 'domestic bliss' is." She grinned irrepressibly. "And why the lovely Sonia and the gorgeous Marsha are not with you."

Joe sighed. He and his long-time girlfriend had begun living together a year and a half ago. Though not yet married they were still enjoying the honeymoon, even with an eight-month old daughter making sleeping in difficult and life, in general, incredible. "I wish they could have come, but Sonia's work is at a bit of a crucial stage." Sonia Pracek, PhD. in some awful branch of physics that Fiona could never quite get straight, was technically a university lecturer, but had been seconded to a government research project over a year ago. At least the government facility was located in their home city of Seattle. Her appointment meant that she did not have to move, but it had certainly focussed their attention on the fact that their work could separate them at any time. Hence the decision to start a family when they did have some time together. "Sonia is wonderful. And Marsha is a doll. You've only seen her as a new-born. You must get out to see her."

"I am sorry, Joe. I keep meaning to." It was hard to explain that her job as a fashion tabloid correspondent was actually important. As cover it was wonderful; as an excuse it failed on all points.

He sighed again. "Marsha has an asthma condition. She should grow out of it. Normal, apparently. But it means flying for a year or two is out." He smiled. "Sonia has really changed my life."

Fiona laughed. "As I am sure you have changed hers. All for the better, in both cases." Her enthusiasm was genuine. She enjoyed the time she had managed to spend with both Joe and Sonia, although limited by her own work schedule. "I was just thinking—I don't get to spend enough time with you, or you three, now. But I did manage to book off three weeks...and let them know that I will not respond to any requests for an early return." She frowned.

"Yeah, I coordinated my return flight with yours. But I might have to sneak in a few on-line hours here and there," her cousin responded. "I wonder what it is Uncle Mack needs us for."

Later, at some thirty-five thousand feet, hurtling over some ice-covered part of northern Canada in BA Flight 3405, the cousins prepared themselves for the dinner service.

Fiona grinned. "You know, I have a friend who is a pilot. On the jumbos apparently they refer to the passengers as 'cattle', and talk with the cabin crew about the 'cattle' being 'fed and bedded'. And the chicken dinner offering is known as 'grey matter in a batter'."

Turning off his laptop, and dropping his tray table, Joe responded. "I noticed our vegetarian choice tonight is the inevitable *pasta prima vera*. Which is never 'vera prima', if you know what I mean? And, of course, your chicken."

Fiona shifted in her seat beside him. "Yeah, but then, they have to stick to the standards, don't they? Who would choose an entre of 'Liver with a Quiver'?"

"Or 'Seriously Limp Shrimp'," her cousin returned immediately.

"Or 'Sham Lamb'."

The bantering continued, like a well-matched game of badminton, the shuttlecock of really disgusting sounding foods gently batted back and forth. The cousins had always played games like this.

After a tasty meal of Salmon Wellington—the aircraft had been provisioned in Seattle, of course—and an elegant sufficiency, as their Uncle Mack always said, of a fine Californian Pinot Noir, the two travellers dimmed their reading lights and prepared to quietly continue the flight, and hopefully, to get some sleep.

"Really Scary Calamari," Joe said quietly.

Fiona groaned then responded with, "Virgin Sturgeon."

"I don't get...."

Then she laughed. "It's so gross, it's never been tried."

"You win," her cousin conceded. "And goodnight."

The British Airways flight landed at Glasgow International at 10:00 am local time; they had travelled one-third of the way around the globe in under nine hours, and because of time zones, had lost a further eight hours. Both cousins had that glazed 'I've travelled all night' look so common in international airport arrivals halls.

An hour later, on their Aer Lingus flight to Cork, the good weather allowed them to watch the islands and mountains of southwestern Scotland unfold below them, before clouds over the North Sea obscured their view. As the altitude of the mid-sized jet decreased, they caught glimpses of the incredible green glow of Ireland, truly the emerald isle. Because they rise directly from sea-level, the off-shore island mountains loom larger than would be supposed from their rather meagre heights. But somehow a one thousand foot Irish tor, rimmed with rocky shores, and crashing seas, is always more awe inspiring than a ten thousand foot peak in a mountain range that begins at already high ground, such as the Rocky Mountains of the American west. They could even discern sea birds, wheeling in to their nests on the cliffs. Fiona pointed out the bay-cum-river that runs up to Cork, just as their pilot announced their descent.

Cork is a provincial airport. They were soon cleared by a rather bored customs officer, then went to meet their rental car.

"I'll drive," offered Fiona. "I've driven on the left before."

"When? Where?" asked Joe. He stowed their bags in the car trunk—thanking the gods that Fiona knew how to pack lightly, then clambered into the passenger seat. He was secretly happy to not have to taunt his night-flight tired brain with the conundrum of left-hand driving.

Fiona moved the little Ford easily through the airport roads and onto the R600, heading south. "Oh, in England, a year or so ago," she said. "But don't worry; it comes back to you."

CHAPTER 3

INNESCARRIG, IRELAND

He had slept badly—as he mostly did now—when the shrill of the telephone wakened him.

"What idiot would be calling at this time?" he muttered, then spoke in his normal professorial tones into the receiver. "Cliffside. Kirby here."

"Hi Mack. Sorry to be calling you so early." It was his friend and favourite publican Jim Grady, owner of Innescarrig House. "But you did say as I should be calling if ever I thought I should."

God, why did he have to talk like an Irishman—everyone knew he was English. Awake and alert now, Mackellan said "That is fine, Jim. What is it?"

"A guest. Late last night. Over a whiskey, which I think he ordered just to be able to talk to me, because he did not seem to know how to enjoy it."

"Jim."

"Yes. Anyway he asks about you. I go all innocent—says I don't know you."

"Did he buy that?"

"No, he did not. Just looked at me, like. You know, like he knew I was lying. Anyway, he is driving a Land Rover, dark green, registration 11-D-122911. Registered here as Martin Froese, booked for three more nights. Hasn't had breakfast yet."

As Kirby noted the plate number he grinned. Once Jim got over his jolly Irish publican persona he reverted easily to himself— retired military.

Grady continued. "He is six one, fifteen stone, sandy hair, big ugly hatchet of a nose, lifeless eyes. Dressed for birdwatcher hiking. You know, walking boots but not the good ones and not broken in. His Land Rover is locked and he's got some stuff stowed in there." He paused, then said "I didn't want to break in, just in case someone was enjoying the view of our car park."

Kirby laughed. "Thanks Jim. One more thing. Did you get your famous 'prickling of your scalp' when you talked to this fellow?"

"Prickling?" Jim reverted to his publican bonhomie. "Sure, I felt like I was being acupunctured by amateurs, a whole lot of 'em."

"I get it. And thanks." Kirby pressed 'End' and replaced the receiver on its stand. He did not know if 'acupuncture' could be a verb, but he did get it. "So, I guess this means my day is all planned out."

Kirby dragged himself from bed, perfunctorily showered,—he skipped shaving for once, dressed and went downstairs for coffee. He looked out at the view of still-sleeping Innescarrig, a low mist hiding in the dips and dales of the countryside, the sun touching the tops of the hills with that early morning light known as alpenglow. "So peaceful," he spoke aloud. "I hope I haven't ruined everything."

When his daily, Mary Todd, arrived at eight o'clock she was surprised to see that breakfast was not only over, but reduced to clean dishes drying in the rack.

"The children will be arriving late tomorrow," he said. "I want the east room ready for Fiona, you know, fresh flowers or something. And I want Joe in the north room."

Mary looked at him strangely. She knew when his niece and nephew were arriving, and the rooms were ready. "Won't you be here to greet them?" she asked.

"Of course I will, I just want things ready," he muttered, and abruptly left the kitchen to Mary's care.

Kirby went to his office and opened a laptop computer. He pulled up a split screen of views from eight closed circuit cameras. They were movement activated, and the only recordings were of a doe and her fawns nibbling his roses and of a no-doubt tipsy old fellow who had knocked his bicycle into the iron Cliffside gates. He was known to Kirby, and posed no threat, at least to anyone not using the road when he was heading home from Grady's pub. Kirby closed down the computer and placed it in a backpack.

The surveillance system was relatively new, and the most clandestine that money could buy. When the installation had been completed the technician had challenged Kirby to spot the cameras. Although he knew approximately where they would be—because every part of the house and its accesses had to be covered—Mackellan could not see even one. They were artfully concealed, in a birdhouse, in the pedestal of a bird bath, in the small pigeon cote that rose above the barn roof, not one was visible to even the most experienced and prying of eyes. The premium he had paid for the system and its installation was worth every penny, well, Euro, Kirby mentally amended. The system was also self-contained. Because it was tracked only by Mackellan's laptop, which was never opened to either the internet or his e-mail account, it was safe from prying, spying and assorted malware.

Kirby made a long-distance call, spoke for a minute then gave the car registration number that Grady had given him. "If you don't mind, I will wait." After a few minutes of silence, he spoke again. "Registered to Manresa? Really? Thank you." Wondering why a vehicle registered to the Dublin Jesuit Centre of Spirituality was in Innescarrig, Kirby wandered about his office, placing various items into the backpack. Then to the gunroom. Then to the basement. Common to most eighteenth century houses, the lower floor was sub-ground level, the kitchen being entered down a short flight of stairs. "Bloody inconvenient," thought Mack, when he bought Cliffside, as it meant all deliveries had to be dragged down the stairs, and all outgoing compost and trash had to be lugged up. He solved that problem by converting the large morning room, at the back of the house, into the kitchen. The old kitchen was closed off from the exterior and was totally refurbished as a wine cellar. Mack liked to keep a good cellar. The actual pre-existing wine cellar and subterranean storage rooms became something else.

CHAPTER 4

INNESCARRIG, IRELAND

The drive had gone well, but Fiona was nonetheless glad to reach the seaside town of Innescarrig. She had been feeling a slight anxiety since she had tried to telephone Uncle Mack on his cell phone. It had gone straight to voice-mail, and her call had not been returned. When she telephoned his land line, his message was that he had gone to Cork for a few days, and could be reached at the Crompton Arms. She thought that was a very strange message to leave on a telephone. And why had he left when she and Joe were expected?

She took the turn onto Cliffside Drive, and soon saw the gates of Cliffside House. The eighteenth century gates, intricately patterned wrought-iron hung from massive stone columns, opened welcomingly, via a very twenty-first century computerized system.

"Wake up, Joe." She prodded her companion. "We are here."

She directed the little Ford through the gates, along the gravelled drive, and around three-quarters of the house itself to the grand porte-cochere. Cliffside House had its back to its own entrance way so that the main rooms, at the front of the house, faced out towards the bay and the town below. Fiona shared her Uncle Mack's enjoyment of that glorious view, but could not help but think what a curious man the builder of the house must have been, to situate his home for the view, in a century when the convenience and security of being close to the road was paramount, and most homes were built with their front doors merely feet—and sometimes, in the villages themselves—inches from the roadways.

She got out, stretched, and smiled. It felt so good to be back at Cliffside. Mackellan Kirby had bought it eight years earlier, and she had only been able to visit once before. Joe, groggy but awake, climbed out stiffly. He looked around. "Wow." His head swivelled, from the sea view to the stone and stucco manor house, the massive double doors opening on to a short broad flight of stone steps.

"Wow can wait," said Fiona shortly, as she opened the trunk, and began retrieving luggage. "I am worried about Uncle Mack." Joe had been asleep when she had phoned Kirby, and Fiona had not had time to discuss the calls with him. "There is something wrong... Oh, there you are Mary," she said loudly and cheerfully. Mary had opened the doors, and was smiling broadly. She liked Fiona, from her previous visit. No spoiled 'I don't drink tea, only Starbucks' from this young American, and Fiona had kept her own bedroom in immaculate order. Mary appreciated such things.

"Mary, this is my cousin Joe O'Connor; Joe, Mary Todd," Fiona made the introductions. "Mary is Uncle Mack's housekeeper."

"Daily," corrected Mary, as she shook Joe's proffered hand.

Fiona continued unabashed. "Who does more in her four 'daily' hours than most people would do all day and night." She hugged Mary fondly. "But where is Uncle Mack?"

Mary tried unsuccessfully to take a bag from Joe. "So strange," she said. "He was so full of plans for your visit here. Then suddenly he needs to go to Cork. But he should be letting us know when he plans to get back, soon enough." Fiona thought it stranger still that, if he was already in Cork, he had not let her or Joe know, as they could have gone straight to his hotel from the Cork airport, instead of driving to Cliffside.

Mary led them into the main hall, "Miss Fiona, Mr. Kirby wants you in the east room. You know the one?" Fiona nodded. "And you, Mr. O'Connor..." she continued.

"Please call me Joe," he interrupted her with a smile.

"Of course, sir. Your uncle wants you in the north room. I will show you up."

Fiona was already on the shining oak staircase. "Don't worry about us, Mary. Come on Joe, let's drop our bags, and I will take you exploring."

Fiona led the way down the upper hall, to a set of double doors. "By the way, I am giving up this suite, so you can enjoy the sunrise over the bay." She was, of course, referring to the East Room. "The rooms make no difference to me—in fact, I think my shower is larger—and really, the dawn is glorious from here." She dropped her bags by the door, then went to open the curtains. A set of ten foot high French doors opened onto a balcony, beyond which shone the ruffled water of Kinsale Bay. "Which means you have to be up by then, but you should be able to handle that, given how long you have already slept today." She retrieved her luggage. "I am down the hall to your right, last door on the right." With her usual almost hyper energy, Fiona swept out. "I'll be back soon. We need to talk."

Within five minutes Fiona knocked on Joe's door, peremptorily entered and started without preamble. "I am worried about Uncle Mack." she said.

"Yeah, I noticed," said Joe, still staring out at the sea. "Your face, earlier, when Mary told us where he was. You were thinking, something."

Fiona made a mental note to remember who she was dealing with. She prided herself on her usual air-headed exuberant persona but Joe was the one person who had always been able to see through that. "Here," she said, handing her cell phone to her cousin. "I've called Uncle Mack's land line. And I want you to listen to the recording."

"Won't Mary answer?"

"No one but Uncle Mack answers this phone. Even when he isn't here, and Mary is."

"Okay." He took the phone from her, and listened, as the message Fiona had heard earlier was replayed. "I see what you mean. Bit weird, a message like that. For security reasons, most people don't say they are away." He pressed 'End' and returned the phone to Fiona. "And why specify his hotel?"

"Exactly." Fiona threw herself into an armchair. "Something is definitely wrong."

CHAPTER 5

INNESCARRIG, IRELAND

Fiona came awake, completely and silently; no annoyed sigh or twitch of the bedclothes announced her sudden consciousness. She lifted her pillow slightly, and slid her hand under it, to the scabbard of the American hunting knife she slept with. Then moving only her eyes, she looked into the darkness of her bedroom. There was ambient light, as there almost always is even on moonless nights, and her eyes adjusted quickly to the tones of grey and darker grey.

Then, there, in the corner near the curtains of the French windows, the greyness became a widening black hole. Fiona immediately processed: the moving straight edge of the yawning blackness meant a door was being opened. Unladylike or not, Fiona snored, and under cover of the rude noise, slipped from the bed to the floor. There, she snored again, and cut it off, as good sleepers do naturally. Her pyjamas were dark, blending well with the deep burgundy of the room's carpet. She tossed her hair across her face—her skin was too fair to go unnoticed in even the darkest room. Then, she waited.

The intruder was not good at his work. He almost stumbled when his feet touched the carpet, then, as he approached her side of the bed, he hesitated. She saw his hand reach out to where she had been lying.

Then she had him. She rose up, smashed him into the bed onto his outstretched arm, grabbed his other arm and twisted it up behind his back with her left arm, and pressed the blade of her Bowie knife against his throat with her right hand.

"Okay, you son of a bitch," Fiona snarled through her adrenaline rush. "Tell me what you're doing, or bleed."

A muffled grumble came from her captive. Then, she noticed his aftershave, a distinctively masculine mixture of sandalwood and bergamot. "Uncle Mack?"

She slowly released pressure on her victim's throat, in order to let him speak.

"Holy Mary Mother of Jesus..." he began, still muffled by the bedclothes.

"Oh, Uncle Mack. It is you," Fiona said breathlessly. "But how was I to know?" she added defensively. "You know better than to enter a lady's bedroom," she paused to think, "through the wall!" She released his painfully bent arm and removed her knife from his throat. Then helped him to stand.

"May I turn on a light? Or is this visit a secret?"

Mackellan turned to sit on the bed, alternately rubbing his shoulder and his throat. "Of course it's secret, you mulligan." Fiona was very glad to hear him use his pet name for her. "Why else would it be past midnight and dark as the witches' Sabbath when I come through, as you said, the wall? Ooh, that butcher's blade really is too sharp." He wiped at a droplet of blood from near his left earlobe. In the still impenetrable darkness Fiona bent to give her uncle a kiss on the cheek.

She sat beside him on the bed. "So what is going on?"

"Why are you here?" he retorted.

"We've come to visit; you invited us."

"No, no," he said. "Why are you here? In this room? I specifically instructed Mary to give you the east room, and this one to Joe."

"That's easy," she said brightly. "Joe has never seen the sunrise over Kinsale Bay, and the view is much better from his room."

Her uncle shook his head, which she could feel but not quite see.

"I should have known. I plan and I plan, but something as simple as the sunrise fouls me up. Well, at least you didn't kill me. For that I suppose I must be grateful.

Fiona nodded. Other men had dared to enter her rooms, in various cities, in various circumstances, and had not been so lucky. And her Uncle Mack knew that. "So, again, what is going on?"

Ten minutes later, Mackellan Kirby and his young relatives were deep below Cliffside, in the original cellars of the house. Fiona had gone to waken Joe, ensure him she was not dreaming, and hurry him back to her room. There, Mack locked Fiona's hall door, then led his charges to the corner of the room and through to a landing behind the corner of the room.

"Wait on the landing, and for god's sake don't fall down the stairs. I have to close the door before we can turn on a light," he had instructed. Then, with the staircase door closed, to again form a part of the room's wainscoted panelling, Mack turned on a flashlight, and shone it down a steep but very serviceable staircase. "We will remain silent until we get to the cellars."

The staircase ended at what Fiona recognized as the butler's pantry just outside the original kitchens. They passed into what was now a wine cellar, and then down into the old cellars of the house. They were now in a room warm with electric heat and thick stone walls, decorated as an office-cum-lounge-cum-bolthole, complete with an array of electronics. Next door, Mack told them, there was a functional kitchenette, a bathroom and a room with bunk beds.

"What is this?" asked Joe, as he tried but failed to make sense of the last ten minutes.

"It's the original wine cellar," said Mack. "I still keep a good supply here. I think a nice Blackman's Port would sit well, right now. Not too acidic on an empty stomach, but rich enough to help you sleep when once you are back in your beds." He proceeded to set out a tray with three crystal glasses and a dusty bottle, poured for them all, and sat in the lounge area of the room.

Their Uncle Mack had always been an enigma. To Joe and

Fiona he was the exotic European relative; half Scottish, half Irish, the one who visited rarely but most memorably; the one who always remembered their birthdays with wonderful mail-order gifts which arrived on time every time; the only adult relative they could discuss their parents with, and know that their complaints would never ever get back to their families. They knew he was a Professor Emeritus of Ancient Religious Studies, having taught for many years at the prestigious University of Edinburgh. On his retirement he had appeared to keep very busy, always sojourning off to the most obscure sites to investigate, dig up, and authenticate various bits of religious paraphernalia. He was a Greek and Latin scholar, he was conversant with various Mideast dialects, and he had at one time served with distinction in the British SAS—Fiona had once discovered a Distinguished Service Medal in a desk drawer, with the commendation letter attached. She had been given severe hell for that indiscretion; that medal never saw the light of day, and Fiona always wondered why the date on the letter was so recent, years after Kirby had resigned his commission in the British army.

He typified the retired academic, even to the point of wearing tweed jackets with leather elbow patches. (Mary complained that elbow patches were getting hard to find; Kirby told her to cut them out of a perfectly good leather jacket). He was fastidious in his habits, kept his still full head of hair regularly trimmed, sported a thin mustache, which he absentmindedly stroked in a 'Mothers—lock up your daughters' silent-movie villain sort of way, that always got Fiona choking with laughter. He enjoyed his groceries, as they say, and equally so his beer, wine and assorted liqueurs, but maintained a healthy trimness through regular and long country walks. He was, to all appearances at least, the quintessential retired gentleman, with leisure and money to spare, and academic interests aplenty. He was the kind of man every local society wanted on its board of directors; he sat on none. Every aspiring hostess wanted him on her dinner party guest list; he almost always made his excuses. And, worst and perhaps most dangerous of all, local widows of a certain age tried to entice him with home baking, which apparently was no bother at all to drop by, in person. Mary had standing instructions to meet these women, divest them of their food offerings, explain that Professor Kirby was not available and then send each one a floral offering and a Thank You note 'signed' by Kirby. (At times Kirby thought he should buy shares in the local florist shop.) But the baking was usually quite exceptional.

Now he sheepishly faced his young relatives.

"What is going on, Uncle Mack?" With that one question Joe managed to sound concerned, confused and slightly miffed. He did not like being awakened at one a.m. by a relative who was supposed to be eighty miles away, not carousing through secret staircases and scaring the hell out of people.

Mack started with the easy answers. "This house was built in the late 1700's; it was never a great house, just a very nice home. There is no grand staircase leading up to the main reception rooms, such as a ballroom and dining room and various withdrawing rooms. When rooms such as those existed, there had to be a second set of stairs for the servants to move between the kitchens and those entertainment spaces. This house has the reception rooms—the dining room and the drawing rooms—on the first floor, in the modern way. And, of course, I moved the kitchens to that floor, a few years ago."

He paused to refresh their port, excused himself and went into the kitchenette area. Within minutes he returned with a professionally arranged plate of fruit cake and white cheddar cheese slices. He passed the dish to Fiona and Joe, and then settled it near to his seat. "I have always thought that the modern predilection to despise fruit cake would not have so many adherents if people only learned to eat their cake with cheddar." He put a piece of cheese on a slice of cake and chewed it delicately. "Really very good, this way."

"Uncle!" chorused Fiona and Joe.

"Yes, of course," their uncle continued. "So, there was no 'official' back staircase. But the architect had fun with the northeast and southeast corners of the house. The east side is the main entrance, and as such has some very grand attributes—columns—heavy stone facings—all of which required some substantial underpinnings. Hence, he found space, at both corners, to install serviceable staircases. Just for fun, really. But useful, too, for servants delivering morning hot chocolate...or for others....," he paused meaningfully, "doing whatever."

He continued. "On the lower floor, the staircases open into closets—that large one in the old drying room, and that butler's pantry off the wine cellar, which used to be the kitchen. Not that well-hidden, if you know where to look. The camouflage in the bedrooms is much better, built into the panelling, and because they are at the corners of the rooms near the windows, the drapes always cover one side of each doorway. Quite ingenious."

"Okay," said Joe. "So that explains your 'entry' into Fiona's room. And thank god, I was not there. I don't think I have the right stuff for handling midnight visitors."

"That was the point," interrupted Mack. He leaned forward, earnestly. "I don't have the...well, *cojones* to sneak into Fiona's room. That is why you were supposed to be there." This last was directed to Joe. Then he turned to Fiona. "Thank you for not killing me." He seemed to mean it.

Now Joe was quite confused, but continued gamely on. "So, given that I am a much easier target than my lovely...," he paused to emphasize the next word, "girl cousin, maybe we can get on to why you were traipsing about in the dark, in any case?"

"Yes, well," their uncle continued, quietly. "That is a rather long story. I will try to start at the beginning, it is just that I am not sure I know what the real beginning is."

CHAPTER 6

JERUSALEM 36 A.D.

As predicted by the Old Testament scriptures, Jesus—as the would-be Messiah— had entered Jerusalem on a donkey, with palm fronds spread along his route to cheers of "Hosanna". But the cheering had all been from his own followers. No one else in the city seemed to be very interested. Sure, another would-be Messiah on an ass; sure, his followers saying he is the one true Messiah; sure, what else is new? It was Passover, the time for all Jews to attend the Temple, or at least the Temple Mount, buy a goat for sacrifice if the year had been good, a scrawny pigeon if it had not. A week of religious fervour, feasting and fun. Who needed the diversion of another homegrown Messiah?

This was the public relations issue facing Jesus and his disciples that evening four days before the predicted solar eclipse. The Roman guard had not become interested in this man from Galilee, even with the shouting and excitement that the disciples had tried so hard to engender. And no members of the rabbinical council had seen fit to confront and chastise the pretender-Messiah. Nothing had happened. The worst of all public relations catastrophes—no one was interested. But if something was going to happen, it had to be soon. A lot of planning had to go into what was going to occur on that Friday, the day of the eclipse, the 'dark' day.

Later, at the villa of a relation of the Lady Mary Magdalene, the group was gathered. Even as their word had spread, and the fame of their leader, as a mystic, a healer, an orator, had spread, the group was seldom well housed. On their sojourns some would be admitted as guests to houses of adherents, but most of them had to rely on stables and dry summer-kitchens as sleeping quarters. Few houses could accommodate up to fifteen guests, some of whom were nobly-born, at one time. So it was, with thankfulness that they all met in the Jerusalem villa of Simon Zealotes. He was a member of the High Council of the Sanhedrin, the rabbinical leadership of Jerusalem, and therefore, of the whole of the Judaic diaspora. He was an important man, but one who was used to the disapproval of his fellow council members, and even imprisonment at their hands. He had suffered excommunication, but had been rescued from it by Jesus himself. Only because of this intervention, did Simon still retain title to his extensive business interests, his lands and this sumptuous villa.

"Welcome to my home," Simon said simply, as he gently embraced Jesus of Nazareth. "Please, have everyone enter within. There are rooms for most, warmth for all, and food for—." He laughed. "Food for a multitude." He was quoting scripture, as he often did, and as often, it made him laugh good naturedly. He was a man happy within himself, and therefore, strong enough to confront enemies with, if not love, at least forbearance.

Simon also embraced the Lady Mary, his cousin, and warmly greeted Mary, the mother of Jesus. "You ladies are welcome at our dinner, but..."

Lady Mary laughed. "Do not worry yourself. We will not tarnish your meal with female company. We are tired; it was a long day today, because, of course, I had to lend my donkey to Jesus!" Simon led her and her mother-in-law into the women's area of his house. A beautiful serving girl—perhaps fourteen years of age—greeted them with a deep bow.

"This is Celia," said Simon. "She is to be your personal servant while you are in my home." The use of the adjective 'personal' meant that she would have no loyalty other than to the two Marys;

she would abrogate her loyalty to Simon and his household, for the duration of their stay. It was the highest sign of respect that Simon could pay his royal guests, and the girl was shyly proud of her part, of the trust that had been thrust upon her narrow shoulders.

She bowed again. "Lady," she said to Lady Mary, "There is heated water for bathing, for you both, in your rooms. Thereafter, I will serve you supper, as you choose." She started to turn to go, then, with a glance at their travel-stained clothes, said "And, of course, there are retiring garments better befitting your dining...."

"Thank you, Celia, you dear," said Mary enthusiastically. "I would like nothing better than to be out of these dirty things." She went to the elder Mary and moved her gently into the anteroom of their separate chambers. "Mother, I will meet you here for dinner in...in the time it takes to get the dirt of our travels off, and clean clothes on." She laughed, and Mary hugged her, then walked off into her own room. "And Celia," the Lady Mary said, as she walked into her room, "I would not say no to a glass of chilled Falerian, while I bathe."

The topic of discussion amongst the men that Tuesday evening, was: What can we do to get attention? Jesus, of the House of David, a known leader of the Zealots, and famous in the Galilee region for his fiery condemnation of the Roman rule, had entered Jerusalem on a donkey during Passover, as the scriptures described the entry of the true Messiah. But not only had he not been named the Messiah by the Jewish populace, he had been largely ignored by the Jews of Jerusalem, who were busy with their own preparations and plans for Passover week. And the prophecy of John the Baptist, argued over for years by the learned men of the Sanhedrin, stated clearly that the Messiah must be so named, by the Jews, by midnight tomorrow night.

James the Elder, as usual, was looked to for political guidance. "We need the Jews of Jerusalem to name Jesus as the Messiah, which means we need their attention. Not the attention of the Romans. We now know that a simple re-enactment—well, not re-enactment because the Messiah has never appeared before, but a simple display of all of the requisites for the coming of the Messiah does not work."

"No one paid us any attention. It was almost embarrassing," commented Peter.

Jesus looked about at them all. "It was embarrassing. Have you ever had to ride a donkey? In public?"

James the Brother laughed aloud and the others smiled. It was good to hear Jesus making a joke of the day's fiasco.

James the Elder continued with his thought. "If behaving like a Messiah does not attract attention then Jesus must act unlike a Messiah, or at least unlike what one would expect of a Messiah. He must do something very bad, something that cannot be ignored. But we need the attention of the Jews; so it is our law that must be broken, the law of God, Jewish law."

"But we want the Jews to name Jesus as Messiah!" exploded Peter. "How can we get them to hail Jesus as saviour and king, if he breaks God's law?"

James swallowed a small mouthful of wine, and quietly smacked his lips. He, amongst all of the disciples, most enjoyed their rare stays in the homes of the rich, most particularly for the wine. "We have faith, young man," he said. "We have faith in the scriptures. It is written that the Messiah will be named King of the Jews, and so, if we believe Jesus is the true Messiah, then we must have faith that he will be so named, tomorrow night."

The simple logic was beyond question.

"I think I have it," said Jesus. "Thank you, James, for, as always, guiding gently with your wisdom and understanding." He smiled. "Yes, I have it. Tomorrow, at the Temple Mount, just follow my lead."

The temple at Jerusalem was a massive fortress, not only protecting the priests from contact with the rabble and ensuring their safety and comfort, but separating them out as a special group, the most beloved of their god. The temple itself gave relevance and status to the priests; an imposing conglomerate of walls and towers of sandstone. The main entrance—the Hulda Gates—allowed access under the Portico of the Sanhedrin, in reality the house of governance for all things religious in all of the Jewish world. The gates opened into the Court of Gentiles, a huge open space that housed the busiest market in all of Jerusalem. Passover is the holiest of weeks in the Jewish calendar, but holy days occur throughout the year, each demanding its animal sacrifices, its auguries, and payments to the priests for their services. The Court of Gentiles made up the outer court of the temple. And during Passover Week it was thronged. For the holiday, merchants were selling cheap souvenirs, food stuffs of all variety, silks from the east, rugs from the south and tents from anywhere. Some of the faithful brought in their own livestock for sacrifice, so the court was alive with the unhappy braying of goats, and the rarer mooing of a calf. Baskets of doves were everywhere. Also, the priests had their own herds and flocks of animals ready to be purchased by the endless stream of the faithful, waiting to hear the divination arising from the priestly interpretation of an animal's entrails.

And the moneychangers were in full force. By the temple law, only the shekel of Jerusalem could be used as payment to the priests. Hence, anyone from any other part of Judea, and further afield, had to change his local currency for the money of Jerusalem. Exchange rates were fluid, flowing always against the interest of the common Jew. The moneychangers grew excessively rich, and paid small fortunes for access to the best tables in the court, the ones near the inner temple walls which provided shade and the protection of a solid wall behind the tables of weighing machines, shekels and bags of all the forms of currency known to the Mediterranean world. By the laws of god, no Jew could charge interest on a debt. They more than made up for that with their rates of exchange. The senior bankers did not even attend at their money tables; they strolled about, meeting with acquaintances from the provinces whom they had not seen for some time, they lolled on couches set in shady corners, eating the finest foods and drinking the best wines that had been transported to Jerusalem, specifically for this week of all weeks. Each merchant had an armed cadre, to protect his money and to ensure that no arguments about the rates of exchange became too heated.

In the late morning, when the court was as busy as it could possibly be, a group of peasants, recognizable by their rough clothes and beards, and strange accents, flooded through the southern gate. In their midst was Jesus and most of his disciples. James the Brother was not there. They stormed towards the richest of the moneylenders' tables, and, after Jesus had personally thrown over a table, scattering coins and gold bits into the dirt, the others followed suit. Tables, scales, the private al fresco foods and dishes were thrown everywhere. Goats were set free to run amok amongst the crowd. Cattle were swatted to make them move away from their pens. And thousands—literally thousands of doves—were released, rising as one into the air, then circling uncertainly, until a few remembered the way home.

The private security forces of the moneylenders scrabbled in the dirt for their masters' coins while children nipped amongst their legs, trying to secure just one little bit of the largesse thrown so thoroughly about. The richest of the bankers backed to the wall, for once more afraid for their personal security than for their shekels. And in this bedlam, the instigators moved as one to the more northerly Hulda Gate, and melted into the unknowing crowds waiting their turn to enter the temple precinct.

As Jesus and his followers walked away, casually, in order to discount their involvement, they were passed by a contingent of Roman legionnaires. Always ready for partisan activities during Passover week, the city's main security forces had been more than doubled, and were barracked around and about Jerusalem, so as to be ready in an instant, should trouble start. Over thirty armed and armoured men quick marched past Jesus, and in fact, pushed poor James the Elder out of their way, in their rush to re-establish peace in the Temple.

"Nasty heathens," snarled James.

"At least it was only your dignity they hurt," teased Peter. "Think how those bankers are feeling!"

They all returned to the villa of Simon Zealotes, set high above the city, on one of the seven hills of Jerusalem, and waited for what was expected next.

Freshly bathed, with her long damp hair forming itself into a mass of shining ringlets, and freshly clothed in a dress of white silk and a robe of ruby red linen, Lady Mary was slightly disappointed to receive a request from Jesus to attend the dinner in the main dining hall. She had so wanted to spend another quiet evening in the comfort of her mother-in-law's company.

Celia conducted her from the ladies' guest suite, through hallways of stone and plaster, the floors adorned with tile mosaics. This was indeed a rich man's home. They entered the dining hall, which was a large room set with one long table, more in the manner of an altar, than a dining table. Celia led her to the only empty space at the board, the seat to Jesus' right. Jesus stood, and helped her to sit, a gesture not physically necessary, but which Mary knew to be done for politics—a politeness which would establish her as a person of importance, a person who was not seated on his right just because it was the last chair left, but seated there, in the seat of honour, because she deserved to be there. Mary had often felt the petty jealousy of some of Jesus' followers, most markedly from Peter, who liked to think of himself as Jesus' favourite. Mary had even begun to wonder if perhaps Peter loved his master—as he so often professed—in a somewhat other than acceptable manner. He had once even complained when Jesus kissed Mary on the lips. She definitely did not like young Peter, whom she secretly considered to be less a Rock—as his name implied—than a mincing attention-seeker.

Mary looked about the table. Of the twelve disciples only eleven were present. Judas was not there. Peter was seated on her immediate right, near enough to his leader that he could reach out and take the bread directly from the hand of Jesus. He pressed himself forward, and reached in front of her, as though still trying to diminish her presence in this august company. Mary just shook her head, so much more an admonition than any words could be. James the Brother, was seated to the left of Jesus; freshly bathed, his hair and beard combed out luxuriantly. Mary was astounded to see how much he now resembled his older brother.

Servants with platters of food and flagons of drink began to appear in the dining hall's doorways, waiting for the signal to begin service.

Jesus blessed the bread and the wine, and the meal began.

CHAPTER 7

INNESCARRIG, IRELAND

Mackellan Kirby was explaining the situation to his niece and nephew.

"Some days ago someone asked about me at my local. Grady, the publican, gave me a heads up. And later that day someone took a pot shot at me, in my own woods. He missed—obviously—but he did get my attention. I don't know if both 'someones' were the same 'someone', but I do not believe in coincidences. You were both already on your way, no way to stop that. So I made a point of going to Cork, telling Mary to tell that to everyone she ran into in the village, and even leaving that answering machine message. I did not want you two arriving to a dangerous situation."

"That message certainly got my attention," said Fiona. "I knew it wasn't...real."

"All I could do, at the time. I wanted that 'someone' to follow me to Cork, get him away from here."

"But then how did you get back, without your secret admirer knowing?" asked Joe.

"Oh that. Just an old trick."

Kirby was not about to explain that trick. It involved a supposedly private, and much coded communication with another ex-SAS member. For reasons known only to themselves, Kirby and Colonel Richard Fitzroy had arranged, years ago, the plan that they had executed so flawlessly only yesterday. The very simplicity of it ensured its success.

Kirby had packed an old leather carry-all, donned a rather jaunty cap, and had headed off in his elderly Jaguar e-type. He had stopped at a petrol station, parking in the space closest to the main door, and gone inside to use the facilities, as they say. In minutes he had reappeared, got into the car, and drove off, back onto the main road to Cork.

Anyone watching would have seen an elderly tweed-jacketed, and corduroy-trousered gentleman enter the station, and then seen that person reappear. Anyone tailing Kirby would have parked many spaces from the Jaguar, to maintain a distance that ensured safety from discovery. That distance also ensured the success of the plan. Colonel Fitzroy was wearing the identical mustard tweed jacket, the identical brown cords, and a jaunty cap, only one size larger than Kirby's. When the Colonel drove the Jaguar back onto the highway, Kirby was watching the petrol station courtyard, and noticed the one vehicle from which no driver alit, and which followed his Jag quickly back onto the road. He noted the make—a Land Rover, the colour—green, and even part of the registration plate—the car was too far away for him to read the whole number, but he knew what it would be. He nodded to himself, went out the back door of the station, and got into a still-warm black Rover.

"Let's just say, the old trick worked. Sometimes we old guys just don't want to bother learning anything new. Especially when the tried and true works so well." Kirby reached for his glass of port, attempting to put an end to that discussion.

"We old guys?" Fiona had her head up, her green eyes glowing. "You don't mean you used that old chestnut? "She saw how discomfited her uncle looked, and she crowed "You did, didn't you? My God, the sheer nerve, and what a chance you took."

"No, men with brollies and London Fog raincoats on a sunny day take chances." He sniffed. "We were much more sophisticated."

Joe looked from his uncle to his cousin; he was lost.

Mackellan continued. "So, my friend went on to Cork, used my reservation number, and is still in his room, apparently with a bad chest cold that prohibits his leaving his bed. Boring for Richard, I suppose, but I would do the same for him."

Fiona got up and started to pace about the room. She looked like a caged, and very unhappy tigress. "But isn't that dangerous for your friend? If you were shot at, and then followed..."

Her uncle chuckled. "Oh, I would think that the danger is all on the head of that 'someone'. I wouldn't like to take on the Colonel. He paused for one more sip of port. "Even if he really did have a cold."

CHAPTER 8

CHARLESTON, SOUTH CAROLINA

The secretary glanced at her computer screen, then rose gracefully, and walked towards the double walnut doors that opened into the inner office. "He can see you now," she intoned. That was the only word for how she spoke—intoned, like someone in the presence of God. Which, when you think about it, is probably how she felt about her work place. She placed one slim and perfectly manicured hand on the right hand door and pushed, without effort. Both doors opened. She stood aside for the guest.

He brushed past her, rudely, really. He hated the sanctified air of this place. It irritated him, and when irritated, he was rude. Wardell was an adept psychologist; he well knew that his rudeness was really just a subterfuge, a replacement for the fear that he had, of this place and these people.

The mellow wood of the floor was as perfectly polished as ever. The thickness of the Turkish carpet grabbed at his shoe soles, as it always did. And the man behind the massive antique desk greeted him with his trademark smile of bonhomie, as though his day would not have been complete, or at least not as wonderful, if his visitor had not arrived. Then the beam was switched off, and he frowned.

"Sit, Wardell."

"Good to see you, too, sir," he responded.

The man behind the desk frowned harder and indicated a chair across the desk from his own.

"Cut the crap. Bourbon?"

Sam Wardell, after more than four years of working for the Congregation of the Holy Baptism was still bemused by the inherent contradictions in the man across from him. The Archreverend Claud Mathieux was the revered leader of his sect, a charismatic preacher of the word of God, a man who professed poverty and obedience. He was also an asshole of the highest calibre.

"Sure," said Sam. He flopped himself down into the maroon leather armchair Mathieux had gestured towards. The whole room could have come out of an Edwardian men's club, from the dark wood panelling, the coffered ceiling, the high and small-paned French windows which opened onto a wrought iron balcony. Over-wrought, Sam sometimes thought. Where the panelling ended bookshelves began, and they were beautifully filled with sets of leather-bound tomes. Whether they related to the Archreverend's work or not, was not an issue: they looked good. And anyway, opening up books was bad for their bindings, Sam had heard somewhere.

"Here," said Mathieux, handing Wardell a lead crystal glass, half-filled with the best whiskey that the state of Tennessee had to offer. One thing about the man, he was not cheap with his liquor.

"You summoned me to your presence," began Wardell.

"I told you to cut the crap," snapped Mathieux. "We have a problem, and I want it gone."

"Problem as in a person; gone as in gone-gone?" asked Wardell.

"What? You have a kid in kindergarten? Gone, as in dead." Mathieux got up and began to pace. He was a big man, not fat, just comfortably muscular. He was good looking, in a dark, fleshy way. Like most of the sociopaths they show on 'American Greed' thought Wardell, irreverently. Abundant and dark hair curled over his forehead, and he habitually ran his right hand through it, ostensibly to replace it, but really for the endearing effect it had on his female parishioners. It was an old habit, from his days at the pulpit.

Wardell sipped his bourbon. It really was very good. "Okay, so who, where, when? And the why, if you want me to know."

Mathieux stood still at the French doors, glaring into the distance. The view from this, the fourth floor of the Bastion—as the central church of the Congregation was known—was panoramic. Situated on a slight rise, in the Mount Pleasant area of Charleston, he could see a portion of both the Ashley and the Cooper rivers, as they became one with the Atlantic Ocean in the misty distance.

"This time you definitely need to know the why. That will help with the how," he said. He returned to his desk, sat, and extracted a manila envelope from a drawer. "These are the details."

Wardell opened the envelope and pulled out a photo, and a paper with a name and an address in Georgia. He was not surprised that Mathieux used paper, given what the research and development department of the church was capable of. Knowing the computer hacking capabilities of their own people would make anyone shy away from using e-mails, computer images and even internet searches.

"Ernest Joyful Clappington. The Reverend Clappington. Earnest Ernie, as his flock call him." Mathieux took a huge gulp of his own bourbon, and grimaced slightly. Drinking while angry always brought on his acid reflux. "The man is a phenomenal snake-handler, and maintains that arcane sport as part of his Sunday sermons. It scares the hell out of everyone, of course, and thereby ensures generous donations." He paused, and looked reflectively at Sam. "Actually, his donation ratio per parishioner is the highest—next to my own, of course—in the whole Congregation. Not that I get to preach very often any more. Anyway, those donations are what has caused the trouble. Ernie," he said the name dismissively, "Thinks the head office keeps too much for itself, thinks his stinking little church should get to keep more. And he has started checking into the corporate workings of the Congregation, even hinting that the Archreverendship is something that should be voted on. Voted by who? No one has the right. This church is mine, and will stay that way." His fist hit the desk, in the classic show of anger. In some instances, this would be funny. When Mathieux did it, funny was the last word anyone would think of.

"So he has to go. And I want it done. With theater, with pizazz. Even in that backwoods community someone should have a cell phone with a camera, and know how to use it. Always good for channel news bits. And I might even get some guest shots on late night." Now he laughed, and if anything, that was scarier than his fist thumping.

Sam Wardell adjusted himself in his seat. He handed his glass to Mathieux when that man held up the bottle, and with a rise of his left eyebrow silently asked Sam if he wanted another shot.

"So, what do you intend?"

"He dies of snake bites. Painful, a lot of ugly thrashing. But, newsworthy. And it should put any of his lets-vote-out-Mathieux converts on notice." The Archreverend smiled beatifically. "Too bad about the rattlers. They will all have to be put down. Nasty little biters." Mathieux swallowed and smacked his lips. "And when you have finished with the Reverend Clappington, we have a problem in Ireland, so make sure some passport is up to date."

A week later Sam Wardell was in his hotel room, in Savannah, near Georgia's border with South Carolina, on his way back to Charleston. He was using a rental SUV, under a false name; one of his many aliases. He had dined expensively on the local lobster specialty, and was now relaxing, with a last glass of a rather fine imported Chardonnay, the most expensive white wine on the room-service menu. He flicked through the television channels, then stopped, and upped the volume.

"A tragedy for the Darkwood, Georgia Congregation of the Holy Baptism," the news anchor said, in his someone-has-died voice. "We now go to our reporter Jase King, in Darkwood." The screen split, showing an image of the anchor at his desk, and a handsome black man standing outside a church, holding a microphone. "Jase, can you tell us more about this bizarre accident?"

"Sure, David," started the news reporter. "I am standing outside of the Congregation of the Holy Baptism church in Darkwood, Georgia, where earlier today, the church's minister, the Reverend Ernest Clappington was killed by multiple rattle snake bites. The deceased was known for his serpent handling, incorporating venomous snakes into many of his services. But today, what is usually a meaningful and integral part of the service, went terribly wrong."

The newscast then went into a voice over by King, as a film clip of the event began to play.

"We have this film coverage from a congregation member, who was recording the serpent handling on his Smartphone."

The film was not as choppy or unfocussed as many cell phone clips are. It showed the reverend, in his long white robe, approaching a large wicker basket, which had just been placed by two members of the church, at the front of the pews but below the altar of the church. The reverend made some hand gestures and spoke, which was not recorded well, and opened the basket.

"Here we see Reverend Clappington praying over the serpents. He opens the basket and reaches his hands into it."

Clappington is shown with both hands in the basket, when he rears back, his face anguished with pain. He falls to the floor, simultaneously knocking the basket down, and showering its contents onto himself. The dozen Diamondback Rattle Snakes—for there must be that many—flail about the man, trying to coil, then striking out at any part of their adversary that they can reach. The camera zooms in to a frenzy of snakes, robes, and the Reverend, gamely trying to fight them off, but failing miserably. He is screaming, then moaning, then still. The snakes are still moving, out of the camera's eye into the area under the front pews of the congregation. The camera zooms out. The church attendees are screaming and running, some of the men stomping onto snakes that are too close to run from. It is truly chaotic. And cinematographically wonderful.

The reporter continues, but Wardell has muted him.

"So it was worthwhile to hire a real cameraman," he said to himself, as he sipped his Chardonnay.

On reflection, although he first considered the job run-of-the-mill, he had to admit that it had been sufficiently different to perk his interest; it had even been fun. And Clappington deserved to die; not because he irritated Mathieux, but because of his predilection for his parishioners' young children.

The hiring of the cameraman was done through an agency screen. They said they wanted footage of a serpent handling for an in-depth religious documentary. They hired the iffiest guy with adequate credentials that they could. They knew he would sell the footage to the highest news network bid, and kind of forget that he had been in place only because he had been hired by the documentary producer. That producer would strangely forgive the lack of manners, and nothing more would be said. The photographer never questioned his good luck—sold his clip for a good price and was never threatened by the producer, or the agency. He did wonder how the network knew how to contact him.

Then there were the snakes. Apparently sermon snakes are kept cool, so cool that the poor things are barely above hibernation; their bodily functions are slowed, including their little reptile brains, and they could no more get up the energy to strike, bite and inject venom than they could compose an ode.

The handling is one-hundred per cent safe. The adept handler can make the snakes appear to twist and squirm, of their own accord, in the most frightening way. And if he keeps their numb and non-aggressive mouths away from his body parts, the visual effect is startling. And very wallet opening, it seems.

On the other hand, there are pheromones—certain chemical odours—which stimulate the sex drive, that is, aggression, of a normally healthy young male rattle snake. Being surrounded by other young healthy and pheromone drugged snakes makes the aggression worse.

A short study of the Darkwood church's security—which consisted of basic locks and no CC cameras— and voila, the serpent basket was moved from a specially chilled basement room and placed beside a hot-air vent, a few feet from the chilled room. The basket was thoroughly sprayed with a made-to-order pheromone mixture—the herpetologist who mixed it needed a quick $10,000.00 for a divorce problem and never met his client. (He did see the news broadcast and was not about to come forward with anything he knew.) The men who carried the basket up to the altar were on a six week rota, it was such a special mark of favour to be given this job. They never stopped to think that the basket was usually in the cold room. Not being in on the temperature trick they never gave it a thought—until later.

The few people who knew anything were not about to come forward. And those few had never seen Wardell. Perfect.

Wardell finished his wine, then flicked through the usual night television talk show fare, looking for the inevitable, the sad but still handsome face of the Archreverend Mathieux. For sure, His Smarminess would have been grabbed as a guest by someone, to further dissect this awful accident. In fact, he thought, as he punched his hotel room pillows into order, the bastard probably had an agent. He fell asleep as a televised Mathieux, in what looked with every stitch to be a Cardin suit, softly voiced platitudes about the holiness of dying in sanctity.

The next day, Sam Wardell again entered the Bastion. He had been requested to meet with Mathieux as soon as he got back to Charleston.

CHAPTER 9

INNESCARRIG, IRELAND

"Anyway," concluded Mackellan. "We need our rest, so if you don't mind...." He started to stand. But the still pacing Fiona pushed him back into his armchair.

She stood facing him. "Not so fast. What is going on?" She realized that her demanding voice was probably not going to go over well with her uncle, so she sat down and started again. "Joe and I need to know more. We need to know who followed you, shot at you, and apparently got you so worried you called in the army. Please." She was actually pleading. Joe was dumbstruck; Mackellan was awed.

"Dick is not the army, as you put it. He is retired SAS. The man who followed me is no doubt the man who stopped at my pub and asked about me, and the person who shot at me could be any bad shot out there." He stood again. "I really don't know any more, and my suspicions can wait. But we will be flying to Spain, ASAP. And I for one need some rest. These early morning hours just aren't what they used to be." He turned toward the room with the camp cots. "I am sleeping here children. You know the way out, right? Good. See you at breakfast. A fine Irish breakfast it will be, too. I'm cooking." With that, he closed the door to the sleeping quarters.

"I don't like this," said Fiona. A worried frown creased her forehead.

Joe got up, rinsed their glasses in the kitchenette and put the remains of the fruit cake and cheese back in the apartment-sized refrigerator, under a layer of cling film. "I do," he said. "I have never seen anyone—not even your mother—handle you that well." He walked to the door, then turned. "Are you coming Fi? I am not sure I remember the way."

The watcher in the depths of the fir copse situated to the north of the house had neither seen nor heard anything. For hours now. He stomped his feet. The night was warm but even so, standing still for so long brought on a chilled stiffness. "God, I hate this job. Night watches are so predictable." He caught himself muttering aloud; and firmly clamped his mouth shut. It would not do to be overheard, by any listening ear, or microphone, for that matter.

When the eastern sky began to pale, still a good hour to sunrise, he quietly walked back to the estate's brick wall. He had left a rope hidden in a fall of wild ivy, and now pulled himself up to the top of the wall, detached his anchoring piton, and climbed down the beech tree conveniently placed on the outside of the wall.

Mackellan was already in the kitchen when Fiona and Joe appeared, at just after eight o'clock.

"Sleep well?" he asked, then grinned. "There is fresh coffee in the percolator—I know how you Americans need your coffee. Personally, I take my caffeine from tea." He turned back to the stove and a huge cast iron skillet filled with smoking bacon and black sausages. As they cooked to an acceptable doneness, he removed them to a serving platter, then grilled a half dozen perfect two inch tomatoes, pushed those to the side and added eggs. "Over easy okay?" he asked over his shoulder. "And Fiona dear, could you please see to some toast?"

Fiona did, while Joe got her a mug of coffee. Mackellan brought the skillet and platter to the table, and they sat. Farm butter, two types of jam and a jar of chow-chow completed the meal. Breakfast was wonderful, as only an Irish breakfast can be.

"So," Mackellan began. "You will be glad to know that my theatrics last night were not for nought." He occasionally liked to use words that were not in common usage with his young American relatives; he thought it gave him an edge of the exotic. It simply annoyed Fiona.

"Yes," he continued. "A little reconnaissance this morning showed me that someone had recently scaled the garden wall near the beech tree." He used his fingers to eat his bacon slices, but did it so delicately, and with such obvious appreciation, that neither of his guests minded. "For certain, someone was in the garden, watching and listening, last night."

"How do they get through your security?" Fiona asked.

"The beech tree on the outside of the wall, which with those big wide branches is so easily climbed, is my security. I know that anyone entering, or leaving, will use that spot. So it is easy to check." Mackellan kept eating. "And camera 7, which you can review on the cc system shows someone entering at 9:00 pm and leaving at 5:30 am. Wouldn't want his bill for the night shift."

They cleaned up the dishes, the table, and the stove. Then sat, over two more cups of coffee and one more cup of tea.

Their Uncle Mack looked seriously at his cup and saucer. "It is time I told you what is going on. And if you want to leave, I will endorse that decision, and see that you get home safely."

"Uncle Mack, you know I will do what I can to help you," said Fiona. She reached across the table, and enclosed his right hand within her own. "I owe you."

"I am sure I owe you, too, for semesters three through sixteen, at Stanford," said Joe. "But before we get into anything, can I ask you one thing?"

The other two nodded.

He continued seriously. "Just how do your Irish farmers get the tomatoes to be a perfect two inches in diameter?"

At Innescarrig House, safely back in his room, although he knew the night porter had seen him come in just before 6:00 am, and that that news would soon be spread about, the man called an international number on his cell phone.

It was answered on the second ring, even though it was only 7:00 am in that time zone. "Si?"

"Your Eminence, it is Brother Martin. The cat is among the pigeons."

"Oh don't be an ass," responded an irritated Italian voice. "Have you made contact?"

CHAPTER 10

FINNESTERRE IBERIA 1075

Bishop Darda looked longingly towards the Atlantic Ocean, to where it crashed incessantly into the cliff faces of Finnesterre. Land's End. A most fitting description for this most western point of continental Europe, in the north of the Iberian Peninsula. He felt content when near the sea, felt his heart slow to the timing of the waves, the ceaseless movement; he felt his spirit soar with the ever-present seagulls and ernes. He was still a man of the sea, should have stayed in his Maltese village, following his papa and uncles into the family fishing business, living a life of hard work but better pleasures, with a wife and babes and sufficient food and drink to make life good. Not just good. Wonderful. The sea always filled him with wonder, and started his yearnings for the joys of home.

He turned away from the west, and patted the smooth cheeks of the horse that stood so quietly beside him. "We might as well get started, old friend," he said quietly. "Our cathedral is waiting."

He mounted, and cantered to the roadway, which was set back a goodly distance from the cliff edge. He could see his entourage waiting patiently at the road, well, track really. An old Roman way that had long ago lost most of its paving stones and was now gently receding into the weeds of the countryside.

The bishop rode to the front of the assembled travellers, and started out. He was accompanied by the smallest escort he had been allowed: some thirty fully kitted knights and an equal number of monks, working monks, from medical practitioners to blacksmiths, cooks, ostlers, launderers, whatever would be needed on a venture of this magnitude. The only one of them without a useful trade was himself, Darda mused—no one needs a fisherman fifty miles from the sea.

Bishop Darda had been entrusted, by His Eminence Cardinal Friere, with the construction of a cathedral in the northern Spanish town of Compostela. The little town, inland some fifty miles from Finnesterre, had for as long as anyone knew, been a magnet for Christian pilgrims, from all of Gaul, Iberia, even Albion and parts of northern Italy. The pious flocked to the insignificant Spanish town, bypassing the great cathedrals that had been raised in cities such as Orleans and Rouen in France, and Toledo and Cuernavaca in Spain. Even in times of civil unrest, plague years, and with the usual dangers inherent in a protracted journey in eleventh century Europe, pilgrims came by the thousands, annually, to the little stone church known as San Diego de Compostella.

Cardinal Friere had seen, in those very numbers, an opportunity, one that Mother Church in Rome should not miss out on. Born in a different time and place, Cardinal Friere would have ascended to the chairmanship of any national bank, or become the minister of finance in any conservative government. But, born in the early eleventh century, the third son in a reasonably wealthy French family, his aspirations were limited. He was brilliant, everyone agreed, but there was also something lacking in his personality, a coldness that could not be warmed. He was destined for the church, and his family members quite happily wished him God speed when he left, at age eleven, for the seminary of the Order of the Franciscans in the city of Navarre in southwestern Gaul.

As a child, Jacques Friere had seen the caravans of pilgrims moving slowly but hopefully along the Roman road that connected Margaux to Navarre. He was, even as a child, annoyed at their expectation of hospitality, merely because they were on a holy quest, as they said. They each carried a scallop shell, which were plentiful on the beaches of that part of the Mediterranean Sea; they used it as both a badge of honour, designating the wearer as a pilgrim, and a drinking vessel. Jacques could not help but think that its latter use would have been more readily serviceable if the travellers had kept the shell safely clean within an oil cloth. Worn as each was, about the pilgrim's neck on a leather thong, which meant holes had to be drilled through the shell in at least two places, the shells were always filthy from road dust and hardly water tight. He would have done it differently, he thought, as he watched a happy dozen walk dreamily past his father's property.

He had risen quickly through the ranks of his order after being invested as a monk at age eighteen. He had caught the attention of Rome, which was inordinately relieved to have a Franciscan who was as competent in economics as most were with the living world. His bishopric had begun a mere five years before the call from the Vatican, from Pope Pious, and his promotion to Cardinal for southern France.

Even when immersed in the scents and scenes of Rome, Cardinal Friere had kept his mind, and often his fingers, on the goings on in his homeland. He knew that the popularity of the pilgrimage to Compostela should be making money for the church, and he often mused about the ways and means of making that happen. The church needed funds. It was building cathedrals throughout northern and central France and parts of Spain. The citizenry could not afford the construction, could not be expected to. The Knights Templar were funding a good deal of the construction, and overseeing the engineering to a large extent, but the church was always in need of acquiring new-found sources of wealth.

Cardinal Friere put his able mind to this and developed his theories. He spoke of his plans to senior cardinals, and wrote a report to the Pope Legate, who awarded him with luncheon with His Holiness, Pious the XII, and his inner sanctum of leading churchmen. They were pleased. He was given a large dish of the new frozen dessert, called gelato, which was usually reserved for

His Holiness alone—it aided his digestion, he said. The ice for the confection was brought down from the Alps, in well insulated straw panniers, loaded heavily onto donkeys, and transported night and day until they reached the kitchens of the Vatican. In winter, when even the local streams filled with ice, the making of the dessert was less costly, but who wanted gelato in January? In any case, Cardinal Friere was feted for his brilliance.

Basically, his plan was to build a cathedral at Compostela, to be known as Santiago de Compostela. There had long been a story that St. James' body had washed ashore there. How it could have, some fifty miles inland from the Atlantic, Friere could never figure out, but that was the story, started many centuries ago. The tale had stood the test of time, so why argue with it, even if the facts did not stand up to scrutiny.

The cathedral would subsume the small church that had stood for centuries in Compostela, and which was reputed to have been built on a much earlier holy site, a site from the first century it was said, predating most Christian activity in Iberia. As the only church, the cathedral would have a monopoly, so to speak. Pilgrims would pay for church sanctioned-proof of their trek—perhaps a specially minted coin of some sort. And every hostel on the routes to Compostela, for there were many by then, winding through the country sides of Spain and France, and even as far as Italy and Germany and the isles of Albion, —every hostel which wished to be seen as a stopping place for pilgrims would be allowed to use the symbol of the scallop shell. And every hostel would pay for that usage. It would be a tax,—the cost of the use of the shell would be based on the number of pilgrims who patronized the tavern, inn, farm house, whatever. Friere did not mind how luxurious an accommodation was, or how mean. All would pay for the scallop shell, based on income. A secondary benefit to the church would be the records of income which the hostelries would be expected to keep. Those accounts would provide good material for tithing from the innkeepers, separately from the scallop shell tax. It was a brilliant and novel concept. And very well received by the vault keepers of the Vatican.

Friere requested permission to leave Rome and travel to Iberia, in order to personally oversee the institution of his plan. He took a retinue of knights and monks, and his second-in-command, young Bishop Darda. Friere had had his eye on the bishop for some time; something about the dark-skinned Maltese excited him, in ways he had hoped the seminary had beaten out of him. It had not. Perhaps nothing ever could. He recognized a mournfulness in the younger man. He yearned to take away that sadness, replace it with joy, with love. Yes, the Cardinal admitted, to himself at least, that he was in love with Darda. Perhaps the long sea voyage, from the port of Rome, through the Aegean and the Mediterranean, to Finnesterre in the north of Spain would provide the time and space...and the loneliness... that was needed to bring the younger man to his bed.

They embarked from Porto Roma on a sun swept morning in April. The *Santa Berenetta* was a three-masted galleon, her superstructure rose some forty feet above the waterline. Her holds, newly outfitted to stable the men's horses, reached an equal depth below the waterline. She could be maneuvered by oars, but every man aboard hoped the captain was canny enough to make moorages by sail power alone. She was the finest ship of her time, leased by the Holy See for the many delegations it sent out into the known world beyond the confines of the Mediterranean Sea.

At sea three days, the Cardinal was feeling the gut wrenching nausea of mal-de-mer. He had not eaten for two days; he was sweating; he was a sickly green colour. He sat on the main deck under a shade created for him from a hank of sail and watched disinterestedly as the men exercised the horses.

Ansted of Rouen, the lieutenant in command of the Templars, insisted on the exercising and grooming of the horses every day. He even made his men walk the heavy draught horses that the monks had brought along, to ferry them and their goods from Finnesterre inland to Compostela, when once they arrived at their destination. He was adamant about the health of both horses and men. Cardinal Friere thought he was a pompous bore, and considered moving himself back to his stateroom below decks, when his heart soared. Bishop Darda came up the ramp from the holds, leading his own saddle horse, a large-bodied Belgium, dappled grey and stomping impatiently for his time in the sun. Darda was dressed in his heavy black robes, the silver rosary and wooden cross at his neck the only signs of his position.

Friere watched avidly, his queasiness all but forgotten, as the bishop walked the animal up and down the main deck, then took him aside to curry him thoroughly. Darda brought a bucket of fresh water for the horse to drink, and the horse, still in high spirits, pushed his head against Darda, upsetting his grip on the bucket. The water flew, mostly over Darda. He just laughed and removed his now sodden woolen surplice, revealing his silken undershirt. It damply clung to his well-muscled shoulders and chest. Friere sighed. Tonight, he thought to himself.

The next morning Cardinal Friere summoned the ship's captain to his cabin.

"I need to be put ashore, as soon as possible, at the very next place you can get me safely off this floating piece of shit." He was screaming, uncontrollably.

"You seem to have hurt yourself, Your Eminence," said the captain quietly. "Your eye is quite swollen." The man had obviously received a pretty good left hook to his right eye. The captain secretly hoped it might have been from one of his crew.

The cleric placed a wet cloth to his bruised face. "I fell, against the door," he said. "It is all this rocking to and fro. I can't stand it anymore. I want off." His voice had again risen to its earlier shriek.

"Of course, sir," said the Captain. "We are but a day from Naples. You can disembark there, in comfort. With an entourage of your knights. For your safe return to Rome." He bowed, left the cabin, and grinned. If it was not one of his crew, he hoped it was the bishop. Nothing much escaped the notice of the captain of one of the greatest sailing ships of its time.

As he walked his horse along the stone track, moving ever

eastward from Finnesterre, Bishop Darda let his mind go back to the Cardinal's last two nights aboard the *Santa Bernadetta*. He knew of men like the Cardinal, but had never been openly approached before. He rather prided himself on not looking 'approachable' to men like that. He had thought nothing of being asked by the Cardinal to come to his cabin, after dinner. The Cardinal often spoke to him of his plans for Compostela. The Cardinal had not planned to stay long in the village—just long enough to get the layout of the construction underway. The Templar engineers would follow a Master Architect's plans for the cathedral, which needed to be approved by a representative of the Holy See, to be sure that the Templars were not just building another Templar church, with that strange eight-sided design. They kept trying to return to that configuration, even though the modern way was for cathedrals to soar, to be built with one main castellation that rose, on arches and pillars, to unheard-of heights. The way they were being built in Lourdes, and Paris, and Toulouse.

Anyway, when the little Sodomite tried to kiss him, Darda had smashed one well-aimed fist into the Cardinal's face. Darda had stopped then. Not that he wanted to. But he was a man of god, a man of peace. He was even slightly—but only just slightly—ashamed of laying even one fist on his Cardinal.

After that, the Cardinal had met with both Darda and Ansted always together. He directed them as to their duties, the expectations of Rome, and provided them with drawings of the construction of similar projects, which Rome had on hand. He told Darda he would expect monthly reports. The last the Bishop saw of the Cardinal, as he waited on the stone pier at Naples for his horse to be disembarked, was a malicious smile and the words thrown at him. "Try to lose that nasty Maltese accent. You will never amount to much if your Latin does not improve."

And that was that. Darda was now in charge.

CHAPTER 11

INNESCARRIG, IRELAND

Still at the kitchen table, and with reheated drinks, Kirby looked seriously at his niece and nephew.

"You know I still work as a historian of ancient religions, although I gave up my professorship some years ago," began Mackellan.

"It does make a wonderful cover, for what you really do," said Fiona, with a wicked smile.

O'Connor looked surprised; Mackellan looked guilty.

"We will discuss, hmmm, that later. But I have been concentrating on my 'honest' profession for the last few years. You may not know, how could you, really, as most of the names have been kept quiet. But the UN's Department of Antiquities gave me the privilege of access to the Quhram scrolls. Since their discovery in 1948, and further discoveries in 1956, 1968 and 2004, in other locations, the texts have been in the control of a world church council. That became pretty chaotic—the Catholics saying they had authority because they run Christianity, the Jews saying they did because the scrolls were found in Palestine, and the Islamic delegation demanding the right of veto on any publication of any material. So control went to the UN. Which did not know where to begin. So it set up a Department of Antiquities. As though that name would take away from the fact that the scrolls are all about religion, not archaic facts about household goods in the first century or clay glazes in the third." He snorted, obviously unhappy with such silliness.

"The head of the Department of Antiquities is, oddly enough, a modernist. A Dr. Leo Farber, an American, but with impeccable qualifications."

Fiona allowed herself a small grin.

"He was actually an undergrad, on a dig with me once, in Morocco. Anyway, Farber quickly realized that the way they were proceeding, with historians, religious leaders, and interpreters all crowded about whenever a new bit of parchment was opened, was never going to work. Not to mention the damage that was wreaking on the scrolls. With funding that I cannot even guess at, the Department decided to go on line. The scrolls media, whether papyrus or skin, are handled by the world's best art restorers. They are then photographed in minute detail. And the photomicroscopic plates are reproduced as images on the Department's Quhram internet site. Some one hundred or so of us, world-wide, have access to the site. We log in through a series of portals, to ensure the site's privacy, etc. etc. You probably know all about such things. Through the joys of technology, I can enlarge any segment of writing, to such a degree that any change in the hand writing can be seen, any erasure, or replacement, or additions between lines, can be noted. And as the scrolls are generally in small pieces, I can compare the writing on various bits, to coalesce them with their sister bits, into a whole. It is exciting, but painstaking work. My specialty is Aremaic Greek."

His young relatives looked questioningly at him.

"I don't know why. Just sort of went there. That was the language spoken by most of the educated classes in the Mideast, from Jerusalem to Constantinople, from about the fourth century BC to the fifth century of the modern era. Most of the New Testament texts were written in Aremaic Greek, or translated therefrom. So it is a handy language, for a religious historian. And a lot of the modern languages in the Mideast descend from it; you can still get along in most of that area with Aremaic and a smattering of modern languages. They just look at you funny."

"So, as I was working through one small but interesting document, I felt....well, I felt a presence."

His audience looked sceptical.

"Not an otherworldly presence. Just something not quite right. My computer paused sometimes, when it should not have; some access was slower than normal, fluttered, as though seen through a strobe light. I wondered if my studies had not become the subject of someone else's concern. So I broached this to Leo. He had some genius nerd-type check things out from their centre. Sure enough, some sort of malware keystroke program was following my work. Leo thought they got rid of the problem, and I continued with my research. But I have reason to believe that my 'watcher' was back when I made the discovery that could rock Christianity to its foundations. I really mean that. Its foundations."

He received two doubtful, but concerned, looks.

"Anyway, I will explain this....some of this, on the way to Santiago de Compostela. Luckily enough there are sufficient faithful Irish to make direct flights from Cork feasible for Ryan Air, weekly on Thursdays. That way they can avoid serving fish, which has become frightfully expensive here. Too bad we can't fly Aer Lingus, they offer better tea. I hope you haven't unpacked yet. It will look better if you take all of your luggage with you."

Joe was not yet used to his uncle's strange divergences from the topic of his own conversation. He skipped over the reference to the economics of airline food, but he had to ask. "Better to who? And what is in Santiago de Compostela?"

"Better to whom. But don't worry about that now. Santiago de Compostela is home to one of the oldest, and most famous cathedrals, in all of Spain. I have never actually visited it, and I think neither of you have either, so we really must go. No time like the present. I need your passport names and numbers, and then I have some calls to make. We should be out of here tomorrow. I'll let you know the flight details. Then I'll meet you at the flight gate at Cork.

"How are you getting to Cork? Your car is still there, isn't it?" asked his nephew.

"Yes it is. Dick will be bringing it back. His is parked nearby."

Fiona could take no more. "Uncle," she said quietly but clearly. "Where is 'nearby', and why is the car 'nearby' and not in your forecourt when apparently whoever you were hiding from found you out?"

Mackellan looked questionly at her.

"The beech tree visitor of the other night. Presumably the same man you and your friend Richard were evading, when you pulled that old switcheroo out on the highway. He must have figured out the scam and got back here, in time to go tree climbing."

Her logic was as good as ever, Mackellan had to acknowledge. "I don't want to make it easy for him. If he has the intel I think he has access to, he has already figured out who Richard is and is watching his car, parked, 'nearby', at Innescarrig House. I will be leaving by another exit from here. A vehicle is waiting. Don't worry. I still know what I am doing." He smiled benevolently. "At least, I think I do."

As instructed by their uncle, early the next morning, Joe and Fiona noisily left Cliffside House by the front portico, humping all of their baggage with them. Joe looked out at the Bay of Kinsale, and pronounced loudly "Too bad Uncle Mack wants us to see the sights with him in Dublin. I will miss this view."

"Careful, Sunshine," whispered Fiona. "That was not an Oscar-winning performance." Then she raised her voice to a normal level, knowing that if there was anyone in the vicinity who should not be, he would have some sort of sound enhancement audio device. "He did say we would all be back Saturday night. And that means we will all be able to attend St. Bridget's for Sunday mass. You have never been to a church service in Ireland, have you?" As they stowed the bags and got into the car, she prattled on. "Now that the priests speak English, they are even harder to understand than when they spoke Latin."

The car doors slammed. Fiona started the car and stopped talking. The little car sprayed gravel as she sped down the curved drive to the already-opened gate. Out on Cliffside Drive she continued to the right, away from the roadway on which they had arrived.

"Where are we going?"

"I just want to check something out," Fiona responded. She continued on Cliffside Drive, and turned off onto a narrow lane that led steeply down, towards the shore road that led into Innescarrig. On this seldom used lane they would actually pass below Cliffside House, as it sat high on its almost sheer rock face.

"Aha," she said, a minute later. They had just turned a tight corner that put the shore road into their sight. Off to the right, a gated path, grassy and unused and almost obscured by an overgrown holly bush, but wide enough to admit a vehicle, albeit a narrow one, rose up and headed along the base of the cliff.

Joe's anguished "What?" got her giggling.

"Uncle Mack has a car—no, probably a small four wheel drive of some sort, salted up above. He left Cliffside through his cellars and made his way to his private parking lot, and is even now ahead of us on this road." She grinned. "You did notice that he disappeared this a.m.? Never even gave his loving relations a proper goodbye? He is on his way, he is ahead of us, and his plans are afoot, as they say."

She maneuvered their Ford onto the slightly wider, and slightly busier shore road. "I just hope he is safe," she added. "And I also hope that he is not driving that stupid Brough Superior."

"Okay," sighed Joe. "What is a Brough Superior?"

"A 1930's motorcycle," his cousin replied. "The same model that T.E. Lawrence rode, after his exploits in Arabia." She entered onto the A1 motorway, and sped the little coupe way beyond the posted limit. "You have heard of Lawrence, right?" she asked.

"Of course," Joe snarled. "But why would Uncle Mack have an

old motorcycle stowed away as his escape vehicle, and what is he escaping?"

"Well, apparently a Brough Superior is a really wonderful motorbike, although ancient, and rather uncomfortable, but...."

"Stop it, Fiona. Now you sound like Uncle Mack. Always changing the subject, just as it gets interesting." He turned towards her, and she saw the concern on his handsome face. "What the hell is going on?"

They arrived at Cork Airport an hour later. Fiona drove their rental car into the short-term parking area, coding its registration number into the ticketing machine, and proceeded to park it in amongst a lot of larger cars and estate vehicles. Joe wondered why they were not near an exit, but he just did not want to ask one more stupid question, especially as he knew he would probably not get an answer.

As they rolled and carried their luggage from the Ford, an official Cork Airport Authority transport cart pulled up beside them. A neatly dressed young man, with beautiful posture, smiled reassuringly at them.

"Miss Kirby, Mr. O'Connor? Please let me assist you to your aircraft." He lifted their bags easily onto the cart's baggage compartment, and with a widespread arm offered them seats on the vehicle. Fiona noticed that his official airport identification name tag carried a really recent photograph; his hair had not grown a millimetre since the photo had been taken.

Fiona thought, then said. "So, Sergeant, is it? Or perhaps, Flight Officer?"

No one had prepared the young man for Fiona's rather mesmerizing emerald eyes and plain directness.

"Flying Officer First Class, ma'am," he proudly said. "Southwest Command." And then added quickly, afraid he might have offended some sensibilities. "Seconded to the Republic of Ireland Air Force, of course."

Fiona was as always surprised by the cooperation that existed between Great Britain and the Irish Republic, but in this age of unknown foreign threats, she thought they both must be making the best of a historically unhappy relationship.

"Not in uniform today, Flying Officer?" teased Fiona, as she climbed into the back seat of the vehicle. When possible she liked to give precedence to Joe. Her own sense of self did not need the benefit of a front seat.

The young man blushed, settled into his seat and drove the baggage cart from the parking lot. "The mufti is for cover; didn't take you too long to uncover it, though," he said ruefully. "But for today I am Manager's Assistant Keith Brutosky.

Fiona grinned. "Well, Manager's Assistant Mr. Brutosky, here's a hint. Slouch a bit. And don't be so cheerfully helpful. Most assistants hate having to meet people on behalf of their bosses."

Joe laughed and Brutosky grimaced. "Where are you taking us, Keith? And why?" asked Joe.

While maneuvering the quick little vehicle through the parkade gates, into the airport proper, and down a long exterior walkway, the young man looked over his shoulder at Fiona, and then at Joe.

"Well, since you sussed me out, no reason not to tell you. Someone thought it would be better if you did not fly Ryan Air today. Something about the hacking potential of all flight passenger lists." He looked a bit abashed. "I am not gossiping, I was told I could tell you that, if you resisted my offer of a lift." He was enjoying these two people; they were not what he had expected at all.

Instead of driving into the airport buildings, Brutosky drove them to a distant and quiet taxiway, up to the staircase of a Gulfstream jet. It carried standard GBA identification letters and numbers.

"Not Air Force issue," Brutosky said. "It's a loaner. But we will be flying you." He proceeded to unload their baggage, and attempted to carry it all up the aircraft's stairway. Joe and Fiona rescued him from that nonsensical effort. "Because you are already in the Eurozone, no violations of international law will be evoked, when we land in Spain."

"Well, good," drawled Fiona. "I was really worried about that."

As they climbed the metal staircase, the young Flying Officer said "Your uncle is already aboard. I will be flying with you today, as third officer. Which means, I serve the tea or coffee." He said that rather shamefacedly.

Fiona could not help herself. "What? No third option? Those first two are classically accompanied with a smile and an 'or me'." She leered salaciously.

The young man gulped and blushed again. Joe intervened, as he stepped aboard, and looked about. "Fiona, stop it. You know very well there will be a third option if Uncle Mack is here—whiskey. And a rare single malt, if I know anything."

They settled into huge and comfortable leather seats, across a small table from their Uncle Mack. He was jauntily dressed in hiking gear, for no obvious reason. Both Fiona and Joe wondered about her heels and his city shoes.

Within a minute a tall man, in his later forties, and sporting the usual, and giveaway, RAF mustache, appeared from the aircraft's cockpit. Fiona noticed that his suit, tie and shirt were identical to those worn by their Flying Officer Brutosky. He introduced himself as Captain Ian Markham, told them the expected take off time—they were only third in line—their expected time of arrival, and some details about the aircraft. Very professional, very military. Finally, he asked "Any questions?"

"Why the twin outfits? You and the Manager's Assistant?" asked Fiona.

Markham visibly relaxed. "Flying Officer Brutosky said you were quick. We thought we should all look like a typical private jet crew, you know, discreetly dressed in non-uniforms that are, in fact, very uniform. So you know who we are, presumably." He continued. "Actually, I am a real captain, well, Group Captain, in the RAF, your second officer is Flight Lieutenant Will Olsen, and you have met our third officer. Our orders are to get you discreetly to Spain, and leave just as discreetly. And," he said in a measured and professional voice, "we will be serving luncheon, just as soon as flight conditions safely allow us to do so." He had just given a very passable imitation of a public airline's steward. He knew it, and allowed a hint of a smile to play across his otherwise stony face. "Welcome aboard, and please," he returned to that polished tone, "Assure that your seat belts are fastened for takeoff." He grinned, and returned to the flight deck.

The engines, which were already warming up, increased in decibels, the sleek craft moved forward and out onto a taxiway, held its position for a few minutes, then began to move out onto the active runway. Lift off was smooth, and fast, and within minutes they had turned out of the flight path of the Cork airport, and were heading south over the Irish Sea towards sunny Spain.

CHAPTER 12

CHARLESTON, SOUTH CAROLINA

"So," Sam Wardell said. "Things went well in Darkwood, don't you think?" He passed through Mathieux' huge office and settled himself on the leather couch. He wanted to put his feet up on the antique coffee table, but forbore that pleasure.

The Archreverend looked at the younger man, his eyes raised above the half-frame glasses he used for reading. "Please sit here, at the desk," he said. "We need to discuss business."

Sam got up and sat down in one of the leather upholstered arm chairs which fronted the desk. He found it was more comfortable than the couch, actually, but he was not about to admit that.

Mathieux must have felt slightly remorseful for his terse treatment of his lieutenant—his able lieutenant, he mentally amended. "I want to show you some photographs. It just works better at the desk," he explained.

"Sure, whatever," said Sam. He knew when he was winning a fight with a bully.

Mathieux opened the credenza behind his desk. "Bourbon?"

Now Sam knew for certain that he was winning. "Sure, why not. I'm not driving, as they say."

Mathieux smiled as he poured generous shots of Dark Horse into two crystal glasses. "Ice?"

"Yeah, sure, thanks."

Sam Wardell held a bachelor's degree, English and Political Science, double honours, from a particularly prestigious east coast university. He understood the nuances, and most certainly the meaning, of every word he said, every expression he used. He just smiled at his host, who, to Wardell's knowledge, had not been able to pass second year at a third-rate business school out west. He accepted his glass, with a smile of genuine appreciation, raised it and said "Here's lookin' at you."

He knew Mathieux hated such triteness, and he grinned when Mathieux grimaced slightly.

"Well, to work," said the older man, now seated at his desk. "And yes, Darkwood went well. In particular, I think my interview on 'Tonight in America' went very well, gave the church good publicity, without being too in your face about it. Did you manage to catch any of that interview?"

Sam had seen it all, and even replayed it twice. "No, sorry, must have missed that one." He sipped his bourbon.

Mathieux looked annoyed. He flipped open a manila folder, turned it to face Wardell, and pushed it towards him. "These people. Recognize any of them?"

Wardell looked through five photographs and what looked like a copy of a driver's license issued by the Republic of Ireland. Sam carefully looked at every photograph the same length of time, betraying no particular interest in any one face. Two good looking youngish redheads, an older but well-groomed man—gentleman—he corrected himself, one middle-aged woman, and one distinctly military-looking man running to a bit of weight.

Wardell pursed his lips, then blew them out. If Mathieux was watching for a 'tell', the sign of a lie, usually shown by the unconscious twitching of tiny muscles at the corners of a person's eyes, the diversion of his mouth movement would cover for him. "Never seen any of them," he said quickly. His photographic memory had been very useful at university. "What have they done? Or are about to do?" he asked.

"This man is Mackellan Kirby," Mathieux picked up the photograph of the man identified by Sam as a gentleman. "Professor Emeritus—whatever the fuck that means—at the University of Edinburgh, in Ancient Religious Studies. And these are his niece and nephew." He pointed to the photos of the young people. "This is Mary Todd, the professor's house cleaner. And this is the professor's local innkeeper, one James Grady. The driver's license belongs to a Richard Fitzroy."

Sam nodded, looked serious, then said, "A real nasty looking bunch. What have they done? Stolen the Crown Jewels? They are Irish, right?"

Wardell, as usual, was irritating Mathieux, but the Archreverend needed his assistance, so he carried on. "The old guy is half Irish, half Scottish. The two young ones are American. We don't know about Fitzroy; could be English. He and the professor served together in the Ninth Highlanders." He paused.

"A crack SAS regiment, I think," said Sam. "You might check to see if this other guy was also SAS. He looks it." He was pointing to the photograph of James Grady.

Mathieux made a note.

Then he handed Wardell another photograph, one he had kept out of the file. "Ever seen him?" he asked.

Sam looked at a full photo of a large man, tall, sandy haired, with a distinctive long and wide bony nose. He shook his head.

"Facial recognition software suggests this is Brother Martin Froese, of the Jesuitical Order." The reverend paused, then smiled. "Of the Catholic Church."

"Yeah, I got that part," said Sam.

The two men discussed the file for another hour, and then Sam Wardell rose to leave, his instructions safely stowed away in his head. When he got to the office door he turned and said "Professor Emeritus means he retired from the Chair."

"What bloody chair?" It was the response Sam had expected of the Archreverend Claud Mathieux.

CHAPTER 13

JERUSALEM 36 A.D.

Five of them were in on the plot. Which meant that most of them, and Jesus and Mary of course, were not. The planning had to be done in semi-secret, always away from the ones outside of the cabal. There was James the Brother, of course; James the Elder because he could always contribute something needful to any situation; Simon Zealotes, though not one of the twelve disciples, because his quick and slick hands would no doubt be useful; Peter for the simple reason that if he had been excluded and somehow found out about the plan, he would run and tell Jesus and ruin everything. Judas was the fifth man. This was the night, the time for the execution of their plan.

The evening meal was done. They had all retired to the gardens of the villa, the gardens known as Gethsemane. They were an extensive planting, a private park in the city of Jerusalem, covering more than an acre. Jesus had spoken to his disciples, describing to them what would occur this night.

Now, Jesus surveyed his flock of a dozen dedicated and loyal followers. Many of them were asleep, perhaps from too much wine at supper, he thought. He walked slowly through the old olive trees, to the low stone wall which marked the edge of the gardens where they overlooked the city, far below. It was here that Jesus stood, and pondered what he knew would be coming on the morrow. He was ready, as ready as he could be, but he was also, deep in his soul, afraid. What if something went wrong? What if Simon could not restore him to life, as they had planned? What if his death was just that—death? And the promised coming of the Messiah presaged someone else, and he was never meant to be the King of the Jews, of the line of David; that they had terribly misread the ancient words of the prophets? He had his doubts, at which he had to smile. They did prove he was human, as he had always known he was.

"Come, Jesus," he heard Peter say, as the younger man approached him. "We would speak with you, privately." Peter draped an arm lovingly over Jesus' shoulders, and led him along the wall, to a dark gateway that opened to a little used path that led back, along a side wall, to the villa. "I would like to know more of how I deny you?"

Jesus smiled gently. "It is not your fault; it is simply what will be." As he was reassuring Peter, he felt strong arms about him, a draping of an acrid smelling cloth over his face, and then nothing.

"By the laws of Abraham, he is heavier than he looks," muttered Simon, as he and Peter and James the Brother struggled to carry their unconscious leader, out of the park and up a staircase, to the walls of the villa.

"Be quiet," hissed James the Elder. He led them, with a lantern shaded to the maximum so that it provided only a minimum of light, ahead and to the rear, to light the way for himself and his fellow plotters. "We do not want to wake the others, not now."

They moved silently through a side door of the great house, and with guidance from Simon, carried the limp and unresisting Jesus to the highest room in the villa, a room that could only be accessed through Simon's own sleeping chamber. It was Simon's laboratory; as a magician of notoriety Simon created elixirs, sleeping draughts, other medicants; he star-gazed, and he read ancient texts in a diversity of languages. No servant was allowed to enter this arcane place—and, to be honest—none wished to. So it was the obvious place to secure Jesus.

They quickly stripped the unconscious man, reclothed him with linen robes, and laid him on a bed, newly prepared in the corner of the room. “We have to hurry,” said Simon. “I think I can hear the clanking of armour below us.”

James the Brother quickly dressed himself in the clothes, still warm from Jesus’ wearing of them. He then splattered the spikenard which Simon had ready for him on his hands, and rubbed them energetically through his hair and his beard. Simon had said that a good deal of our sense of recognition of someone comes from their odour, whether pleasant or repellent. Jesus was always identified with a slight hint of the spicy and expensive spikenard, which the Lady Mary purchased for him, usually against his wishes.

James then went to the recumbent form of his brother and leader. He knelt beside the bed, and stroked Jesus’ face gently. “Elder brother and my Messiah,” he spoke softly, as tears began to drop slowly from his eyes. “I have always loved you. But never more than now. I am so grateful that I can do this for you.” He stood up, and slowly released his hands from the sleeping face. “I wish you a long life, the life that you deserve. I am eternally grateful for being able to help that happen.”

The other men tried, rather unsuccessfully, to hide their own tears.

“We really have to hurry,” said Simon. “I do hear the soldiers. I know Judas can divert them for a few minutes, but you need to get down there. I will stay with Jesus. That medication should not wear off, until late tomorrow, but one has to keep watch.”

As the three other men left the room and clamoured down the stairway, and through his bed chamber, he said quietly “And good luck to you all, but mostly to you James. You are a braver man than we deserve.” He looked at the unconscious man, laid out on the cot. “And, you, My Lord. Will you ever forgive us for what James is about to do?”

CHAPTER 14

CHARLESTON, SOUTH CAROLINA

Sam Wardell was enjoying a fine coq-au-vin in a quiet bistro off Market Street. When I next come here, it will probably be crowded with the 'cheffie' people, he thought. He had discovered the place, and its southern Louisianan 'French' chef, some months earlier, and ate there as often as his waistband allowed him to. He was thinking over what the good Archreverend Claud had told him, the reasons behind the proposed murder of the old guy in the photos Mathieux had showed him. Sam liked to know that the people he killed deserved it, and his innate curiosity meant he did like to know the reason for his hiring. The Archreverend's explanation had fallen a bit short. Something the old guy was doing was a threat to the Congregation of the Holy Baptism. Okay. That off-shoot of Christianity was threatened daily, by the real Baptists, by religious weirdos, by the Internal Revenue Service which was forever investigating its status as a charity, and on and on. So why the old Irish guy? Mathieux had hinted that the guy, one Mackellan Kirby, was getting close to a discovery that would destroy the Congregation. And by that, Sam knew Mathieux meant destroy the steady income stream that the church enjoyed from its adherents. What on earth would stop southern Christians from being members of the Congregation, one of the largest by number of adherents, strictest in belief in the truth of the Bible stories, and richest by far, of any church in the USA? And what was the involvement of the beautiful red head, whose photograph Sam had recognized instantly?

"I will just have to check out this Kirby, myself," he said quietly to his glass of Pinot Noir.

Sam Wardell lived in a loft condominium, overlooking the Battery area of Charleston. The building had once housed a cotton manufactory, conveniently situated near the old port, from which it had received its bales of raw cotton, and from which it shipped bolts of the best southern chambrays. The business had thrived, and moved when more space was needed for the larger and heavier machines that cotton production in the twentieth century had demanded. So, after having sat empty for over half a century, the building was one of the first manufactories converted to housing. That explained the vast space that Sam enjoyed—in a later time his loft would have been outfitted as three rental units, at least. He had a view of the port and beyond to the Atlantic Ocean, and a side view of the commercial downtown of Charleston; he had three floor levels, and he had over three thousand square feet. It really was an unnecessarily luxurious space for a single man. But, on the other hand, it increased in value by at least a hundred grand each year. And anyway, Sam liked it.

Sam watched the port traffic for some minutes, then went up two flights of stairs to his computer room. As a trusted consultant to the Congregation of the Holy Baptism, Sam enjoyed almost complete access to the archives of the church's computer system. He knew that system was one of the largest in the USA. He was sure the CIA system was larger, and he thought the IRS data storage would be larger, based on annual tax returns alone. But after those, the Congregation might be third, certainly not more than fifth, in sheer size, breadth, depth, however you describe a computer heavyweight. For some reason, before the advent of Claud Mathieux, the head of the church, the Godfather, as Sam liked to think of him, had decided that computers were the way of the future. The World Wide Web proved him right, of course, and the Congregation had continually stayed on the cutting edge. Thousands of analysts, programmers, geeks and nerds were employed by the church, through its totally owned adjunct, Dawning Day Industries Ltd. Wardell knew the company produced as much new software as Microsoft did; made a fortune selling the second-rate programs, and an even larger fortune using the first-rate programs for its own purposes. The Congregation used to be funded, and amply so, by the generous donations of its members. Now it was mostly funded through slick on-line 'convenient' services. The church had introduced monthly donations, automatically made from members' bank accounts. Sign in once, you never escaped. Tithing was a tradition of the Congregation, and heaven help the member who thought he could hide his true net worth and income from the hackers employed by Dawning Day. There was a lot more to the fund raising; Sam just did not want to know anymore. And he steadfastly refused to become a member of the Congregation, claiming it would constitute a conflict of interest. A conflict with his own best interests, he told himself.

Sam accessed his Google app, typed in 'Professor Mackellan Kirby' and noted there were over 3000 entries. He then accessed the data base of Dawning Day, with the same request. Result: 5600 entries. Yeah, he knew which site he wanted to search.

He first searched for references to the Ninth Highlander Regiment. Apparently Kirby had been an officer during the Falklands war, and thereafter resigned, with distinction. Nothing more.

The entries on Kirby himself were restricted to material about his professorship, his chair of Ancient Religious Studies, his publications, and some of the many consultations he had made, mostly in the Middle East. He had retired and was now living in Ireland. There were no references to his personal life.

Next, he keyed in Richard Fitzroy, Ninth Highlander Regiment, and SAS. The entries were fascinating, connecting Fitzroy with the Falklands, and with SAS actions in the south Atlantic, and later in various theatres of war in Africa, the Mid-East and even Spain.

"Oh, yeah. That separatist stuff with the Basques, I bet," Wardell thought. There was some pretty in depth stuff here, more than the Special Air Service of the Royal Air Force would like to have made public. And the funny thing was, although a lot of other commissioned officers were named as Ninth Highlanders and SAS in the descriptions of the various actions they had taken part in, there was no mention of Colonel Kirby. Not a one.

"Pay dirt," muttered Sam to himself. Sometimes the absence of information is even more informative than an encyclopaedia on the subject. "Wow. I can't even guess at what this guy did in order for his people to go to the trouble of erasing all mention of it," Sam mused. "Or what he still might be doing for them."

CHAPTER 15

COMPOSTELA 1075

Darda was exhausted. Weeks ago, he had successfully herded his troupe through the wilds of northern Iberia, from Finnesterre to Compostela. Axles on overladen carts had broken, horses had gone lame, the Templar knight guard had proven to include two drunken bullies, and he himself had never felt so far from what he knew. He loved his church, but this building of a cathedral was nowhere near the church work he wanted to do, needed to do, for the sake of his soul. He felt exhausted, mentally, physically, but worst of all, spiritually.

The renowned architect Bernard Gelduin, and his assistant Robertus Galperinus had arrived some weeks before the Bishop's party. Gelduin was the architect of the great Romanesque cathedral of Saint Sermin, in Toulouse, in southern Gaul. It was his intention to model Compostela after that successful design. Before Darda had arrived, he had already ordered his workmen to raze the little wooden church that stood on their building site, and they were so engaged when the Bishop arrived.

The labourers had removed all the wood of the first level of the church, and were beginning to break down the stone wall that they had discovered in the church's cellar.

Darda had been enraged, when he had crested the last hill, on the way to Compostela, and had seen what was going on. He galloped down into the town, outdistancing all of his guards, even the knightly Templars.

"What are you doing?" he shouted, as he neared the churchyard. "Stop! Stop now!

The foreman of the workers' gang, in midswing with a huge iron sledge, roared back at him "And who do you think you are?"

Darda's face flushed. "I am Bishop Darda, the Pope's Emissary here, and the authority on this site." He stayed astraddle his horse. It gave him height, and presence, and a sense of protection from this unfriendly-looking gang of men, every one of whom was armed with a tool of some sort.

The foreman dropped his hammer, pulled off his cap, and bowed. "My apologies, Your Grace. But you might want to talk to Master Bernard." He nodded his head towards an old man, who even now was striding towards the group.

As one, all of the workmen walked slowly away from the site, leaving the bishop and the architect alone, in the middle of the destruction of the church.

"The Most Reverend Bishop Darda," the old man said, in French-accented Latin. "We have been expecting you." He bowed but only minimally. Perhaps his back was stiff with age, thought Darda, or perhaps with pride. He would soon learn which.

The bishop had managed to stop the destruction of what remained of the ancient church—one stone wall inset with a projecting cedar beam. The Master Architect had argued. But Darda has persevered. This was an ancient church, at least 900 years old, perhaps more. And Darda felt instinctively that it should not be erased from existence. Apparently the workmen, especially their foreman Breg, the erstwhile hammer swinger, had never wanted to tear down the stone wall, had felt that was wrong. They were all secretly glad of the timely intervention of Bishop Darda, and held him in respectful awe for his handling of Master Bernard.

The master architect, in conference with his assistant, a master architect in his own right, agreed that the stone wall could remain, as a part of the lowest level of the new church's crypt. They could not dig through the granite it sat on, in any case, and any church of any importance needed a multi-tiered crypt. Hopefully, the congregation would be burying its dead for years, centuries even, and who knew how much space would be needed. The stone wall could easily be incorporated into the cellar walls. And the argument over the ancient wall and its cedar shelf was resolved. That the altar of cedar had been carved by James himself had been forgotten in the passage of time, through the passage of a millennium.

For the past five years, the Bishop had been housed in the finest house in Compostela, the Casa Parador, or Lookout House, for its placement on a hill overlooking the townsite. He had insisted that its owners remain in residence, and he occupied only one small wing, with a sleeping chamber and an office for himself, a bathing area, and rooms for two servants. He ate with the householders, for which they were both proud and grateful. It was all he could do, each evening, to dress for dinner, and have himself displayed to the friends and relatives, and then business associates of the home owners. He wanted only to retire to his own chamber, remove the heavy and costly robes of a bishop, and kneel at his own prie-dieu. Thank Heaven, it was in his bedroom. The householders had wanted to remodel a large formal room of their house into a private chapel for him. He had steadfastly refused. The prie-dieu was enough, and often now, late at night when sleep eluded him, he would kneel before the little altar, and pray for guidance, and, more often than not, relief from the troubles of his mind.

Darda was a simple man, who through intelligence, perseverance, and true faith had risen far above his expectations. That he could handle. But the building of this cathedral, this copy of one of the great churches of France, he knew was too much for him. The building progressed so slowly. Even the marking out of the site, the locating of the walls, entrances, supporting buttresses, everything—that had taken months, with Masters Bernard and Robertus working diligently with their squares and sextants and other arcane technology, the use of which was apparently known only to them and their senior assistants. There were now hundreds—no, perhaps he had missed a day or two—by now there might be a thousand workmen on and about the site. And the guilds—woodworkers, masons, stone carvers, metalworkers all jockeyed for space in the available workrooms of Compostela. Never had the town known such activity, never had it flourished as it did now. Every room was rented, every ale house was full, and every whore was sleeping through the day. Darda shook his head, as he walked through the town. He just hoped that the church would justify its cost and the changes it was making in the little town. He had always known that he would never see the completion of the cathedral. The building of such an edifice took a century or more. But he had hoped to see just a bit more done. And, he had to admit, he was really quite useless on the site. The architects were the designers, and would brook no suggested change of plans. The Templars were the bankers of the construction and the guards of all shipments of supplies. He was simply the Pope Legate, apparently the man in charge, but in reality, in charge of nothing. And not often needed.

So it was with surprise, and he had to acknowledge to himself real joy, when Breg, the foreman of the labourers ran up to him, in the street outside his residence.

"Your Grace," he said, bowing deeply as he swept his cap from his head. "My Bishop, at the church, we have found something, something you should see." The man was so excited he could barely speak.

Darda walked swiftly with the man, towards the building site.

"It's that stone wall, the one you saved," Breg said. "We have at last started to build the foundations. Master Robertus needed to know if that wall was sound, or did it have to stand on its own, not supporting anything else. They are fussy, these architects." The man spoke excitedly. "Anyway, we were told to check it out. And sure enough, part of it is false. Well, not false," he amended. "Just not like the rest of it. So we prodded about. And...well, you will see."

The Bishop wanted an explanation now, of what was so animating this usually imperturbable fellow, but Breg was adamant, and grinning. "You will see, My Bishop. I do not want to ruin your surprise."

Workmen stood aside, all smiling, when Darda and Breg walked onto the site, and up to the stone wall. It reminded Darda of a chimney revealed when the rest of the house has burned down, lonely and a little fragile, as though it knows it cannot continue to exist without the support of its erstwhile building.

"See here, Your Grace," said Breg. He bent down below the cedar beam, and pushed at the rock face there. "This rock was placed here, years, perhaps decades after the wall was built. The rock and the concrete are different. We think this beam, which is too low to have been a supporting beam of any sort, was actually more like a shelf, with a space beneath it. That space was closed in by the newer rock face."

The rock face, which had been earlier loosened by the workmen, was lifted away by two burly fellows Breg had called in to help. The rock panel was about three feet wide, and two feet high. Well built, it showed no cracks, even while being moved.

"Now, this," Breg said excitedly, "This is what you have to see." He pulled out a cedar chest that had obviously been designed to fit the space, behind the rock panel. "We did not open it; we wanted you to be here."

Bishop Darda, who knew he should have more faith in human beings, was stunned that these simple workers would not have opened such a find. Most likely it contained the riches of the early church, sealed away during a time of war, to protect the paten and chalice, and perhaps even gold candlesticks, from an invading army. Why the labourers had not taken the box and its contents, he would never know. He did know that he needed to work on his trust issues. He also knew, that given the looks of excitement and expectation on the faces of the men all around him, he would have to open the chest here, in front of them all.

The cedar box was placed gently at Darda's feet. He said quietly, "Open it, Breg."

The big foreman knelt and pulled at the chest's lid. Its leather hinges had long ago rotted away, and the lid had to be pried with a knife blade, all along its edges, from the main body of the chest. Breg felt it loosen, then lifted the lid away. Revealed within was a smaller chest, stone of some sort, perhaps marble. From the look and size, an ossuary, thought Darda. And stacked beside the stone box were a number of scrolls. Papyrus perhaps? Darda had seen such scrolls in the library of the Vatican; he knew they were old, very old indeed.

The bishop stood erect, and went over to the cedar beam. "I think this was an altar." he said. "And these scrolls tell the story of the person whose bones lie within this ossuary." He absentmindedly touched the beam, where the now dull pink cross was still visible. "Such beautiful carving, such care. Of course this was the altar, how could I not have guessed that?" He stood deep in thought, the men silent around him.

Then he smiled, a radiant smile of delight. "Please close the chest and carry it to my rooms." He set off behind Breg and the man who was assisting him, still smiling. "I believe I have found something useful to do," he said to himself. Perhaps it was finding the chest, or perhaps it was because he touched the rose cross, but Darda was seen to smile a lot, after that.

CHAPTER 16

Over the Irish Sea

Mackellan Kirby liked to fly in small planes—or jets, as this one was, he corrected himself. He had always found it difficult to believe in Boeing 747s; to accept that an object weighing some three hundred tons, given its cargo of persons and baggage, could actually fly. What on earth held it up? It was easier to accept that a small, elegant, and hawk-like machine, with incredible groundspeed, could carry them safely into the troposphere. He stared out of the porthole at the side of his seat, until the cloud cover obscured his view of the waters of the Irish Sea. He had also needed the time to think.

He turned to his niece and nephew. "You have been patient, but it is time I told you what I know of what is going on."

"High time, Uncle Darling," said Fiona. Joe nodded.

The older man sighed and sipped his San Pellegrino. "Okay, where do I start?" His silence grew too long.

"Perhaps at the beginning?" suggested Fiona.

Her uncle laughed. "No, no, that is far too far back. Alright. I just start. And if you get confused, just interrupt. Anyway, have either of you heard of the St. James Conspiracy?

"No," his listeners chorused.

"Good. Not many people have. It was an idea floated about, starting some fifty years or so ago. The precept is that Saint James 'stood in' as it were, for the Christ, at the crucifixion." He looked a bit shamefaced, as though he did not want to give credence to such an idea, by even voicing it.

Fiona leaned forward. "Saint James, as in Jesus Christ's brother?"

"The very man. Many Christians, certainly most Catholics, like to believe that Mary was a virgin when she bore Jesus, and remained so throughout her life. Hence the many churches named for her virginity and pureness. I mean, really, why suffer through an immaculate conception if you are going to do it the easy way, later?"

"Uncle Mack! I may not be a practising Catholic, but that is really...really in bad taste," remonstrated Fiona.

"Sorry. Anyway, some of the Quhram scrolls suggest...no, they state quite clearly, that Jesus had two younger brothers, James and Joseph. James has been identified, in a number of texts, as one of Jesus' twelve disciples. He is identified as James the Brother usually, to separate him from James the Elder, also a disciple. Sometimes the list of apostles names only one James, so things do get confusing. But the accepted texts from which the gospels of Mark and John have come to us, definitely describe James as the brother of Jesus."

"I don't remember learning that at Sunday school, but, given your professional cred, I'll accept that," Joe said seriously, to the mirth of his companions.

"Of course, you did not learn that. You were raised a nice Catholic boy, by a nice Catholic family. I should know. Your mother was so straight-laced as a girl we all thought she would become a nun. Thank god she met your father at college."

"Not perhaps the entity to thank, but, please continue," said Fiona, with a twinkle in her eyes.

Their uncle continued, as the jet soared over the waters of the North Atlantic, where it divides into the Irish Sea and the English Channel, unseen, so far below them through the cloud cover.

"Regarding the 'stand in', as I referred to it, there has been conjecture, some in-depth scholastic work and some out and out fiction, suggesting that Jesus did not die on the cross. There are so many inconsistencies with the crucifixion as related in the gospels.

For instance, the obvious ones: Jesus and the disciples were in Jerusalem during Passover and yet, the Sanhedrin, the high priests of the Jews, were meeting, and initially 'tried' Jesus before handing him over to the Romans. By law, the Sanhedrin could not meet during Passover. Secondly, this crucifixion was not public, in that onlookers had to stay a distance away, and it occurred in a private estate, near a private tomb. The man on the cross died within hours, not days, as was usual."

"Days?" asked Fiona, clearly appalled.

"Oh yes, three or four usually. That is why the legs were often broken, so that the victim could not support himself by his feet. Without his feet helping to support his weight, the chest cavity fills fairly quickly with water, and the man suffocates. Better that, than hanging there for days while the wounds in the hands fester, and..."

"Enough. There is a reason I didn't go to medical school, okay?" Joe looked queasy.

"So, was there a substitute, or was Jesus rescued from the cross, before death? The story of the sponge, dipped in vinegar, looms large here. You remember, when Jesus was near to fainting a rag or sponge of some sort, dipped in vinegar, or sour wine as some translations put it, was raised to his lips. He then reportedly said something, which has been quoted in at least three gospels and is different every time, and then died. Vinegar would have revived him, not hastened his demise. And then the body was given to his relatives. For burial. That never ever happened. The criminal's body remained on the cross, until it was eaten by birds, or it rotted off, as a warning to other would-be traitors to Rome. That part of a crucifixion was almost as important to the authorities,—for what it did to the populace—as the putting to death of the criminal. There are a lot of other inconsistencies, and stories. For instance, Essenes always dressed in white, so maybe the angels that were reportedly seen in the tomb were really Essene doctors, brought in to assist with the recovery of the victim, et cetera, et cetera."

"What do you think?" asked Fiona quietly.

"Honestly, I do not know. I have read a lot of the books on the matter. Some are really very well researched, but leave gaps. I have read most of the texts from which the bible is created, in their original Greek or Aremaic. My Hebrew is not very good, so there I have to rely on translations, but I tend to trust the translations. I've paid for a lot of them myself, so I know they are not slanted one way or the other. And the biblical texts, too, leave gaps, perhaps purposefully. In the case of the Bible, the disciples whose names are attached to the gospels John, Mark, Luke, et al, did not write them. Most were written two, even three hundred years after the history they profess to record. So that muddies things up. Then, many texts were ignored when the Bible was compiled; many more were left out than were included. And many more texts were edited, so to speak."

He looked at his two young relatives. "I do know that questioning Jesus' death on the cross questions the foundation of Christianity."

Joe intoned "That Jesus died for our sins, and through him our sins will be forgiven, and heaven can be attained."

"You were a good boy at Sunday school, weren't you?" said Fiona.

Joe looked somewhat abashed. "It's just...it's just hard to imagine, that the Easter story is not true. That it is not all true."

Their uncle looked at each of them, and continued. "I am sure most adherents of any religion feel that way, that it would be hard to believe that their particular religion was false, or at best erroneous, and hence baseless. And therefore useless. But, I think we can all agree that there is no Valhalla, that Pele does not control volcanic eruptions in Hawaii, and that Neptune does not dwell in a palace below the waters of the Mediterranean."

"Yes, but..." started Joe.

Mack interrupted him. "No buts. I just referenced three world religions, all of which once had devout followers, who could not conceive of any other world, or any other religion. Perhaps Christianity is no different.

"You mean, it has a 'best before' date, like those others?" asked Fiona seriously.

"Well, I would not have put it quite that way, but yes." said Kirby.

They were all quiet for some minutes. Then Fiona said "So, what has all that got to do with us flying first class to the prime pilgrimage destination in Christendom?"

Her uncle was glad to be brought back to their present situation. He really hated that look of confusion when Christians were faced with the fact that their religion was like all the others, no better, no more important, no closer to god, if there was such an entity. Joe was definitely wearing that expression.

"Actually, I think Jerusalem or Bethlehem might claim that distinction. They certainly would if travel there was safer. I need a drink," he interrupted himself. "Where is young Keith?" He reached for his call button, but Fiona stopped him.

"I'll get what you want, Uncle Mack," she said, then dropped her voice to a whisper. "I don't think Mr. Brutosky really enjoys serving drinks. I think he would rather chart our flight coordinates, or whatever it is that Flying Officers do."

Her uncle harrumphed. "Since the advent of computerized on-board navigation systems, Flying Officers have become redundant. Almost. They are left to serving drinks, if there happen to be any on board. In this case there is. A lovely Islay single malt. And I need some, now. It's got to be noon somewhere."

Fiona undid her seatbelt and stood up, laughing. "It's already two o'clock in this time zone. But isn't the expression 'it's got to be five o'clock somewhere'?"

"I go to bed early, so I get to start early."

Fiona moved to the front of the cabin, and disappeared through the curtain that Brutosky had closed, to give the passengers privacy. Mack and Joe heard Brutosky's deep voice and Fiona's answering giggle, and then waited, and waited.

"Whatever is that girl doing?" fretted Mack.

Joe, straight-faced, said "Oh, chilling the glasses, I should think. What else?"

Fiona did return, with the bottle of Mack's scotch, some bottled water, and glasses. Flying Officer Brutosky followed her, with a tray of crudité vegetables, a dip, and a variety of sandwiches. From a cupboard near the table, he retrieved silverware, cloth napkins and small china plates.

As he set the table, he said "We have beer and wine, juices, soft drinks, tea or coffee. Sorry to have to serve you sandwiches, but at least they were requisitioned from a good café in Cork, this morning. If you saw what I cook for myself, you'll be glad I was not asked to prepare anything." As he straightened the silverware, he continued, good-naturedly. "Actually, I was ordered to stay away from the cooker. Sorry."

Fiona and Joe were happy with the water, so the Flying Officer excused himself, and returned to the forward cabin.

"You certainly warmed him up," said Joe, directing his glance towards Fiona. "Even his tie looked looser."

She merely flipped her hair, and said in her most imperious voice. "I will have you know, I never touched his..." she grinned, "... his tie."

"Children," said Uncle Mack, pouring a healthy measure of Islay's finest into his crystal glass. "I could devour that egg salad, if no one else wants it."

Ham and cheese long gone, roast beef with lettuce and tomato but a memory, and the vegetable plate reduced to some lonely broccoli pieces, Fiona finally asked "So, Uncle Mack. Why are we here?"

The older man carefully placed his fork and knife side by side and face downwards on his plate; he folded his napkin into a triangular shape and placed it on the table beside his place setting, leaned back and took another sip of his drink. As Fiona cleared the table, he began.

"Remember, I have been at this for over forty years. It's difficult to condense. But I'll try. There have always been, suggestions, whispers really, if text can whisper, that Jesus may not have died on the cross.

The Koran even says openly that Jesus watched the crucifixion from a place of hiding, and rejoiced in the confusion of his enemies. That interpretation was not known until recently. But, the most telling information is from the gospels, and the conflict between what they say, and what is known of both Jewish and Roman law, in the first century. And if that were not enough, now the Dead Sea Scrolls and more recently found Egyptian papyri seriously contradict the gospels. The inconsistencies just pile up. You do not know what to believe after a while. You can only hope for something new, some heretofore undiscovered source, which will clear everything up. That is what we are after."

"Like a well written mystery story." said Fiona. "Every fact must fit the story, and red herrings must be ignored. Until every fact is known, the mystery cannot be solved, the story cannot be complete."

"Exactly," said Mack. And reflected that her perceptiveness had been honed by her training; never look for confirmation of what you believe; look for the inconsistencies, the crucial elements that distort the expected pattern. She had learned her craft very well.

"There should be no inconsistencies. At least none that can't be explained by either sloppy translation, intentionally misleading information for either political or religious reasons, which can fairly easily be determined, by the way." He paused. "Or perhaps a cover-up of such magnitude it has lasted for centuries. No, almost two millennia, now."

He continued. "So, we are seeking that cornerstone inconsistency. The 'fact' that is the key to the whole truth, or, as Fiona has said, the solution to the mystery. And I have reason to believe that we can find it at Santiago de Compostela. In the cathedral, to be precise."

He went on. "In the Dead Sea Scrolls there is a document titled 'The Testament of Ephes'. From the terminology, and then the lettering, I expect it is a third century Greek copy of a document written in Greek or Aremaic Greek, originally written in the first century. The letter shapes, the spacing, all clues to the date of the document. But it is the text that is important."

He took a sip of whiskey. "No, not important. Riveting."

Fiona and Joe were transfixed.

"I have never heard of Ephes, the man. Ephus the city of course. It's in Turkey, somewhere, right?" asked Joe.

"That is E-P-H-A-S-U-S. This man's name is two syllables: E-P-H-E-S. Without question a Greek name, and an uppity one, if you know what I mean. A noble name. Not common. In the way you don't expect a coalminer's son to be named Clarence or Rupert."

"Whereas 'Jim' or 'Joe' are normal," Joe said quietly.

His uncle glared at him. "Your mother named you after a favourite great-uncle. And Joseph was his middle name. Would you have liked to have been saddled with Montmorency? That was his first name, poor sod. Can you imagine the ribbing he took at school? Being nicknamed 'Cherry' from his very first day? And he was a wonderful fellow, more a 'Joe' than a 'Montmorency', in any case."

"Why 'Cherry'?" asked Joe.

"Montmorency is a type of sour cherry," said Fiona. She was beginning to get impatient with the interruptions to the story. Joe wondered how she knew the names of rare fruit varieties.

"Back to Ephes," said Fiona.

Her uncle continued. "It is believed that all of the Quhram scrolls, and that would include the Testament of Ephes, were available to the assembled clergy at Nicaea, in the fourth century, when Constantine was having the church hierarchy determine the texts for the bible. As I said, many more texts were left out than included. Thank god, or the Gideon's version wouldn't be readable by anyone without a microscope."

"Uncle!"

"Yes, well. The Quhram edition of the Ephes testament is not complete. It has long passages missing, or rendered unreadable."

Joe asked "But isn't that normal with those scrolls? They are so old, and were subject to degradation from all sorts of sources; the elements, animals, even the human beings who found them."

Their uncle looked down at his now empty glass and set it aside with a sigh. "The unreadable passages have, in some instances, been inked over. Sections appear to have been removed. The numbering of the chapters is not consistent; whole chapters, whole paragraphs are missing. And it was found that way. There was little or no damage to the papyrus itself."

"Sometimes a scroll is damaged at one point, transversely, through all or most of its layers, from rot or some other damage of some sort. So, as the scroll is unrolled, you have a consistent pattern of damage running vertically through the scroll medium, beginning at every ten inches say, and slowly reducing to four or five inches, as the scroll gets tighter, near its centre. We have all seen that; it's expected. But in the text of Ephes, the deletions were obviously intentional."

He drank some water, stretched his legs out, luxuriating in the space provided for passengers in the private jet.

"I have read references to an Ephes in other documents. Letters from him to family in Alexandria, a name in a census, and on a title deed. They all relate to an Ephes in Iberia, in the late first century. A man who lived near Finnesterre, in a village then known as Compostela."

Fiona leaned forward, her right elbow on her knee, her chin in her hand. She was engrossed, as she always had been by a good story, whether tales of dragons and witches when she was a child, or Nancy Drew mysteries when she was a young teenager. "Could it be the same Ephes? The author of the Testament, and your man in Compostela?"

"I think there is a possibility. Ephes is a rare name. And both of our Epheses—if there are two—were literate and rich. Education was expensive. Writing was not a poor man's pastime."

"But," said Fiona, "If, as you said, Ephes is an 'uppity' name, isn't it possible that if your name was Ephes that you were both well-educated and rich? To use your example, like every Clarence or Rupert in Great Britain?"

Mackellan Kirby nodded. "Yes, you have noticed that flaw in my thinking. But, I still think there is a strong possibility that the Ephes who lived in Compostela, is the writer of the text."

"Given Fiona's argument, what makes you think that?" asked Joe.

"Because the Testament of Ephes is set in Compostela."

CHAPTER 17

COMPOSTELA 39 A.D. LETTER FROM EPHES

Ava Cousin Bartholemy:

My father and I am well, as I hope and trust in the gods that you and your family are.

We are now resident in the area of northern Iberia known as Compostela, the place of bones. Not real ones, thank the gods, just the show of a very white granite through the earth, in places. The outcroppings look like bones, if you happen to suffer from nightmares. Hence the name.

Father and I have been travelling for years, as you know, conducting caravans of merchants, and whatever, wherever they needed to go. But Father seems set on staying here, with his last paying pilgrims, one Sir James and his wife, Lady Mary, Jews from Jerusalem. We met them in Margaux, in south Gaul, when we were bringing our caravan east to the Pyrenees. We meant to travel north, on the eastern rim of that great mountain range, then cross eastward into Iberia, and out to Finnesterre on the Atlantic. Apparently James and Mary were also heading there, so they hired our protection. They are gentle people, and travel with a married couple, one Rhus and Liara. Rhus and Father have become firm friends, and I am allowed to listen to their converse, at the evening meal and fire. I have heard all about their journey. Apparently they arrived in

Margaux, by sea all the way from Judaea fully across the Mediterranean Sea, a few days before our caravan. Their story:

The captain, a squat and ill-featured man, from the Levant brought the low-drafted barque alongside the stone landing, ordered the drop of the single sail, and agilely leapt to the pier, encircled a bollard with the fore landing line in one smooth movement, then grinned back at his passengers. His boatman secured the stern line to another stone bollard, and the little ship was moored. The movement of the barque ceased, except for a gentle roll with the wavelets of the calm Mediterranean Sea. But Lady Mary was still feeling the incessant movement of the ship; two weeks at sea she had endured without seasickness; now she was off-balance with a stomach turning dizziness. "This too, will pass," she said to Liara. Then she bowed her head and thanked god for the safe passage.

"James, come, let me help you," she said, turning to the slender man, standing now, beside her. It came naturally to his fellow travellers to want to help him. But the sea voyage had changed him. The ethereal wasted husk of a man who had shipped out of Acre only weeks ago was now healthy and newly tanned. He smiled at Mary.

"You are the best and most steadfast of ladies. I must remember to never travel without you, and I promise you that," he said. His green blue eyes darkened to the colour of the midnight sky and he took her hand in his. "Thank you, for all you have done, for us all." Barely in time, Mary remembered not to bow.

The man known as James, his uncle Joseph and the Lady Mary, with their two servants Rhus and Liara, a young married couple whom Joseph had seconded to the voyage, disembarked. Their baggage was scant.

The little group moved from the stone pier up the dirt track to a public house, overlooking the anchorage. The town, for it would have been so described in that early time, consisted of some large stone and mortar buildings near the port, the domains of traders and small manufacturers. Then many more rough wooden houses; the homes of the townspeople who worked the surrounding farms.

Joseph, his nose wrinkled against the smell of drying fish overladen with the usual noxious odours of a town, spoke quietly to James and Mary. "I do wish you would allow us to continue to Finnesterre. I know the trip is far longer by sea, but at least you would have Captain Fallah and me at hand." He moved protectively close to his nephew, and looked alertly about.

"Uncle," James laughed, "There is no need to seek out our enemies here...we have none. And thank you, but I know the tides of your trade. I want you to make your summer expedition." James knew that Joseph, a trader from Arimathea, prospered only if his vessels sailed in accordance with the seasons of the year, in particular with the stormy seasons of the east Atlantic. He needed to return to the ports of the east Mediterranean without delay, in order to have his fleet ready for the long voyage to the Albion Islands, in time to safely return before the winter storms set in. "If you do not get back to Alexandria for a cargo of spice within the next few weeks the season will be lost to you." assured James. "And, in any case, I believe we are meant to travel this way."

Joseph knew better than to argue. He had known this strange person since his birth, some thirty-four years before. If his nephew thought he should walk from Margaux on the coast of the Gaulish lands, through to Finnesterre, some two months travel though the Pyrenees Mountains, out to the Atlantic, then perhaps that was what needed to happen. Joseph knew enough to know he knew far too little to understand the whys and wherefores of the man he called nephew. So he fell into step beside him, as they wound up the shell strewn road to the beckoning inn.

Captain Fallah and Joseph welcomed one night's stay at the inn, with its offering of a warm bath and hot food. The second mate stayed with the ship, of course, but a ramekin of still-steaming food was sent down to him.

James, the Lady Mary and Liara and Rhus would stay a few days at the inn, and seek out a traders' train to travel with. Their destination was Finnesterre,—end of land in the vernacular Latin—at the far reaches of the Iberian Peninsula, far to the northwest. They had heard of a group of zealots there, turning from Judaism and Roman mythology, now preaching the coming of a Messiah. Apparently their ship had floundered there, in the violent Atlantic seas, and the few poor souls aboard her had taken their safe beaching as a sign that this was their ordained place in the world. James and Mary planned to seek refuge with this tiny enclave of their exiled countrymen.

The next morning James and Mary said their goodbyes to James' uncle. When next Joseph passed this way he would be admiral of a fleet of trading ships, all far grander—and more heavily laden—than the agile little barque. Joseph was saddened to say farewell to his nephew and the beautiful woman who stood so steadfastly beside him, both waving and smiling. He looked down at the small piece of thorn wood that James had given him, and wondered again about the instructions he had been given.

"Take this to the Albion Islands, and plant it in a holy place. The people of that land will be true to our beliefs, and will even be ruled by namesakes of my brother, many years from now," his nephew had instructed him. We all knew the twig had been part of the circlet of thorns which had so ignominiously crowned the Messiah prior to his crucifixion. Joseph sighed, placed the prickly branch safely into a thick piece of dampened carpet, and placed that in a soft leather pouch that he attached to his belt. "May no *lestus,*"— he used the Greek word for foul thief— "think this is gold." Then added softly "I think it may be worth so much more." He leapt down from the pier to the deck of the barque, and waved one last time to his family on the shore.

James and Mary wandered slowly back to the shops of the town. They had been told that a train of traders was expected in the next few days, so they prepared to wait, and to enjoy the sights and sounds of this pleasant seaside town and its outlying farms. They took a trail away from the shore, up into the hillsides, where small farm lots sat amongst the myrtle forests. They could see that the native trees were being replaced, slowly, with olive groves, and the natural grasses with fields of wheat and barley. At a distance they saw a child herding milk cows out of a crude byre of stone, going out to the meadows after their morning milking. As they neared the byre they saw another child with one remaining cow. The little girl—perhaps ten years of age—was stroking the black patch between the cow's large reflective eyes, offering her some fresh daisies, and talking to her urgently.

"Come on, Malla, you have to come out to the meadow, you need to eat, too," the child implored. But the cow stood resolutely in the low-walled byre.

"Is Malla not cooperating?" asked James.

The child looked up, fearfully, then saw who it was, and smiled. "She is old, and does not like to move much anymore." The child added quietly "But she has to keep moving, or her calf will not be right, and then..." her voice faded away.

James and the Lady Mary both petted the cow gently. "She is old to calf," said Mary.

"That is what father says, but the bull got at her." James looked shocked by what farm children knew of breeding; Mary just laughed.

"You are Tila, right?" James asked. "Your mother cooks at the inn?" The child nodded shyly. "What kind of calf do you wish for, Tila?"

The little girl considered. "A bullock would be good, because he can be fattened and sold and we always need money. But a heifer would be good, because we need more cows. My mother makes cheese from the cows' milk—it is sweeter than goats' cheese," she added knowledgeably. "And the visitors like it, so we always need more milk. So, I don't know." She paused, troubled. "I really just want Malla to be all right. She is my favourite."

James smiled "And I think that you must be Malla's favourite, too." He rubbed the tufts of hair just below the cows' ears, looked her right in the eyes, and said "Malla will be fine, and she deserves a quiet retirement after this birthing."

The cow tossed her head, over her shoulder, and began to move out of the stone enclosure. Tila went quickly to lead her, then smiled back at James and the Lady Mary. "Thank you," she said, then hurried to keep up with the now trotting cow.

"We had best get back," said James, turning towards the trail to the seaside. "We would not want Rhus to be late for his midday meal, of which he is already thinking." He laughed. "He would never forgive us."

Mary turned and saw Rhus, a stone's toss away. He kept a respectful distance, but was always with them, not close enough to be obtrusive but near enough to be effective protection.

Rhus is a burly man, but slim-waisted as fighting men often are. He carries the short Roman sword, the gladus, in a scabbard on his back, held by a thick leather strap; in the band of his Arabian-style breeches he always secures a deadly sicarri, the dagger so beloved by assassins throughout the eastern ports of the Mediterranean. Whatever other weapons he might have been familiar with, or even carrying somewhere about him, none of us wish to contemplate. We are only thankful that Lord John had seconded Rhus to James and Mary.

For Rhus' part, he was glad of his assignment, somewhat of a holiday, he thought. He was protecting and serving two undemanding—and could he say it—charming people. James never asked much of him, in the role of manservant. And he was invariably kind and gently-spoken, something Rhus had not experienced in masters, until he had been purchased by the Arimathean.

Rhus grinned sheepishly, when James asked him about his morning hunt. "Nothing to report, sir," said Rhus, bowing.

"But you never know, do you?" asked James.

"No, sir, you never do." The big man turned to walk behind his charges. "So, if you do not mind, I will walk back to Margaux with you, and stay a bit closer as we approach the town."

As James suspected, Rhus had been thinking of his midday meal, in particular the woman who would be overseeing its preparation. The holiday part of this adventure—well, honeymoon really— was that he was travelling with his wife Liara, who was the Lady Mary's maidservant. In most households only servants of status could court and marry. Rhus had thought he would never be able to offer for Liara, who worked at Lord Joseph's house as maid governess to his young daughters. So Liara was a household servant, while Rhus was only a corporal in Lord John's household guard.

A week before their voyage began, Lord John had requested Rhus to walk with him in his gardens. A slightly strange request. And then things got stranger still.

"I think you have feelings for Liara," John began.

"Well, I....," stumbled a tongue-tied Rhus.

John plucked an early camellia and continued, "And I understand the feelings are returned?"

At this, the big soldier blushed. "Well, I would not know that, never having...having..."

"Rest yourself, Rhus. I know you have done nothing impertinent. But, if you and Liara should wed, within the week, I have a new duty for you both, which I believe you will welcome." He then turned back to the villa, and on the way, discussed his proposal with his favourite soldier.

So now Liara and Rhus found themselves in southern Gaul, on the adventure of their young lives, admittedly without a clue as to where they were going. But strangely at peace with that, none the less.

That is the story as I have heard it related by Rhus to my father. And that cow incident was only the first of a series of rather strange events that beset—no that is not the word—blessed us on the trip northward

Our caravan of horse-drawn carts, overburdened mules, and armed guards arrived in Margaux late in the day, from Naronne to the west. The train was taking the northerly route, along the already ancient Via Domitia, north along the coast then north-west along the foothills of the Pyrenees. The route is easier on both beast and man than the more direct, but more mountainous Roman Via Augusta, so Father prefers it.

The landlord of the inn told Father about the travellers wishing to join the train, and he met with James and Mary in the quiet inner courtyard of the inn. You know that my Father Torgas is....

Torgas was a well-muscled, well-scarred giant—he had to be that big just to carry all of the weaponry and jewellery he had suspended on and about his body. He wore Roman leather armour, carried two scabbarded swords, and the handles of at least two daggers were visible in the waistband of his sirwal—the fine cotton pantaloons popular in the Mideast. His hair was braided, and held back from his face by a circlet of gold. Gold adorned his wrists, and throat, and waist. But no rings were allowed to endanger his hands. He could have been from almost anywhere in the Roman Empire, with his dark skin and darker eyes. So it was with surprise and relief to James when he spoke in slightly accented but perfect Arimaec.

Torgas bowed, slightly, as he assessed his would-be clients. "I understand you wish the protection of my caravan," he said, "as you travel through Gaul to Iberia?"

James indicated a stone bench in the courtyard, set near a table laden with a flagon of wine, some olives and cheese, a new round of bread, and three goblets. "Thank you for seeing us, Captain Torgas. But as you have just arrived, in our home as it were, please sit, and refresh yourself."

The large soldier smiled slightly, circled the bench and table, and then sat. He was not used to being treated courteously, as an equal of those who bought his services, as a guest at their table. "I am in no man's army, so I am not a captain, but thank you." Mary poured the wine and bent towards Torgas, to offer the first cup. She then sat beside James, at another bench, and smiled softly.

"Please," said James, indicating the food.

Torgas delicately cut a slice of cheese, slid it onto a chunk of bread, and ate. "The landlady here is justly famous for her cheese," he said. "And just as famous for her wine," he said, grinning.

As they ate, Torgas spoke. "So, I understand you and two servants wish my protection to Land's End? It is a long but not perilous journey. You could travel with the Roman tax collector, who is due through here within the week. His train travels slower but would provide more comfort."

"No, we do not wish to travel with the Romans," said James. His narrowed eyes dared the caravanner to comment.

Torgas leaned back and laughed. "So, I take it that you will not want to be staying at any *mansios* along the way? They really are comfortable, well-provisioned, they rent good horses...." He was referring to the Roman system of way stops along the main *iters*, the Roman roadways, in the Empire. Spaced a day's cart travel apart, the *mansios* were stopping-places for travellers on official Empire business or carrying Roman passports. And every *mansio* was garrisoned with a few to dozens of soldiers depending on the location and the neighbourhood's degree of civility. Roman officials did not enjoy the threat of kidnapping; tax collectors in particular did not enjoy being used for ransom.

Calmly, James replied, "No, we will not want to overnight in *mansios*."

Torgas' large teeth shone as he laughed again. "That is fine with me, friend." And he proceeded to attack the cheese and olives.

"Your man wants your attention," said Lady Mary quietly to Torgas, as she motioned to a slight but armoured young man who stood hesitantly at the gate of the courtyard

My Father frowned slightly. He said "That is my son Ephes. He would rather be a scribe than a caravanner chief, so, of late, I have been bringing him with me on these trips." He hesitated. "To broaden his outlook on life, real life."

"May we meet him?" asked James.

"Of course." Torgas motioned for me to come forward, and I did so, keeping my shoulders straight and back like a proud soldier, but I also managed to shuffle slightly, like a hesitant boy. Lady Mary is just so beautiful, but she did smile. Such a difficult time, between manhood and childhood.

Introductions were made, and after politely saying no to the food offered to me, I told Father that he was needed at camp.

Torgas rose and put his arm about my shoulders. "Excuse us. And thank you for the refreshments. We can negotiate your price later; now, other duties call." He bowed to them both and we went to confer with his second-in-command.

As we were leaving I saw Lady Mary lean close to James. "We will be fine with him," she whispered. "He washed before he met with us. I could smell our landlady's lavender soap when I passed him his wine."

Obviously cleanliness is next to goodness, for Mary. I saw James absently eat an olive, and he said "And he bothered to put back on his armour. He is careful; he has his son with him; we will be safe."

I liked them both, immediately.

Supper at the now over-crowded inn was a noisy, smoky and boisterous affair, marked with some minor skirmishes but generally gay with bonhomie. Some members of our caravan stayed in their encampment, near where the mountain brook which served the town, flowed into the sea. The land there was grassy and level, and well enough above the waters to provide dry quarters. The camp fires filled the air with smoke and the redolent odours of freshly acquired foodstuffs cooking. Men wandered from time to time into the village and up to the inn, to refill wine jugs. A lucky few of our caravan found rooms at the inn; and most of them ate and drank there. The landlady was justly famous for her cow's cheese, her high-rising white bread, and all types of baked, seared, and stewed meats and fishes. Having enjoyed a milky stew of oysters and leeks, gently teased with chervil leaves and a local white wine, Mary and James waved off the second course of roasted venison. They did let Liara bring them some local berries, richly purple and almost sweet, before sending her off to tend to Rhus and their own preparations for the next day's journey. James and Mary retired early, and as they left the dining space, James told me that he appreciated that Torgas' guards were all now imbibing only water, while the caravan traders and followers were still gulping down the local wine, beer and whatever the stronger spirit was that was being poured from the stoneware pots, which now appeared from the inn's storehouse so regularly.

James's party was outfitted by my Father with two horses and two donkeys. Their baggage was minimal, so it could be shared amongst the beasts, leaving room for saddles and riders. Earlier Torgas himself had led over a muscular, well-blooded stallion, outfitted with military saddle and sword sheath. "I think this fellow will suit your man," he said to James. "If I am right, young Rhus has seen some military service. He just might be useful on the road." He handed the reins to Rhus, who was staring transfixed at the fine horse, fidgeting and stamping at his feet. "And if I have need of Rhus, he will have need of this piece of nastiness." He grinned and walked away.

Rhus, of course, tried to give the war horse to James, but James laughed. "I have been thinking that I just might trade my horse for Liara's donkey. There is no way I am attempting to ride that behemoth!" He sidled carefully past the great horse. "And please, keep him from stamping on me...or my donkey."

Still early enough to have the sun glinting off the seawater to the east, the caravan left Margaux and headed slowly to the northeast. We would follow the coast road for some days, turn inland at the eastern escarpment of the Pyrenees, then follow the foothills into Gaul.

As our caravan came within sight of the first Roman outpost, a collection of barracks and stables surrounding a grander, porticoed building, all tucked within an imposing dirt wall, James drew up beside Torgas, and I heard them converse.

"Will there be any trouble from the mansio?" he asked.

"No, I would not think so," replied my father. "Most caravans pass right on by, these days. On to the open—or non-Roman—hostelry which will be located within an hour's ride." He shushed at his horse to slow it to the pace of James' donkey. "You know, when the road was built, some two hundred years ago they say, there was nothing here. The mansios were instituted to provide the Roman columns with a safe resting spot, new horses, medical aid if needed. And food, of course. Then, as travellers became more plentiful, and the mansios were hard-pressed to service the traffic of the empire, men of business began to establish the open hostelries. You know how it is—when someone has a good idea, others sidle in. One tentmaker will make a profit at his end of

town, so three others will see that as a good place for tentmakers; a potter will find a good cache of clay and begin to produce fine products and five others will arrive to use the second-best clay and make second-best pots, and no one will profit. That is the way it has always been. But out here, on the via, the Roman soldiers welcome their competition; they don't see themselves as landlords and ostlers in any case. So as we pass by they might wave, if bored, or ignore us entirely if asleep." Father laughed his usual deep belly laugh. "All depends on the time of day, really."

As predicted, our caravan passed the mansio without incident, and within an hour we came within sight of our first wayside inn, now the centre of a small but quite complete village.

Strangely enough, over the following days and weeks, our caravan was never inspected by any Roman contingent. The hunting was better than we had ever known it to be, providing plenty of fresh meat for the cooking pots. And the usual arguments and occasional fighting which have always been a part of any such trek, were non-existent.

I have rambled on far too long. May the gods keep you safe. I will write again soon, of the continuing saga of Compostela.

Your cousin Ephes

CHAPTER 18

CHARLESTON, SOUTH CAROLINA

Sam Wardell was not happy. "I am getting seriously pissed off," he yelled into his cell phone.

"I am sorry you are not having a good day," responded the female voice. Unctuous bitch, he thought.

"I am having a good day—a wonderful day." Sam screamed back. "I am not hungover. Now, let me speak to someone with an IQ in the triple digits. Now."

He had called Dawning Day Industries Ltd. but some telephone glitch had connected him to the main switchboard, instead of his intended party. When Sam gave her the name of the man he wanted, the receptionist had assured him that such a person was not and never had been, employed by Dawning Day. Okay, so that's a secret, but when I ask for the man by name, can't the idiot figure out that maybe I know he works there, and that maybe I really want—and need, to speak to him, and him only? Oh, well, Sam thought to himself, she no doubt has the required assets of receptionists, and those do not always include intellectual capacity. He tried gamely to calm himself. He was of an age when blood pressure should be kept in the medium range.

"Please, connect me to extension 007."

"Of course, sir. I will ring Mr. Bond now."

Mr. Bond? Of course that would be his alias; his extension was 007, so it should have been obvious. But Wardell was not that used to working with childish dingbat geniuses. Dingbats, yes; geniuses, yes; just not usually combined in the same person.

The telephone rang, and a hesitant voice answered. "Hello?" Sam hated the now common use of the up-speak, as though the speaker was asking a question, when he was really making a statement. Another childish habit.

"It's Sam Wardell."

"Oh, hi. The switchboard computer is having an issue today, refusing to forward extension numbers. They have to be dialed directly from the switchboard. I guess you figured that out?"

Again with the up-speak. "Yes, Mr. Bond," he emphasized the name. "I did figure that out. And ten to one your first name, in the office, is James."

He heard an embarrassed laugh. "I always wanted to be...well, important... and famous. But with the work I do, I can't even use my real name. Too much of a security risk. No one will know when I do something phenomenal."

"Look Carl, I don't need phenomenal, I need competent." He paused, then said "If no one knows your real name, why do I?"

"Because you are important, Mr. Wardell, real important."

No argument there, thought Sam.

"Carl, what the hell is going on with the Irish?

There was a long pause. "We don't know."

Again a pause, as though he was hoping Sam would say something.

Carl continued gamely. "And, since two of the three are American, and one is half Scottish, then the reference to 'Irish' is not really....."

He was interrupted by Wardell. "Carl, you knew who I meant so I guess the moniker is clear enough. Now, where are they?"

"Mr. Wardell, are you in Charleston?"

"Yes."

"Could you come in please? Telephones make me nervous."

Telephones make one of the nerdiest but best computer hackers in the world nervous? "Be there in forty minutes."

"Wonderful. I will let security know." The connection was ended.

CHAPTER 19

COMPOSTELA 1080

The cathedral was rising slowly. From the doors of the church that had been hastily constructed, across the square, Bishop Darda could see the progress, slow as it was. The church he was standing in was new, built quickly by the workmen, in order to give the townsfolk, and the members of the work force who were so inclined, a church in which to worship. The cathedral itself would not be consecrated for another one hundred years; in the meantime a church was needed. The small wooden church on the cathedral site had been the only one in Compostela, and it, or course, had been razed in order for the construction of the cathedral to commence. So Darda had a new church, and a new parish priest. Father Timothy was a Gaul, a big friendly man who enjoyed his food and drink in equally large amounts. But he was a caring, empathetic man, and the congregation adored him.

Which meant that Darda, who never interfered with the building itself, and now without priestly duties to the Compostela congregation, had time to spend on the manuscripts. In his office, the cedar chest had been placed on his work table, and there it sat. But he had removed the scrolls, had opened each one, took note of the opening lines, and hence had sorted them, as best he could, into chronological order. Some opened with a date, which helped; others referred to previous entries. So it was a doable job.

The ossuary he left intact. The lid appeared to have been concreted with some material, to the four sides of the box, and would not easily be removed. Darda was not even sure it could be opened without damaging the delicate marble that it was made of. There was no inscription anywhere on the marble that Darda could discern. Perhaps the scrolls would identify the contents, for contents there were; they could be heard sliding about when Breg and his men had brought the cedar chest in. And now, on occasion Darda moved the ossuary gently from side to side and up and down. When he did so, he could hear things sliding and rolling.

Darda sat at his work table and opened a large wooden-bound volume. It was a notebook, pages of vellum bound together by leather laces and the wooden cover. He opened it to the page where he had ended his transcription earlier that week. Then he slowly unwound the scroll that he had been translating. He rolled it carefully to the point where he had stopped work. The afternoon was early, so the light in his room was sufficient for easy reading, although the text was cramped and foreign.

Darda would not have been able to make anything of the text, if not for his exposure to similar writings, when he had studied at the Vatican, as a young initiate. As a Maltese, his mother tongue was an amalgam of a Siculo-Arabic language. His written language was Greek. This stood the young initiate in good stead, when it came to translating the ancient scrolls sequestered in the Vatican Library. The very old ones were written in Aremaic Greek, Hebrew and Arabic, or a combination of all three, with lapses into the vernacular of the writer. Somewhat complicated, but Darda, who was a favourite of the Head Librarian, had learned to scan various documents until he saw some similarities; similar geographical setting, the repetitive use of names, which were easier to recognize than most other parts of the writing. In this way, he trained himself to recognize scrolls which were copied from earlier writings. If one was in a language he was more familiar with, then he could translate the unknown writing, and thereby learn that older language. He was a naturally gifted linguist, a talent the Head Librarian recognized and abetted. He gave the young Maltese never before granted access to the oldest, and therefore most fragile scrolls in the library, most of which had never been unrolled, much less translated or categorized.

Darda took to them willingly. Translation of biblical texts was not only a holy chore, it was an exciting challenge, a puzzle he eagerly sought to solve. And the great library in Rome provided an endless supply of scrolls.

In Compostela, some twenty years later, the bishop was happily surprised that his ability to read the tight curves and cramped lines of Aremaic Greek returned to him so easily. Perhaps it was the ink. The Compostela scrolls were written with a deep purple-black ink, incised with a clean stylus. The ink must have been sourced locally, from plants or a natural tar or coal pit, or a combination thereof. The writer had obviously been a fine technician of inks, for his was still relatively dark and clear.

Darda hummed to himself, as he read through the words of the scroll, then transcribed them, in Latin, in his work book. He could not help but think, what a wonder it would be if his translation lasted as long as the original text had,—a millennium, if the dates of the scrolls were authentic.

Hours later the light was beginning to fail when Bishop Darda leapt up from his writing table. He dropped the ancient scroll from lifeless fingers. Both hands shook, and he was simultaneously chilled and sweating. He stepped away from his table and made the sign of the cross over himself. He went to his prie-dieu, knelt and began to pray. He arose only when the afternoon light had almost totally failed. He lit a candle, then a few more about the room. He draped his alb about his neck and shoulders, and went to his cupboard for a vial of holy water. He approached his desk, crossed himself, and splattered the water over the scroll he had been translating. All the time he prayed, an act of absolution, a prayer of cleansing. When nothing happened he approached the scroll and checked it for burning or other damage. It was as whole as it had been, when first he placed it on his work table. He had expected the water to cause ignition of the old papyrus, or at the very least, smoke. Perhaps the holy water was somehow diminished, so he went to the font just inside his door, dipped the vial in that, and again dropped water onto the text. Nothing.

Darda began to pray in earnest, his prayers as heartfelt as ever they had been. He had one question in mind; God must answer him. Even with his head bowed and his eyes tightly closed, the bishop sensed the light in the room. He opened his eyes to a shaft of a brilliant sunbeam entering his window aperture, and lighting up the scroll on his desk. The light was the last ray of the setting sun; it had emerged under the clouds at the western mountains which formed the horizon in Compostela. It was a totally natural occurrence—something Darda had seen often enough—but today it felt like a sign, nay, it was surely a sign, the sign he had asked for.

Darda walked slowly to his work table and touched the scroll. It felt as it always had. It was neither hot nor cold, just slightly damp. He sat, and opened the scroll to his previous place. And he laughed. With relief, and joy. If God wanted him to translate this.....thing, he would do so, as he now felt instructed to do. And he would do that duty with joy. The Testament of Ephes and its account of the St. James conspiracy would be saved for posterity. And God help Christianity.

CHAPTER 20

JERUSALEM 36 A.D.

Judas met the contingent of well-armed temple guards, at the main entrance to the villa, as planned. He knew he might have to delay them for a short while, in order to allow his co-conspirators to get into position.

"I have not received the bounty I was promised." He spoke quietly to the officer in charge, hoping that his soft tones would suggest a need for secrecy. In fact, it was important to not rouse the sleeping disciples until the coming action was well advanced.

The officer looked pityingly at Judas, a traitor to his master, a despicable wretch, by all accounts. "I have your... reward," he intoned the word with sarcasm. "Right here. I was told you would demand it." He handed Judas a small leather pouch, then spat onto the ground at Judas's feet.

Judas opened the pouch, and proceeded to count out the pieces of silver. There were thirty, as promised. He carefully replaced them into the bag, and stowed it under his outer garment. As he did so, his hand brushed the hilt of his *sicarri,* his assassin's dagger. His skill with the needlepointed dagger so beloved of the zealots, had earned him his nickname of 'Iscariot'. He was ready to use it, if their plans went awry, and Jesus was in danger of capture.

The armed men jostled behind their leader. The temple guard were never as disciplined as the Roman soldiers. Their officer raised his right hand to quieten them. "Your price is paid, now where is this Messiah?"

Judas, again with a quiet voice, answered. "Please, keep your men quiet. Most of Jesus' followers are asleep, and it is best they remain so. I will lead you to him." He turned toward the villa and began to walk slowly forward, towards the garden gate at the left of the villa's courtyard. "I will embrace him; that will identify him to you."

As arranged, Peter, James the Elder and James the Brother were standing just inside the garden gate, in an area unlit by any flambeaux, or light from a villa window. Judas walked up to the younger James, put both hands on his shoulders, and kissed him on the cheek. James returned the embrace, without hesitation.

Then confusion reigned. The temple guard rushed at James, grabbing his arms. One soldier held a short sword to his throat. Peter, perhaps because of adrenaline or perhaps because of a penchant for drama, stabbed at the only unarmed man, and managed to cut off part of his ear. They learned later that this was the secretary of Caiaphus, the High Priest. That man's piercing scream, the clatter of armour and arms, and the roars of anger from the soldiers at this assault, roused the sleeping disciples. They woke, alarmed, and somewhat still confused by drink, saw soldiers arresting their leader, identifiable by his white robe and red surplice, and ran, each man for himself, for every exit from the garden.

The soldiers dragged the unresisting James from the garden and through the courtyard of the villa. They marched him down to the palace of the High Priest, as ordered. Peter slunk through the shadows, well behind them; he had to know what was happening in order to report back to Simon and James the Elder.

The whole of the Sanhedrin and most other elders had known of the plan to arrest Jesus, and they were all in attendance, at the palace that night, awaiting Caiaphas' judgement of this would-be messiah. The lower levels of the palace and the entrance courtyard were filled with common Jews, come to either support Jesus's claim or to insult him as a false claimant to the throne of David. Here Peter waited word of the High Priest's decision.

Caiaphas was not a particularly pious or learned priest. He had inherited his position from his father-in-law. But he did enjoy the trappings of the High Priesthood: his residency at the palace, his adulation in the streets of Jerusalem, even his frequent visits to the home and table of the governor of the province. He enjoyed the power. He did not want his High Priesthood usurped by the one true King of Judaea, who, would perforce, also take the position of High Priest.

Scriptures of the Jews spoke of the arrival of the king of the Jews. The true claimant to the ancient throne of David would be a rabbi of the House of David, he would enter Jerusalem on an ass, and palm fronds would be laid as a path before him. Caiaphas had had members of the Sanhedrin research Jesus's lineage and he knew that through his mother Mary, Jesus was of the House of David. He was a trained rabbi and a charismatic theologian. From spies he knew that the man had entered Jerusalem as the scriptures ordained. He had also been told of the teachings of this man, the wide extent of his following, and the miracles he had allegedly performed. The possibility—no, the probability, that this bearded and ragged wretch, now bleeding and torn from his violent arrest was the true Messiah, weighed heavily on Caiaphas. It weighed on him, and had he been a religious man, perhaps that weight would have tipped the scales of justice and he would have acted differently that night. Perhaps he would have knelt and welcomed his king. But Caiaphas, High Priest of Judaea, was not of a religious nature. Power meant everything to him.

Many men had claimed to be the messiah, and the Roman government had slain them all. It was sedition against Rome to claim to be king of Judaea. It was not against the rabbinical law. Caiaphas questioned the prisoner, trying without success to make him say something blasphemous, for, it was within his rights to put to death a blasphemer.

The elders asked for witnesses to come forward, to testify to the prisoner's blasphemy.

Many people in the crowd came forward, all clamoring to testify, to be heard, to have a moment of glory in the palace of the High Priest. One motley-skinned old man pushed others aside.

"I know he has blasphemed."

"What did he say or do?" asked the clerk of the Sanhedrin.

The oldster moved proudly forward. "First, my name is Ezra, son of Josiah. I have a spice stall in the market; only the finest spices from the east, and...."

The clerk interrupted him. "What did this man say?"

"I heard him say he could ruin the Temple and rebuild it in three days."

"That was all that you heard?" asked Gamaliel, a Sanhedrin elder, and a respected lawyer.

"Yes," exclaimed, the old man, so excited that spittle was flying from his lips. "Yes. That was enough. I did not want to become poisoned by his blasphemy, so I left." He was clearly pleased with his piety.

Gamaliel turned to the other members of the Sanhedrin. They were seated in a semi-circle around the outer wall of the chamber, on a raised dais, to separate them from the body of the courtroom. This room in the palace of the High Priest was a copy of the High Council Chamber in the temple itself.

"That was not a threat to the temple. He said he 'could', not that he 'would' destroy the temple. And rebuilding in three days? That is only boastful." He turned to the rabble before him, and continued. "And if it is a capital offence to boast, then surely we would have not one Jew left in the world."

The witness retreated, red-faced, to the laughter of both the Sanhedrin councillors and the general citizenry.

More witnesses came forward, and gave similar testimony, all useless, and some patently false.

Caiaphas decided he had to take back control of the council. "Do you say you are the Christ, the son of god?" Caiaphas taunted him.

The man answered. "You have said that."

So he would neither deny nor confirm that statement.

But then the prisoner spoke, almost out of context.

"Hereafter you will see the Son of Man sitting on the right hand of power, and coming in the clouds of heaven."

As soon as he had spoken James realized his error: he had spoken of the Son of Man in the third person, not the first, as he naturally would have, were he really Jesus. He began to sweat.

Caiaphas seemed not to have noticed the grammatical error. He began to rant that the prisoner had just now been blasphemous, and that the council must find it so. They did. Immediately the crowd began to beat at James, pummelling him with their fists, and some striking at him with their leather belts. Finally he was led away to the cells of the palace, and no one seemed to notice the ghost of a smile that crossed his swollen and bloody face. He had passed himself off as Jesus, and with luck, that meant that his brother, his Messiah, could live.

The council chambers were cleared of everyone, the citizens of Jerusalem and the visitors there for Passover. The scribes left to record the evening's testimony. The priests and council members moved to a withdrawing room, where the High Priest's servants provided them with a late night meal of wine and sweet cakes, fruits and cheese. It was only a few hours before sunrise, when Caiaphas finally withdrew to his own rooms. He paced about until his wife Judith, who had been waiting up for him, told him to order in the slave girl who played the lyre so beautifully. She arrived, bleary eyed from being roused from sleep, and obediently took up her harp and began to play softly. Judith motioned Caiaphas to a divan, removed his outer clothing, and began to massage his shoulders.

"Husband, your muscles are as knotted as the roots of a great tree." she said, as she applied oil to the nape of his neck and his upper back. "What is troubling you?" She paused, wondering how much she was allowed to know. "Is it this Jesus, this false messiah?"

The big man relaxed under her hands. "I am not certain he is false. I think perhaps I have met the anointed one, the rightful King of Judaea." He reached for a beaker of wine, and drank it down. "And now, I do not know what to do with him."

Judith continued to work on his shoulders. "But he is a blasphemer, as the Council determined."

Caiaphas smiled. It was always revelatory to see how quickly news spread in the palace.

"Perhaps. But I have thought about what he said. On reflection, I do not think he claimed to be the Son of God, or of Man, whatever that means. There was something not right about what he said." He relaxed under his wife's ministrations, the sounds of the soft music, and the alcohol in the wine.

"That is enough, Judith. Thank you, my darling." He had noticed that the intensity of the massage had decreased; no doubt his soft-handed wife was tired. He leaned back onto the silk of the couch, more relaxed than he had been all day. He reached for his wife's hand, and kissed it lightly.

"This Jesus is famous for his parables, his way of telling a story that seems to say something obvious, but, when thought through, really means something else, something far more reaching. And the predictions in the scriptures have all been met by him. If he is the Son of God than who am I to judge him to be blasphemous?"

He sighed. "How can I, as the High Priest of the Jews, allow the Jews to stone their Messiah to death? That will be noted in history. I will not be remembered well. And yet, he has been sentenced by the Council, to death. So what can I do?"

Judith relaxed on the divan, pushing her ample bosom against Caiaphas' chest, as she snuggled under his left arm. "Do you want him to live?" she asked, simply.

Caiaphas laughed. "No, of course not. If he is a blasphemer and a fake, he should be stoned. If he is the Messiah, and I let him live because I believe that, then I will be out of a job. No, I want him dead, but I do not want to be responsible for his death."

Judith sat up, her dark eyes glowing. "Then, Husband, turn him over to the Romans. He claims to be King of the Jews. That is treasonous of the rule of Rome. The Governor always deals with that crime with crucifixion." She smiled down at her husband. "Then you have no hand in the death of this so called messiah. If he is what his followers claim, the Romans, not you, will be blamed"

"You are both beautiful and brilliant, Wife." Caiaphas smiled. "And I seem to remember something we used to do, often." He grabbed for Judith, who giggled loudly, and the lyrist quietly stole from their chamber.

Judas left the Garden of Gethsemane, weeping openly. Embracing James had been the hardest thing he had ever done; he had condemned an innocent and brave friend to death. But... there is always a 'but', he thought contemptuously to himself. It was for the greater good as they had argued over and over. The saving of Jesus meant there was a chance that he could later arise, as the Messiah, the anointed one, the King of Judaea. And relieve them of the yoke of the Romans. Judas spat in disgust at the thought of the Romans. Even worse were the men of the Temple Guard, supposedly good Jews all, but really in the service of the empire, through the connivance,—and no doubt bribery— of their ultimate leader, the High Priest. It was almost more than his stomach could bear; it had wanted to revolt by puking on the boots of the officer of the Guard, when that man had sneeringly paid him the thirty pieces of silver.

He strode angrily towards the temple, which even at this late hour had one courtyard open to the public, and at least one priest on duty. He brusquely told the guard he needed to see a priest, and pushed past him. An acolyte, a very junior member of the priesthood quickly appeared before him.

"Take back this blood money," Judas said. He opened the money pouch and hurled the coins at the quaking young man. "I have no need of it." He turned and walked back through the courtyard, and added "Or of you."

The acolyte carefully picked up the money.

Judas was angrier and more sorry than he had ever remembered being. He went into a tavern and ordered a pot of wine, he knew he needed more than one beaker. As he drank down the sour brew, he kept smacking his fist onto his table, his frustration numbed the pain to his knuckles.

The pot of wine was not yet drunk when four of the disciples entered the tavern, saw Judas, and surrounded him at his table. They were four inconsequential followers of Jesus, hangers-on, really, Judas thought. Young men who left their farms and their fishing boats for the adventure, not for the mission.

"Judas, we would speak with you," said Mark.

Judas looked up at them all angrily. "Well, I would not speak with you."

The largest of the four said "We would speak with you. Because of what you did tonight we are all in danger. We must hide or be imprisoned with Jesus. All because of you."

"You treasonous bastards! You knew what we were planning was sedition, and you walked into it openly, because you thought Jesus would save you. Now you know he cannot even save himself." He took a drink of wine. "So run along, run away. Not a one of you was ever man enough to be a true follower of Jesus."

The verbal attack was too much for the stressed and frightened men. As one, they grabbed Judas' arms, and dragged him from the tavern. The other patrons accepted their behaviour; they were countrified Galileans, from their rough clothing and speech, and no one else in Jerusalem cared about what they did, as long as they did not break any tables or stools while doing it. The barkeep shrugged; he had been paid for his wine.

The four men dragged Judas through the dark and narrow alleys of Jerusalem, keeping away from the wider, more heavily trafficked streets of the city. They pulled him into a quiet and particularly dark byway, and stopped.

"At least give us the money you got for betraying Jesus."

Another said "Then we can escape back to Galilee. We need money for that."

Judas laughed at them. "Too late. It is gone."

One man pulled Judas' left arm tightly behind his back, and upwards, until the position was painful.

"What? You never could have drunk it all away?

Another whined. "And really, it is ours, at least a share. Jesus was our leader, too."

Judas spat. "It is blood money. No one honourable would want it."

The four vigilantes slammed Judas against a rough stone wall, and started to search his clothing. He pushed them away, as he slid his sicarri from its sheath, and held it pressed backward along his right forearm, the flat of the blade against his own arm, the two sharp edges pointing outward. The most defensive, and professional, way to hold a knife. Any attacker trying to disarm him would be met with the razor sharp blade, yet the weapon was protected by his closed fist from being kicked or slapped from his hand. Judas moved backward, along the wall, to give himself some room.

"You forgot that I—Iscariot—would be armed?" He referred to his nickname,—in translation, 'the Knife'. The four wine-befuddled, sleep-deprived and really frightened men, cowered in front of him.

"You are all too pathetic," Judas said, and dropped his dagger to the ground. "But you are my brethren, through the good graces of our Messiah, and I will not harm a hair of any of you." He turned and began to walk away, further down the dark alley. His attackers could not take this last demeaning sign of Judas' disdain for them. As one they rushed him, knocked him down, and tied his hands behind his back, with his own head scarf. They lifted him up, and began walking him to a desolate graveyard, in the slums of Jerusalem. There, they dragged him to a thorn tree, and by knotting together their belts, created a rope with which to hang Judas.

"Tell us where the money is, or you will hang," snarled Mark, their apparent leader.

Judas calmly replied. "You have searched me. You know I have but a few coppers in my purse. Your purse, now. The silver shekels I threw back to the priests, at the temple. Go ask the priests for them, if you dare." He laughed without humour. "Tell the priests why you deserve your share".

The youngest of the group, John, slapped Judas' face. "Do not mock us. You will die tonight, as the betrayer of our Messiah deserves." He tossed the end of the rope over a branch in the thorn tree, and the other end he wrapped about Judas' neck, and tied it securely. The four Galileans began to pull on the untied end of the rope, until Judas was pulled upright, and almost off his feet.

Judas gasped, as the thong of leather tightened about his throat, and began to take his weight.

"For god's sake, make it look like suicide, or the Roman legions will be hunting you down." He could barely breathe, but managed to croak almost inaudibly. "Untie my hands and place a rock near my feet, or they will know I could not have done this."

It was his last act of caring for these poor sad men. He had, earlier that evening, quit caring for himself.

CHAPTER 21

CORK, IRELAND

Brother Martin Froese watched the small jet taxi out and take off from Cork International. It was required to file a flight plan but as a private aircraft, that flight information was not accessible by the public. He telephoned Rome.

"Si?"

"Your Excellency, this is Brother Martin. I am in Cork."

The irritated Italian voice responded. "So? I should send a postcard? Where is Kirby?"

"I do not know."

"Why not? It is your mission to know where Kirby is. At all times. Why can you not..."

Brother Martin interrupted what he knew could be a lengthy diatribe about his shortcomings. "They just took off in a Gulfstream G600, registration G-OJFT. His niece and nephew are on board, also. That aircraft has a range of 5000 kilometres; virtually anywhere in Europe."

The voice was calmer now. "I will have this matter looked into. Wait at the airport. I will get back to you about your destination."

"Thank you, Your Eminence." Brother Martin ended the call.

The cardinal in Rome telephoned another number.

"Father Carstairs speaking. How may I help you?" The educated voice spoke in perfect Italian, although Greg Carstairs was American born and raised. On his appointment as a priest, he had been seconded from St. Patrick's Cathedral in New York to the Vatican Library Special Research Division. He was an ace computer hacker; the e-world was his area of special religious research.

"I need to have an airplane traced."

"Traced as in ownership or traced to a destination?"

"We need to know its destination."

Carstairs made some long-hand notes. "What information have you?"

The Cardinal gave Carstairs the aircraft registration number and said that it had left Cork Airport at 11:00 that morning.

The young priest smiled to himself. "That should be no problem, Your Eminence. I assume this is priority, as in, you wish to know where the aircraft is landing even before it does so."

"You got it. And phone me. I don't always read my computer mail. Ciao." And click.

Greg Carstairs ran his fingers lightly over his keyboard. This was too easy. The most menial priest in his department could handle this inquiry, but it was the Cardinal so he would do it himself. His fingers flashed. And anyway, he thought to himself, it would take just about as long to describe the task as it would take to complete it.

First he would hack into the Irish National Air Traffic Control system. With the aircraft registration he would be able to access the Gulfstream's flight plan, with, presumably, the aircraft's intended destination. In the data base, he skewed to the aircraft's registration, and there it was: leaving Cork at 11:00 GMT; arriving Glasgow International with an ETA of 12.15 GMT. That would mean the plane had already landed. Carstairs turned his interest to the British Air Traffic Control, Scottish arena. He checked landings at Glasgow international. No mention of the Gulfstream. Then he checked the radar data at that airport.

Every aircraft in the world—excepting some puddle-jumping pre-World War II singles, have a Mode C transponder. After filing a flight plan, the pilot is given a four digit code which the pilot enters into his aircraft's transponder. Throughout the flight the transponder signal is picked up by every ground radar station whose space the aircraft enters. The radar station records the location, altitude and flight direction of the aircraft. The radar station at Glasgow International had no record of the assigned transponder code entering its airspace.

"Okay," said Carstairs. "This just might get interesting." His fingers moved quickly over the keyboard of his computer. He overlaid a map of northern Europe with the location of radar installations, and starting with an epicentre at Cork, moved the search outward concentrically. Cork International recorded the aircraft as heading eastward, as expected on a heading for Glasgow. But it never got close enough to Glasgow to be recorded. So he searched south. Sure enough, Dublin had the aircraft enter its eastern sector, now heading due south.

Carstairs set up a simple algorithm so the computer would scan through the radar installations' entries for the transponder code. When it made a 'hit' it would alert Carstairs, who then moved onto the next radar station, again moving the search outward in a concentric pattern from the last known radar sighting. Given some time, he could have created a program that would have done all of the legwork—that is, finger work, for him, searching through radar data bases by itself. But this would not take long, and it was a game, really, to follow the flight of the Gulfstream almost manually, down the Irish Sea, across the Channel, and along the coast of France.

Mode C transponders automatically provide the altitude of the aircraft to ground radar—important at busy airports—so Carstairs knew the Gulfstream was maintaining an altitude of 25,000 feet. So, not landing soon, he thought. And he was catching up fast. The aircraft was now nearing the northern shore of the Iberian Peninsula, as recorded on both the Bilbao and the Santander airports' traffic control systems. It was still heading generally south west. Now it was descending. Carstairs skipped his program ahead, to the radar stations in the line of flight. There it was. The aircraft had just entered the airspace of Oviedo, but its altitude was much too great for a landing there. So where? Yes, Santiago de Compostela. The last airport before the vast Atlantic Ocean, which even the plucky Gulfstream would not be able to cross without refuelling. The priest grinned. This had been fun, something he did not get enough of, at the Vatican.

He telephoned the Cardinal, who answered immediately.

"Your Excellency, they are heading to Santiago de Compostela. Unless there is a lot of traffic today, they should be landing in approximately thirty-six minutes."

He was quite proud of himself for that extra calculation until the Cardinal asked "Which runway?"

The priest stammered. "I can check for the active...."

The Italian was now laughing. "That was a joke, Greg. A joke. You have to get out more. Thanks, and ciao."

CHAPTER 22

Over the Bay of Biscay

Mackellan Kirby was trying to not sound like a university lecturer, but the subject was dear to his antiquarian heart and he could not help his excitement about being able to share his findings and theories with his young relatives. For their part, Fiona and Joe were transfixed.

"Ephes writes in Greek, so his name for the place is not Compostela, which is of Latin derivation. There is some confusion about the name—some saying it means 'Field of Flowers', but nowadays most scholars agree that the name means 'place of bones' in Aremaic Greek, named not after real bones, but after the outcroppings of granite that occur through the area. Apparently they made someone think of clean white bones, poking from the earth; hence the name."

"What is the date of Ephes' writing?" asked Joe.

"He dates it according to the reigning Emperor in Rome, which translates to about 60 A.D."

Joe continued. "Then how was it named for St. James? Didn't he die in Rome? Did he ever even get to Spain?"

His uncle smiled. "Good questions. There is some really silly legend that the body of St. James washed ashore there, covered in scallop shells. And that many centuries later his tomb was found somewhere in the area. Doubtful, really. At that time he was not yet a saint, and who in Finnesterre would recognize a man he had never seen, and worse, a man who had suffered the ravages of having been dead long enough for scallops to attach themselves. Think about it."

Fiona grimaced. "I would rather not, actually."

Her uncle continued. "Right. He would have been a mess. Hardly recognizable to his closest relatives, much less foreign strangers. That legend fails on a lot of points. No, the city—or town at that point—was known only as Compostela, the Santiago, or St. James, was added later. How much later? Hard to tell, unless we get lucky, and Ephes lets us know what is going on."

"You have not read his complete text?"

"Not yet. The Quhram text—which I believe is a copy of the original, written perhaps a century later, has been severely redacted. Great chunks are missing." He leaned back in his seat, and looked out at the never-ending clouds.

"I have guessed at a lot of the Testimony of Ephes. And if my guesses are correct, it is going to be in a lot of peoples' interest to keep me from finding the original." He sighed. "But there is more to this story than just the Ephes text."

He offered the bottle of Scotch to Joe and Fiona, got their negative head shakes, and proceeded to pour a goodly dram into his glass. He savoured the strong bite of the malt, then continued.

"It is one thing to suppose that Jesus did not die on the cross. Another to expostulate that. But if not crucified in Jerusalem in 36 A.D., what happened to him? And if he was not crucified, buried and arose to forgive us our sins, then what is the world Christian church built on? It's like saying the Buddha was never enlightened, just stole his ideas from some cave-dwelling hermit. Or that Mohammed was really a low-life money-trader who had connections with slavers. Knowledge, in this case, could be dangerous."

He looked at his reflection in the porthole window, and nodded slowly. "And I am very afraid that I have brought you both into the ambit of that danger."

Fiona grabbed for his hand. "Uncle, if you are in danger you know there is no other place I would want to be. I would insist on being here."

Joe had the feeling he was missing something, something private between his two relatives. But he gamely said "Yeah, me too. I mean, when have I ever actually had the chance to do something dangerous? I've led a pretty sheltered life, really." He looked sad.

"As well you should have," his uncle asserted. "Anyway, in for a penny in for a pound. The rest of the story. What do you know of the Holy Grail?"

"The wineglass used by Jesus at the Last Supper?" asked Joe. "Sought by the Grail Knights, because of the magical powers accorded to the vessel that had held his wine, which he likened to his blood."

"Which never made sense to me," interrupted Fiona. "I mean, it was his wine glass. Or beaker of some sort; I don't suppose they had glassware in those days."

"Roman and Egyptian royalty did," said Uncle Mack.

"Exactly. He wasn't either. Now if this grail had actually held his blood, I can understand how it could be considered to be magical. But why wouldn't the cutting board or platter that held the bread, which he called his body, be just as important? No one goes on a quest for a holy bread basket."

Her uncle tsked audibly. "Now Fiona. I think you are being purposefully sacrilegious." She grinned wickedly, and he continued, "But I agree with you, totally. The grail story never made sense. And that nonsense got intensified when the Arthurian legends got so popular. If Malory had never been imprisoned we may never have even heard of King Arthur and his Knights of the Round Table. But another theory of the Grail has become popular. The book *Holy Blood, Holy Grail* put forward the concept that the Holy Grail could mean the bloodline of Jesus, not an actual goblet. In French, or at least some ancient type of French, the words *Sang Real* mean Blood Royal. And of course, *Sang Real* easily becomes San—or sainted, holy. Add the leftover 'G' to Real and you have 'greal' or 'grail'. And there you have it. Holy Blood becomes Holy Grail."

His audience looked confounded.

"I have had a long time to study the matter. And I believe this is the true derivation of the term Holy Grail."

"So the Arthurian legends are all about seeking out Christ, or his descendants?" asked Joe.

Mack snorted. "Who knows what the Arthurian legends are all about? Malory just kept writing, hoping that as long as his captors were happy to read his tales that he would be kept alive. Worked for years, that theory. Seems he was imprisoned a God-awful long time. But executed in the end. I mean, really, he combines Celtic legends with Biblical parables; German folktales with French chivalry, and even manages to play with necromancy and alchemy. Who knows where he would have got to if he had survived his imprisonment?"

Joe spoke up. "I once tried to research the word 'grail'"

"You did?" asked a surprised Fiona.

"Yeah, well I was kind of into the whole Knights of the Round Table thing."

"Really?"

"I was eleven years old. Okay? Anyway, later, when I checked it out on Google, I found nothing. The word just does not mean chalice, or glass, or even beaker in any known language. Is that right?"

His uncle nodded. "Yes, the word grail does not relate to any known item, other than in Malory's stories. It is suggested that the shape of the grail, the accepted shape that is, the broad V of a modern martini glass, is actually an ancient representation of the female. The 'V' accepts the pointed male. Very phallic and quite chauvinistic. Some modern authors have suggested that the 'V' was used in some ancient manuscripts to represent the female, a sort of shorthand. Later scholars, not knowing the background, took this to be the shape of a wine glass, or chalice. And there you have the five-minute pedigree of the Holy Grail."

Fiona grimaced. "The female becomes the vessel."

"Get over your feministic bent and you will see that that designation is right on point. The woman is the vessel for the bloodline. In really ancient times, try tens of thousands of years ago, the only truly ascertainable parent of a child was the mother. Pregnancy and birth could hardly be disguised, even to people just out of caves. That is why in so many ancient cultures women were the hereditary leaders of their families. Only through the mother could the family line be known for certain and kept pure."

"I suppose worse has happened," smiled Fiona.

"So what about the Holy Grail, Uncle? Why tell us about it, if it doesn't exist, and never did apparently?" asked Joe.

His uncle sniffed his near empty tumbler of Scotch and nodded with satisfaction. "No, no, Joe. I never said it did not exist. Just not in the form you immediately thought of, when I mentioned it. I do not believe it was ever the chalice that Jesus drank wine from. I believe it was always a reference to the mother of his children."

"Jesus had children?" Fiona almost screeched—as close as such a refined female could come to screeching.

"Probably," her uncle answered. "Actually, most likely. Jesus was a rabbi, and in the Jewish faith rabbis are required to marry. He was also the heir of the Davidic line, so he would have been schooled in the Messianic traditions from childhood. They are quite complicated, involving celibacy during marriage, short periods of nuptial sexual relations, and calendar-driven pregnancies."

Joe snorted. "And a simple carpenter from the village of Nazareth believed he was supposed to practise celibacy?"

"He was not born in Nazareth. He was born a Nazarene, a priestly sect of Jews. The two words got mistranslated at some point; easy to see why. And yes, I am certain that as an intelligent young man, who knew his mother was of royal blood, that he both studied for and accepted his fate."

Fiona and Joe both stared at him.

"Yes, quite complicated really. But we do not need to get into that. Just be assured—Jesus had children."

"But they are never mentioned." Fiona was perplexed. "What happened to them?"

Her uncle quickly responded. "When we know what happened to their father, we might be able to ascertain what happened to them."

"Don't we know what happened to Jesus?" asked Joe.

"Not really; not definitively." He looked at his relatives. "Do you think I could risk a little more Islay? I think this is going to be thirsty work."

Fiona poured him a good shot, looked at it critically, and poured more.

"Now talk, Uncle."

"Yes, well, it gets complicated. There are so many strands, which don't seem to bear any relationship to the other strands, but I have the feeling that they all weave together, and the pattern will be clearly seen, eventually. Okay, there has long—and I mean long, going back to the first century—there has long been a tradition of Mary Magdalene landing in southern France, Gaul as it then was. This is not controversial; why wouldn't she escape Jerusalem after the crucifixion? She may even have been wanted by the Romans, on some charge or other."

"Are you proposing that Mary Magdalene was the mother of Jesus' children?" asked Fiona.

Quick as ever, Mackellan thought. "Yes."

"But wasn't she a prostitute?" asked Joe. The other two stared at him, and he blushed slightly. "I mean, would Jesus have slept with a prostitute? Wasn't that forbidden to a rabbi? And for sure, to the scion of the House of David?"

His uncle shook his head. "Mary was no prostitute. She was a lady. Her family probably owned most of the land around Magdala, a fishing village on the Sea of Galilee."

Joe continued. "But doesn't 'magdalene' mean prostitute?"

"Not until the Catholic church decided it should!" snapped his uncle. "Sorry, Joe. It is just that it makes me so angry when people believe that revision of history. She was landed gentry, if they had such a designation in that time. She was rich enough to pay for most of the expenses of Jesus and his followers, she was likely the cousin of Simon Zealotes, and she was probably married to Jesus at that famous wedding in Cana. She was a lady, but not a 'Lady of the Night'." He took a deep drink of his scotch. "Of course that was his wedding. Why else ask him to provide the wine?" he muttered to himself. He then continued:

"The Catholic church, especially under the leadership of Peter, who had been jealous of the love and esteem Jesus held for Mary, began an organized campaign to blacken her reputation. Actually, blacken is the perfect word. You have heard of the Black Madonnas? Many historians believe Mary is the model, or the basis, for those. The church itself held her in disrepute, but many artists of the Renaissance period, by making her the black Madonna, were making a social and political statement, much like satirists today." Kirby leaned back, rested his elbows on the padded arms of his seat, and touched his fingertips together. "Speaking of artists, there are all those codes and clues contained in the works of Leonardo da Vinci, which must have something to do with his being the Grand Master of the *Priore de Sion*."

"The what?" asked Joe, just as Fiona said "I have read about that."

Their uncle continued. "The *Priore de Sion*, or Priory of Sion was one of the many orders started in the twelfth through fourteenth centuries. It reputedly took over from the Templars, re: the protection of the seed of Jesus, the so-called Holy Grail."

"I am starting to get an inkling of the pattern of all those strands," mused Fiona.

"And I am getting a headache," said Joe. "So, we have Mary Magdalene, who might be Jesus' wife, living in southern France. Did the Templars travel with her and protect her?"

"The Knights Templar were not in existence in the first century. They started as a loosely-knit group of European knights who went to Jerusalem to protect pilgrims, tenth century or so. Then, when the Persians attacked Jerusalem, the knights were organized to fight in the crusades to take back the Holy Sepulchre, the Temple. They became an official order in the eleventh century. Way too late to help Mary. They fell out with the Vatican, probably something to do with their banking abilities, and were hunted down and eradicated sometime in the thirteenth century."

"So who protected Mary, and her children? For over a thousand years?"

"There has been a lot of supposition about Mary in Gaul, about her descendants marrying into all of the royal houses of Europe, starting with the Merovingians in the ninth century. What happened between the first and the ninth centuries, though, is a bit of a blank. We are never going to find a book titled *Whatever Happened to Mary*. But we can interpolate."

"You know how North American native people have a myth for every animal, for every body of water, for the start of the world, known as creation stories? And amongst most nations, although separated by distance and language, many of those myths are similar? So it is with European Christian mythology. There is a persistent Grail Quest myth, tightly interwoven with chivalry throughout western Europe. Who knows how it got started or how it spread? No doubt bards and troubadours had a lot to do with it. They were travelling entertainers; they would steal each other's material; they would misinterpret, mistranslate or mispronounce words. Hence the ongoing similarities, but differences also, in the folklore of various nations. And there is a reason for the term Dark Ages. That was the period from perhaps the fifth century through the eighth or ninth. It varied from country to country, or kingdom to kingdom, as they were then."

"I thought the expression Dark Ages was being frowned, on.

That it seems pejorative of that period of history." Fiona looked at her uncle.

He leaned forward, intently. "Yes, I have heard that argument. But personally I think the term Middle Ages is threatening, in the extreme. If you have 'middle' then you must have first and last. We are now some eight centuries past the Middle Ages, so how much future do we have, do you think?"

"Put that way, I think we should stick with Dark Ages" commented Joe. He was back to being laconic, no longer panicked by the revelations about his faith. All good, thought Mack.

"Back to Mary, and the family of Jesus. There is some evidence that the family survived the trip to Gaul, and perhaps to Iberia. There are those horrific stories of the Desposyni, the descendants of Jesus Christ, who were hunted down and murdered by the Romans in the first and second century. But some scholars believe 'descendant' has been mistranslated from the word for family, so the Desposyni could be the descendants of his siblings and cousins. He had a number of siblings, besides James. There are rumours—scholarly rumours, mind,— that the early Christian church was so well established in Rome by then that perhaps the church hierarchy itself had something to do with hunting down the family of Christ, in order that no new Messiah could claim to be the head of the church, in place of the Bishops of Rome." Kirby shook his head. "Really, if you look hard and far enough, you can find two unsupported myths for every fact in the story of early Christianity. Telling the difference is the art of archaeological religious studies."

Flying Officer Keith Brutosky knocked on the cabin door, and entered. "We will be landing in just less than an hour. Is there anything I can get for any of you?" He smiled particularly at Fiona, who had the good grace to remain unblushing.

Uncharacteristically, Joe spoke up. "I could do with a beer, Lager if you have one, please." Joe did not really enjoy the dark British beers he had been exposed to at Uncle Mack's house.

"Oh well," said Fiona. "I do know it is five o'clock somewhere.

I would absolutely adore a glass of white wine. Chablis if you have one, please," she paused, then said "Keith." Fiona was unusually low-voiced for a woman, but the flying officer's name came out like a deep but happy moan. An orgasmic moan, Joe privately thought. For his part, Brutosky reddened immediately. Mackellan shook his head, and asked his niece for another shot of his Islay.

"I think we are all glad for the interruption," he said. "I think you two were nodding off. I am familiar with that glazed look from my days of lecturing."

Fiona poured his scotch, handed it to him, and sat back down. "No, Uncle Mack. This is fascinating."

"But so multi-layered," said Joe.

Mack laughed. "Well, to be fair to you, we have covered more ground than you would in a whole term of 'The Politics of Ancient Judaea'. But I need to have you both up to speed, when we land."

Joe grimaced. "Can I at least enjoy my beer first?"

CHAPTER 23

CHARLESTON, SOUTH CAROLINA

Dawning Day Industries Ltd. is headquartered in an impressive modernistic tower in the high-rent district of downtown Charleston. Actually, it owns the building and is the sole occupant, although the lengthy list of corporate names on the directory in the main foyer suggests otherwise. Strangely enough, no one ever asks for entry to the offices of any of those 'tenants'. And no one gets through the foyer without a visitor's pass around his neck and a metal bracelet on his wrist. The pass includes a photograph. The metal bracelet includes a high tech monitoring chip. Walk through the wrong door, and that chip screams at the central computer, and guards appear, soon, very soon. Try to remove the bracelet, and those guards appear even sooner, and all surrounding doors are automatically locked down. The system constantly annoyed Wardell; what impressed him was the spacious underground guest parking facility. The elevator took visitors to only the main entrance. When receiving the visitor's pass, you simply told the receptionist the model and license number of your car. You could park all day, provided that you left the garage within ten minutes of checking back through the receptionist's desk. Sam had no idea what happened if you overstayed your welcome in the carpark; spikes probably rose out of the concrete parking surface and punctured all four tires. That would fit with the general eeriness that pervaded the offices of Dawning Day Industries Ltd.

Outfitted with pass and bracelet, Wardell took the elevator to the fifteenth floor and ambled down the hall to Carl Rutger's office... excuse me, James Bond's office.

Carl met him at the door and ushered him in, careful to lock the door from his desk, when he sat down. Wardell sat in a very comfortable armchair. He wished Carl would leave the blinds open; from this height his office had a perfect view of the Cooper River, and John's Island, keeping the Atlantic Ocean at bay. But the blinds were drawn, as usual, to keep reflected sunlight off Carl's desk computer screen. The office was outfitted with a number of computers and a multi-dimensional flick screen, useful when Carl needed to pull up a number of images and browse through them. These lined an interior wall. His desk held only a keyboard and a screen, which at this point were both withdrawn into their cavity under the sleek wood surface of the desk. The room was free of any personal items: no photographs, no diplomas, no dirty coffee cups.

Carl smiled awkwardly. "How are you, Sam?"

"I'm perfect," replied Sam. "Now, the Irish."

Carl fidgeted with an oversized jack, like a child's jack, which he had just removed from a desk drawer. "We have people on the ground, in Innescarrig, at Cliffside House—that is Kirby's house." He paused to explain.

"I know. I have read the file. Not particularly onerous, given its size."

Carl continued. "In Dublin, and now Cork."

"I thought they were in Dublin."

"Yes, well, that was the general consensus. From what we heard. But when none of the highway cameras picked up their rental car we knew that was not where they were headed."

Sam silently acknowledged that this was going to take longer than it was probably worth, but he was here now, so he might as well let Carl prose along until he got to the point.

"I replayed the tape of the conversation O'Connor and Kirby, that is, Miss Kirby, had outside Cliffside. Obviously O'Connor was playacting, and badly too, when he said they were going to Dublin. So now we know that both O'Connor and Ms. Kirby are in on the scheme, whatever the scheme is." As he talked, Carl kept twisting the jack over and over, running his fingertips over the four spheres at the ends of the crossed pieces. Sam stared at the constantly moving fingers, then let himself smile. Carl was not just nervous; Carl was stressed, and like a child he needed his soother, his 'blankie'. At least it is not a real baby soother, or a real blanket, either of which would have looked pathetically weird, even for Carl, thought Sam.

"Our facial recognition software system is scanning surveillance tapes for Cork International Airport. Highway cameras showed that they arrived there Friday morning. And our person on the ground confirmed that their rental car is parked in short term parking." He sat back and looked straight at his visitor. "And that is where we lost them."

"Lost?"

"As in, never saw again."

"They didn't check in with any airline?"

"Not on any passenger list, and our FRS would have picked them up."

"What about being picked up by another vehicle, in the parking area?"

"Not likely. Highway cameras are no good for FRS; they are mounted so high that tall people are obscured by the roofs of their vehicles. But the cameras on the exits of the parkade pin point the faces of the driver and front seat passenger, if any. We got nothing there."

"Okay." Wardell began to think. "What about their cell phone GPSes?" He knew it was illegal, and difficult, to trace a cellular telephone's GPS signal. But he also knew that neither of those restrictions would deter Dawning Day.

Carl shook his head. "They left them, both, in the trunk of their rental car."

"So they knew we would use the phones as a trace."

"Knew someone would. Maybe not us. I mean, how could Kirby know about us?"

Yeah, thought Sam. How would someone who was a world-class religious scholar, someone working on a document that could destroy Christianity if it got public, how could that person not know about the world's second largest Christian church, second only to the Roman Catholics?

He got up and walked over to the windows, and opened the blinds. The view really was magnificent, on this golden fall day. He wished he was sailing.

"Yeah, how would they know about us?" He closed his eyes and thought. "What about private aircraft? They don't have to file lists of passengers, but they do file flight plans, which usually include the number of persons on board, destination, ETA, etc. etc."

Carl Rutger stared at Sam, his mouth agape. "We never thought of private airplanes. None of us."

Nerds, thought Sam. They could compute a spacecraft's trajectory to Mars, but they might just trip on a crack in the sidewalk.

"Get on it," said Sam, back in his chair, his head leaning on his right hand. "I'll wait. And I want a gin and tonic." He thought about it, then added "Thanks."

CHAPTER 24

OVER THE COAST OF THE IBERIAN PENINSULA

"So, what have I glossed over?" mused Kirby.

"Oh, I don't know?" said Fiona. "We have Mary Magdalene, who is a lady not a whore, giving birth to Jesus Christ's children, in Gaul. Or maybe Iberia. We have Jesus not dying on the cross, so maybe he is with the happy family. But if he wasn't crucified then who was? We have an ancient scroll written by this Ephes guy, which apparently holds a secret that could blow apart Christianity. He may have been in Compostela, where we are headed. Although, from the first century to today, I would say his trail has gone cold. No, icy." She paused for a sip of wine. "What else? Oh, yes. We are flying in a premier private jet, crewed by the Royal Air Force. And you were shot at in your own park. Have I missed anything?"

Her Uncle Mack tut tutted. "Sarcasm is not becoming, Fiona. Even though you do it beautifully." He smiled. "But I can tell you more about the man who died on the cross. I believe it was James, the next younger brother of Jesus."

Joe sat up. "Is there another secret text, or something?"

"No," said Mack. "But there is a painting. The Last Supper, the Leonardo da Vinci masterpiece."

"Oh no," Fiona faked dismay. "Not *The da Vinci Code* again."

"Actually, that was a very fine read," said Mack seriously. "Brown got a lot right. But he missed some things. Have you ever studied the painting?

Joe looked up. "I do know what was said in the book; that the disciple on Jesus' right is really Mary Magdalene. That person does look rather feminine. And then there was that hypothesis that the angle between that disciple and Jesus forms a perfect 'V', which is suggestive of the Holy Grail shape."

"The representation of the female," said Fiona.

"Good. But what no one has ever commented on is the disciple on Jesus's immediate left. The man is bearded, bears a striking resemblance to Jesus, and inexplicably has his arms spread out, at right angles to his body. Like this." Kirby sat forward, tilted his shoulders somewhat, and spread his arms out straight. "Remind you of anything?" His eyes sparkled. Excitement or scotch, wondered Fiona.

Mack continued. "I believe that da Vinci was telling us that James was the one crucified. The position of the arms is the giveaway."

"But how did...how would... Leonardo da Vinci know that?" asked Joe.

"Because he was the Grand Master of the Priory of Sion," Mack grinned triumphantly.

So it was excitement, not the scotch, amended Fiona to herself. "Of course he was," she dead-panned.

"The Priory of Sion?" Joe asked.

"Yes, I was starting to tell you about that. And really, Fiona. Be nice. The Priory of Sion, or Prieure de Sion as it was known, was one of those many orders founded in the late Middle Ages, sometime in the eleventh century. It was entrusted by the Knights Templar with some arcane secrets. The knights knew they were in danger from the Vatican, probably the only entity which was powerful enough to threaten them at that time. There is some old story about an elm tree at Guise being cut down, and that meant the Templars and their allied Orders were severed, giving rise to the Priory. I don't know.

That is medieval history, not my forte. But certainly the Priory did exist, still does actually."

"Have either of you read *Holy Blood, Holy Grail* by Baigent, Leigh and Lincoln? Brown referred to it, in his book. Anyway, it was published in the early eighties. One of the first books to question some of the biblical stories. It gives a concise history of the Priory of Sion. And a list of its Grand Masters."

He paused. "And sure enough, Leonardo da Vinci was the leader of the Priory. And as such, he would have been privy to its secrets. And, like a naughty child with a secret, he just had to hint about it. Children usually hint too broadly, and their secret is out. Da Vinci hinted, but for over five hundred years, no one has figured him out."

"Until now," said Joe, with awe.

"Yes, well," his uncle said rather diffidently. "I do have a few years of study under my belt."

"What secrets?" asked an unconvinced Fiona.

"They are secrets. So how can any of us know, for sure? But one of those secrets was worth a fortune, to the man who discovered it. In 1891, a small town priest, in southern France, was undertaking renovations on the local Catholic church and grounds. He found something in a concrete pillar. The story is that it was documents. But soon thereafter, this poor priest was building a villa for himself that today would cost millions. He and his housekeeper lived like the proverbial king and queen, of their village, until his death in the forties, and her's in the next decade. Whatever their secret, they took it to their graves. There was never any explanation for their sudden wealth. But the Priory of Sion was very definitely involved, if you believe Baigent.

"So, to add to the mix, just in case it wasn't complicated enough, we now have a rich country priest?"

"I know, I know. It is starting to sound like a novel, and maybe not even a good one. But I swear, that is all true."

"What do you think the priest found?" asked Joe. He really

could be some comedian's straight man, thought Fiona. He always asks the obvious question, at the obvious time. Right on cue.

Their uncle leaned back, looked out at the northern coast of the Iberian Peninsula, just appearing in their portside windows. The waters of the Bay of Biscay crashed relentlessly into the rocky coast, forming huge sprays of white froth. But the land beyond the breakers looked warm and inviting. He really, really wanted to be able to enjoy this trip.

"I think he may have found a copy of the Testament of Ephes. And he sold it to the Vatican. For a fortune."

"So if you find another copy of the Testament, will the Vatican pay you a fortune? With the rise in the cost of living computed in, of course." The economist in Joe was still alive.

"To be honest, with you both, I think finding the testament could be a death warrant. I have to wonder who shot at me, at Cliffside."

Now Fiona was confused. "But, didn't you say that it was the Testament of this Ephes character that you are looking for, at the cathedral, in Santiago de Compostela?" She shook her elegant head. "Why look for something when the finding of it could mean..." She struggled over the words 'your death', and substituted "trouble?"

"You did see that old Michael Douglas movie *Romancing the Stone* didn't you? And Harrison Ford's *Indiana Jones* movies about the crystal skulls and the Ark of the Covenant? Well, archaeologists have for centuries put themselves into situations of very real danger seeking after such things. And religious studies archaeologists seek after the true history of Jesus Christ. We just can't help it." He took a sip of scotch. "Even if it is dangerous." He muttered this last in an undertone, but the two members of his rapt audience heard every word.

CHAPTER 25

Compostela Iberia 48 AD Letter from Ephes to his cousin Bartholomew of Alexandria

Ava Cousin

Thank you for your correspondence. I fondly remember young Bethany, and cannot believe she is now a married woman and a new mama! I can see you being a very proud grandpapa, though. Congratulations.

You did not write of it, but I am aware of the persecution you and our family must be suffering. In northern Iberia we are not so separated from civilization so as not to be aware of world politics, that is, Roman politics. I know of the troubles in Albion, of the attacks of the Vandals on Rome itself, and of the foment of revolution within the Jewish province of Judaea. I know the new religion—Christianity—is being blamed for all of these troubles, and more. But I believe that Rome has rotted from the inside; like an overripe fruit, it can hang on to the glory of the top branch of the tree for only so long.

Near a decade ago, as I told you, father led our caravan to this spot, on our way out to Finnesterre. But when we arrived here, our paying guest, one James of Judaea, spoke to my father:

"Torgas," said James. "My family will be staying here. Thank you

for your protection, and, I would like to think, your friendship. You are a most competent caravanner, a good soldier, and a fine man." James looked about, at the shallow green hills rising from a base of granite, so white it looked like bone.

My father studied James. "But we are only five days from Finnesterre. There is a port there, merchants, hostelries..." he paused. "People."

James smiled. "There will be people here, many people." He walked across a patch of exposed granite. "In this place of bones, this Compostela, will rise a church." He said that dreamily, his eyes focused on the far distance, as though in a trance. Then he shook his head, and said "And I will build that church."

My father also looked about, at the verdant land, the copses of wild olives that showed that there were rivulets of water running down the slopes. He looked out from the granite outcropping that was so smooth and level it almost begged to be a building site. He looked down at the gentle dips and swales that ran away from their perch of stone; those spoke of deep loam and good farming earth.

"You know," he said quietly. "We might just stay with you."

We camped at Compostela for some days, on that first visit years ago, and surveyed it as best we could. Father and James then travelled to Finnesterre, the nearest Roman administration centre. There they bought the land they had marked out, from the Roman Empire, in the personage of the local magistrate. They were secure with their titles—the Roman Empire is often corrupt, but it does function well, and deeds of land are well understood and not often interfered with. James even purchased a good sized property with farming potential, and registered it in the names of Rhus and Liara. He gave it to them on the birth of their first son, some six years ago, now. Although as land owners they could live independently, Rhus and Liara remain in the household of James and Mary, as senior servants in charge of both the household and the substantial grounds. And of their church, of course.

I will tell you of our church, and the strange stories that surround it:

The people of the caravan had no pressing need for permanent houses—their tents were tough, weatherproof and commodious. And easily repaired by the resident tentmaker. So the church, or synagogue, had been one of the first buildings.

Soon after the settlement of Compostela, the sect of Judaic zealots living in Finnesterre, having heard of Sir James, moved to join his colony. So ours is a community of Jews and these new Christians. Whatever the background, whatever the homeland, the religion of their fathers, the secret arcane abilities of their mothers, we are all living together in harmony.

Mary often receives letters from her brother Lazarus from Bethany in Judea. He learned that after the departure of James from Judea, that the disciples—led, strangely enough, by Saul of Tarsus, a man James had met once during his escape from Judea, spread the word of the Christ who had died for all of mankind's sins, and through whom, one could be forgiven his earthly transgressions, and enter into the kingdom of heaven. James thought that seemed a bit farfetched, when Mary told him of the church's spread from Galilee, to Greece, and even to Rome itself.

So the church, built on the white granite, the 'bones' of the 'place of bones', is an amalgamation of what anyone in the community thought a church should be. It is made of stones, mortared together with a mixture of clay and lime, which we found locally. Angular chunks of granite sit incongruously with round river rocks. The doorway faces east, as is proper, and no door bars entry—the way is left open and welcoming. Liara, it was discovered, is a gifted artist, and with paint made from mixing plant juices and ground rock pigments into the local clay, adorned the area behind the altar. She drew the prophets looking towards a golden cross, a crucifix to commemorate the awful event that had given birth to the new Jewish sect of Christianity. She added doves and fishes, and lambs, and even a scallop shell, because she enjoys drawing these things.

The altar itself is made of cedar. A nearby grove of old cedars had one tree harvested for the purpose. The trees are so beautiful, and so beset with mythology as the homes of woodland gods and goddesses, that it was a communal decision to preserve the rest. The one tree provided a trunk substantial enough to encompass the whole altar. It needed to be fitted to the church, and carved and shaped in order to function. James happily took on this task; he had worked with wood when he helped his father Joseph with the simple joinery jobs that were called for in their Galilean village. He obtained a rudimentary saw and a plane from the metal mongers in Finnesterre and joyfully worked the wood, opening it to expose its bursting reds and sunny yellows. He planed the altar level, through a week of hard work. Then he began to decorate the frontispiece with carvings of the natural world. While carving an owl, perched in a tree, James nicked himself with his knife. His blood dripped onto the leaves of the tree, a group of four leaves, with their stems forming an 'X', and they remain stained to this day. Cedar turns a rosy hue when stained with haemoglobin, and the pinkish colour of the cross stands out clearly from the cedar wood of the altar. As the story goes:

James had just cut himself, when Rhus entered the church-to-be, saw the blood, and ran forward.

"Lord, you are hurt?" Rhus quickly brought a bowl of fresh water and cloth to bathe the cut. He sat an ashen-faced James down on a workroom stool, and set his hand to soak gently into the water. He then went over to the tree trunk, and traced his finger on the leaf motif. It was already dry. "It feels warm," he said.

"It should," laughed James, rather ashamed about his near faint. "It should have all the warmth of my body, within itself. May it flourish with my life blood." He said the last as a joke, a dismissal of his cut, and the marring of his work.

But Rhus looked seriously at the leaf pattern, looked at his strangely tingling fingers, and stroked the wood again. "No, definitely. It is still warm."

And that, of course, began the miracles. Or at least, the tradition of the miracles, which to this day—though I should not be so prideful—maintains the widespread fame of our little church.

That afternoon, Rhus went hunting in the chestnut groves where boar were known to root for grubs and mushrooms. He was hunting with bow and arrows, in order to cause the least damage to the meat of his prey, although he did carry his gladius in its sheath on his back, and a dagger in his belt. He was hunting with two others—Captain Torgas being one of his companions, as he often was on these hunting forays. As the story goes, and it has been recounted since the day it happened, Rhus came upon an adult male pig enjoying a roll in the muddy banks of a woodland stream. It turned suddenly, large and mean-eyed, to attack. Rhus let off one arrow, which went wide of its mark, when Rhus missed his footing on the muddy edge of the stream. As the boar surged forward, Rhus notched another arrow, and, on his back, let loose the bolt. The great boar died, an arrow through its throat to its brain, its tusks only inches from Rhus' stomach.

Torgas had heard the noise of the confrontation, and arrived within seconds. He helped Rhus up, then studied the boar. "If those tusks had got to your gut, you would be a dead man. And how did you ever get an arrow off with your hands covered in mud?"

Rhus looked down at the wet and filthy thumb and index finger of his right hand; they were covered in mud. He should not have been able to notch an arrow and draw back the bow, requisite for a straight and powerful shot. He wiped his hands on his jerkin, which he knew would give rise to an admonition from Liara later, and said "I do not know. I just know they are still tingling."

"Tingling? Your hands?" Torgas turned towards the boar again, slit its throat to begin the butchering process, and stood back as the blood spurted. "I know I would be a bit more than 'tingling' as you say, if that great ugly beast had come as close as that to goring me. It's a miracle you are not dead."

The story was told, again and again, as such things are. In the tent of the ale maker, now accepted as the place to gather for refreshment before dinner, or for gossip afterwards, Torgas and Rhus enjoyed free drinks in exchange for the tale.

This incident would not have been sufficient to start the tradition of the miracles. That took a few more events. Like the cleaning woman who was dusting the altar, and, touched the four leaf carving with her fingers, in order to remove dust hidden within the grooves of the wood.

She said she felt a tingling, in her belly, and within two months she was pregnant, to the great joy of her husband and herself; they had been married for some years, but were, until then, childless. And the child with fits, who touched the rose cross, in wonder at its colour, and then, strangely, never succumbed to an epileptic seizure again.

Of course, there is an element of chance, or coincidence that plays out, whenever miracles are attributed to a place, or a stone...or a rose-coloured cross carved on a cedar altar. People who do not experience a beneficent change to their circumstances do not report the failure of the miraculous font; they simply say nothing, perhaps out of a sense of personal failure, for not being worthy to be the recipient of a miracle. And some of the miracles reported were perhaps, not quite all that miraculous, but just a bit of good luck come into the lives of people who were used to the other kind, and were grateful for just a modicum of surcease of their problems. Such as 'I touched the leaves, then won at dice.' Or 'I asked to see the face of my love-to-be when I touched the rose cross, and then I turned and there you were' when all along the man accompanying the young lady to the church was already courting her.

Undeniably, something happens to most people, when they touch the small part of the carving of the altar that depicts the cross formed by the stems of four oak leaves, stained a rosy hue from the blood of James. A peace comes to each one, and a sense of love, and with that in their hearts as they leave the little stone church, surely it is not unreasonable to accept that then good things happen.

The story of the pink cross spread, as these things will, and soon strangers, traders, and farmers made their way into Compostela, in order to touch the icon. Pilgrims all, they are welcomed, fed if they are poor, charged for room and board if they can afford it. The lucky ones who feel a 'tingle' usually buy a round for everyone, at the tent of the ale maker, in celebration.

Some pilgrims stayed, and Compostela has grown from a small settlement to a sizable town. Tents were replaced with wooden, thatch and stone houses. Part of the river running down to the valley was diverted to a millstream, powering a watermill wheel, which was outfitted to cut timber into planks. Another mill, on a smaller stream, became a grist mill, grinding grain between its massive circular stones. The miller's wife has become famous for her breads and cakes. Her son and his wife opened an inn, generously serving bread with every meal. Other farmers with grain to grind hire teams of horses and carts to carry their product to the mill. An ostelry opened, to service that requirement. And so it goes on. Some pilgrims simply moved to Compostela, to be near to a source of miracles. Others, women of impugned reputations, moved here just to be near to the deep pockets of well-off pilgrims.

And through this change to the village, James and Mary continue to live and raise their family. They are known as 'Lord' and 'Lady' although James preaches on the Sabbath at his church and Mary teaches the town's children, which includes their own five, the rudiments of writing and mathematics. They are acknowledged by all as the founders of the town, and by common gossip as nobility from the east. They are respected, and more importantly, loved. They succor the sick; they provide for the poor, they bury the dead. Which is starting to pose a problem.

We still follow the practices of the Jewish synagogues. Bodies are buried for a year. Then, on the first anniversary of the death, the bones are disinterred, are placed in a stone box or ossuary, and the ossuary is placed permanently in either a private tomb or the crypt of the synagogue. Because our church is built on solid granite, which has forestalled all efforts to dig into or under it, and the church itself is now too small to comfortably hold the adherents who arrive every Saturday, the solution was clear: build a larger church over the present one, and use the lower level as the ossuarium. The stone walls of the tiny church, which are now to some degree held vertical by the massive cedar altar, will serve as a foundation for the new church, so they, and the altar, were left in place, to become one end of the cellar of our new church.

That is the tale of our famous rose cross. I trust I have not unduly bored you with its telling. May the gods be with you,

Ephes, son of Torgas

CHAPTER 26

SANTIAGO DE COMPOSTELA

They could hear the two Pratt and Whitney engines winding down, when Keith Brutosky came into the main cabin to inform them that they would be landing in ten minutes. He removed the cutlery and dishes. Fiona had already put everything that did not need washing back in the storage bins, and had surreptitiously stowed Uncle Mack's bottle of Islay Malt into his computer bag. They were ready to land.

"How long will you be in Santiago?" the young Flying Officer asked Fiona.

She smiled at him. "I have no idea. This whole scheme is Uncle Mack's party. How long will you be here?"

"We drop you off, refuel and head right out. Someone important wants his plane back."

"I don't blame him." Fiona smiled, she could not resist a slight flirt. "So, where is home base?"

"I am stationed at Hatfield. Just outside Liverpool. But the aircraft is being returned to a private aerodrome in Suffolk. We will have to hitch a ride from there."

"Will you be coming back for us?"

He grinned. "I do believe that is in the cards. And then, of course, we will have to stay over in Cork. To debrief," he explained.

"Well then, Flying Officer, we will have to see what there is to do in Cork."

He was blushing when he left the cabin. Mack audibly tsked, tsked, and Joe commented quietly "So what is your head count, now, Fiona? Or have you lost count?"

"I am just being friendly," his cousin said, as she sat down and fastened her seat belt.

After a smooth landing and exit from the active runway, the Gulfstream moved quickly along a taxiway. Joe and Fiona watched, as the aircraft moved past the tower and main airport buildings, through a grouping of hangars to the local flights area of the airport. Luggage in hand, they walked through the smaller airport building and out onto the street. An SUV sporting the name of a local but famous hotel pulled into the curb and a uniformed chauffeur leapt out smiling, scooped their bags into the rear of the vehicle, and settled them into the front and second-row passenger seats. He managed to do this so quickly, not even one horn was honked, to encourage him to vacate his parking spot even faster.

Their driver silently, but masterfully, directed the vehicle onto a freeway towards the city. It was a strangely European mixture of modern square structures surrounding a town centre of ancient baroque buildings, the whole being dominated by the majestic double towers of the Basilica de Santiago, the Cathedral of St. James, proudly lifting its famous head over the city. Their driver manoeuvred through ever smaller and more congested streets, heading, it seemed, directly to the cathedral. Only a street away, he turned and parked in front of a large but plain façade.

"The Hostal Abbe des Soeurs Negras," said their driver, proudly. "We can no longer drive through the Plaza, itself. Only guests of the Hostal des Reis Catolicos have that privilege."

Once inside, Fiona saw that the hotel was like so many grand Spanish buildings; they show a bleak exterior with a plain wooden door, which enters, by way of a short alley under the upper stories of the façade wall into an open courtyard. The building surrounds the courtyard on all sides. Only when in the courtyard proper does one have a sense of the height and breadth of the building. The Abbe, as Fiona soon learned was the vernacular for the hotel, had once housed the Black Sisters, the nuns of the Benedictine order. The Abbe had been begun in 1499 under the aegis of King Ferdinand and Queen Isabella, to house the sisters who were needed to assist with the management of the nearby Basilica of St. James. It also acted as secondary accommodation, when the nearby Hostal des Reis Catolicos was filled with the thousands of pilgrims who travelled to Santiago de Compostela yearly. That hostal, a hotel—or hospital—as they were then known, was also commissioned by those two very forward thinking monarchs..

Their bags in their rooms, the three went out the main reception hall to the Plaza de Obradoiro.

"Oh my word!" breathed Joe, when to their immediate left he first saw the Basilica itself, its two baroque towers rising up into the cerulean Spanish sky, their flanking side buildings covered with statuary.

"It really is a magnificent building," said Mackellan. "Somehow they managed to integrate the original Romanesque, with the Baroque and the Gothic beautifully. Not something a lot of buildings can boast."

They began to stroll towards the cathedral. It was as though the wondrous church simply drew them towards itself. Into the plaza some fifty feet, Mack told them to turn back and look at their own hotel. This was the front entrance proper, the one that had been in use for five centuries. The original doors, wide enough to allow the entry of a carriage or wagon, with a small inset door for people, had been replaced in the eighteenth century with carved wooden doors, covered in a thin layer of brass, still as shining and golden as the day it was emplaced. The Abbe, next to the basilica, looked understated but still stately, not ornate but quietly ladylike, like the nuns themselves who had for so long swished their long habits silently through its cloisters. The façade was stone, rising some four stories, with a fifth attic level tucked under the tiled roof.

Joe tilted his head back, to get a view of the whole of the building, and then looked over to the basilica.

"It looks rather plain, next to the cathedral, doesn't it?" he said.

Fiona snorted. "Plain like Dame Maggie Smith compared to an overly exposed Marilyn Monroe?" She smiled at the Abbe. "I know which one I would rather have lunch with."

"Supper first, please," said their Uncle Mack. "And you are both right, of course." He turned back towards the cathedral. "The cathedral was decorated to the teeth, as all medieval cathedrals were. The better to garner donations and to impress the lowly congregants with the glory of their god." He turned back towards the Abbe. "The Abbe was built for service to that same god. And still manages to be beautiful, in its own right." He put an arm around the shoulders of each of his young relatives. "I cannot tell you how much it means to me, to be here with you both. I have been wanting to come here for so long."

Fiona looked over at him. "You mean you have never been here? And you a religious archaeology professor?"

"No, it always seemed a bit pedestrian. You know, tens of thousands of pilgrims slash tourists arriving yearly. A thousand a day, in the high season." He stared absently at the cathedral. "And I never thought that there might be anything of interest to me, here."

Joe was slightly embarrassed by the obvious emotion in his uncle's voice. So, on cue as ever, he asked a question that would get them out of any emotional wringer.

"So, you sometimes call this the Cathedral of St. James, and sometimes the Basilica Santiago de Compostela. What is the difference between a basilica and a cathedral, anyway?"

His uncle smiled and replaced his arms at his sides, as he led them across the square to an alley that led them to the patio of a tapas bar. "That one is easy. A cathedral is a church of a certain size, usually with a bishop or archbishop affixed as the head of its clerical team. A basilica is a cathedral with the added pizazz of having the bones of its namesake—a saint usually—interred somewhere within its depths.

Joe gallantly indicated that Fiona should precede him down the narrow cobblestone way to the tavern.

"So that is why there is never a basilica named after the Virgin Mary, or Christ?"

"Right. They do get some wonderful churches, though. Notre Dame in Paris, for one. Though there is some controversy about the churches named for 'Our Lady'. Some experts think the name could refer to Mary Magdalene, not Jesus' mother. Of course, 'Our Lady of Perpetual Sorrows' or anything mentioning the Virgin would refer to Mary the mother. That is why there are no basilicas in the USA. St. Patrick's Cathedral in New York is as fine a church as any basilica, but no saintly bones. Although there is a basilica in Quebec City in Canada, now. A native Indian lady was inducted into sainthood, so of course, her last resting place is now a basilica."

"Is 'inducted' the right word?" asked Fiona, archly.

"I would have thought that question—and attitude—would be more in line for Joe, him being a good Catholic boy." Their uncle ushered them up to the bar of the little restaurant they had been heading to. "And I do think 'inducted' is a fair word. As in inducted into the-whatever-Hall of Fame. Do you have any idea how many saints there are, in the Roman Catholic Saints' Index?" He caught the proprietor's attention, who, politely, would not approach a patron until that person indicated he wanted service.

"It is very much like any Hall of Fame, especially the sports ones. Some inductees are deservedly there; some people just paid for the privilege. Now, let's have some tapas with a very good *fino*."

CHAPTER 27

CHARLESTON, SOUTH CAROLINA

"E-e-ureka! We have them," shouted an excited Carl Rutger.

Sam Wardell was sipping his third gin and tonic, which had been delivered, one by one, every ten minutes by a shy but willowy young lady from Rutger's 'bull-pen' of tech nerds. He had commissioned a few of them to trace the trail of the Irish, as their quarry was called. They had been reporting back to Rutger via his desk computer, which was the monitor he was now viewing.

"They left Cork in a Gulfstream G600 today at 11:00 a.m. GMT, or 6:00 a.m. our time. They have now just landed at SCQ." he said.

"What, or where is SCQ?" asked a still clear-headed Sam Wardell.

"Sorry, that is aviation-speak for the Santiago de Compostela Airport. Those are the three letters identifying that airport. Three letters identify every airport in the world."

Nerd, thought Sam Wardell to himself. Two minutes ago Rutger did not know the code for the airport at Santiago de Compostela; now he was pretending to be so familiar with it, he used the code instead of the name. Show-off fucking nerd. But he still needed him.

"Is that the Santiago that pilgrims walk to? Somewhere in northern Spain?"

Carl grinned at his computer screen. "Right on. You do deserve the big money."

He was being funny, or thought he was. Wardell did actually earn very big money.

Just to irritate Rutger, Sam said "So book the CHB Leer to get me from CHS to SCQ ASAP."

"CHS?" asked Rutger.

"Charleston International," said Wardell, downing the last melted ice infused ounce of his drink.

Within thirty minutes Sam Wardell was at the Charleston airport. He had passed customs and was heading out onto the tarmac, in an airport motor cart, being conducted to his flight, a shiny Leer jet patiently waiting for its only passenger.

When the vehicle arrived at the extended staircase of the Leer, his driver grabbed Sam's bag and handed it to a uniformed man standing at the base of the staircase, a member of the crew. When the crewman turned to walk up and into the aircraft, the driver of the motor cart handed Sam an aluminum attaché case.

"I was told you will be needing this, sir." he said.

Sam took it. "Yes, I think I might." He grinned. The Congregation certainly looked after their operatives. No guns, for civilians at least, could be cleared through customs. Something to do with some international aeronautical treaties. So an attaché case with everything he needed, arms wise, was a useful and important adjunct to his luggage. He slipped the driver a twenty.

As he climbed the aluminum stairway up into the aircraft, he wondered if he would be met by just such a helpful airport employee in Spain. Probably. And when he thought about it further, he thought that it really must be true that handguns are just not that available in Europe. Otherwise, no need to import this one. However it worked, everything always seemed to work for employees of the Congregation of the Holy Baptism.

CHAPTER 28

SANTIAGO DE COMPOSTELA

"Now," said Mackellan Kirby, "when in a tapas bar—that is, a proper tapas bar in Spain no less, because they aren't proper unless they are in Spain, in my humble opinion..."

When has his opinion ever been humble? Fiona thought. Then mentally chided herself. Uncle Mack was just having a good time, telling his young relations about Spain.

"With every order of drinks the proprietor provides a tapas or 'covering' for your glass. When flies, or other forms of airborne detritus were plentiful, the tapas was served on a small plate which covered, and thereby protected your drink. The more you drink the more expensive or ornate the tapas becomes. Typically the first drink is worth a plate of peanuts or perhaps olives. Then we move on to their famous Spanish omelette, little squares of the most delectable potato and cheese omelette. Then, we can expect *scampi aioli,* the traditional garlic shrimp. And on it goes." He smiled benignly at the tavern keeper, and asked for a very good sherry all around. "This *fino* will help your appetites. It always does mine. So, if we drink enough we get rewarded with a wonderful meal."

Their host returned with three glasses of a beautifully hued amber fluid. The glasses were juice glasses, Fiona noticed, small and flat bottomed. Not like North American wine glasses. Their host also brought over a saucer of mixed olives and slices of an ivory coloured cheese.

"Oh yes. I forgot," enthused Mack. "Because we are drinking sherry we must have cheese. To have no cheese with sherry would be like having a hotdog without mustard." He grinned, waiting to see if Joe or Fiona had picked up on his subtle attack on American culture. Fiona had, and showed that by rolling her eyes.

They clinked glasses and sipped at their sherry. It was dry and delicious, and made Joe realize that he was, in fact, reasonably hungry. He looked around for a table. Eating while standing at a bar seemed so...well, foreign. Then he kicked himself: they were in foreign parts.

"It's normal to stand at the bar," said Uncle Mack. He delicately wiped his lips with a tiny paper napkin, then made a show of dropping it to the floor. His young relatives looked shocked. "If we don't drop our used napkins, there will be no need for someone to sweep the floor, and then that person—usually an elderly woman—would have no job."

Fiona noticed the bartender glaring at Mack, so she quietly retrieved the discarded napkin. Their host nodded in approval. "It seems that minimum wage may have arrived in medieval Santiago," she said.

Mack looked chastised. "Sorry, kids. I haven't been to Spain since the late seventies. I forget that things change."

Joe patted him gently on his forearm. "That is because nothing does change in your world, Uncle Mack. Your world of ancient texts and long lost languages."

Fiona looked thoughtfully at an olive impaled on a toothpick. If I am right, she thought to herself, Uncle Mack's world was one of incredible changes, and had already, or soon would, change dramatically.

They proceeded to drink and eat their way through a series of seafood appetizers, spicy beef sausages and a wide array of pickled vegetables. Tapas are a true Spanish national treasure, concluded Joe.

CHAPTER 29

SANTIAGO DE COMPOSTELA INTERNATIONAL AIRPORT

Group Captain Ian Markham listened intently to the voice on his headset, then turned to his two flight crew members. "We are grounded."

"What?" asked his co-pilot Will Olsen.

"Seems the av-gas guys noticed a leaking hydraulic line in the landing gear. This bird has a dual back-up of course, but no reason to chance it. And it was made bloody clear to me that we better return this to Prince..." he caught himself. "We have to return this lady in good nick to its owner."

He listened to another voice on the headset. "We are to taxi to Hangar 28, to our left, down C-18. Here Keith, you take her down." He stood up and out of the left seat, and indicated that his young Flying Officer should sit. "I'll be right here, and Will isn't taking his hands off any of the controls." The older man grinned. "You may never get another chance to pilot a Gulfstream G600."

Flying Officer Keith Brutosky tried in vain to keep his face set to serious and responsible. Guiding the sleek aircraft down the indicated taxiway to Hanger 28 posed no difficulties. It was just fun to check those precision-made instruments and experience controlling such a powerful little beast. His grin lit up the cockpit.

Once in the hangar, the three flight crew members exited the aircraft. They were approached by a middle-aged man, whose name tag identified him as Jorge Gutierres, with Sita Avionica, a large and dependable aviation repair company, with facilities at most Spanish airports.

"Gentlemen," he said. "We have been instructed to take care of the hydraulics issue."

Markham reached to shake his hand. Gutierres looked awkward, then took the proffered hand. He did not extend a greeting to either Olsen or Brutosky.

"We will keep the aircraft overnight. For one, the repair may take some time. When one hydraulic line goes we of course check all others. Just a precaution. And for two, we have no AME available at this moment, who is certified on the G600."

Markham frowned. "Okay, if that is the way it is, that's the way it is. Brutosky, you will stay with the aircraft."

"Yes sir." Brutosky barely managed not to salute. But they were still under cover, so to speak, and civilian flight crewmen did not salute each other.

Gutierres shook his head. "I am sorry, Captain Markham." He said the name as two words, 'mark' and 'ham'. Otherwise his English was almost unaccented. "Company protocol, no one other than the Sita night watchman remains on the premises, overnight. An insurance matter, I believe."

Markham's frown got deeper. "Just one minute, please," he said to Gutierres. He walked some distance away and made a call on his cell phone. He spoke to someone, nodded, and ended the call.

"Seems our office," he emphasized the word for Olsen and Brutosky, so they would know he meant RAF at Hatton Field "They are good with this. Not the way I like to do things, but apparently Sita is certified for," again he paused, "our repairs."

His men got the message. Group Captain Markham had just been ordered to leave the aircraft under the care of Sita Avionica.

He smiled at Gutierres, in an attempt to take any sting out of his questioning of that man's trustworthiness. "And it seems we get a night out in Santiago. Brutosky, our go-bags, please."

Brutosky was hurrying back to the Gulfstream, to collect their overnight bags, always packed, even when the flight was expected to be a simple turn-around, when Olsen piped up. "Did you ask her what hotel they are staying at, just in case, Keith?" Brutosky, as usual when Fiona was mentioned, blushed.

CHAPTER 30

IBERIA 51 A.D. LETTER FROM EPHES TO HIS COUSIN BARTHOLOMEW OF ALEXANDRIA

Ava dear cousin. I trust all is well with you and my so beloved cousins.

I am no gossip—I hope. But I must let you know what has transpired here. Someone beyond our little part of the world must know of this.

As you know, my father and I have lived happily here for many years, and life is good in Compostela. The peacefulness of Lord James seems to touch anyone who comes here, and everyone is imbued with his gentle spirit, his true devotion to his god, and to the people of this town. He and Mary are our royalty, for one knows upon meeting them that they are highborn. But they are also natural leaders, caring, resourceful, and deserving of their people's admiration and loyalty.

But all is not perfect here. Recently there came to Compostela a man renowned for his preaching of the word of Christ, his faith in the story of the resurrection, of which he claims to have first-hand knowledge, and his unflagging belief that we all may enter into Heaven, through Christ, our Lord, who died for our sins, so that we may be forgiven them, and dwell with God, His Father.

That man is Saul of Tarsus. He came with Timothy. They have travelled most of the known world, preaching this new religion, which, of course, was not new to us.

Saul of Tarsus—or Paul as he is now known, came here. And he met with James, whom he claimed to have met once, on the road to Damascus. Lord James said to him "But you have written that you met the Lord Jesus on that road, and you were enlightened. So how could you have met me, his brother?"

But Paul continued to harangue Lord James, and to remind him of places, and people, and the horrors of the crucifixion of our Lord. He argued with him, and in the end our Lord James met with us, the men of his church, and he said to us "I must return to Judaea, for the Jews need me to lead them out of their servitude to Rome. This will be the second coming of their Messiah, for I am him. And it is foretold in the scriptures that the second coming of the King of the House of David will free all Jews from persecution."

He bowed his head and said quietly. "I have lied to you. I have lived a lie. I am Jesus, not James."

As his tears flowed, the men of Compostela, came to him, and embraced him, and kissed him. We had known for many years that James was in fact Jesus, for at times his language faltered, and he referred to God as his Father, made reference to his brother James. And his wife Mary could only have been the Magdalene, of whom word had spread, even to Landsend, in western Iberia.

But Paul of Tarsus was also at this meeting. And his anger reddened his face, and caused spittle to fly from his lips, when he said "But the true religion is based on the resurrection. Faith in the resurrection is why men become Christian; because they believe that their sins will be forgiven through their faith in Christ, and they also will be saved, and will become housed in Heaven."

James looked sadly at Paul. "You have done good works, espousing Christianity to the Jews and the Gentiles of the known world. And I wish you well with that calling. It is a beautiful credo to live by. But I always knew I would have to return, at some point, to give truth to the scriptures that speak of the second coming of the Messiah. I must return to Jerusalem. It is written."

Paul glared at Lord James. "That is ancient scripture, Jewish words. Do you not realize how Christianity has spread beyond you? It is no longer the man; it is the message." He stomped up to James, and pressed his forefinger into James' chest. "And I have dedicated my life to the spreading of that message. I will not have that work destroyed." He began to walk away, then turned. "By anyone, even Jesus Christ himself." He spat, and left the meeting room.

I see the joy and the sadness in Lord James' face, and I am afraid that something bad will come of this confrontation between Paul and our Lord.

I will write to you of the outcome.

Your loving cousin,

Ephes, Son of Torgas

CHAPTER 31

COMPOSTELA 1085

Bishop Darda rerolled the fourth of the five scrolls of the Testament of Ephes. He sighed deeply. He did not know what the reading of the scrolls would do to his faith; it should shake it to its roots, no, it should tear it, roots and all, from his consciousness, so that it could never possibly live—must less flourish—again.

He carefully placed the scroll back into the cedar chest, next to the first three parts of the testament. The fifth scroll remained on his work table, as yet unread. He knew he should be devastated, as any man of god, whose faith is so shredded, would be. But, he felt a familiar relaxing of his face muscles, and knew that he was smiling. And crying. Tears rolled down his cheeks, so in conflict with his beaming face. He was happy, elated, ecstatic. And perhaps this was how every good-hearted Christian would feel, when the testament was made known to him, or her, he mentally amended. Although women were eschewed from any place of participation or leadership in the Roman church, and he himself had remained wary and watchful of them, Darda had a new respect for the female of the species, and their role in his church. He had to have, after reading the testament.

Darda worked in his shirt and knee-length pants because of the heat in northern Iberia. He now put on his heavy woollen robe, tied it with a piece of rope, as was normal in his order, and went out, into the streets of Compostela.

He saw them in a different light now. Perhaps in a beam from the very heavens, he thought, and that thought caused him to giggle like a child. He walked down into the town, to the huge square that Master Gelduin had decreed to be fitting for what would be a most magnificent church when completed. The church was rising, slowly but surely, and it would no doubt be as magnificent as Gelduin and Galperinus envisioned. But Darda could not help but remember the remains of the tiny church that had stood on this site since the days of Ephes. The little church with the cedar altar. And the newer church which ensconced the altar and its rocky foundations in the burial chambers of the cellar, newer, yes, but still built in the first century.

Darda shook his head at the wonder of it all. To be alive at such a time. And to know what he did.

He wandered past the alehouse, and even raised his hand in a friendly benediction when he heard invitations for him to come inside. He did sometimes. It was not forbidden in his order. And the townspeople seemed to enjoy a bishop who could drink his posset of ale with as much relish, and speed when he was dry, as the next man.

He wandered until the darkness came down, when he returned to the Casa Parador overlooking the town. He knew what he would do. He would write his Cardinal. And thank god, it was not Cardinal Friere. He had been promoted to a different and more important jurisdiction. Darda grinned; not even thinking about Friere could dim his good mood.

Darda was quietly and humbly very happy with himself. His letter to Cardinal Legare had had an immediate effect. It had, in fact, caused that most respected of Cardinals to send a Papal Delegate to see him. Word had arrived by messenger; the Delegate would be arriving within the month. As Darda knew well, it was no easy feat to travel to Compostela, and he was pleased that the Cardinal took his correspondence so seriously that he would spend Vatican resources to underwrite the trip.

Bishop Viandicondi, a lord in his own right as a member of the noblest family in Navarre, arrived with pomp, at the head of a party of some twenty knights, and only two other clergymen, both of whom acted as house servants to their bishop. He initially demanded possession of the Casa Parador, but thankfully, found that Master Gelduin, that redoubtable architect, had spent his free time from the building of the cathedral, arranging the building of a fine villa on the Plaza de Obradoiro, close by the cathedral grounds. That villa was certainly more modern than the Parador, and so he stayed there, and paid Gelduin whatever tariff that learned businessman thought he could extract.

After that initial confrontation regarding Viandicondi's living arrangements, Darda determined to be somewhat guarded in his relations with the man. This turned out to be too easy—Darda could simply not enjoy the man's company. The bishop was pompous, vainglorious, demanding, rude, and worst of all, unapologetically un-Christian. He was a bishop because of his family, not from any calling to serve his god. That was abundantly clear, from his demands on the town's resources of fine wine, good meat, and beautiful whores. He used them all, voraciously.

But meet with him, Darda must. Viandicondi, through one of his clergymen, sent a request to Darda that Darda attend at Viandicondi's hostel, after terce, the third period of the monastic day, the afternoon. Darda was used to getting business done in the earliest hours of the day. Oh well. Perhaps the man meant to give him his midday meal; it would be nice to vary from the bread and cheese that was his usual fare.

At the main door of the great hostel built by Master Gelduin, Darda pulled the chain which rang an interior bell. The door was immediately opened by one of Viandicondi's young clergymen. He bowed to Darda and led the way through the entrance passageway, into a cloistered courtyard. Two of Viandicondi's guard sat there, partially dressed, and even less arrayed in armour. They nodded at Darda over the brims of their tankards. The bishop took that to mean he was allowed entry, but he could not help but compare them to his own knightly guard, who stood at attention when he passed, and who were always fully armed and presentable.

From the cloister Darda was led into a large reception room. The walls were plastered in the new style, and were painted with pagan Roman scenes. The subject matter of the friezes made Darda blush, and he averted his eyes, as best he could, to the stone floor. It was covered in rich and deep rugs identifiable as Middle Eastern by their intricate floral designs, he noticed. The room was obviously meant as the gathering hall for all of the guests when more than one party was residing in the hostel, but now most of the furniture had been removed, to be replaced by an oversized worktable-cum desk, set in the middle of the vast space.

Bishop Viandicondi was seated behind the desk, and remained seated when Darda was announced. His robe was black silk, Darda noticed, not the usual woollen habit of the Benedictines. Viandicondi looked up and indicated with his hand that Darda should sit. The only chairs were set far from the desk, but as Darda walked towards Viandicondi the young clergyman ran forward to drag one chair over towards the table, and bowed to Darda.

"You may leave us, now." Viandicondi glared malevolently at his servant.

"Thank you, Brother," said Darda quietly as the young man passed by him on the way to the door. He knew that would annoy his host.

The Papal Legate opened the conversation with an angry "You idiot!" Darda was dumbstruck. He did not like the other man, but courtesy was the norm amongst high ranking churchmen.

"What sort of an idiot are you?" Viandicondi spat the words. "To think that the Vatican would celebrate the knowledge that Jesus Christ did not die on the cross, but lived out his life in this miserable hell-hole?" Spittle flew from his angrily compressed lips. He dabbed at his mouth with a silk and lace handkerchief, and took a sip from a golden wine goblet. He did not offer Darda similar refreshment.

Not that Darda could have swallowed anything just now. His throat was constricted with anger. And, he had to admit, fear. He was not used to such blatant rudeness and unfettered animosity.

"Christ had to die on the cross," Viandicondi continued, "or all of Christianity is built on a lie. And the Vatican will never accept that, or allow that filth to be promulgated." He paused, then smiled humourlessly. "Especially by a Maltese turd like you."

There it was, as Darda had expected. The nadir of every argument that was reduced from theological to personal, by anyone he was debating who felt threatened. Darda did not know how he threatened other churchmen. He would never know that it was his own unfaltering faith in goodness that brought out the evil jealousy in his opponents.

Darda consciously gathered himself, and said "Thank you, Lord Bishop." He looked down at his clenched fists, then forced himself to relax them. "I did think that the leaders of the Church of Rome would celebrate the life of Jesus. He lived a holy life, and imbued his love for his god into everyone who knew him. This is why this region has been Christian for over a thousand years." He paused, then said "He caused miracles."

Viandicondi absently stroked the beads of his rosary. Darda noticed that they were at least four times the size of the silver alloy beads which adorned the rosaries presented by the Pope to every man raised to the status of bishop. And Viandicondi's beads looked to be pure gold. Even the cross at the base of the rosary was huge and gold. Darda's was wood, as was traditional.

"Any saint worth his salt has produced miracles," Viandicondi snorted. "We have more than enough miracles. What we do not need are people questioning that God did not allow his only son to die for us. So that our sins, through the intercession of the church of course, would be forgiven in the name of Jesus Christ. We do..."

Darda interrupted him. "But what if there is a more important lesson to be learned from the life of Jesus? What if living the words of the Sermon on the Mount is the lesson our Lord Jesus meant to leave us?" He looked at Viandicondi's sneering face, but continued anyway. "The Ten Commandments are simply laws, such as are incorporated into every realm's code of jurisprudence. Of course you cannot kill, or commit adultery, or thieve. No state would be without turmoil if it did not forbid such behaviour. But the Beatitudes. Live the Beatitudes and you live a holy and happy life. Was that really his message?"

Viandicondi shook his head. "I don't care what his message was. I do know I do not care to be preached to by a Maltese peasant." He stopped, waiting for the expected reaction of anger. It did not come.

"Tomorrow, you will deliver to me the chest with the ossuary and the scrolls you wrote of. And if you have a copy of the letter you wrote to Cardinal Legare, you will destroy that." He looked at Darda's clouded face. "No, you will give me any copy of that letter, so that I may personally see that it is destroyed. Now leave."

Darda rose, bowed his head only fractionally, and said "You are justly renowned for your hospitality, Lord Bishop." He turned and left, before a furious Viandicondi could think of anything to say.

Instead of returning immediately to his lodgings, Darda stopped at the alehouse, not usual for him but he felt the need to cleanse his mouth of the taste of his meeting with Viandicondi. And he needed to speak to the barman.

The barman waved away payment for the beaker of ale, but Darda drew him over, with a silent crook of his forefinger. When the man came to his table, Darda passed him a coin, and said quietly "Can you find Breg and ask him to come to the Parador garden? Through the back gate? As soon as possible?"

When full dusk had enveloped Compostela, Darda had his plans well underway. His ever-helpful hosts were happy to provide beer, a lot of beer, to the two knights Viandicondi had posted at the front entrance of Casa Parador. A servant had then gone out to the two knights standing not very inconspicuously at the rear entrance to the grounds.

She was the prettiest of the housemaids, and coquettish by nature. "We have provided your friends with beer. There is enough for you, if you hurry." She smiled. "And perhaps some of the house staff will join you. There are benches at the entrance courtyard for us all."

"Will you be there?" leered the older of the two soldiers.

"I just might, if I know you will be." She winked, and walked back to the house, her hips swinging invitingly. She had been surprised by her usually proper employers when they had instructed her to behave so. But she gamely played her part perfectly; she enjoyed it, and looked forward to the gossip her exploits would enliven.

When the soldiers posted at the rear garden gate made their way to the front courtyard, which took very little time, a candle was lit in an upper story room of the Parador. Soon two figures, carrying a wooden box, walked silently through the gardens, through the gate left ajar for them. At the casa they were met by Darda himself. He conducted them to the wing of the house used by his retinue, and into his private quarters.

Darda pulled Breg into a brotherly embrace, and shook the hand of Breg's companion. "It is Will, is it not? From Rheims?" Breg was once again surprised by Darda's ability to recognize every workman in Compostela. "I apologize for my manners, but we have no time for chitchat." He went to his table where the old cedar chest was already packed with the ossuary and the scrolls. The men lifted it from the table, and placed their chest in its place. The resemblance was quite remarkable, given the short notice.

"I made it myself," said Breg. "Better that way, I thought."

"And is it difficult to open?" asked Darda.

The foreman's teeth shone in the candlelight. "It will prove reasonably difficult, My Lord. No," he amended, "Very difficult. As you suggested it should." His grin grew even wider.

"Good," said Darda.

The two workmen lifted up Darda's cedar chest between them and silently moved back through the house, out the rear entrance, and through the now unguarded gate. Darda relocked the gate when they were through, and returned to his own rooms. Only a few minutes had passed since the candle in the upper room had been lit.

CHAPTER 32

SANTIAGO DE COMPOSTELA

"Now," said Mackellan Kirby, as he pushed away an empty plate. "If we have all enjoyed an elegant sufficiency, as my grandfather used to say, we can think about what's for supper."

Joe groaned. "Uncle, how can you always be hungry? Especially when we have just eaten?"

Kirby sniffed. "I did not say I was hungry. I just like to be prepared. And the Spanish do dine late, ten, eleven o'clock. By then you will be starving."

"By then I will be in bed," replied Joe.

The three travellers left the tapas bar and retraced their steps through the alley and out into the Plaza de Obradoiro. As they entered the vast square, they were watched by a good-looking middle-aged man, presumably American by his clothing and by the rum and Coke set before him, at his table outside a café. He lazily let his glance slide over them, then returned his attention to the façade of the cathedral, now behind the trio. The cathedral was the obvious building a tourist would study; burying his face in a tourist guide book would simply draw unwanted attention.

But attention he had. A clergyman, most likely Catholic from his white Roman collar, watched him. He was ambling through the plaza in the company of two fully robed priests, presumably attached to the cathedral. He was wearing a light weight grey suit, well-tailored, very continental. It looked strangely at odds with his hard planed face and hatchet nose. Brother Martin allowed himself few indulgences, but bespoke suits were one of them. He turned his face away from Kirby and his relatives, to speak to one of his companions. He did keep an eye on the American, playing with his rum and Coke.

"Oh to hell with this." muttered Wardell to himself. "A decent glass of Godello might not be touristy but I don't give a damn." With that, he signalled for his waiter, and ordered a bottle of the elegant white wine, grown so masterfully in Galicia, the province which is home to Santiago de Compostela. The waiter removed the rum and Coke with obvious relief.

Fiona faced the cathedral directly, but watched the American through the side of her sunglasses. Yes, it was him, she was certain. She had to deal with this.

"Excuse me, for a minute," she said to Mack and Joe. "I think I see someone I know. I will catch up with you later, in the Abbe." She smiled convincingly and neither Joe nor Mack were alerted to her tense posture. Her companions left her, and she walked directly to the American's café table. He watched as she approached, and a smile lit up his face.

He stood up. "Well, well. Miss Fiona Kirby, here in Santiago. Sometimes I do get all the luck." He spoke with a hint of a Southern accent, the one that so annoyed Archbishop Mathieux. They embraced in the fashion of Europeans, forearms touching shoulders, lips airbrushing a kiss on both cheeks.

"I see you finally learned which cheek to 'not kiss' first," Fiona said, somewhat archly.

"Yup. That and other things. Such as your real name." He pulled out a chair, and stood behind it, then pushed it gently towards the table as she sat. The ever watchful waiter appeared immediately with another wineglass and a white linen napkin, and as quickly melted away when his client said "*Mi gracias*" in a good Spanish accent, and handed him a five euro note.

"You are looking wonderful, darlin'."

"Cut the crap and that fake accent. It always was annoying," Despite her words Fiona was smiling. "What are you doing here, Leo? Or do you have another name now?"

Sam Wardell smiled dreamily at his guest. "Waiting for you, darl.... Waiting for you, Fiona." They touched glasses, said *salute* in chorus, and sipped the wine.

"Really. I thought I might have to sit here all night. And maybe tomorrow. I thought you might be incognito. You know. Dressed like a nun, or something."

She shook her head. "So am I to assume that you have been ogling every Sister in the plaza?"

"And every Mother Superior," he said.

They both laughed.

Sam reached tentatively for her hand, and covered it in his. "Seriously, you do look good. I thought black hair and blue eyes suited your Celtic complexion to a tee, but, girl, you are a wonder in your new look. Those green, green eyes."

She knew he was flirting with her, to divert her from her first question, but she could not stop herself from responding. "This is the real me," Fiona insisted.

"Sure."

They continued to reminisce, without regard for the gruff blond clergyman, across the square, who was now speaking on a cell phone.

"Your Excellency? I transmitted photos of the man a moment ago. It is definitely Miss Kirby he is speaking to." He paused. "They look friendly. Are they together in this?"

Cardinal Contini bowed his head. "I do not know, Martin. But I soon will. You shall hear from me. Ciao." He ended the call and immediately speed dialed another number. "Monseigneur? Good, good, I am well *gracias.* I am sending you a photo. I need the man identified. Pronto. *Si.* Absolute priority. *Molte Bene.*"

CHAPTER 33

COMPOSTELA 1086

Darda started his day early, writing a hastily composed letter to Bishop Viandicondi. He had his acolyte deliver it to Viandicondi's lodging, some hours before anyone but the servant brothers would be awake.

Then he continued with his day. Having returned from the lauds service in the temporary church in the square, and starting on his breakfast of gruel with currants and fresh cow's milk, Darda was interrupted by a pounding on the door to his portion of Casa Parador.

His acolyte Joaquim answered the door, began to say that his Lordship was at breakfast, when the door was pushed wide, and a contingent of Viandicondi's knights strode into the room. Joaquim, pushed backwards, tried none the less to stand between the fully armed guard and his bishop.

"You may go, Joaquim," said Darda quietly. He stood. Joaquim turned to him, and was heartened to see that his bishop, dressed in the simple robes of a churchman, still managed to look more threatening than any of the fully armoured knights. It is those two creases between his eyes, and the throbbing vein in his neck, Joaquim thought, as he quickly exited the room.

"We are here for that chest," said the captain of the squad of knights. He pointed to Breg's wooden box, sitting on Darda's worktable. The man immediately behind him and to his right, cleared his throat, loudly. The captain looked at him questionly, and the man pantomimed a writing motion. "Oh yeah. Some letter too."

"I have no copy of the letter I wrote to Cardinal Legare," said Darda. This was in fact true; the only copy was in the old cedar chest, so technically he was not lying. "That chest," he pointed to his worktable, "I intend to deliver, with its contents, directly into the hands of His Excellency Cardinal Legare. I informed your Bishop of this, by letter, delivered this morning." He paused. "Perhaps he has not read my letter? I understand he does not attend to business until after midday." He raised his eyebrows, questioningly.

The captain sent two of his men forward. They hoisted up the box and walked with it to stand again behind their leader.

"Oh yeah," he snarled. "He attended to business all right. That is why we are here. At bloody dawn."

His leather and metal armour groaned, as though unaccustomed to either oil or polish, as he moved back to the door. "Do not worry, Bishop." He spat that last word. "His Lordship will see that your precious chest is delivered to Legare." With that last rudeness, he led his men from the room.

Darda crossed the room to close the door, then returned to his breakfast. The currants are really sweet this year, he thought.

CHAPTER 34

SANTIAGO DE COMPOSTELA

Sam Wardell and Fiona Kirby talked through the bottle of old vine Godello. They had years of catching up to talk about. Fiona remembered clearly the last time she had seen Sam, or Leo Schmidt as he was known to her. He was climbing into an American forces helicopter, from the American air force base at Kandahar City, Afghanistan, eight years ago.

Wardell was CIA, but had been on the ground as a field worker for a non-governmental organization rebuilding water systems in Afghani villages. The war devastated hundreds of American families when they received the flag-draped coffins of their sons, brothers, fathers. But it had devastated thousands of Afghani families, innocent mountain shepherds and farmers whose lives were blown to bits; their houses razed, fields burned, water systems obliterated, as often as not by their own countrymen.

Fiona was there as a news reporter for the Canadian Broadcasting Corporation. Although she was American born, her father, her Uncle Mack's eldest brother, had been born in Scotland. His accent, some of which she had absorbed through her childhood, and her mother's insistence on good grammar, made her sound passably Canadian. That, together with training, helped the accent. Apparently it had been more difficult for her bosses to convince the CBC to cooperate than it had been for her to convince news watchers that she really was Canadian. It might have been safer for her to not be used as on-camera talent, but using such an obviously beautiful woman in any other job could easily have caused unwanted suspicion from the factions in Afghanistan.

So Fiona and Sam met in Afghanistan, neither knowing the other was CIA. He thought she was a spoiled and somewhat vapid 'Is my hair okay?' television reporter; she thought he was a pacifistic do-gooder, who should never have gone to a war zone. Their mutual disregard grew, as it often will, into mutual lust. Or was it love? Perhaps it could have been, if they had been given time.

"I tried to find you, when I returned to the States. Apparently your NGO never existed, and neither did Leo Schmidt." She made this a statement, but the question was obvious.

"Golly," her companion drawled. "Least they could 'a done was treat me like a hero, kill me off at some well-site, or somethin'. At least in writing."

"You were CIA then?"

"I didn't say that. And I most certainly am not CIA now." His face darkened, and Fiona had the feeling that he was, now at least, telling the truth.

"And what about you, Miss Kirby? Still with the CBC?"

She laughed. "I moved on to KOMO in Seattle, then went east. Now I have a blog. Sounds silly but it does allow me to travel. I comment on fashion trends, more specifically, the unsanctioned borrowing of indigenous patterns etc. by high-end fashion houses and mass-production lines. It's fun."

Fiona had just convinced Sam that his first opinion of her was still correct, a woman beautiful enough to move through the world by doing nothing useful at all. He stared at her, somewhat disappointed.

"So darlin'?" How's about dinner?"

"How's about you tell me your name, drop that stupid accent, and tell me why you were waiting for me, in the Plaza de Obradoiro, of all places?" She smiled, to take the sting from her words.

"The name is Wardell, Sam Wardell." The Dixie tonations had been replaced with a passable British accent. Fiona laughed; she had picked up on the Bond impersonation. "And my boss said I would find you in Santiago. Dinner?"

In the main dining room of the grand Hostal dos Reis Catolicos they ate the local speciality of turbot, lobster and scallops, gently cooked as a stew in a white wine sauce flavoured with herbs known only to the chef.

"*Calderada dos Reis*? *Hostal dos Reis Catolicos*? Is the dish named after the hotel?" asked Fiona.

Sam dipped a piece of crusty bread in the last of his sauce. "Should think it might be the other way around. The dish was so enjoyed by King Ferdinand and his Queen Isabella that the locals renamed their plain old *calda mariscos* for their beloved royals. The hotel was commissioned by the pair in 1499, as a hostel for the pilgrims who flocked here. It was the Parador de Santiago, then, and renamed centuries later." He delicately finished mopping out his earthenware dish.

"Really? Ferdinand and Isabella? They are the only king and queen of Spain I can name. They built this?" She looked around her, at the splendour of the dining room. "In 1499?"

"Well, they commissioned it then. It took a while. They must have been incredibly forward looking people. And westward looking, of course. Else we might not have passports."

Fiona looked seriously at her dinner companion. "Thank you for a wonderful dinner Le....Sam. Now I really should get back." She sighed, and twirled the stem of her wine glass. Thoughtful.

Sam leaned across the table and gently touched her fingers as they encircled the glass stem. "But you have not yet had dessert. You simply cannot miss *filloas*."

"*Filloas*?"

"Oh yes. The most delicate crepes filled with caramelized apple cream. And secret liqueurs, of course." He leaned back. "I don't ask; I just enjoy."

Fiona was already sufficiently well fed, but her sweet tooth was beginning to ache, just a touch. "Then so shall I," she laughed.

After dessert, Fiona had needed only gentle urging from Sam to visit his room,—conveniently at Dos Reis—for a final nightcap. Both of them knew a glass of Spanish Cava would not be the end of their evening.

When Sam and Fiona left the restaurant table, a nearby diner made a call on his cell phone.

He said quietly "Miss Kirby and Wardell just left together. My guess, from their body language, they went to his room."

"Good. The more distracted both of them are, the better. And how goes the other project?" The speaker gave the last word a particular emphasis.

"All is in hand. Gutierres proved pretty easy."

"Keep me informed."

CHAPTER 35

COMPOSTELA 1086

"Breg, I need your help again, if I may?" said Bishop Darda quietly to his guest, at an outside table at the alehouse. No one was near them, but Darda was taking no chances.

Breg grinned. He was proud to be the bishop's confidante. Normally men of the cloth left him cold, but this bishop was different.

"I need a tomb."

"My Lord! You are not ill? You look hale."

'No, no, not for me." He considered this next step. Once his request was spoken there would be no taking it back, and he hoped that he was putting his trust in the right man. "For those poor souls whose bones are sealed in that marble casket."

Breg took a draught of his ale. "The ossuary? Souls? More than one?"

"Yes. I believe that the cas...." He had not known that Master Breg would have knowledge of the Jewish word for the burial casket. "I believe that the ossuary holds the bones of two people, a lord and his lady, who ruled in this town a long time ago. A very long time ago."

"Were they good?"

What a strange question, thought Darda. "Yes, they were very good." Then he smiled. "They were Christians."

"Right then," said his companion. He had noticed Darda's tense surveillance of the courtyard. "I take it, this is to be kept private?" Darda nodded. "But to do a good job I will need to call in a stone carver. My men can dig the foundation, and emplace the stones of the tomb. But I will need a stone carver. To give proper value to the interred."

Oh, if only every Christian priest had such sensitivity. "Breg, if I am not being too inquisitive, where did you go to school?"

The big man laughed. "I usually cannot use words as I have been using, with my mates, or even the engineers. I went to a school for orphans at a seminary, in Grenoble. But they soon found I was more useful with my hands than my head. And I was moved on to an apprenticeship with a church builder." He paused, studied his Bishop. "And I have never been sorry about that." He laughed self-consciously. "I like to think that Lord Jesus guides my hands, I know that sounds stupid, but..." He looked down.

Darda clasped his friend's hand. "Not stupid. Enlightened. That counterfeit chest you made, was definitely guided. Will they ever be able to open it?"

"Yes, but they will destroy it by doing so. Irreparable damage."

"So if Viandicondi is to deliver it to Cardinal Legare, he cannot open it beforehand, without the Cardinal knowing?"

"Exactly," smiled Breg. Both men leaned back and enjoyed their ale.

CHAPTER 36

Santiago de Compostela

Sam Wardell's room at the Hostal dos Reis Catolicos was a suite. The sitting room and bedroom had twelve foot ceilings, with commensurately tall narrow windows, opening onto small balconies enclosed with carved stone balusters. The view from the sitting room was into the Plaza, now lit up for the nightlife that is such a part of modern Santiago. Pilgrims might develop tired feet, but apparently their stomachs and throats know no fatigue.

Sam handed a chilled glass of a very fine *cava* to Fiona, then gently stroked her shoulder with his still cold fingers.

"Umm." She shivered. With cold, delight, anticipation? She actually did not know. This was not like her, usually in such total control. But Leo....Sam, this man she had started to love, then had not seen for so many years. This was not like a first date; it was more like a reunion. And, she reminded herself, he was business; what was he doing in Santiago and why had he expected her to be here? She told herself she would do what she had to do to find the answers. Then laughed inwardly: she would do what she wanted to do, and would let no sense of duty interfere with that.

That decided she turned towards her host. He was standing so close she could feel the heat of his body radiating through his clothes. He bent his head and kissed her. She so enjoyed a man tall enough to have to bend his head to hers, she thought errantly, as her body and mouth responded without conscious direction from her brain.

His hands moved to her waist, pulled her towards him, then one hand moved to her breast. She felt her nipple harden immediately, as did he. His kiss went deeper and she felt the thrust of his pubis against her.

"Why waste any of this?" she said, and moved him towards the bedroom, her arms wrapped around his neck, her thighs tightly touching his.

Their lovemaking was fast and furious, then just furious. Then slow and delicious. Fiona had nearly forgotten what good sex felt like—nothing else on earth, and yet somehow dirty and human. Her pushing abdomen and encircling arms wanted this man to stay inside her forever, and he agreed, with a fast and deeply thrusting penetration. She purred, he yelled, and it was over. For now.

Lying in bed, with a glass of the local *cava*, in hand, Fiona was stretched full out in the bed, without coverings of any sort. He was running his chilled glass over her belly, and she was giggling.

"So," she said, "What brings a nice guy like you to Santiago de Compostela? And what made you expect to find me here?"

"That'll wait 'til morning." he said, now nuzzling her left aureole. She could barely think.

My left aureole is a very small part of my body, so I will overcome its mad desire to be sucked by his lips, here, and... No, she would be professional.

She sat up. "Sam, I think I need to know who you are working for."

He answered sleepily. "Now? Really? Fiona."

"Well," she said archly. "If my calculations are right, I think we probably have about a half hour of free time." She looked at his well-used and now flatulent member.

"I will remind you of that, in half an hour."

She laughed and pulled him to her, in a full body embrace. "You won't have to. I'll remind you. Promise." She then sat up, her back against the headboard. "But really, I do need to know how you knew to look for me here."

Sam looked at her. He knew she was not what she pretended. He was quite sure she worked for some agency or other. Although he could not even hazard a guess why any American agency would have a senior operative here in Santiago. He got off the bed, refilled their glasses, and sat in an armchair.

"Okay. I'll tell you. I work for the Congregation of the Holy Baptism, headquartered in Charleston..."

"The what?" she laughed. "A Baptist church?"

"The Baptist church. Next to the Roman Catholic Church probably the most potent Christian organization in the world. And when I say potent, I mean that." He hesitated. Should he be telling her any of this? Probably not, but would it really matter? Probably not.

"We traced you to the Gulfstream, and the Gulfstream to Santiago International. Pretty nice kite, by the way." He grinned. She remained silent, not wanting to show her surprise at his employer's abilities to trace people, some thousands of miles away from its headquarters. Damn computers, she thought.

"I have been sent to take the scroll from your uncle. If need be, by force, deadly force."

This caught her attention, hard, in the solar plexus. "My uncle has no scroll."

"Not what I've been told."

"No. Really. I think he is looking for one. But....but," she was searching for a way out of this. "Whatever happened to your work with World Waterworks Inc.? Also known as the CIA?" She hoped that would divert him.

He grimaced. "Some intel suggested my cover was blown in Kandahar. So I was removed." He took a sip of wine. "Nothing new in that. But when I asked about you, I was told you had returned to Toronto, married your cameraman, and was busy producing little CBCnicks."

"You didn't believe them?"

"Not unless your cameraman's taste in lovers had suddenly switched to the other team. He was gay to his toenails, which, really, he should never have polished hot pink."

"Seriously? He did that?"

"Of course not." Then he added "As far as I know."

They both laughed. Lovemaking made the mood so good, how could anyone take spies or assassination missions or world politics seriously?

CHAPTER 37

COMPOSTELA 1086

Darda felt suddenly free again, riding his big Belgium gelding through the north Iberian countryside. Breg drove the heavy transport cart pulled by two wide-bodied nags; his two helpers sat on the rear plank of the cart, with their legs dangling. This was like a holiday; a ride in the country. Even the blindfolds both workmen wore did not take away from their pleasure.

They came to a place where hills rose to the south, and to the north the blue of the far distant Bay of Biscay could just be seen, past an ocean of dark green forests, and paler fields of grasses.

"This will do," said Darda, dismounting, and unsaddling his horse. He let the horse go, knowing it would not wander far from him. It nudged his shoulder then went off, in search of the perfect stalk of grass.

The two workmen, newly released from their blindfolds, began to dig a hole, where indicated by Breg.

"It need only be two hand spans deep," the foreman told his men.

They quickly dug through the heavy turf and into the rich loam below. When the hole was dug, the men dumped gravel, which they had carted with them, into the hole, and spread it evenly. This would allow drainage, so that no build-up of water, from errant spring floods, could damage their cenotaph. Then they struggled, with Darda and Breg both assisting, to carry the concrete tomb to the readied space.

The tomb had been fashioned at Compostela, by a trusted stone carver. He had emplaced the marble ossuary in layers of cloth, then straw, and had covered this all in a concrete made from the local clays and limestone sand. The result was a quasi-rectangular shape, some three feet long and wide, and two feet in height. He had carved a Latin inscription into the fresh concrete, as directed by his bishop. He had also carved, or more correctly incised, lines into the marble of the ossuary itself, again as directed by Darda. The stonemason did not know the meaning of the straight line patterns. How could he know that Darda had him writing a dialect of ancient Aremaic Greek?

When the concrete chest was levelled to the satisfaction of Breg, he poured a specially prepared yogurt, ingrained with moss fragments, over it. His two helpers proceeded to plant local, fast-growing vine seedlings around the site. Then they ate, and drank, a truly wonderful midday feast. Darda had felt it manifest that he do at least this for the men. They had accepted the conditions of the day's outing without demur, so secure did they feel in Breg's leadership. After the last bit of pastry and good wine had been accounted for, the men loaded the cart, Darda whistled up his horse, and Breg replaced the scarves over his men's eyes.

"It is for your own good that you do not know where we are, or how to return here," he said. They nodded. Stranger things had happened, to both of them.

The saddle horse and the two cart horses moved off, back the way they had come. As they neared Compostela Breg drove the cart in a roundabout way amongst the farms surrounding the town. Then he told the men to remove their blindfolds. And so, Breg and two workmen drove an empty cart back into Compostela. Darda had already gone his own way, back to the Casa Parador.

When Breg neared the cathedral site, he stopped. "Here," he said, and gave each man a silver coin. "A gift from the Bishop, to obscure your memories." The men smiled, and nodded agreement.

"And do not spend that all in one place," he laughingly admonished them.

CHAPTER 38

SANTIAGO DE COMPOSTELA

The Gulfstream G600 gleamed like a jewel in the semi-darkness of the Sita Avionica hangar. Jorge Gutierres walked to it, and patted its prominent nose cone.

"Too bad, my pretty friend. Too bad."

He knew the guard was outside, doing his exterior rounds, but he looked around anyway, then climbed aboard the aircraft. He was carrying a soft-sided workbag, they type that had replaced the metal tool boxes, usually bright red, which were once the insignia of workmen everywhere. He carried the bag carefully.

He went straight to the storage compartments at the rear of the passenger cabin. He had had only one day to think about this, but that was long enough for a man of his experience. There was no way he could place the bomb next to the fuel tanks of the aircraft; the fittings there were just too tight, no room for anything. And those areas were typically inspected, especially by such a professional crew as the RAF pilots. No, nowhere near the fuel tanks. Actually, it did not really matter where the detonation occurred; anywhere on the aircraft, at thirty thousand feet, would do. At that altitude the outside pressure was so low that the effects of a bomb would be magnified many times over. Any breach in the hull at all, and the aircraft was doomed.

He had thought of using a simple heat source. He thought it

would be ironically funny to have a kettle set off the bomb, as an English crew was certain to want a 'cuppa' tea at some point in the flight. But then he realized that they might want one before takeoff, so that idea had to be scotched.

He could not use a timer. No one knew when the aircraft would lift off. The cabin was pressurized, so a detonator activated at a specific altitude would not work, either. So, it had to be at a specific place, somewhere over the ocean. It was almost too easy, really, particularly for someone whose training had started in boyhood, assisting his separatist father with home-made bombs with which to fight for Basque independence from the monarchy of Spain.

Gutierres was not political, never had been. He just enjoyed making bombs. And he was good at it. His father, God rest his soul, had taught his very capable son well, until the young Gutierres had quickly outstripped his tutor. The older man was glorified by his mates for his bomb-making expertise; he never let on, to anyone, that it was young Jorge who was the designer and fabricator of the most intricate devices. Not that he was not proud of his son; it just would have been too dangerous to have the youngster known as a bomb maker. And Jorge did not mind that he was the unsung hero of many a fatal incident in their finally unsuccessful bid for freedom, three decades ago.

Gutierres had decided to attack the aircraft's elevator controls, the flight surfaces on the tail section of every fixed-wing aircraft, which allow the pilots to alter or correct the aircraft's attitude, its flight pattern relative to the earth's surface. Destroy the elevator controls, and the plane was fated to crash.

In the rear of the storage compartments Gutierres removed a hatch cover, allowing access to the elevator controls, in the tail of the aircraft. Off to the side of the hatch cover, inside the compartment, he measured the wall space, then screwed in two small metal hooks. To these he affixed his standard white-with-a-red-cross first aid kit. No one ever checked the contents of a first aid kit; everyone just assumed everything would be there, when required. Yes, well, in this case, everything would be there. In the metal case, the eight ounces of C4, in a stable paste form, fit snugly with the detonator—pieces of a cell phone, which he had cannibalized. Then he resealed the hatch. If anyone opened the hatch, and no one would have any reason to do so, Gutierres doubted that he would even notice the first aid kit. They were virtually invisible, in that no one noticed them.

Then Gutierres moved to the outside of the aircraft. He climbed a tall step ladder so that he was just at the level of the top of the jet's rear section, near the ailerons and tail assembly. In the very centre of the top of the fuselage, a place that was out of sight of anyone conducting a ground inspection, he attached the device he had made, only last night. It was a metal O, approximately two inches in diameter, and three-eighths of an inch thick. The centre of the disc was what appeared to be a circle of aluminum foil covered with a thin piece of glass. The centre was about one inch in diameter. The outer ring was fitted with four miniscule metal screws, which he drilled into the aircraft. He then sprayed the whole with an aerosol can of the standard white Gulfstream paint, being careful not to overspray the body of the plane. He wanted no variation in the gloss or the wear of the paint to give him away. When completed, the nearly flat disc was not visible from the ground, and barely visible from any angle. Gutierres proudly thought to himself that not even a head engineer for the aircraft's manufacturer would spot the anomaly.

The one inch metal disc was a GPS, paired by wireless electronics to the trigger of his bomb. Out over the Bay of Biscay, when the aircraft crossed north 45 degrees, 30 minutes, 0 seconds latitude, the bomb would detonate.

At 6:00 a.m. the three RAF officers were on the tarmac, in front of the Sita Avionica hangar. The G600 had been rolled out, her repairs obviously complete. Gutierres came out of the hangar office and walked up to them, smiling.

"She is ready for flight. Only the one line was compromised, by a loose fitting. It would never have caused any trouble, but better to be certain, hey?" He handed over the mechanical log to Captain Markham. "Our head mechanic has made the required entries and has signed it off. His name and contacts are there, in case anyone has any questions or concerns. She is fully fueled. Your water tanks are filled. All batteries charged."

He followed Markham and Olsen as they did their ground check. Brutosky stowed their kit into the aircraft. The two senior officers, happy with the readiness of the aircraft, climbed into the cockpit, and began their run up protocol. After receiving instructions from the tower, the sleek aircraft moved slowly onto a taxiway, its pilot waiting for take-off clearance. It was 6: 32 am.

CHAPTER 39

SANTIAGO DE COMPOSTELA

"You murderous son of a bitch." Fiona spoke quietly, through clenched teeth. Sam had just come from the shower into his bedroom, his hair still wet, a hotel bathrobe wrapped around his body. He was totally unprepared for the closed fist that smashed into his left temple. He spun sideways, off-balance and in a lot of pain. Only a rookie slugs the jaw of an opponent; the temple is much more sensitive. Then he took a well-directed knee to the crotch, his naked crotch. Bent now in pain he straightened slowly when he felt his hair pulled sharply back and a blade at his throat.

"I should kill you now, but I'll wait, until I can get away with it, you fuck!" Now her voice was rising with the hysteria she was trying to keep back.

"What the hell, Fiona?" he spoke as best he could without moving his Adam's apple, which was so perilously close to the knife. "What's wrong?"

She was standing behind him, and with a painful grip on his hair she pointed his head in the direction of the room's television set. She had turned on the local news channel, an old habit when travelling abroad; it helped to improve her accent in whichever language the telecast was in. Television de Galicia was still on the news flash which had arrested her attention.

Sam watched for a few seconds, then said "Oh my god."

Even without a thorough knowledge of Spanish, the story was clear. A private aircraft had gone down over the Cantabrian Sea of the Bay of Biscay, at approximately 7:20 a.m. local time. From the news helicopter, there was a panning camera shot of the smooth waters of the bay, centering on an oil slick, and some as yet unidentified bits of airplane and seats, crumpled sheets of painted aluminum, and what else, Fiona did not want to think about. The aircraft was identified as a Gulfstream G600 that had departed from Santiago International Airport at approximately 6:40 that morning. Of the three passengers and three crewmen aboard, there were no survivors. The names of the deceased were not yet known, but the aircraft was registered in Great Britain.

"They think we were aboard," she snarled. "You fuck. You meant to kill us."

He tried to turn, but his head was held painfully facing the television set. "Fiona. I did not do this." But he was beginning to get angry, thinking about who had done it. "Look, I can prove it wasn't me. For one thing, I know you were not on that flight. For Christ's sake, you are here. And when would I have had time? I've been with you, since about two hours after you arrived here."

"You would have had someone else sabotage the aircraft. You wouldn't want to dirty those dainty fingers." She splayed out one of his hands on the coffee table and smashed the back of it with the handle of her knife. With the force of the blade removed from his throat, Sam thought about fighting her off. This was his chance. But her face was now almost beside his; she had had to move to strike his hand. He could see the hate there. She wanted him to make a move. Then she would kill him. He could see that in her face. So he froze.

"For god's sake, Fiona. It wasn't me. Remember, I told you I needed to get your uncle's scroll? Why would I tell you that, it I didn't want things to be peaceful?" He felt her grip loosen only slightly. "And I knew none of you would be aboard that aircraft. The perpetrator obviously let out the news about the passengers. He did not know he did not kill you all. I would have known that. Think, Fiona." He sensed a hint of panic in his voice. He had to get control.

The pure hatred in Fiona's face turned somewhat towards pensiveness. "But it had to be one of your crazy Congregationists. No one else is after us." She released Sam, and moved away into the room. She drew a Beretta from her handbag, and still held the knife in her right hand. Sam knew she was probably equally proficient with both hands with any firearm. Or knife.

"How do we know that?" he said. "You must know the contents of that scroll have a serious impact on the Roman Catholic Church? I'll bet they are here, in masses."

Despite herself Fiona grinned a bit.

"Sorry. Unintentional pun. And I am the agent here in Santiago for the CHB. The only agent."

"You sure?"

He thought about that. Of course Mathieux would cover his butt with two teams on the ground, if the trophy was that important. What was that scroll all about? Obviously not just another piece of antiquity of museum quality.

He thought for a minute, then said quietly, "What is the scroll about, Fiona?"

She snarled again, and Sam felt a frisonne of equal parts fear and lust waft over him. "Like I would tell you, shithead." Then she realized her mistake. "Even if there was a scroll."

But her denial of knowledge of the scroll was too little too late, and they both knew it.

Sam looked calmly and directly at her. "I will find out who did this, Fiona. I promise."

"You better, fuckface." She secretly hated how she always became verbally abusive when angry, but could just not stop herself. That would probably get in the way of promotion, one day, she knew. "Let me know what you find out. No, let my uncle know. You won't be seeing me again."

With that she smacked him in the face with her semiautomatic, and backed from the room, slamming the door behind her.

"I think I am in love," Sam said to himself, as he wiped blood from his nose and mouth.

CHAPTER 40

THE VATICAN

"Your Eminence," Greg Carstairs said into his headset microphone. He was still seated at his computer. "I do not understand this." He paused, then added, "But perhaps you will. The man in the photograph you sent me has been identified as one Leo Schmidt, an American national, a volunteer with a non-governmental organization known as Water Works Inc., operating in Afghanistan. He left there some eight years ago. No known reason. And here is where it gets weird. Since then, nothing on this guy. I mean, absolutely *nada*."

"Have you checked facial recognition software?"

"Just starting. I was working from the photograph first, checking his ID for more hits. FRS has now been brought on line."

"Good. Let me know."

"Ah Cardinal. Something coming in." Carstairs stared at his screen. He had never seen this notation before. It read 'NO ACCESS'. Something big was blocking the usual FRS program. Or someone big. He described the screen to his Cardinal. Then said "Don't worry, sir. We will work on this problem."

"You might check USA service data bases. Just a thought," said the Cardinal.

Within the hour Carstairs' computer screen signalled that it was getting responses. His back-door search of the USA armed forces brought up a service ID photo that looked a lot like Leo Schmidt, and a much younger rendition of the stranger in Santiago. It had to be the same man. One Samuel Clemens Wardell was a colonel in the Special Operations Group, retired. Current address unknown. Current employer unknown. No entries since his retirement seven years ago. His service record was not accessible, which suggested he had been special ops, or undercover. Given time, Carstairs could delve through the layers of obfuscation that the Pentagon had placed over their records. But he had enough.

"Your Eminence? The man's name is Samuel Clemens Wardell; he is a retired Colonel in the Special Operations Group of the American armed forces. His work now is not known. In fact, his record is encrypted, not available."

The Cardinal spoke slowly. "He could have worked as a spy for the CIA. They do co-opt regular armed forces members into their Special Activities Division. The Special Operations Group is seconded to that division." Carstairs could hear the Cardinal humming for a few seconds, a bad telephone habit he had, when he was thinking.

"Yes, I believe this means the man is a spy, a very high level spy, working within the aegis of the United States of America's foreign office. Or was. We need more current data," the Cardinal concluded.

Carstairs replied, "Of course, sir. We will keep on this." But he thought: if the Pentagon really wants to keep Samuel Clemens Wardell a secret, a secret he will be.

CHAPTER 41

Santiago de Compostela

His bloodied nose staunched, and his lip iced, Sam moved somewhat stiffly around his hotel suite. Fiona had left no trace of herself; he had to admire her tradecraft. But what of his tradecraft? How could he have got so much wrong? It was only 9:10 a.m. in Spain. Five hours earlier in Charlotte. Too bad. He telephoned a number he had memorized.

"What?" came the exasperated response.

"Mathieux? This is Wardell. What the hell are you playing at over here?"

"Give me a minute, Sam." The voice was well modulated, calm. Obviously his wife was sleeping next to him, not that common an occurrence if Sam's sources were up to date. He heard footsteps, and a door opening and closing. Then Mathieux came back on.

"What the fuck do you mean, calling at this time of night?"

"Morning actually, boss. Check your clock. And my reason? The aircraft that just got dumped in the Bay of Biscay. Don't pretend you don't know about it." Sam was keeping his voice calm, but his fingernails were digging into his palms.

The voice over the telephone was suddenly soft and smarmy. "Oh, that. Yes. Well. I wasn't sure you could put your heart to 'the sticking place' as Macbeth would have it. So I had someone else see to things." The voice got suddenly angry. "We could not be sure you were up to the job."

"Well maybe your new guy wasn't up to the job. Despite reports to the contrary, the Irish were not aboard the Gulfstream." As soon as he said it, he realized his mistake. If they thought Fiona and her relatives were dead they would no longer pursue them. Now that he had told them, Fiona was again in danger.

Mathieux tried to think, but his mind was still blurred from sleep. "Not on board?" He calmed his voice into an unctuous baritone. "Are you sure?"

Sam was quicker. "No I am not. But neither are you, or you wouldn't ask. Who do you trust? Me or your new recruit? Think about it and let me know. And oh yeah. That was Lady Macbeth you were trying to quote, not her laird, asshole." He slammed off his cell phone. Why had he let his anger override his characteristic caution? Oh well, it was early in Charlotte, the call did not sound taped, and maybe Mathieux would misinterpret what Sam had said, maybe he would just think it was the blathering of a disgruntled and jealous employee. Yeah, and maybe the moon was made of cheese.

"You have to fix this now, kid," he said aloud. "This is on you." He put down his ice pack and began to dress.

The dining room at the Abbe was nearly empty, and Sam thought he had missed his chance to see Mackellan Kirby and his niece and nephew. But Kirby and O'Connor had waited for Fiona, and when, at 9:00 a.m. she had not yet appeared, and was answering neither her room telephone or her new cell phone, they went down to a late breakfast. They were reasonably unconcerned about the absence of Fiona; she was like that. And, as Kirby well knew, she was more capable of self-sufficiency than either of her male relatives.

Thankfully the kitchen of the Abbe had become used to American and British tourists, so *jamon* and eggs were available, although the toast was made from a sweet yeast bread. Joe was enjoying his coffee, in particular. It was rich and dark and unmuddled with either milk or cream, either of which would have been an affront to their very Galician waiter. The ham was locally grown and cured, the egg yolks were a bright orange, not yellow in the least. Joe, who had believed that breakfast in continental Europe had to consist of a sugary bakery product, was happily surprised.

"You should try the churros with hot chocolate, at least once," Kirby was telling his nephew.

Joe swallowed, and replied. "That sounds more like a midnight snack, after overindulging with liquor."

"That could have been its start," his Uncle Mack considered. "They do eat supper late here, and continue to imbibe even later. So perhaps churros and chocolate for breakfast really is a hangover fix. I will have to check that out."

Joe was imagining what that investigation might entail, when a tall, well-dressed American leant over their table.

"Excuse me, Professor Kirby. And Mr. O'Connor." The man smiled slightly, and Kirby noticed the split in his bottom lip. "I am an acquaintance of Fiona. May I sit?"

"Of course," said Kirby. The stranger took the seat beside Joe, so he was facing the restaurant entrance. Kirby noticed that, too.

"Coffee? Some breakfast?" offered Kirby.

"Just coffee, thank you," said Sam, and slid his cup and saucer across the table towards the approaching waiter.

When the waiter had retreated, Wardell spoke. "Have you seen Fiona this morning?"

Both Kirby and O'Connor shook their heads, both wondering why they were being asked about Fiona by this rather pushy stranger.

"Thought not." He stirred sugar into his coffee. He was thinking, hard. "I work..." He amended that. "I used to work for an American interest. It wants you dead, all of you." If that did not get young Joe's American dander up, and his uncle's British reserve to drop like a broken jaw, he did not know what would.

"Really?" said Kirby, as he dabbed at his lips with his napkin.

"Who are you and what are you talking about?" Joe was

beginning to rise from the table. Both the stranger and his uncle motioned him to sit.

"Sam Wardell. Neither of you have seen the Spanish news this morning? Thought not. The Gulfstream that you flew in on yesterday has gone down, in the Cantabrian Sea." To answer Joe's unspoken question, he added. "The south-east edge of the Bay of Biscay. A bit east of your flight path yesterday. Maybe they were sightseeing. Whatever, the G600 is gone. And its flight crew with it."

His table companions stared at him, shocked, and perhaps frightened.

"The *Television de Galicia* report this morning said three crew members and three passengers were on board. All lost." He took a sip of coffee. "Those passengers were supposed to be you."

"So who...? Joe began to ask.

"No one, I think. I believe the report was wrong. Someone thought you were on board, maybe was even told that. And reported your...," he paused. This was awkward. "And reported your involvement. Probably in order to secure a pretty hefty bonus."

Kirby studied his guest intently. "And why are you telling us this?"

"Because, dammit, I was trying real hard to avoid earning that bonus!" Kirby's sangfroid was really too much to take. "I'm sorry. I hate dropping into poor grammar. Please excuse me."

"But?" said Kirby.

"But? But, as you say, you are all in danger. And it is close. I know these people. They will check, everything. They will learn you were not aboard. And they will come after you here." His eyes slid about the room, while his face remained still. "They may already be here."

"Well, hardly," said Kirby. "Besides the staff, who all look very familiar with the place, i.e. have been employed here for some time, the only other person here is that rather sickly looking elderly lady dining alone." He nodded towards a distant table. "And she was here before us, so I hardly think she is following us. Unless she is prescient, of course."

In spite of himself, and the frightening things just said by this stranger, Joe felt a smile tug at his mouth. His uncle really was something. Face him with murder and mayhem at breakfast, and he just began to talk like a professor giving a lecture, a rather boring one. His cold mode, Fiona called it.

Sam sat back and sighed audibly. "Okay. So they are not here. In this room. But they are in Santiago. They are after you. They want you dead. I would like to prevent that."

"So would I," said Kirby. "As the professional here, what would you suggest?"

As the three of them conferred at the breakfast table, Kirby saw the old lady rise from her table, lean on her cane, and limp painfully from the room.

He stood suddenly and said "Excuse me, for a minute. The coffee, you know."

He walked quickly through the dining room to the main hotel anteroom, leading to the washrooms, front desk, and elevators. Out of sight of Joe and Wardell, he stopped at the desk, and asked for a sheet of paper. He quickly wrote something down, then walked slowly back, studying what he had written. Although the old lady was trying gamely to limp past him, he just managed to gently bump into her.

"*Perdone, senora,*" he said, as he put out a hand to keep her from falling. His other hand brushed over her large and out-of-date handbag. "*Por favor, acepta mis disculpes.*"

She looked up at him through rheumy pale blue eyes, and for a minute he thought he had made a mistake. "*De nada,*" she said. Then winked.

Kirby returned to his table, in a quietly self-congratulatory mood.

CHAPTER 42

Iberia 61 A.D. Letter from Ephes to his cousin Bartholomew of Alexandria

Ava dear Cousin. Thank you for your correspondence. I know what I wrote to you last must have been a shock to one who follows the new religion. And I am so relieved that you, and your co-religionists, are so accepting of the fact of your Saviour's continued existence. Of course, as you said, how could the Messiah return to Judaea if he were truly dead?

We have been making arrangements for Lord James' return to Judaea. (I still cannot name him other than that, as I have known him most of my life.)

Rhus and Liara invited my father and me for the evening meal, at their villa.

Rhus had begun to construct the stone house when his children began to be borne, one regularly each year, he was proud to say. As a lay Jew, his sexual relations with his wife were not proscribed, as they are for rabbis of the faith, which in general means a child could only be expected every four years. He is now the proud—too proud Liara would have said—father of six strapping men and three beautiful daughters. Thanks be his daughters have taken after their mother.

When their older children had come of an age to serve in the household of Lord James and Lady Mary, Rhus and Liara moved permanently to their villa, ready to retire from service. They felt secure that their own children would continue to serve the Lord and Lady, with the conscientiousness and love that had imbued their own years with James and Mary.

Their oldest children could not wait for their parents' retirement. Their son Jonathan is proving a very able steward of the royal household of Compostela. And their daughter, Myrna, is very happy to be recognized as the head of all servants, and companion of the royal daughters.

"More caldo, Torgas?" asked Liara. She still feels a bit impertinent to call this great soldier by his given name, with no formal word of address. But many years before Father had insisted on this. Rhus is his best friend, and his friend's wife should be a friend, also. He is an enlightened man.

My father leaned back, smiling at her. "Liara, if I eat one more piece of lamb, I will not fit into my armour. And then where would we be?" He said this pleasantly enough, but I think we all felt an underlying seriousness to his words.

"Another beaker of wine, Torgas? Ephes? In the gardens?" asked Rhus, standing. "They are cool, this time of the evening."

My father took the hint, and so did I. I thanked my host and hostess, and said I needed to get back to my desk. Both Rhus and Father looked relieved to be left alone, and as I left Rhus and my father wandered out into the night.

Liara sighed, then helped her housemaids to clear the table. Force of habit, that; her well-trained servants needed no assistance.

Rhus conducted Torgas across the stone floor of the porch which opened off the dining room, to the baluster guarding its far edge. From there they could look out over Rhus' property—that same land James had purchased in his servant's name, when first they settled in Compostela, so many years earlier. Neat rows of vines ran down the shallow hills. Leas for their sheep and cattle were situated at the bottom of the slopes, where the land levelled out, and through which a stream meandered most of the year. From here, the farm buildings were hidden from them, on the other side of the villa. The two men walked companionably down an exterior staircase and into the gardens. They walked towards the surrounding wall, and again, admired the view.

"Let us sit, Torgas." Rhus indicated a stone bench, set to allow enjoyment of the view. "I feel you are troubled, this evening. What is it?"

"I am worried for Lord James." There, it was out. Torgas had been debating this matter with himself, since the advent of Paul of Tarsus and his companion Timothy. They were still in Compostela, and still being an irritant to the peace of Lord James and to the community. They were apparently the apostles of Christianity—of James for they now knew him to be Jesus Christ. But there had been nothing but discord since they had arrived. What should have been a joyous reunion of saviour with early adherents, had been reduced to shouts and threats. And Torgas knew that Paul, under the guise of a faithful follower, was daily taunting James.

Torgas took a sip of wine. "I do believe that James will be leaving soon, for Judaea. He is struggling within himself, to know what to do. He believes he is the Messiah, and so must return to free the Jews of Palestine from the Roman yoke."

"As it has been written," said Rhus.

"Yes, well. Perhaps anything and everything has been written, depending on your interpretation. I lived long enough in Egypt to learn that. The deadly crocodile is a god, a wild hound is a god. The sun was a god, until Pharaoh decided it was not. So what is true? What is myth?"

Rhus leaned back, and drew in a deep breath of the cool evening air. "I have never been of a particularly religious mind. I was raised with the Roman gods, the powerful ones honoured in the Pantheon, and the more accessible ones who dwell with us within our households. I know that when danger is near me I tend to believe. And when I am without cares, I tend to be without religion." He shook his head. "I think I am not a good person."

"You are perfectly good, Rhus. Good! God! Do you not think the two words are of one? To be good is to be godly. I begin to think that beliefs, and animal sacrifices, and payments to the church are not what real salvation is about. I believe in goodness." He laughed at himself, for this very serious tirade. "I am sorry. This wine is stronger than I knew."

Rhus laughed.

Torgas looked to the sky, at the thousands of stars shining there. "I think there is nothing wrong in believing that a towering cedar may house a dryad—who would not want to live in such a house? And the clean cold water flowing by stones in the stream must house naiads. Why not? I believe we should celebrate the summer solstice which brings us our crops. And then the winter solstice, which is the harbinger of a promised spring, and renewal of the world. I pray to the sun, to the moon, to Horus, and Yaway. And, of late, I have been praying to the father of Christ, the god who led us all here."

"You are a truly religious man, Torgas," commented his friend, a chuckle almost, but not quite, hidden in his voice.

"No. No. That is not what I meant to lead you to believe. I just...," he paused. "I am happy with my belief in James and Mary and of the way we live here. If that makes me Christian, than that is what I am. But I do not think my belief in the Christ means I must discard all of the rest. That would make life," again he paused, "so small."

Rhus signalled to the servant who had quietly been waiting, out of earshot but within striking distance should any danger present itself to his master and his guest. That man quietly approached and poured them each another draught of wine.

"So. To business," said Torgas, in a no-nonsense voice. "If James is set on travelling to Jerusalem, then we must ensure an army goes with him." He stood, and began to pace across the low-growing and fragrant thyme in front of the bench.

"An army?" asked Rhus. He was thinking about the resources of Compostela.

"Well. A guard, then. A goodly guard. One that anyone, even the Emperor, would think twice about engaging. If it is written that the Messiah will return to Judaea, then I believe we need to ensure that he arrives there. Intact." He was now looking straight at Rhus.

"And, my friend, if he is the son of god, then it is our duty to ensure that his family, his royal blood, is kept safe.

Torgas returned to our villa, hours past midnight. He was annoyed, but more pleased, that I had waited up for him.

"Father. You had a good evening with Rhus?"

"Of course," said Torgas. "I always enjoy visiting them both. Liara must be the best cook in Compostela."

I laughed, as I took Torgas' outer cloak from him. "Perhaps in all of Iberia. How many meals have I enjoyed there? They are without count." I am proud to be regarded as a young uncle by the children of the Rhus household, being some decades their senior, and almost as a younger brother by Rhus. I like to think I am a popular guest, with my endless supply of stories of eastern lands.

He regarded his father closely. Torgas was beginning to show his age, and tonight looked tired and worried.

"Father, would you like a warm posset? Some milk and spices?" He went towards the fireplace, and stirred a pot which was sitting to the side of the flame. "I have been keeping this warm for you."

Torgas nodded, and sat. Ephes poured a portion of the drink into a stoneware beaker, then poured another for himself. He sat, cross-legged, at the feet of his father.

"What problems of the world were you and Rhus solving this evening?"

Torgas respected his son; knew that his learning, his ability to read and write did not make him any less a fighting man. He did wish Ephes would marry, because grandchildren would be welcome, at his stage of life. He accepted his drink with a nod.

"We have been talking of Lord James' wish to return to Judaea. We believe that a guard must be readied to travel with him. He must be kept safe."

"Safe from the legions of Rome, or safe from his own self-named apostles?" rejoined Ephes. His undisguised anger took Torgas off guard. He had not known what high disregard his son held for Paul of Tarsus and his travelling companion Timothy.

Torgas loosened his chest-piece of thick leather. It was not armour, but it was capable of stopping an arrow, or deflecting a sword blade. Torgas was perennially on guard. His son lifted the leather piece from his chest and back, and draped him in a soft woolen night robe. Torgas then removed his trousers, still the wide Arab dress which he still wore, after all these years.

"There. You can relax now, Father," said Ephes. "You work too hard. You know that." He bent to the charcoals of the fire, and blew them into flame. He placed a piece of split wood on the nascent flames, nestling it in, to hurry it into fire. "Even on a mild evening, it is good to have a fire."

"Yes," said Torgas slowly. The milky drink was calming him; knowing that his son loved him was also calming. "Looking into the flames is something I never tire of. I wonder if we have always done this."

"What is worrying you, Father? The guard that you must mount for James?"

His father looked at him. "It is more than just James, I think. You know he is our Christ, the son of man, the son of god. He is holy. As are his children. As with anything so pure and good, there will be evil in pursuit." He moved fractionally closer to the flames.

"Rhus and I have spoken of a guard. A permanent guard, that will outlive us both, and even James and Mary. And even you." He smiled at Ephes. "We must look to the future, of our Messiah, and of his progeny."

"I agree, Father. In fact, I was wondering when I could broach this to you. I have been aware for some time, since when the pilgrims started to arrive here, that James needed protection. This visit by his....." here the young man spat. "This visit by his disciples has only intensified this belief. You know I will be happy to be a founding member of the guard."

Torgas knew his son was a very able fighting man; not only skilled at arms, but unequalled in his ability to foresee the progress and the pitfalls of a campaign. Life in Compostela had mostly been peaceful, but when hill tribes, wild groups of men without land or occupation, had seen fit to attack the thriving community, it was Ephes who had corrected Torgas' plans of attack.

They talked on, and Torgas felt a weight being lifted from him. It felt so good to pass the responsibility on to the next generation, a generation which was ready.

"We must ensure that the guard is continued. Perhaps for a hundred years," said my father.

"No, we must know it can continue as long as it is needed. One hundred years, one thousand. If the guard is well structured, there is no reason that cannot happen." I smiled an inward smile, already thinking how to structure such an entity. "What name do you have for this guard?"

"I thought the Guard of Sir James?" Father said, with a question in his voice. He knew it was a terrible name.

"But we will be protecting not only James, and Mary, but their children, and their scions, forever. We will be protecting the bloodline of our Lord and Lady," I said, and smiled. "The blood of James has always been one with the rose cross, on the altar of the church; the grantor of miracles. Why would your guard not be known as the Guard of the Rose Cross?"

"You always have had a way with words." Torgas said, saluting me with his near-empty beaker of warm milk. "Yes, the Guard of the Rose Cross."

So. The Rose Cross. You may just be hearing of us.

Take care, and take care of everyone you love.

Your cousin,

Ephes.

CHAPTER 43

SANTIAGO DE COMPOSTELA

The elderly lady, moving painfully, limped into the bathroom marked *damas,* went into a stall and opened her handbag. She retrieved a piece of paper. On it she read 'Hello Fiona." Damn, she thought, how did he know? Kirby had also written down a local telephone number, presumably the number of a new cell phone he had acquired from the ever-so-helpful hotel concierge.

She would wait to call him, until he was no longer with Wardell. What was Wardell doing with her relatives, anyway? Not asking for her hand in marriage, she laughed. More like asking for reparation payments for the damage she had done to him. She made her slow way through the back entrance of the Abbe, the street exit, and asked the doorman for a taxi. It came immediately, she was gently assisted to the back seat, and gave directions to her driver. He winked at her: good, the company had come through again. The taxicab meandered through the narrow old streets near the basilica, then headed into a part of the city which was nearly as old as the Plaza de Obradoiro. Within minutes she was parked in the area known as Las Gallerias, a mixed residential and commercial area which could best be described as a bohemian village. Tavernas, cafes, butcher shops mixed with accountants' offices and pharmacies lined the streets. But Fiona had been told about Las Gallerias' best kept secret. Narrow gates, set between the commercial spaces, opened into tiny squares or courtyards, which were overlooked by the apartments built over the commercial spaces. Here, laundry hung from balconies, bright pots of bougainvillea spilled colour everywhere, and splashing fountains cooled the air.

She looked about discreetly, then lifted her cane and walked with her usual quick step up three flights of stairs to the top floor of the building and knocked on an apartment door. Celeste Robles opened the door immediately, and grinned at the apparition she saw.

"Caro, you are perspiring! Old ladies do not run up stairs! They wait for elevators." She was laughing as she led Fiona into her salon which doubled as a workroom. Celeste was a retired cinematographic make-up artist. Supposedly she was semi-retired, but still working her make-up magic, mostly on brides these days and their entourages, or modelling wantabes who needed some portfolio head shots. She had been hired by 'an American firm' to transform Fiona into an infirm elderly lady, in a matter of minutes, not hours, just that morning. She had worked for that client before; they paid extremely well. In a non-taxable form. So she had gladly accepted the job. And she had been pleased to meet Fiona, someone without artifice, so non-threatening—some of the clients of the American firm, in the past, had been downright scary.

Fiona kissed Celeste on each cheek, and pulled off her wig. "Whoo! That thing is hot! Glad I don't usually wear wigs."

"Would you like a *café*? asked Celeste. "One of my good ones, with milk and cinnamon and a touch of chocolate?"

"Well, when you put it that way," laughed Fiona.

Celeste Robles had spent many years in Hollywood, honing both her talent and her English. So Fiona was immediately at ease with her. She had tried, but her Spanish was still not that passable. Her Urdu, now, or her Czech? Perfection. Somehow, Spanish eluded her.

Savouring her coffee, and enjoying the street view from Celeste's salon window, Fiona finally admitted, "My uncle knew me immediately."

"Uncle? Didn't they know what you looked like?" Celeste was referring to the personification of the USA, Uncle Sam.

"No, no, not those guys. My real uncle, Uncle Mack. He looked around the room, and nailed me."

"Did he see you walk?" asked Celeste.

Fiona thought. "My table was some distance from theirs. I stood and left the room. He got up as I was leaving. I was moving slowly, with that stupid cane. So he had time to pass me, write me a billet-doux, bump into me, and then stuff the note into my bag, as he apologized for his clumsiness. Lovely Spanish, I think."

"Ah Caro. Let me see you walk, with the cane."

Fiona put her shoes back on, placing a little stone in her left one, as Celeste had instructed her earlier. Not even an amnesiac can forget to limp, with a stone in her shoe. Fiona then walked across the room, leaning heavily on the cane in her left hand.

"Ah, *si*." said Celeste, with a nod of her head. "People think the cane should be used on the side of the...the crippling? The deficiency? Yes. But people who limp for real, support themselves on the outside of their good leg, to make up for the weakness in their bad leg or foot. There is more stability that way. The cane is further from the weakness." She retrieved Fiona's cane, and demonstrated. It did look very convincing the way Celeste limped through the room.

"You know? I have never noticed that before," said Fiona. "But obviously Uncle Mack has."

"He was in a war, correct? He probably saw many men with real injuries." Celeste sounded pensive, and Fiona wondered if she had lost someone, somewhere.

"Yeah," replied Fiona slowly. "But now I need another persona. I don't want 'Limping Old Lady' to become a familiar figure leaning over certain peoples' shoulders."

Celeste put her coffee cup down on the metal counter in her miniscule kitchen. "Of course. And as you are in Santiago de Compostela, what better disguise than the cloth?"

"But....the guy I don't want to recognize me told me he has been watching out for every Sister and Mother Superior."

Celeste smiled, and went to her closet of costumes. "Yes, but was he watching for Padres?"

"Not unless he has experienced a sea-change."

Celeste laughed, and got to work.

CHAPTER 44

SANTIAGO DE COMPOSTELA

Brother Martin had been instructed to meet the Cardinal at the airport at Santiago de Compostela. He was usually a patient man, but today he was angry, and that negativity eroded his usual passivity.

He strode through the arrivals area of the airport, impatiently. His bluntly ugly face and short blond hair were at odds with his obviously continentally styled suit. Which, again, was at odds with his Roman collar. He was a big man, well-muscled; his tailor had to employ some artifice to allow room for the pistol holster he habitually wore. Part of his job, part of his service to his god. The god with whom he was, at this instant, very angry.

The arrival of the flight from Rome was finally announced. Normally the Cardinal would have flown in Vatican One, as the Pontiff's Lear jet was nicknamed, after the USA's president's Air Force One. But a new age of cut-backs on perks, and a general restraint on spending, meant that Cardinal Contini was flying on a scheduled Alitalia flight.

No doubt in first class, though, thought Martin Froese. He waited at the side of the arrivals hall. No reason to press forward, with a 'Cardinal Contini' sign held hopefully in his hands. He hated the way overly sycophantic hotel reception staff were so prone to greet their more famous guests. Or more paying, he amended. The Cardinal knew Martin; he could come to him.

The Cardinal was also in plain clothes, as they called them. Not even with a collar. Just an open shirt, with its collar points spread over his light sports coat. And jeans. Really. Jeans. They fit well, and the Cardinal was a youngish man, for a Cardinal at least, not yet fifty. The only sign of his rank was his ring, a gold signet inset with a magnificent sapphire, proudly glowing on the third finger of this right hand. A discreet sign that could easily be missed by most of the thronging crowd, even if any of them happened to be aware of its meaning.

Cardinal Contini was pulling a carry-on sized suitcase behind him, with a computer bag over his shoulder. He looked like any other businessman. Martin approached him, and took his suitcase from him.

"I would kiss your ring, My Cardinal, but you appear to be in disguise," he said. His sneer was not well hidden.

"Brother Martin. So good of you to meet me." The man spoke politely. "Regarding my clothes, I see no reason for the good folk of Santiago de Compostela to wonder why a Cardinal is visiting their fair city. They might assume it has something to do with the Basilica. Which, of course, it does not."

With Brother Martin brusquely leading the way at an almost rude pace through the crowds, they walked out to the arrivals level, and then across the roadway to the short-term parking garage. Froese opened the door of his rental SUV for the Cardinal, and tossed the bag onto the back seat.

"You are staying at the Basilica, I expect?" asked Brother Martin.

"No. No. I thought I would remain incognito. I have a reservation at the Hostal dos Reis Catolicos. You know it?"

"Of course. I am not an idiot." The response was barely above a snarl.

Cardinal Contini was an intellectual, yes, but a churchman first. He could feel the antipathy radiating from Froese.

"Brother Martin? Have you had lunch yet?"

"I am not hungry," was the terse response.

"But perhaps you are thirsty. I know I am. And I do believe that any thirst is easily assuaged in Galicia. Or perhaps a simple ice cream. In a park. Whatever. But I do want to know what is so irritating you."

Martin Froese parked his rental SUV in front of a tavern. "I could do with a beer. My Northern European roots showing through."

The two men sat at an outside table, and ordered a beer for Froese and a Campari for the Cardinal.

When the drinks were served, the Cardinal said "So, what is the problem, Brother Martin?"

Froese squeezed his big hand around his beer, to the point that the Cardinal had fears for the glass' continued existence. Then he took a drink.

"I have worked for you for years, Your Eminence. I have never questioned your requests, accepting them all as my duty, to my God. But..." Here he faltered, and took another draught of his beer. "But why did you have to kill Kirby? And his niece and nephew, and those innocent airmen? How do I know that we are on the side of the..." here he paused, and added, irreverently, "..the angels, when we do things like that."

He glared down at the table, not able to look at his Cardinal.

"Ah. So that is the problem." The Cardinal leaned back, and lifted his face to the early afternoon sunshine. "I assure you, we do not want Professor Kirby dead; much the opposite." He leaned forward, and touched his companion's forearm. "You know I requested that when shooting at Kirby, in his woods, that you shoot wide?"

The priest nodded.

"Does that suggest I wanted him dead? Think about it."

Martin Froese had to acknowledge the simple truth of the Cardinal's point.

"I believe that the motivation behind the downing of the aircraft was to frighten Professor Kirby. But that is supposition, and because we do not know, for certain, the motivation, we also do not know who the criminals are who committed that crime. But we do have reason to believe that Professor Kirby and his family members were not aboard that flight. And even more reason to believe that they are in danger. Grave danger, as that bombing suggests."

Brother Martin nodded. He might look like any other paid muscle, goon, enforcer, whatever. But he was a Jesuit. They took only the brightest into their seminaries. And Martin was indeed, very bright. Muscle, yes; bright, yes. The two did not often coincide. Brother Martin was an asset that Cardinal Contini valued very highly.

"So, now what?" asked Froese.

"Now, we continue to do what we meant to do when we 'inspired' Kirby to come to Santiago. We wait for him to recover the original Testament of Ephes."

Martin felt a change in the air. His Cardinal did not usually tell him what a mission was about.

"The Testament of Ephes?" he asked. Then, as an afterthought, added, "Sir?"

"You know, Martin. I tend to be a secretive man. I keep myself to myself, and my thoughts even closer." He chuckled at his little joke, but Martin was not smiling. "Okay, but right now, in this sunshiny city dedicated to the remembrance of Saint James, I feel, somehow, the shadow of.....of death, perhaps. That plane crash was no accident. It makes me feel....the brush of angel wings, if you will."

Martin wondered about the strength of Campari compared to beer. He had had a pint, to Contini's four ounces.

"Your Excellency? If you would like to discuss this matter, with me, as I think you do, then may I suggest lunch? The Scallops St. Jacques are good. I know, I know, it is a bit touristy, and French if the truth be told, but here they do it very well. The piped potatoes around the shell itself, might just be better than the scallops." At a nod from his Cardinal he signalled for their waiter. "And perhaps a bottle of this area's very fine *Albarino*. Yes, you will enjoy this very much, I think."

The Cardinal knew he would enjoy his lunch very much, because, finally, he had decided to tell Brother Martin what everything was all about.

CHAPTER 45

THE VATICAN 1086

Papal Legate Bishop Viandicondi was announced into the stateroom of Cardinal Legare. The Cardinal officiated over an important aspect of the library of the Vatican, and thus commanded a grand stateroom, or outer office. Most business was conducted, at that time, in the stateroom, where the cardinal met with visiting dignitaries, discussed the problems of the day, and generally displayed himself as minor royalty. Only a selected few were received into his private office. Very little of a librarian's business needed to be so secretive that it had to be conducted without the benefit of comfortable furnishings, servants, good food and drink, as the small, plain, and priest-like interior of his office demanded.

Viandicondi was led in by an officer and four of his soldiers. Four more marched behind him, two of them carrying the cedar chest on a wooden litter, the other two were laden with hammers and axes, instead of the standard issue halberds.

The Cardinal stepped toward the Bishop, then extended his right hand to allow the lesser churchman to kneel and kiss his ring. When the Bishop stood, the Cardinal placed one hand on the other man's back, and guided him to a chair at a table, bathed in full light from the vast windows. The library of the Vatican had seen improvements over the centuries. And one such was the installation of the best glass windows known to Christendom. They rose from near the floor, to a height of at least twelve feet, and their crystal clarity allowed the full passage of the Italian sunlight.

"May I see what you have?" the Cardinal said.

A bit peremptory, thought the Bishop. It had been a long and arduous trek, to outer Iberia and back. Could the Cardinal not at least be grateful?

"Of course, My Lord." Viandicondi signalled for the two chest bearers to approach. Their officer placed a rough cotton sheet on the Cardinal's rich carpet, and the soldiers placed the chest there.

"What is within it?" asked Legare.

"I do not know. I thought the honour of the opening should be yours alone." He smirked and bowed. Legare just looked at him.

"So, open it."

Viandicondi signalled to the two soldiers. One fitted a metal wedge into the line between the top of the chest and the side, and the other man lifted a hammer, ready to swing at the wedge.

"Wait!" said Legare, standing. "Will they not damage the chest, this way?"

One of the soldiers, the older and less politic one, spoke up. "Won't open, otherwise. We've tried."

Viandicondi had the good manners to blush slightly, and bow his head. "Yes, we did try to open it. Just to be sure there was something there, something to bring to Your Lordship. But when it resisted, we stopped. I did not want to damage the chest." The Cardinal looked steadily at him. Viandicondi whispered "It purports to be a thousand years old."

"So if it gets damaged, it gets damaged on my watch?" The Cardinal nodded to the two soldiers. "Open it."

They finally had to splinter the wood to open the chest, so artfully was the wood of the top dovetailed into the wood of the sides of the chest. They found an iron locking mechanism, which had also affixed the lid to the body of the chest, which had been set when the lid was closed.

Viandicondi looked upward, seeking inspiration, or perhaps salvation. Nothing about this box looked first century.

Inside, they found a smaller stone box, a cris, or modern ossuary, empty. And a scroll.

Cardinal Legare opened the scroll, read for a few minutes, then tossed it down, onto his table. "This is from Bishop Darda. He sends you his greetings. And he asks me to invite him to Rome, so that he may present the text of the scrolls to me personally. Personally." Legare was a small man, but somehow he managed to put a definitive stomp into his walk about his stateroom table and Viandicondi's chair. After three complete circumnavigations, he stopped.

"Go back to Gaul. There is no place for such as you in modern Rome. We need thinkers, politicians, bankers....we do not need would-be Papal Legates who cannot garner even the trust of a simple bishop."

"But," spluttered Viandicondi. "But...let me return to Compostela. I will show Darda just who he is dealing with." He dropped to his knees in front of Legare, and grabbed at his right hand. "I will do this, for you, my Lord, and to punish this upstart for his impertinence." The angry words made him feel better already.

"We also do not need bullies in the Vatican. That ended in the fourth century. And I am 'Your Excellency', not 'My Lord', although I am certain that your failure to address me properly when me meet, will not be a problem, ever again. Leave."

When alone Legare mused over the other paragraphs of Bishop Darda's text, the ones he had not told Viandicondi of. Apparently Darda's scrolls gave him reason to believe that the ossuary in his possession contained the bones of two people, not one. And if he was correct in his translation of the language of the scrolls, then the Roman Catholic Church had a very serious problem to contend with.

CHAPTER 46

COMPOSTELA 1087

Bishop Darda had not heard back from Cardinal Legare, although Bishop Viandicondi had left the town some four months earlier. That was sufficient time to have received word, but he decided to wait a fortnight longer. Perhaps the Cardinal had not been amused by his charade with the chest

His translation of the Testament of Ephes was complete. Parts of the papyrus were illegible, from rot or dryness or a combination of the two. But he had taken careful note of the width of the unreadable spaces, and had notated his own copy with what he guessed to have been written in the original. But the tale it told was indeed sad. And Darda knew that it was affecting him badly; he seemed unable to shake a deep sadness such as he had never experienced.

To occupy his days, he wrote a second copy of his translation. This was not in a wood-bound notebook, but was instead, neatly penned on folios. The folio, a large sheet of paper, when folded correctly, produces eight pages on which to write. When bound, and then with the folds slit, the whole becomes a book. He had requested that Breg find a workman who could bind his folios—there were only six—and the book now sat on his work table. It was beautifully bound in leather, a slim volume of less than fifty pages. The binder had incised 'The Testament of Ephes' into the leather, and had even created a frontispiece from a partial folio he had at hand, which said

'The Testament of Ephes' as translated by Bishop Darda, 1086'. In this copy Darda had again reproduced, as best he could, the missing text, marking each such insertion, so that the reader would know the text, so marked, was supposition, and not a direct translation. The book was written in modern Latin as was the notebook.

The little book, for it measured a scant inch thick, some four inches wide and six inches high, now sat on Darda's desk. His notebook was wood-bound and filled with scholarly discussions referencing the Coptic Greek, and what the writer might have meant to have said, and the different interpretations which might apply to some of the ancient words. The notebook was a masterful scholarly piece. And much larger and heavier than the tidy little volume.

He decided to write again to his Cardinal. In this letter he said when he intended to begin his trip to Rome. Given the time of year, he would not be going to the port at Finnesterre. The north Atlantic weather was too untrustworthy in the months of autumn. He would travel, instead, overland, east through the Pyrenees, then southward along their foothills in Gaul to the port of Navarre. The roads were still decent, old Roman stone paved routes from the second century, but maintained to some extent and passable easily by a party on horseback, as long as they got through the mountain passes by mid October. He would not wait for a reply, this time, simply go. He knew the Testament of Ephes had to get to Rome, had to become recognized as an important—perhaps the most important—Biblical text of all time. This was his duty. This was why he had been sent to Compostela. Not to oversee the building of a grand cathedral—about which he knew nothing. No, he had been sent here, to decipher this text. He had the training, from his younger days in the libraries of the Vatican, he knew the languages as very few people would, and he had been there when the scrolls had been discovered. Of course God had sent him. And now he must complete this task, his task. With that decided Darda became a more contented man, not happier perhaps, but at least, now with a goal, he once more became the pleasant man he had always been, to his friends and underlings.

A group of pilgrims who had been visiting Compostela hand delivered Darda's letter to a barque in Finnesterre, where it was included in the Roman Catholic correspondence directed to various bishopric sees along the way to Rome. When the dispatch bag arrived at the port of Navarre, Bishop Viandicondi, as had been his wont since his return some months earlier, had all of the correspondence brought to his office. There were many boring accounts, a report from Master Bernard Gelduin to Cardinal Benestus, the head architect at the Vatican, regarding the progress of the cathedral at Compostela, and many rather peevish reports from parish priests claiming to be overworked and underpaid. Finally, his secretary found it. A letter from Bishop Darda to Cardinal Legare.

"Leave that on my table," he ordered his secretary.

"But, Your Grace, this is a personal letter, it is marked so. It is sealed. It is not general church business."

"It is very personal to me," snarled Viandicondi. "Leave it. And go."

Viandicondi smiled when he read the letter. Just like the impertinent Maltese upstart, heading off to Rome without an invitation. He knew, of course, why Darda had never received word from Legare. The Cardinal's letter to Darda had been one of his first interceptions, when he was so conveniently on board the same ship that brought the letter. That was when he instituted the custom of having every Roman Catholic communications bag stored for safekeeping in his palace in Navarre, until the ship which had brought it in was ready for the ongoing journey. It worked perfectly. He appeared to be watching out for the Papacy and its smooth operations in the west Mediterranean. No one had raised a questioning priestly eyebrow, until his secretary, earlier today. Perhaps it was time for that young man to seek a mission somewhere in Africa. Or worse yet, Albion in the north. Whatever, he would not long remain in the Bishop's Palace in Navarre.

Viandicondi smiled. Finally his troop of knights would be worth their keep.

On a bright September day, Bishop Darda's party left Compostela. Darda took only his acolyte Joaquim, who could act as both travelling companion and servant, and a retinue of seven knights and their seven servants. The bishop did not feel the need of a servant for himself; he had for a long time been a particularly self-sufficient man. But he understood that the politics of the day required that a churchman of his rank must not be seen tending to his own laundry or cooking, and that when needs be, a servant was required to serve both Darda and any guest along the way whom he might be constrained to entertain. He would much rather have travelled with Joaquim as his sole companion, as a simple transient priest might do. But a bishop was invested with power, and authority, and presumably the ear of god. That all required some pomp. He did, though, insist that no cart would be included in the entourage. The knights would have to do with what their servants could load onto their horses.

Truth be told, the knights in Captain Ansted's—yes, he had received a promotion, as he thought just for years of service, not for valour or accomplishment—the knights in his command had for years felt underutilized in Compostela. They were bored. So for the last two weeks they had been devising ways and means of determining who got to go on the trip with the Bishop: the man who won at sword practice at the end of a complicated tournament process, which allowed every contestant the chance to try again, if he was beaten once; the strongest man, determined by lifting stones for the masons—who thought that was a wonderful game—; again, in a tournament, the best chess player, for they all played the game that was supposed to develop battle strategy but really only whiled away the hours. The seventh place was reserved for Captain Ansted himself. He too, was feeling rather pent up in Compostela. Yes, the pilgrims did need some controlling at times, especially when one who had touched the famed rose cross began to feel touched by god, instead of just by the wine he had imbibed. Or a merchant was caught short-weighting grain or meat. The knights in Ansted's patrol had become the police force for all of Compostela.

They rode decorously out of the city, pennants flying on uplifted lances, the colours of the See of Northern Iberia raised high. They followed, but in reverse, the northern or French pilgrims' route. Along the way they were met by throngs of pedestrians, as the various holy routes drew together, the closer they neared the city of Compostela. The troop was cheered lustily, by the by-now very bored pilgrims. And Bishop Darda blessed every single person they passed, to the point where his voice grew hoarse, until Joaquim suggested he just raise the first two fingers of his right hand in greeting, the accepted sign of a blessing from a holy personage. Darda was so grateful for this advice he determined he would cook supper at their next stop. But his cooking skills were not soon required.

Although they had the gear required to sleep and cook rough, the pilgrims' routes, in northern Spain and through to the Pyrenees foothills which flanked the mountain range as they moved southward through France, were well serviced by hostels, inns, taverns, stables, and anything else travellers might need. When hostels were sufficiently large, Darda had everyone, even the servants, stay as a paying guest. He knew most of the hostels charged the true pilgrims only a very minimal amount or nothing at all, and tried to bring up their revenues by surcharging the well-to-do and quite obviously holidaying travellers. Darda paid for everyone. As a bishop he received a reasonable stipend from Rome, and he never spent more than a miniscule portion of that, so why not splurge on this trip? The men were grateful for such luxurious treatment, and they in turn dealt kindly with their horses, which meant that all of them, man and beast, travelled in good health and good spirits.

At the smaller hostels some of the servants had to sleep in the stables, or, on the calm and starry nights of autumn, camped in the hostel's grounds. Only on rare occasions did the whole entourage find itself, at nightfall, without accommodation. Then they bivouacked, and as is the way with Templars, the food on those evenings was well-cooked game, simmered in wine, with their travel bread for dipping. One of the knights—the strongest man, Darda was told—was a very passable baker, and he renewed their bread at every hostel which boasted a decent oven. Usually the lady of the house was both flummoxed and thrilled that a very large knight asked for access to her kitchen, and then proceeded to prove his abilities as a baker. The landlady usually learned something she had not known about testing the crust, or kneading the dough, and she certainly enjoyed the novel idea that men do have a place in the kitchen. Truth be told, the landlords were not usually so pleased by this culinary display, although they were happy, to a man, to test the resulting breads and brioches.

The pine forests of the Pyrenees descended to the road, on their right. The aspens and chestnuts of the foothills forested the left of their route, and at times opened up into the vast natural meadows of western Gaul. They passed through farmed areas, where the trees had been hewn and the land cleared for vineyards, or pasturage for dairy animals, or tilled fields for food crops. The beauty of the land, with the colours of autumn just beginning to show, was unsurpassed, by anything he had ever known, thought Darda.

Captain Ansted drifted his horse back through the troop until he was beside Darda.

"That Belgium looks more fit today than he did a decade ago. You must exercise him often."

Darda laughed. "He exercises me. It is never the other way about. But is this not a spectacular land, so beautiful in the colours of the fall?"

Captain Ansted looked about, as though seeing the countryside for the first time. "It is beautiful, yes. Perhaps we should have taken a journey every year, just to see the colours." He smiled. "This reminds me of my home, near Rouen. There are more vineyards there, and many small holdings, so there is a sense of civilization. That is missing here." He looked about again. "Which I like."

They rode on in a friendly silence.

Then, "Bishop Darda, do we have any reason to expect trouble? I have a forward scout and a rear guard, as always, but should we be doing more?"

Darda thought about that look of hate that he had seen on Viandicondi's face, and the rough rudeness of the bishop's guardsmen. "I hope not."

After an agonizing night of reflection and consideration, Darda asked Ansted to again ride beside him.

"I have thought of what you asked me, yesterday. About precautions."

Their horses walked amicably together. Darda's was a gelding, and the Captain's was a stallion, which will not typically allow a gelding near it. But the captain's horse accepted Darda's gelding, and, in fact, after being ridden beside each other for two days, they began to whinny to each other, if their masters happened to be riding apart. Darda thought that was quite endearing; Captain Ansted found it embarrassing.

"Yes, My Bishop?"

"In one of Joaquim's saddlebags there are four scrolls. They are old, so we packed them in cloth, in a stout leather sheath. It is some six inches in diameter, and less than two feet long. The scrolls are of infinite value. If anything should happen, they must be kept safe." The bishop rode on, distracted. "Whatever it takes, they must be kept safe."

CHAPTER 47

SANTIAGO DE COMPOSTELA

"Brother Martin, thank you for sharing your knowledge of Coquilles St. Jacques." The Cardinal touched his lips with his linen napkin, then took a drink of the brilliant white wine in his glass. "And of this Albarino. A most remarkable combination. So, thank you."

"You wanted to tell me something?"

"Yes. Over coffee. May we have coffee?"

"Of course, Your Eminence." Brother Martin expertly signalled for their waiter and made the order. "Any dessert, sir?" A head shake for answer, Froese waved away the waiter.

"Yes," the Cardinal sighed. "This story begins in a French village called Rennes-le-Chateau in the Carcassonne region of France. The village had a church, consecrated to Mary Magdalene in the eleventh century. In the southwest of France, and in the neighbouring parts of Spain and north into the Galician region there was almost a cult-like belief in the Magdalene, seen nowhere else in the Roman Catholic Church. Except possibly Scotland, but that is another story. Anyway, in 1891 the local priest, while undertaking repairs to the church, found some scrolls, long hidden in the support of the christening font. Apparently, the base, which appeared to be carved of stone, was in fact a hollow tube of concrete, with a stone facing. Details of those scrolls are sketchy, at best. But thereafter the poor parish *cure*, one Berenger Sauniere,—and I mean poor; his annual wage was only a few hundred francs— began to exhibit signs of wealth, and....well, social acceptance. He was often seen at Parisienne soirees, especially those hosted by known members of the occult." Here Contini shrugged. "I have no idea what that means, or what it refers to. I think no one does."

"What happened to the scrolls?"

"Well, again. Who knows?" The Cardinal sipped his espresso. "But the wealth exhibited by the Cure Sauniere began to be commented on. He built a villa, for himself and his housekeeper." Here Contini raised his two forefingers in the air and twitched them, to indicate air apostrophes. "His housekeeper lived with him for years, from when she was only eighteen."

"That happens."

"Yes. But, the cost of that villa, in today's terms, would be millions, quite a few millions, of Euros. This country cure was rich, beyond belief, and yet, he appeared to do nothing but be a simple parish priest. After he found the hoard of scrolls."

"So where are the scrolls, and/or what do they say?" the always pragmatic Brother Martin asked.

The Cardinal had to respect a man who could introduce a forward slash into his speech. That so reminded him of university. "Two of them made their way to the Vatican library. The other two, we believe, were purchased by Leopold II, the Hapsburg king, at the time. There is some supposition that Leopold purchased all four, but allowed the first two to get to the Vatican. Sort of a teaser, if you will. The Hapsburgs, the ruling house of most of central Europe, were fighting a significant but silent battle on the home front. Did Austria want to be Roman Catholic or Lutheran? England was clearly Protestant, or, to be precise Anglican, which has always been a mirror image of Catholicism. Although the state religion in Holland, Belgium and Luxembourg was a long-established Catholic tradition, the people were adopting the protestant concepts. Their Huguenots were fleeing in droves to Protestant England."

"So, in 1891, some papers are found that are apparently worth, in today's terms, millions. The Vatican records show that payment was not made from its coffers. So, the Hapsburgs? And if the Hapsburgs were funding Sauniere, why? What did they expect to receive, that would compensate them for that quite hefty cost? But at that time the Hapsburgs had a secret. They wanted to join the Protestant revolution. I believe they blackmailed the Catholic Church, with what was written in those scrolls. Blackmailed the Vatican to allow them, and their empire, to become Protestant."

There, he had said it. Something he had never done before. Cardinal Contini had spent decades in the libraries of the Vatican. He had had access to every piece of paper—or papyrus—enshrouded therein. But this was one mystery that he still struggled with. What did the Sauniere scrolls say? And why was what they said so important to the Hapsburgs? What would induce that royal house to make most substantial payments to a small town priest? And did the conversion of the Hapsburgs to Protestantism so soon thereafter bear any relationship to the puzzle?

Brother Martin sipped his espresso. And frowned. "What do you think the scrolls said?"

"Whatever they said, the mere ownership of them meant the preeminent empire of the European continent was allowed to adopt Protestantism without any resistance from the Vatican. Ergo, the scrolls hold a secret, a secret so unacceptable to the Roman Catholic church, that it was thought it was better to lose the Austro-Hungarian Empire to another religion, then to have that secret revealed."

"And that secret is still such? Still a secret?"

"It is to me," the Cardinal said, and shrugged eloquently. "And, remember, I have free access to all documents in the Vatican libraries. I know, I have not reviewed them all. Who could, in one lifetime? But I have also had the resource of my librarian trainees, for many years. I have had all scrolls and papyri read and reread, by my students. Nothing." Here he smiled. "Well, not nothing, really. I have actually found quite a few interesting bits of news, some of it over a thousand years old, some more recent, which would, in every instance, make for a wonderful Hollywood movie. But I doubt that we will ever see any of that on the screen. I could so easily become a blackmailer, myself."

His companion allowed a look of shock to flit across his face.

"Oh, not that I would do that. I love my church. And, at nearly two thousand years of age, one has to expect some foibles, some lack of judgement, some dirty dealings. Especially when the popes were selected from the ruling class, instead of the true clergy. That is another of my rants, which I will not bore you with, at this time. But what really stumps me is that I thought I might come at the problem from another direction. So I have reviewed all correspondence between the Vatican officials and the Hapsburg government, from 1891 through to the destruction of the empire. Nothing. Just trite politeness.

Brother Martin signalled for the waiter and, with a nod from the cardinal, ordered a bottle of a decent local cava. Brother Martin did not want the story to end just because the meal had.

"So, you believe Professor Kirby has the scrolls?"

The Cardinal thought for a moment. "No, I do not think he has them. Yet. But I believe he will find them. That is what he does. He is a very famous religious archaeologist. He has found other artifacts."

"But why have we pushed this man, this retired university professor, into danger? That matter of the aircraft. It was just by chance that Professor Kirby and his relatives were not aboard. Perhaps you were not personally made aware of the danger, but you know now to what extent some people will go to protect their secret. So why leave him in this mess?"

The Cardinal could hear in Froese's voice the strident sounds of confusion and disappointment.

Their waiter returned with a bottle of the local champagne-style white and two wine flutes. After the falderal of opening, and sniffing, and testing, he poured two glasses. The Cardinal lifted his glass. "*Salute*."

"*Salute*, Your Eminence."

"The good Professor has resources, shall we say, which should relieve him from any 'mess' as you term it." He sipped his cava appreciatively. "They always have, in the past. No, Dr. Kirby should be safe enough, but the scrolls themselves might not be, after he has found them. That is where we—or more to the point, you come in. I believe that whoever blew up an aircraft to either kill Kirby, or to frighten him severely, will stop at nothing to keep the scrolls a secret. The most efficient way to ensure that is to destroy the evidence before it can be verified. And perhaps, to destroy whoever knows of it. So, be careful Martin.

The use of his Christian name without the title of brother, caught Froese's attention. And he silently vowed to himself that he would be careful on behalf of his Cardinal, also. And he had to wonder about the Cardinal's reference to 'whoever' when it was clear to Martin that that personage had to be a Vatican operative.

"When you told me Kirby was headed to Spain I presumed he was heading to the south, to the Carcassonne. I thought he would begin his hunt in Rennes-le-Chateau. That town was on the pilgrims' route that heads north along the French side of the Pyrenees. An ancient hamlet. Some people think that Cure Sauniere had discovered the famed Knights Templar treasure, and was spending that. But there was never any evidence of Templar era artifacts being sold off to finance his building schemes. So I do not believe that. Though there is a ruin of a Templar fortress near the village."

"Sounds like an interesting place. Will we be going there?" Not such an innocent question. If the Cardinal wanted to head to some village in the south of France, Martin had research to do, and people to put into place. His usual duties.

"No. We have had treasure hunters search that area for years. Still have some, actually. They haven't found anything, but they do work cheaply, in the expectation of a big payday when they discover the hoard." He shook his head. "At least it keeps them out of other mischief."

CHAPTER 48

SANTIAGO DE COMPOSTELA

"Where can I park these contacts?" asked Fiona, as she reached to her eyes to eject the two lenses. "Not only did they look awful, they hurt."

Celeste laughed. "They are supposed to look awful, as though you are near blind with an eye infection. I developed them myself. For a Scorsese production. He loved them." She scooped up the contact lenses and placed them in an alcohol wash. "But this time, I think you do not need the contacts. I think the right eyebrow colour and white on your eyelashes will make you look so pale behind your glasses that no one will notice your eyes."

Fiona sipped her coffee. "Nice touch with the cinnamon. Do you grind your own sticks? Does that make it fresher?" Celeste nodded. "And I will wear contacts again if a have to. I just hate it when I shock myself when I look in the mirror." She grinned.

Celeste led her along a line of clothes racks in her studio. "Here," said Celeste, "I think this will work. It is a soutane, not worn by every priest anymore, just the more conservative, or provincial. The skirt will disguise your legs and feet. And no one really looks very masculine in a soutane, so with a little acting you should pass." She twitched the soutane over Fiona's head, and smoothed it down over her hips. "You are so slim that no provocative curves should give you away. And, there is room under your skirt for concealment of a weapon. Should you have one." She smiled. "That is often a requirement of my costumes for your bosses." She found a pair of black leather boots, of indiscernible age and style and had Fiona put them on.

"Well," said Fiona, studying herself in a full-length mirror. "I kind of always thought I looked good in black, but, really..."

"No one looks good in a soutane," rejoined Celeste. "Which is why it should work." She indicated that Fiona should walk up and down the room, as though really modelling the clothes.

Celeste laughed. "No, no. You are not on a runway. Walk like a man."

Fiona shrugged.

Celeste demonstrated. "Men walk with their hips back, under their abdomens. Women thrust their hips forward, and stride from their hips. Men walk from their knees. Their knees go forward, like this." She thumped about the room. "And their feet are always placed flatly. No arch in the foot. And directly under the body."

Fiona practised, as Celeste had prescribed. She had never particularly studied how men walked, but as soon as she saw Celeste demonstrate, she recognized the differences between a typical female and male movement. The differences were subtle when understood, but made a manifest difference in perception. Within minutes, with Celeste's coaching, she was parading about in front of the mirror, doing a passable rendition of a man in a skirt.

"And you never, never put your toes down first. That is a holdover from wearing high heels. You always put your heel down, with a heaviness, and let the front of the foot smack down after." She demonstrated.

Fiona practised for a minute or two.

"Yes, you have it now," enthused Celeste. "For a naturally elegant lady you walk like a man very well."

"Should I thank you for that?" asked Fiona.

They both laughed.

"And now your make-up," said Celeste, walking towards a huge wardrobe. It was separated by shelves, and each level held plastic bins. She looked hard at them, pulled out a few, opened their lids, and then slid them back. She extracted one. "This should do."

She held up a full face mask, made of a soft and supple rubber. "I hope you have not that allergy, to latex. Or to glue." She sat Fiona down in front of a well-lit mirror, and placed the mask over her head and face. The latex fit closely, covering Fiona's hair with what appeared to be a balding male skull, complete with tufts of long and thin white hairs. Her face became aged and ugly, with a bulbous nose, a straggly mustache and thin beard.

"You will need to glue the area around the eye holes to your skin. As with the mouth. But the hair of the mask will disguise the edges, just so." Celeste demonstrated, pulling the thick white eyebrows down over the plastic of the mask. "The bottom of the eyeholes will be disguised with mastique. You will look as though you have a wrinkle just under each eye, as old men do. And these glasses will help to disguise that area. But first, the white mascara on your eyelashes." She fussed about Fiona's face for a few minutes, stood back and said "Voila! "

Fiona looked at her reflection. She saw an ugly old man, with an almost bald pate, bushy white eyebrows, and aged and blue-veined skin. "You are amazing," she wheezed, in a barely audible but deep tone.

Celeste laughed. "I have had a lot of practice. And that was a pretty good mimicking of an old man's voice. But remember to speak French, or Spanish, or best yet, Italian. American priests do not wear soutanes, I think. And now we must work on your hands," said Celeste. "You are not going to like what I am going to do to your manicure."

CHAPTER 49

NEAR NAVARRE
FRANCE 1087

Bishop Darda's group camped for the night, far from any village, or even a farm. They had the hillside, which sloped down from the roadway to a stream, all to themselves. Darda himself did not like to camp below the road; that gave him a sense of being overlooked, of being observed. He would rather be above any traffic which might pass by. But the lay of the land dictated that they camp below the roadway, so that was that. The men all seemed happy with the arrangements, finding small plots of level ground on which to unroll their bedding, and working out an efficient path to the stream, for fetching water for cooking and washing. The horses were roughly corralled with ropes and tree boughs, near the stream, so they could water themselves, and still have access to grasses and mosses growing beside the water. It was almost perfect.

The main campfire was burning brightly as the knight who charged himself with their cooking was making the servants hustle about, securely emplacing the metal stands for his rotisserie rod and crank. He had expertly butchered and skewered the three rabbits which the men had encountered earlier that day, and was instructing the servants regarding the saucing of the rabbit as it turned gently on the spit. The smell of roasting meat and chestnuts stewing with the wild onion and parsley which the servants had freshly harvested that afternoon, was making Darda's mouth water with anticipation. He knew, as a man of God, he should deny himself worldly pleasures, but surely a camping trip was a time to enjoy all of life's gifts, was it not?

After a really fine meal of roast rabbit, chestnuts, and fresh camp bread, Darda walked with Ansted down to the brook, to look at the horses. Their own mounts walked up to them, to be stroked, and petted; in their equine minds this placed them above the other horses, because they were loved by and important to these two men. The other horses did not even notice, so busy were they browsing the rich grasses and sedges of the streamside.

Darda petted his Belgium, walked a few steps away, then paced back.

"What is it, My Bishop?" gently asked Ansted. He had come to admire this man, this quiet cleric, this man who could have been such a successful soldier with his muscle and attitude. No, he amended mentally. He had come to love this man. There was no shame in that. Darda was worthy of unfettered affection.

"I do not know." Darda strode about, looking upward, to the roadway far above them. "I just do not like to be....to be below anything. Like the road." He laughed, without humour. "It must be something from my childhood. Perhaps a bat flew in from an upper window, one night and frightened me. Or perhaps, as a Maltese, I am only happy when on the sea, with everything level with me. I do not know. I just feel unease, here, in this beautiful place."

The Captain looked about, as usual, on guard. "If you feel unease, my Bishop, I could place more guards tonight. I do have, as usual, a man in the rear and the fore, a few minutes away, watching the road."

Darda turned to him. "You mean you have two knights positioned away from camp? Have they had dinner?"

Ansted smiled. "The ones on earlier duty have now come in and enjoyed the meal. The men who replaced them ate before they left camp. I try to maintain the basics of civilization, even out here."

Darda kept striding about the paddock area. He was restless.

"Shall we walk, My Bishop? Is there something troubling you?" He gently touched Darda's elbow, and moved him further along the streamside. "Is there reason to be especially on guard?"

So Darda told Ansted about the animosity he had felt from Bishop Viandicondi, and the rudeness of his guard.

"He is a prince of the royal house of Navarre. And we are nearing that city," said Darda.

Ansted looked about, as usual, ever vigilant. "We are a few days still from Navarre, My Bishop. But perhaps tomorrow evening we should encamp within Castle Rennes, the Templar fortress near the hamlet of Rennes-le-Chateau. That will make it a long day, but we should get there, near twilight or just after."

"Yes, Ansted. You did tell me of Castle Rennes. If we mean to be entertained at a Templar castle I must send word ahead." Then he laughed. "Or ask you to send word. That might mean more."

"Your word is good with all Templars, My Bishop," said Ansted. Usually a bishop was addressed as 'Your Holiness' but Bishop Darda had encouraged the more comfortable address Ansted used. And somehow the use of the word 'my' made Darda feel secure in the protection of the people who used that term. "I will send a man off before daybreak. That will give the Master of the Keep some hours in which to prepare for our arrival."

"Thank you, Ansted. I am sure there is nothing untoward in this peaceful place, but....but, until we are past Navarre, I would appreciate you taking the leather sheath from Brother Joaquim, and keeping it close to yourself. When we return to camp, I will go with you to Joaquim's sleeping place. To get the scrolls." He looked up into the swaying branches of the chestnut trees. The rising moon was just coming into view, over the low horizon to the east. "I would like you to have them. They must be kept safe."

In the semi-darkness of early morning one servant—a squire, soon to be promoted to knighthood—left the camp. His horse was the fastest, and could gallop for hours without stress, particularly when his rider was without armour. The squire should reach the Templar fortress in the middle of the afternoon, with the news of the imminent arrival of the bishop and his troop. It was not a lot of notice, but it would be sufficient for a well-run castle to prepare a welcome feast fit for a bishop, and to accommodate his entourage of fifteen men. Darda would be happy with bread and cheese, and a stable for himself and his men, but politeness required that he give notice of his arrival, and allow the Master of the Keep to provide the best he could for his guests.

The squire, Henri of Rouen, Captain Ansted's own nephew and squire, rode easily through the morning. He stopped at times to water his horse at rivulets that ran down from the Pyrenees and under short stone bridges, built by the Roman engineers, some thirteen centuries earlier. The road was smooth and straight, and he made good time. He had been authorized by Captain Ansted to change horses at a pilgrim house in Rennes-le-Chateau, but his animal was eager to go on, and was showing no signs of fatigue or strain. So he rode on, through the hamlet of some forty homes, a mill, a market area, and a newly built stone church.

From the village he could see, high on a mountain to the west, Castle Rennes. In truth, it was built on a craggy foothill of the Pyrenees themselves, but from the plains below, it looked high and distant. At the junction of the road to the castle and the highway he was on, the squire led his horse down to a stream that he had seen, gurgling through scrubby pines and boulders, below the roadway. While his horse filled his belly with the cold mountain water, he heard the unmistakeable rumble of shod hooves, and the voices of men. They were moving fast. The squire tethered his horse to a bush near the water, and moved quickly and silently up the trail to the road, squatting just out of sight of the riders. He counted over thirty fully armed knights, under banners showing a black animal—at this distance he could not discern which one—on a white field, with a red bar across the top. He did not recognize the banner, but he did take the time to remember it.

When the men and horses had passed, and were out of sight on the road to Rennes-le-Chateau, he remounted and rode, as fast as he dared on his now tiring horse, up the rocky road to Castle Rennes. Something about that group of men made him nervous and wary. He pushed his mount to a steady but ground-covering canter. It was only mid-afternoon; he had made good time, but now he felt a special urgency.

As he approached the castle, the great doors were opened, and he rode directly into the castle yard. A Templar sergeant, recognizable from his brown chemise with a black cross on the chest, worn over his coat of mail, greeted him. One man alone, unarmed but for a still-sheathed sword, was not a threat, so the sergeant met him alone. The squire noticed, though, that he was being carefully observed by many other men. Within minutes he was being conducted into the castle itself, to meet the Master of the Keep, and his horse was being led to the stables, for a well-deserved feed of grain and a bucket of water.

As the sergeant took him through into the inner rooms of the castle, Henri asked "I saw a mounted troop of men. Riding towards that little village I passed an hour ago. Whose arms is a black animal on a field of white, with a bar of red above?"

The sergeant kept walking but replied. "A black leopard? That would be the royal standard of the House of Navarre. The red band on the top means it is the personal standard of Prince Renaldo, the Bishop Viandicondi. He believes he will soon be promoted to cardinal, hence the red band. Cardinal, red. Get it? But the little shit has not been rewarded with the berretta yet." He turned to look at the squire. "We all hope he never will be. So, how many men?"

The Templar sergeant led the squire into a work-like office. It was plain to the point of poverty, he thought. One man sat at a table, a quill in his right hand, writing down the words being dictated by an older man looking pensively through a casement window.

"My Lord? "said the sergeant. "A messenger from Bishop Darda of Compostela. And Captain Ansted."

The older man turned, revealing the dull red cross of his surplice, and a handsome bearded face. He smiled at the squire and came towards him, his hand extended. "I know the Captain, and I have heard good things of your Bishop. Welcome to Castle Rennes."

The squire managed to shake the proffered hand, then bowed, and felt totally out of his element. He managed to mutter through his message, regarding the advent of Bishop Darda and fourteen other men, besides himself, hoping to rest within the castle for the night.

"Of course. Of course. Arrange that, Rene." His secretary stood, bowed and left the room. "I am Marshal de Clury. To whom do I speak?"

"Excuse me, My Lord, I am Henri, of the House Morigne, from Rouen. I am Captain Ansted's squire. And his nephew."

"And soon to be knight?"

The younger man blushed. "Yes, sir. I should be raised at the Yuletide festivities, this winter. There are some others posted at Compostela, who will also receive their spurs."

The sergeant, having heard enough niceties for one day, cleared his throat.

"Yes Sergeant?" asked de Clury.

"This young fellow saw a troop of horsemen, well-armed, riding under the banner of our Lord Bishop Viandicondi." The way he said the last three words was telling of a warm disregard.

The Marshal's head snapped up, into even better posture. "Where? When? How many?"

The squire answered.

The Marshal regarded him. "Why do you think they were riding, as you report?" His eyes bore into the young man.

"I have no idea, My Lord. I just know they made me uneasy." He stopped, then added, "Uneasy for my Lord Bishop."

And for your uncle, the Marshal thought, but no Templar-trainee would allow himself to bring concern for his own blood into the discussion.

The Marshal considered for a heartbeat, then said "Sergeant, mount a troop. I will be with you. They have thirty men. We will take sixty." Then he turned aside to Henri. "Whenever you can enjoy strength of numbers, do so. It is not particularly heroic, perhaps, but is usually effective." With that he strode from the room.

CHAPTER 50

Santiago de Compostela

Mackellan Kirby and Joe O'Connor were back in Kirby's room at the Abbe. Their breakfast conversation with Sam Wardell had shaken them both. Kirby paced, sat, stood, paced again.

Kirby said his people would let Sonia know that none of them had been aboard the downed Gulfstream, as various European news services were sniffing about, and then suggesting they knew who the three as-yet-unnamed passengers were. It was only a matter of days before their names broke into the headlines. But Joe could not stand it. He telephoned Sonia early afternoon, 6:30 a.m. Seattle time. He used the Abbe switchboard, knowing that cell phones could be compromised.

"Joe," breathed Sonia. "I am so glad to hear from you." She sounded somewhat strained.

"I'm sorry it is so early. But how are you and Marsha?" he asked. "I...I have been concerned."

"Marsha's asthma is fine. She even insisted on going for a buggy ride yesterday. In the rain. She even tried to hold the umbrella. You know, your big black umbrella."

Joe winced. "That's great. We are all fine. No problems to speak of. Safe and sound at Uncle Mack's." He hated lying, but then decided that as Uncle Mack was paying for the suite at the Abbe, this was, in fact 'his place'. They spoke for another few minutes, about ordinary things that ordinary people have to talk about. Then: "I will call again soon. I love you both."

"I love you too. Goodbye, Joe."

Christ! thought Joe. He ran from their common sitting room into Mack's bedroom. His uncle had stayed there to give his nephew some privacy. "Uncle Mack!" he shrilled, his throat muscles totally out of control. "Something is wrong with Sonia. And Marsha."

Uncle Mack looked up, over his eyeglasses, the way he did. "What's wrong?"

"I don't know. But something. Something bad." He moved quickly but directionlessly all about the room. "She said the word 'umbrella'. Twice."

"Oh my. A code word, is it?" The strained look on his face belied his light tone.

"Exactly." Joe threw himself down into an upholstered side chair, near the desk. "We use the word 'umbrella' if something is wrong. Like we can't talk, because her mother is on Skype, or her boss is over her shoulder, or....or whatever. But it means trouble."

"And at 6:30 local time neither her boss nor her mother would be present. I see."

"And she said it twice." Joe was almost moaning.

His uncle came to him, awkwardly patted his shoulder. He knew how to hug a female, but his own male flesh and blood was another animal. "I will see to this. Now. I need some privacy."

"Can't I help?" asked Joe.

"No, not really. I will see you in ten minutes."

Joe went back to his room and paced. He had wondered if his Uncle Mack was in trouble when he had called and asked Joe to visit, telling him that Fiona would be there too. Joe knew Fiona had an incredibly busy schedule, doing quite what he did not know. And he himself did not get that many weeks of holidays. But it was for Uncle Mack, who had been a mainstay of their lives since earliest childhood. So, of course, they had agreed. It was bad enough that their private aircraft had crashed, really bad actually, but with this added trouble in Seattle, his fears began to take over his usually very competent brain.

Within the projected ten minutes Mack knocked at Joe's bedroom door, and said "Let's sit out here," indicating their joint drawing room. "People are on their way to your condo. It might take a while; they have to be a bit circumspect."

"Uncle Mack?"

"I told you I should never have got you involved. I never thought it would extend to Sonia and your daughter." Mack looked as though he wanted to cry. "Please, now, go home."

Joe straightened his shoulders. He had played forward in his college's rugby eleven, and his shoulders were not something to ignore. "Whatever is going on, Uncle Mack, if...when... Sonia and Marsha are safe, I will stay here with you."

Within thirty minutes Mack's new cell phone trilled. He answered, looked pensive, listened for what Joe thought was an inordinate length of time, and then laughed. A huge belly laugh. "Thanks," he said.

Joe looked at him. Mack beamed. "You have a bit of a hell-cat in Sonia. My guy was just talking to her. She will be calling you in a minute, on the room telephone. Seems she had a visitor at the condo very early this morning. He bypassed the access system, came right to her door. He said he was a friend of yours. He apparently did not bother to hide the fact that he was carrying a handgun. At about that time you telephoned her. Hence the 'umbrella' references. He made her nervous. So she claimed Marsha was starting an asthma attack, and she had to see to her. The thug followed Sonia into the nursery. Of course he was not going to let her out of his sight. And she managed to get him into view of the nanny cam. It's hidden apparently, in some teddy bear or something?"

Joe nodded.

His uncle continued. "Sonia adjusted the arm of the toy, and in doing so set off some alarm?"

Joe nodded again. "For security reasons, no one at Sonia's lab is allowed to keep their cell phones on. A hacking issue. But because of Marsha's asthma, Sonia wanted to always have immediate contact with our babysitter. So rules be damned, Sonia fixed things her way. The nanny-cam transmits to her computer in the lab, so she can check it at any time. And she got some IT nerd friend to set up an alarm on her computer, which is activated from a switch—the teddy bear sits on the switch. That way, our babysitter can alert Sonia without leaving Marsha in the nursery, and can talk immediately to Sonia through the nanny-cam audio. It is totally illegal of course, probably violates some Secrets Act prohibition."

Mack laughed. "I don't think anyone is going to be too concerned about that. In fact, the powers that be may just borrow Sonia's technology. She set off the alarm and then got some good shots of the guy. The alarm was responded to by the night guard at her lab. Sonia's computer was displaying the nanny-cam video, and the guard didn't like the looks of the guy, and called in security. The thug was just forcing Sonia, with Marsha, to leave with him when a bimboish babysitter-type—their words not mine—turned up at your condo, exclaiming how she was sorry she was a bit late, etc. Marsha was safe with Sonia, so the 'babysitter' disarmed the thug. And disarm is the operative word; apparently his right shoulder is severely dislocated. But she did stop herself from shooting him, although she voiced her regret at that." Mack rubbed his hands together, obviously very satisfied with his news. "I know Sonia's work is very hush-hush, but I had no idea how much protection she merits. I do like the way you Americans handle security. That babysitter ploy was brilliant. Lucky they had a young Quantico alumna on hand."

Joe still looked shaken when he answered the telephone. It was Sonia. They spoke for some time in the privacy of his room, then Joe came back to the sitting room, where his uncle was staring disconsolately through the open window.

"Sonia and Marsha are safe, and in protection. And I want you to get on the first flight out of here. Go home," said Kirby.

"Uncle Mack, I am not leaving you here. Sonia agrees. No,

insists. I know you said not to worry, but we don't even know where Fiona is, so you would have no one. I am not leaving." He looked belligerently at his uncle. His arms were crossed over his chest, and Mack could swear that his red hair was standing on end.

"Look, Joe," his uncle said, and then sat in the room's second armchair. "I should never have asked you and Fiona to come with me. In the beginning, I honestly thought the trip here with you two would be fun, like in the old days when I used to take you with me on digs and hunts. And when I thought there might be a chance of danger, I quite honestly wanted you two with me. You know, safety in numbers, that sort of thing. But not now. If something happened to either of you, I could never get over that. Facing whatever dangers there are, alone, will never be as bad as having something untoward occur to you or Fiona."

"And I can make the same argument. I could never live with myself if I left now, and something happened to you or Fiona. There. A tautology, for you."

"Technically speaking that is not a tautology, because we were saying different..."

"You know what I mean, Uncle Mack. I mean I am staying."

Kirby looked at his nephew, then nodded. "Alright then. The quicker we find what we are looking for, the faster we can get out of here." Mack looked at his watch. "Come on, Joe. I.....we, have an appointment with one Monsignor Manuel Torres." He hustled Joe up and out of the room.

Once out onto the Plaza De Obradoiro Kirby strode toward the Cathedral of St. James. He spoke quietly so no passersby could overhear.

"Let's use that mathematician's brain of yours. One: In the Dead Sea Scrolls there is a fragment dated 70 A.D., written by one Ephes, who writes about being in Compostela."

"The date could mean that Ephes met, or at least knew of Jesus and Mary. You did say there was some story of them leaving the Holy Land for Gaul," Joe said.

"There has long been that supposition," said Mack, musing. "The Dead Sea scrolls are thought to be part of a collection of hundreds of manuscripts, all brought together for the Council of Nicaea, in 325, to be considered for inclusion in the Holy Bible being underwritten by Emperor Constantine. None of the Dead Sea Scrolls were included in the Bible."

"But someone, or more likely some group, thought the papers were of value. Perhaps not as part of the Bible, but having some value. I take it there were different factions, arguing over what should be included and what excised?" asked Joe.

Oh yes. Fairly bitter it was, too, by all accounts. Hence, the later split of the Christian church into the west and eastern orthodoxies. Two: the Testament of Ephes was not included in the Bible by the Council, but the copy I have read has been heavily redacted. Not unknown but rare. Why redact a document if you did not intend to use any part of it?"

"Perhaps some guy at Nicaea thought the text was so controversial he just could not allow it to exist, in its then current form. But why not just destroy the whole thing?" asked Joe.

"Yes. Good question. So perhaps there was some part of the text that was considered to be important, and which existed in no other document. That is the only reason to not destroy the thing outright."

Nearly at the cathedral, Kirby turned to skirt the left tower of the great church. "The main entrance is for pilgrims and tourists. We need the office." Sure enough a door marked 'Officios' allowed entry into a mundane and unfurnished office, with a grill, a guard, and a rather bored secretary.

"Si?" she asked, through the grill.

"Buenos Dias, Senorita. I have an appointment with Monsignor Torres. Professor Kirby."

"May I see your identification papers? And who is your guest?"

Kirby handed both his and Joe's passports through the bottom of the grill. "This my nephew, he is working as my research assistant."

She telephoned to someone, spoke, then assured Kirby that he was correct. "The Monsignor is sending someone for you. You may wait in the anteroom, Senor." She made a signal to the armed guard, who bowed Kirby and Joe through a heavily secured metal door, into a chamber of such beauty, Joe's breath was virtually taken away. Now this was a waiting room, worthy of its name. You could wait in here, forever, thought Joe. The room was furnished sumptuously with small groupings of upholstered chairs and sofas, all in a pale mint green velvet. The drapes at the windows, which, in Spanish fashion soared to the sixteen foot ceiling, were of a soft gold silk, shantung came to Joe's mind, although he did not know why. And somehow, the artwork covering the walls, and the sculptures resting on tables, brought it all together. It was a waiting room fit for visitors to a cathedral.

Joe was still wandering about, admiring everything he saw; and mentally adding up the value of the furnishings. His mathematical training just would not shut off, even in the face of the most ineffable beauty. He was thus engaged when the double doors at the far end of the room, crashed open, and in rushed a large, black suited man, wearing a Roman collar. And a smile, Joe was glad to see.

"Professorio Kirby!" He almost ran to Mack, and grabbed his right hand in both of his, and pumped it up and down vigorously. "You honour our cathedral, with your presence." Then he released Kirby, and bowed. Not a curt nod of the head, but a real bow, from the waist. Joe did not think he had ever actually seen a real bow, before.

"Monsignor Torres," responded Kirby warmly. "It has been many years, too many."

"Yes. When you used to visit the Vatican Library." The big man put his hand on Mack's upper back and conducted him towards Joe, who was waiting quietly. "And who is this young man? You used to work, alone Professorio. Except for those 'students' of yours, who could never come into the library proper because they could never pass the metal detector." Then he laughed, a huge belly-laugh.

"This is my nephew Joseph O'Connor. My sister's eldest, and visiting from Seattle, in the USA."

The two men shook hands, while Kirby abashedly thought back to when he had last been to the Vatican. It was true that in those days he always had a guard with him, in civvies, but militarily armed. He just did not know that the Vatican staff had been so well aware of everything.

"Ah, a nephew. I think I see a family resemblance." Then he turned back to Kirby. "So, he is your nephew? Not another one of your *vigilari*?"

Kirby laughed. "He is my nephew. I haven't needed a guard since I retired. Years ago."

Torres was now conducting both Joe and Mack through the double doors he had used. He walked quickly through a broad stone-tiled hallway, made one turn, and they were walking through a colonnade, a wall on one side, columns on the other, separating their walkway from a tiny but perfect courtyard garden, complete with a three-tiered fountain. "We are now in part of the original buildings. This was the monks' cloister. The Baroque tower has a smaller cloister. Not for monks, of course. Nothing less than a bishop was expected to stroll there."

"Not very democratic, or Christian."

Torres glanced sideways at Mack, and slid his eyes upward. "The Vatican may be a country unto itself," he said, "but it is not a democracy." He kept moving quickly, and muttered. "And sometimes I wonder if it is even Christian."

CHAPTER 51

NEAR NAVARRE, FRANCE 1087

Captain Ansted had his men on the road some two hours after the messenger had left camp. It was an early start, but he knew that Castle Rennes was a long ride away. His troop walked their horses, to conserve their energy and increase their stamina.

By late afternoon they were just coming up to the village of Rennes-le-Chateau, when the autumn sun sank behind the mountains to their west, and the evening shadows darkened. The Captain saw one rider, cantering fast towards them. It was his outrider, his forward scout. Ansted spurred his big stallion into a gallop, and rode out to meet his man.

"My Captain." The man bowed in his saddle. "There is a mounted troop heading this way, perhaps a mile distant. It is a goodly number, I think, from the dust and length of the group. They are moving fast."

"Thank you, Sir Raoul. You may rejoin the troop." Both men returned to the main body of their party, the Captain turning to ride alongside Bishop Darda.

"My Bishop. There is a mounted troop within minutes of us. Coming our way."

Bishop Darda kept his big Belgium ambling forward. "Other people do use this road. Pilgrims, for instance." He looked about, at the sere landscape they were now in. A rocky scree to their right, gave evidence of the proximity of the Pyrenees Mountains. And to their left, open meadows of dry grasses and gorse stretched to the low hill which protected the village which lay just ahead. "And, even if I wished to, I see no way to avoid meeting this group."

"You could leave now, My Bishop," said Amsted, sitting very straight in his saddle. His face was grim. "They might never even know you were here."

"Thank you, Ansted. I appreciate your concern. But it might be difficult for you to explain that the Bishop is not present, when the men are carrying the pennants of the See of Northern Iberia." He grinned wryly. Then looked down at his pommel. "No, I will stay here. I have served as required. This will be as it must be."

Ansted thought that speech was a bit esoteric, but this was his bishop and his friend, so he just nodded.

The troop of men encountered Darda's group within minutes. Ansted had all the knights close up ranks, with the servant squires in the centre of the fighting force. Ansted rode at Darda's right, at the front of the group.

The knights of Navarre rushed at Darda's group at a full gallop, which was just barely restrained before the two groups met. With a great huffing and puffing of the straining horses, their forelegs braced for a quick stop, the Navarrese troop filled the breadth of the roadway. Their leader, that same soldier Darda had met in his rooms in Compostela, spoke up.

"Bishop Darda. We understand you are carrying documents to Rome. To ensure their security, we are here to request that those documents be given over to us, for the Bishop Viandicondi." Here he stopped, and then looked gloatingly at Darda. "For their safekeeping." He could not—or did not bother —to keep the smugness from his voice.

"Captain," said Darda, with a smile. "I trust the Most Reverend Bishop of Navarre is well?" He looked about, as though searching. "Bishop Viandicondi is not with you? Too bad. It would be nice to have his company—and his protection—when we enter into his city." Again he smiled.

"Bishop, we know you are carrying documents. I demand you turn them over to us," responded the Navarrese leader.

By now, the knights of the French troop had surrounded Darda and his followers. They did it subtly, but Ansted's men were fully aware of their own vulnerability.

"I am a delegate to the papal symposia. Meetings to be held three months from now, in Rome. I demand the protection of the Christian realms I am passing through." Darda said this quietly, but his back had straightened, and he somehow looked inches taller and broader.

The captain of the Navarrese sneered. "Tough, Bishop. I just want your fucking scrolls." Then he spat, to the right foreleg of his horse.

At that diversion, Joaquim kicked his horse out of the encircling Navarrese, and shouted "My Bishop, I will protect the scrolls with my life." With that he galloped full bore into the meadow land to the east of the road. Some ten of the Navarrese raced after him. But the odds were still all wrong.

"Oh, my God, Joaquim, no," muttered Darda. Had Joaquim forgotten that he no longer had the scrolls? No, of course not; he was creating a diversion. Darda prayed for the man's soul as he thanked him for his bravery. At Joaquim's run, all hell broke loose. One third of the Navarrese were in pursuit, but that still left some twenty armed men to Darda's group of seven knights and their servants.

They fought bravely. But the attack had been unexpected. They were not ready. They were at the end of a long day of riding. Darda could not believe that he was seeing swords slashing at his followers, mowing them from their saddles, hobbling horses when desperate soldiers decided to bring down the horse, if they could not touch the rider. Blood flew through the air, emitting its bitter smell of iron. Darda felt his loyal Belgium fall; leapt from the saddle, and raised his sword against too many attackers. Through the dark of early evening he saw Ansted ride toward him, his feet kicking at men, his sword cutting through the soft sections of the armlets and the guises of the Navarrese armour. Ansted was coming for Darda, when Darda yelled "No, Ansted. You know what you must do. Go now. God be with you." Those were the bishop's last words, as his head was nearly severed from his body, by the full swing of a Navarrese long sword.

Darda knew he was dying, or perhaps even dead. He stopped hearing the horrible sounds of the fight, the screams of pain from men and horses, the ugly thunk of weapons tearing into flesh. He saw the sea again, with the light of a moonrise crossing to him, coming for him. He sighed, and tried to speak again.

CHAPTER 52

JUDAEA 36 A.D.

Joseph held tightly to his niece's shaking shoulders. Then he turned her face away from the spectacle, and into the soft wool of his robe. "You should not see this, Mary. Let my servants take you home."

"And you will stay here, Uncle? And watch this horror? Because I have not the stomach to do so?" She was very angry, which Joseph knew was an improvement over sorrow. "No, Uncle. I must stay. He is my son. I cannot desert him now."

They watched as her son, tied loosely to a wooden post, and stripped of his outer garments, was flogged. The Roman soldier entrusted with the whipping was a huge man, and he was putting every ounce of his considerable strength into his lashes. The whip itself had many shorter leather thongs attached to it, each with a tip of iron, so that when the whip raked down the prisoner's back and thighs, the metal bits dug and tore at his flesh, while the leather thongs themselves opened long welts in his skin. The prisoner bravely bit off his screams of pain, then involuntarily began to moan softly whenever the whip struck. When his blood was dripping from most of his back, and had pooled at his feet, the flogging was stopped. It was not desirable to have a condemned man die before his crucifixion.

He was untied from the post, his cruel crown of thorns was righted on his head by the centurion, and he was told to pick up his crucifixion pole, a hefty oak post the length of two men, with a cross-beam half that length, set at right angles to the post, and placed a few feet from the top of the post. It weighed too much for the poor bleeding wretch to carry, so he braced himself under the cross-beam and dragged it over the stones of the roadway.

One man came forward to help the prisoner, then seeing that the soldiers did not use the lash to whip him away, others followed suit. They might have been the good Jews who had condemned him as a blasphemer the night before, at the palace of the High Priest, or they might have been good citizens who could not stomach being witness to the pain of this human being, without trying to help in some small way. They eased his burden, all the way to Calvary. At the base of the hill, very near to the place of execution, Joseph instructed Mary to wait. He went to the condemned man, his great-nephew, and told the guards he wished to say his farewells. As a council member of the Sanhedrin, and a rich and respected trader, Joseph of Arimathea was known to Jews and Romans alike. They allowed him to approach the prisoner. Joseph held his nephew's head, one hand on each cheek, and kissed him on the mouth. It was a long embrace.

The Hill of Calvary was littered with old crucifixion posts, some still erect and carrying the blackened and rotting remains of condemned men, some lying down, awaiting the newly condemned. Soldiers took the crucifixion post from the crowd of Jews who were now openly assisting their Messiah. The long end was placed just over the lip of a hole, some four feet deep. Then the centurion ordered the prisoner to lie down along the beam, and two soldiers stretched his arms out, along the cross-piece.

That is when the prisoner bit down hard on the tiny tin capsule his great-uncle had passed into his mouth from his own mouth, under the masquerade of his farewell kiss. A sudden taste of bitter acid flooded his mouth, then he felt no more. He could hear the sound of the great iron spikes being nailed through each palm, to attach his hands to the cross-piece. But he felt no pain. He heard the ugly crunching of bones in his feet, as they, too, were nailed together to the long beam of his cross. The length of time on the cross that a man could survive was greatly enhanced if his feet were nailed, or sometimes bound, to the post; that gave him a perch, on which he could rest his weight, which meant that the fluids flowing into his chest pooled slower, and his eventual suffocation from water-filled lungs was delayed and his suffering thereby stretched out, sometimes for many excruciating hours, even days for some. He thought: they really want me to suffer. But he felt no pain.

Ropes were attached just above the cross-piece, and a cadre of soldiers pulled the cross up, until its butt end slid into the prepared hole. Other soldiers filled the space around the beam with rocks, placed handily in a pile nearby. These were tamped down somewhat, but that would not matter; even if the cross swayed slightly, it could not topple. And the looser the rocks, the easier they would be to remove, and pile neatly aside for the next crucifixion, when this cross was eventually lowered.

In the crowd below he saw his mother, weeping, great gasping sobs exploding painfully from her throat. He did feel that pain, and closed his eyes to it. There are some things a man cannot bear.

Some three hours later, in the strange murkiness of that day of the total eclipse of the sun, the man on the cross began to speak. Joseph listened attentively. He was aware that the nostrum he had passed to his nephew, the work of the best alchemist that Joseph's money could buy, was finally failing, and pain was taking precedence. Joseph asked the centurion if he could offer a sponge dipped in sour wine to ease the thirst of the poor wretch. This was often done; it seemed to revive a fainting man. Why his great-uncle would want to revive him, the centurion did not know, but he authorized the act. Joseph's servants brought forward a stick, with a sopping sponge attached to its tip, and raised it to the sufferer's lips. He tasted it. Then turned his face upwards. To most of those watching he appeared to look heavenward. Joseph knew he was looking toward the hill of

Gethsemane, across the city. He said "My Lord, it is done." Then his head drooped in death.

Ever on guard for faked deaths on the cross, especially as in this case when death had come so unexpectedly soon, the centurion ordered a soldier to slash the prisoner's torso with his spear. This was ostensibly done to determine how much water had accumulated in the victim's lungs; in actual fact it served as irrefutable proof of death. No one could survive that slashing wound, from the breast down though the soft internal organs to the hip.

The cross was lowered, the iron spikes removed from his hands and crossed feet. The centurion pocketed the nails, and surreptitiously wiped an errant tear from his cheek. He ordered his men to leave and he, too, walked away, to leave the lady mother in peace with her burden. Anguish was clear in her eyes, in the lines newly etched into her face barely visible now in the dimness of the day when darkness had come so early. She hugged the body to herself, and gently—although no further pain could reach that poor sad thing—she gently removed the crown of thorns from his forehead. The lady stroked the scratched and bloody face without concern for the hem of the sleeves of her mantle. The red blood stained the deep blue of the cloth to a purple fit for the kings of all the world.

She cried out: "Oh my son. What have they done?"

Joseph of Arimathea watched his niece weep over the body of her son. Then he signalled his servants forward. They gently wrapped the body in a soft linen cloth, then lifted the body onto a length of coarser, heavier linen, folded in the sides and used the ends to lift and carry the body. Joseph had received special permission to remove the body immediately after death. Usually the Roman administration wished to have the victims of crucifixion remain on their crosses, as carrion for flesh-eating birds, and hungry dogs, or just to rot from the inside, to semi-mummify with the skin turning into a blackened leather. This was to serve as an example to other would-be malfeasors.

In this case, though, it had been considered that the body of

Jesus might become, in itself, a rallying point for Jews who believed him to be the Messiah, the one to lead them from the tyranny of Rome. It would have been too ironic to kill the man, and then have his dead body cause the very political uproar that his death was supposed to quieten.

So Joseph was made welcome to the body, and had even been requested to move it quickly and quietly to a hidden place. His servants gently moved their burden across the Hill of Calvary and down the hillside to the graveyard of Golgotha. The Place of Skulls had been a burial site for centuries, the ancient graves now being dug up and destroyed as new tombs were constructed over the old. It was a sad place, but for all that, a holy place. And a most desirable location for a tomb. Joseph's was a newly-renovated family tomb, with rock shelves sufficient to house many generations. The most recent work had just been completed, as requested of Joseph by Simon Zealotes. The servants carried the body into the tomb, laid it on a stone table as instructed, then waited outside. Joseph, Mary and two of her ladies-in-waiting sat with the body, as two Essene priests opened the linen coverings and washed the body with a mixture of sweet-smelling frankincense and water, rinsing the blood from its many wounds. The two priests shrouded the body in fine linen, and then in the coarser stronger linen which had been used to transport the body. Mary and Joseph said their tearful farewells, and everyone left the chamber. A great wheel-like rock was rolled across the doorway. The entrance to the tomb was sealed.

CHAPTER 53

NEAR NAVARRE, FRANCE 1087

Ansted continued to fight, turning his huge stallion in tight turns, as he slashed and hacked with his sword. He felt the satisfaction of pulling his weapon from the flesh of one man's abdomen, and saw one knight's right arm part from his body at the shoulder, so powerful was Ansted's sword work. But he also felt a slash across his left shoulder and a spear tore up his right thigh. Then he felt his Bishop's words ringing out. "You know what you must do. Go now. God be with you, my friend."

And Ansted, in contradiction to all of his training, all of his beliefs, rode from the fight. It was a slaughter, they were done, his bishop and his men all dead. But still, it felt so wrong to gallop away, to quieten his frightened horse, to hide in the farm lots of the village, as the men of Navarre searched for him. His adrenalin urged him to return to the fight, for one last showing. But his mind, and his heart, held him firm to what he must do. He must protect the scrolls. His bishop had told him this was paramount, so paramount it became, in his battle-wearied brain.

In late twilight he neared the town of Rennes-le-Chateau, on a slight rise above the copse he had ridden into. As he eased his horse to start up the rocky slope skirting the woods, the animal shuddered, lowered his great head, and sank to his knees. As his rear legs splayed out, Ansted dismounted to a searing jolt of pain to his injured thigh. His horse turned to look at him, and Ansted could swear he saw tears in those huge black eyes. Then the eyes closed and the stallion died. Only then did Ansted see the sword-slash across the stallion's left haunch; from the amount of blood streaming therefrom and dried on his lower leg and hoof, Ansted realized he had bled out this best of all horses. He unbuckled his saddlebag, removed the leather sheath, touched the horse's still forelock, and limped slowly away. He had seen his men slaughtered, he had seen his bishop killed; so why was he wiping tears from his eyes and snot from his nose, over the death of one horse?

Ansted moved slowly upwards, and into the village proper. Candle and lamplight shone from the windows of most of the houses. He did not want to involve anyone in his trouble, so he kept moving. There, in the centre of the village, gleamed the new rockwork of their church. He limped, then finally managed a lurching crawl to its unlatched wooden doors.

He had seen Bishop Viandicondi's men make short work of Darda's acolyte Joaquim. Despite that young man's brave dash across the meadowlands, the soldiers dispatched to the chase had soon caught up to him, and murdered him outright. But when the search of his packs did not locate the scrolls, they would scour every bloodied body, every saddlebag on every dead horse. And when the scrolls were still not found, they would come after him. If they had not already.

These thoughts flashed in an orderly way through his head. He was a trained soldier, and a trained soldier he would continue to be. He entered the church. The stone walls kept out any of the ambient evening light and in the impenetrable darkness, Ansted groped his way down one wall, then stumbled into something solid. He braced himself with his full weight on it. He felt the shape of a bowl, it felt like stone, then the bowl clattered to the floor. The baptismal font, he thought, as he heard water splashing the stone flags of the floor. A baptismal font should not fall apart, he thought, through a haze of pain. "What if?" He groped his right hand into the base of the font. Yes, it was wide, and hollow. He placed his scroll sheath into it, felt about to be certain the sheath had dropped to below the lip of the stone base. Then, using both arms although his shoulder screamed with the effort, and his thigh muscle began to spasm, he lifted the bowl of the font back into place. Thank god for the lazy workmen who thought that the mere weight of the bowl was sufficient to keep it in place.

Ansted's last coherent thought was to get away from the church. If they found him here, they would see the spilled water, and then, even an idiot would take the time to check out the font. He must get away. He hoped he had not left a telltale trail of blood. He made his way back to the great doors, crawled outside and closed the doors. He painfully turned his body, so that he would appear to be approaching, not leaving, the church. That done, he slowly exhaled his last breath of the cool night air.

CHAPTER 54

Hatton Field Royal Air Force Base, Great Britain / Santiago de Compostela International Airport

"Gentlemen," announced the Air Marshal, in clipped public-school tones. "This seriously pisses me off."

A group of nine men were meeting in the wardroom of Group Captain MacLeod, the ranking officer at Hatton Field Air Force Base. Today the Group Captain gave precedence to visiting Air Marshal Neil Patterson, who had flown in earlier that day, in the rear seat of a Tornado GR4 combat jet. Yes, he needed the speed, but he also yearned for that remembered thrill of supersonic flight. The assembled officers did not realize how lucky they were—the flight had put the Air Marshal in a good mood.

"Three officers down." He smacked the table top with the bottom of a closed fist. "This was supposed to be a simple taxicab mission. Now this. Whenever the bloody SAS get involved, we know there will be trouble, every time. But three officers...." His voice faded.

"To say nothing of the aircraft," Flying Officer Michaels spoke up. His rank might indicate differently, but F.O. Michaels had not flown anything for years other than his computer desk. He was the base's quartermaster, the watchdog of operations expenses.

The service men joked that his rank should be CFO, not for chief financial officer, but for not capable of flying officer. "That was a civilian aircraft, and pounds to pennies, the owner's insurance will not extend to cover military flights out of country."

He raised his glasses by pushing them up with his right index finger, and continued in the face of a glaring audience. "This will cost us millions. Improper flight plans, foreign repairs, alcoholic beverages on board,..."

Patterson interrupted him. "Foreign repairs?"

"Yes, sir. An issue with a hydraulic line. I have the bill here." He indicated his I-Pad.

Patterson nodded as though answering a silent question of his own. "That is how they got the bomb on board."

"Sir?" said MacLeod. "We do not know it was a bomb. It could have been any number..."

Again the Air Marshal interrupted. "Look. Kirby was involved. It was a bomb. What do we have on the AME who did the work? His assistants? His boss?"

"The work was done by Sita Avionica. Air Command OK'ed them for the work," said Michaels. "But, of course, we have to pay for it, out of operations."

MacLeod spoke up. "Group Captain Markham did send in his daily log. I know he mentioned the name of the Avionica service manager to whom he entrusted the aircraft. The aircraft log was lost, of course, but Avionica will have a record of the work done and the employees who had access to the aircraft."

"This meeting is over," said the Air Marshall, standing. The men jumped up in unison, so as not to be seen sitting while their superior was standing. "MacLeod, you are with me." With that the highest ranking airman to have ever graced Hatton Field strode from the room.

Investigators from the European Aviation Safety Agency, sent from EASA headquarters in Cologne, Germany were at the Santiago de Compostela International Airport within forty-eight hours of the downing of the Gulfstream. Other team members were on two French Coast Guard ships, collecting the meagre debris which marked the crash site in the Cantabrian Sea.

The EASA investigators questioned the men who had fueled the air-craft and discovered the hydraulic leak. One of them seemed nervous, so the lead investigator, Herr Otto Schorn from Austria, quietly drew an asterisk beside his name, in the margin of his notes.

They questioned the aircraft mechanical engineer who had repaired the hydraulic line. He had correctly entered the repair into his own work log, and into the computerized records of Sita Avionica. When questioned he said that the hydraulic line was not damaged, that the leak was from a loose connection, which was repaired by simply tightening it and installing a self-tightening nut so that the connection could not loosen again. He acknowledged that the men in his crew, five including himself, had full access to the aircraft for all of the hours of their shift. He added that the Service Manager, Jorge Gutierres, as their supervisor, also had access.

They spoke to Gutierres, who gave them the complete list of the names and addresses of every man who had had access to the aircraft while it was in the Sita Avionica's hangar and the watchman on duty outside the building. Schorn noticed that he had left his own name off the list.

"You spoke to Group Captain Markham when they brought the aircraft in?" The investigator was looking down at his hand-written notes.

"Yes," said Gutierres. "That is part of my job, as Service Manager. I deal with the clients, then write up the work order."

"That was when?"

Gutierres brought something up on his I-Pad. "It was 15:34 hours, on the Friday. The work order was complete by the end of the workday, 17:00 hours. I signed it off."

"And you were here when the flight crew arrived in the morning?"

"Yes, at 06:00 hours."

Schorn was getting annoyed with Gutierres' constant use of the military clock references. He, himself, was quite capable of dealing with pm and am references.

"Long work day. For management." As he said this he was looking directly at Gutierres, and was somewhat pleased to see the tightening of the muscles around the man's eyes. He would have missed the 'tell' if he had not already been looking directly at the service manager's face.

"For Sita Avionica I do what is required of me."

Untrustworthy and pompous, thought the lead investigator, and mentally drew two asterisks beside Gutierres' name.

They questioned the watchman, who had seen nothing, of course.

The team from EASA said they might be back if the recovered wreckage raised any more questions. Then they went directly to the office in airport security which had been provided for them. The leader conferred with his team members, then sent a terse request to EASA headquarters in Cologne. He asked for background checks on two men: the fuel man whose name he had starred in his notes, and one Jorge Gutierres.

When the team left, Gutierres waited for one agonizing hour, then another. He had nerves of steel, a requirement for bomb-makers. But then he folded, and made a panicked call from his cell phone.

"EASA was here," he said. "I think they know something."

"How could they?" The voice was cool, distant. "There is not enough of that plane left to prove anything."

"I do not know what they know, or how. But believe me, they know something."

The man he had called could hear the stress in Gutierres' voice, and made a quick decision. "Do you wish to meet?" he asked quietly.

"Yes. Yes. As soon as possible." Then his self-survival instincts conflicted with his natural greed. "I think I should disappear, and for that I will need adequate funding."

"Of course," replied the quiet voice. "Just what I was thinking." At least the first half, he amended to himself.

The EASA team, and some guests, were meeting in Cologne. They had just read through the background check on the aviation gas employee. It proved him to be a man in a lot of debt—one wife and two girlfriends can do that to a man—and he had a criminal record for various misdemeanours, since his early twenties. Nothing particularly nasty, more stupid than anything.

"That fits," said Lead Investigator Schorn to the room. "Let's get the Guardia Civil to pick him up. They'll put the fear of God in him."

With advice from Air Marshal Patterson, the EASA research into Gutierres had been directed into the area of bomb-making. Gutierres' infamous father was flagged immediately, and from there supposition based on human nature and the odds against coincidence, pointed them straight at him.

"We will need a search warrant for Gutierres' apartment, his vehicle, his work place, anywhere that can hold a trace of the explosive he used. And a search of his bank records for any recent 'bonus' he might have received, etc. A report to the Guardia needs to be prepared forthwith," Schorn said. "Do you have anything to add, sir?"

Air Marshal Patterson looked up and smiled, if granite can smile. "Yes. Firstly, thank you for extending your welcome to me and allowing me to attend this meeting. I know that is...." he paused. "Slightly irregular." It was not irregular, it was bizarre, thought the lead investigator, to allow anyone to be privy to their investigations into air crashes, before their public report. But this man was an Air Marshal, and the RAF had lost three officers in the crash. So accommodation of the RAF brass had been ordered.

"I applaud your work, and your conclusions. And, I just might be able to help you with the Guardia. I have a friend who, I am certain, will entertain the immediate apprehension of both men. If your report can get to the Guardia within forty-eight hours of their arrests, I am sure the Colonel will have no trouble holding them."

"The Colonel?"

"Colonel Roberto-Fernando de Calles, second-in-command of the Guardia. I trained his squad on the Tornado, years ago. Troubles in Algiers. Thought the problems might spread to Morocco and hence, irritate Spain. Years later he gave up the air force for the police. Sometimes it's nice to have friends." He smiled again. "Even if they are policemen."

Schorn's I-phone, lying on the conference table, beeped quietly. "Excuse me, gentlemen." He was speaking to them all but was addressing Patterson. "We are waiting for a report from the second half of our team, the men on board the French Coast Guard ships. Patterson nodded.

"Schorn here." Then a long pause as he listened. "Are you certain?" Pause. "I am going to put you on speaker phone."

He placed the cell phone on the table. "We can all hear you now."

"Hello," came the distant sounding voice that the speaker app always produces.

"Please start at the beginning, then continue your report," said Schorn.

"Yes sir. The main body of the aircraft has been located. Luckily it crashed over the continental shelf, shallow enough for us to send a photo submarine unit down. The cockpit and galley were destroyed, possibly from impact. There may be evidence of an explosive device. That is yet to be determined, when the flotsam from the wreck site can be analyzed. The main cabin is quite intact. It shows no sign of passengers."

"No sign?" asked the Air Marshal.

"Yes sir. By that I mean, no baggage, no personal effects, and....uh...."

"No body parts?"

"Yes sir. Exactly."

"Anything else?" asked Schorn.

"Not yet," came the disembodied voice. "We will have more when the wreckage can be analyzed."

Thank you," said Schorn. He turned off his telephone. "We have followed up on the information to Television de Galicia, regarding the report of three crewmen and three passengers on board the aircraft. Seems there was a telephone call from a public telephone at the airport from someone claiming to be an airport employee. The name does not check out."

"What does that tell us?" asked a member of the team.

Schorn answered. "That someone wanted the word out that three passengers were involved."

"Gutierres knew Kirby's group was not on board," mused Patterson aloud. "Because he was there that morning when the flight left. And, as the bomb-maker, he is the only person who had any interest in making that false telephone call. Why? Because he wants someone to think he succeeded? He's afraid to have failed?"

The EASA members were silent. They knew the Air Marshal's questions were rhetorical, an aid to thinking.

"Herr Schorn. Can you keep a lid on the absence of passengers, just for now?" asked Patterson.

"We will not be making our report public until we have analyzed the wreckage that we have recovered so far, studied the photographs from our robot submarine, and determined whether or not we need to raise the balance of the wreckage. We would not expect to make a report for many months."

"Perfect," said Patterson.

Schorn, who usually was the brunt of frustration from people wanting a quick end to an EASA investigation, asked "Sir?"

"Professor Kirby was the target. I am certain of that. So, by not officially refuting his death, we may just help him to stay alive."

The body of Jorge Gutierres was found twelve hours later. It was in an alley, in the nightlife centre of the city. His throat had been slashed. His wallet, watch and cell phone were missing. A robbery gone wrong? That did not explain the obvious marks of shackles on his wrists, and the fact that very little blood soiled the alley.

CHAPTER 55

COMPOSTELA 1088

Springtime in northern Iberia is a season of gentle and life-giving rains, new growth in the vineyards, and a general greening of the usually sere hillsides. It is a time of rebirth, and of new births, Breg thought, as he watched a group of new-born lambs running freely, but never out of sight of their careful mamas. Breg sighed. Even the new season could not lift his sadness.

Young Henri was the only man who returned alive from Bishop Darda's fateful journey. He was a changed man, no longer young, in one fortnight he had become mature and quiet, inward looking.

Henri told them what he knew of the attack by Bishop Viandicondi's troop. He had begged to be allowed to accompany Marshal de Clury, and that experienced soldier, knowing he might need someone who could put a name to the dead, provided him with a fresh horse, and let him ride at the rear of his troop. And ride they did. Henri was used to a quick-gaited horse, but he had never experienced riding with a troop of three score men, at a full gallop. De Clury was hoping to arrive in time. The pace ate up the distance, and Henri soon recognized the village of Rennes-le-Chateau on its slight rise. Full darkness had descended soon after the knights left Castle Rennes, but the full moon, and the good surface of the old Roman road, allowed them to move fast.

At a distance de Clury could see the flames of torches dipping and bobbing on the road ahead, and he knew he was too late, by only minutes. He angrily spurred his horse into even greater speed, and his men scrambled to keep up.

They found six men of Bishop Viandicondi's troop, including their captain, searching the bodies of the slain, and the baggage of all the horses, by torchlight. As men will, they were keeping what they wanted, and tossing the rest aside. They did not even take the time to tend to their own wounded, two wretches who would die of their wounds before morning, and two more who were less seriously hurt. Bishop Darda and his men had made a good account of themselves—the balance of the Navarrese troop were dead.

"Arrest them all," De Clury quietly ordered his lieutenant. It was as though only by forcing himself to speak quietly could he dampen his rage.

The Navarrese captain tried to control the situation. "We are here under the order of Bishop Viandicondi, Prince Renaldo of the House of Navarre. You have no authority here." He spoke brazenly, but was looking desperately around, at his now tiny cadre of men.

"You are not in Navarre, and I am the authority out here. If I cannot lay the murder of these men at any particular pair of feet, at least I can see that you are all hanged for the robbery I have seen you all committing. Hanging for theft is just as final as hanging for murder. Arrest them."

They left a guard of men, to keep the bodies safe overnight. The rest of the troop returned to Castle Rennes with their prisoners in chains. Henri stayed with the guard, and went slowly through the rubble of the battle site, identifying his friends, the young squires of Compostela, and their knights. He knelt beside the body of Bishop Darda, and crossed himself. A man of god should not die so, he thought.

In the morning they found the body of young Joaquim and his horse, a goodly distance away from the main skirmish.

"He must have run for it, poor sod," said the sergeant, the man in charge of the guard. Henri knew Joaquim would not desert his adored Bishop. He just shook his head.

The Sergeant Templar studied the ground, then spoke again. "No, he ran to divide the Navarrese ranks. There were a lot of horses here. He must have drawn off six or more soldiers." He indicated the area where Joaquim and his horse had been killed. "I think his last act was one of bravery, not cowardice. And his family must be made aware of that."

A villager reported the finding of a body of a very large knight on the doorstep of the church, and the carcass of a great stallion, in a wooded area just below the town. Henri recognized his uncle's horse. Somewhat to the sergeant's distaste, he checked the animal's saddlebags. Ansted had pledged Henri to silence about the scrolls, and told him to ensure their safety, should anything happen to his uncle.

"He was carrying something important," said Henri. He hated to see that look of disgust on the face of the sergeant whom he had come to respect.

"Well, if it had any value, at all, you can bet some early-rising villager is already trying to sell it."

Henri did not think so. There were still valuables in the saddlebags, money for the excursion, and Ansted's signet ring. No, those bags had not been rifled. If the leather sheath was the only thing missing, then it must have been Ansted himself who took it.

Then Henri sadly identified the body of his uncle, Captain Ansted of Rouen. He could see the leather sheath was not near or on the body. And that is when Henri went cold from the shock of seeing his uncle's body, the trauma of what he had seen at the site of the ambush, and the knowledge that he too would be dead if he had not been chosen to be the messenger. He went still, and quiet. The sergeant, who had seen this reaction to the ugliness of death before, gently urged him back onto his horse, and led him away, while other soldiers attended to Ansted's body.

The men of Captain Ansted's troop were accorded Templar

internments in the grounds of Castle Rennes. But Bishop Darda's body was returned to Compostela for burial. After some consideration, he was placed to rest in the lowest crypt of the rising cathedral, near to the ancient altar of cedar and its supporting walls of mortared stones. He was laid out in a stone sarcophagus, marked with his name, places and dates of birth and death, and adorned with a carved bishop's mitre. Breg had ordered the sarcophagus to be made with two compartments, each with its own lid. When there was no one about to notice, Breg placed the bishop's workbook, within that second smaller casket, protected from the decaying remains, but still close to the man who had laboured for so long over it. The workbook had been a constant companion of the bishop's for years; Breg knew it had given him great joy in life; he hoped it would continue to do that in death.

Months later, when he had recovered from shock, Henri would wonder what had happened to the leather sheath. But he did not know the significance of the scrolls, he did not know what they held. Nothing seemed important, really, after what he had seen and smelled. So, in time, he forgot about them. If he had ever mentioned this to Breg, that man might have known the significance of the missing scrolls, and the history of the Roman Catholic Church might have taken the turn that Bishop Darda had hoped it would.

Before he left Compostela for Rome, Darda had given Breg the bound book of six folios, the book with the title *The Testament of Ephes* embossed on its leather cover. Breg knew it was a copy, in Latin, of the ancient scrolls Darda and he had found in the cedar chest, in the altar below the floor of the old church, years earlier. Darda had worked on his translation for years, and then for months more copying his text onto the folio pages of the book. Breg had demurred at the receipt of the gift, aware of how Darda valued the little volume. He had accepted it, but only for safekeeping, until Darda returned for it. Now, with Darda gone, Breg did not have the heart to read the manuscript; the manuscript that had meant so much to his old friend. He kept it, for years, in his room at Compostela.

And when he retired from his work there, he took the book with him when he returned to his birthplace, the city of Grenoble in the Alps. In his last years Breg became a brother novitiate at the monastery attached to the seminary where he had been raised. He spent his time constructing dove cotes, and hen houses, and tripods for climber beans. He was happy in his retirement. When he died, peacefully and painlessly in his sleep, in his 104th year, the book found its way to the monastery's library. Breg had never read the book.

CHAPTER 56

JUDAEA 36 A.D.

Outside the tomb of Joseph of Arimathea, in the graveyard of Gethsemane, three Roman legionnaires walked, stood and sat desultorily. Because of the victim's notoriety and the spreading word of his expected resurrection, the Procurator Pilate had stationed the guard to keep watch, to ensure that the great stone was not rolled back and the body removed. There were four shifts of guards, throughout the day and night. The last shift took up their duties just before midnight on the Sabbath following the crucifixion. It was to this group that Joseph sent his comeliest house serving girl, with a basket of freshly-baked squab pies, and a clay vessel filled with a yeasty honey beer. If they had been presented with wine, the sharpest of the three might have discerned a trap. But beer? Nothing was more agreeable to a soldiering man than a beer. And they accepted the food and drink without a thought.

The honey disguised the somewhat acrid taste of the white henbane seeds which Simon Zealotes had ground into the beer. He had measured the amount judiciously; this was a dangerous poison if over imbibed, while if properly controlled it caused only deep sedation and some hallucinations. Simon hoped that, for their sakes, all three guards would drink a reasonably equal amount of the intoxicant. He did have faith in the universal greediness of soldiers for beer. And this was his only plan.

Joseph's servants waited until the earliest cock's crow, when the night's blackness still seems impenetrable, until one waits a few moments in the dark. Then shapes begin to show themselves, dark pale against less black, a colourless but still visible world. This was when Joseph's servants moved with care through the graveyard, to the treed knoll which formed the rear of their master's tomb. There they hastily but quietly moved a few rocks and bushes which were covering the mouth of an adit into the tomb. Most tombs had an adit, or air-shaft, to prevent the build-up of noxious fumes during the first year of the emplacement of the body within the tomb. The adit was usually narrow, and shielded with a fine metal mesh to prevent rodents and snakes or lizards from entering the space. This shaft had been widened, recently, to allow it to be used as another entrance. Or exit.

Two servants lifted the shrouded body from the tomb shelf, climbed with it through the adit, and passed it to their confederate on the outside. They exited the tomb, and carried their burden down the rear of the knoll, to a waiting wagon. The third man rolled rocks into the adit, until the narrow space was filled. Then he replaced the rocks at the entrance, dusted them with sandy soil, and pulled over the branches of a nearby shrub to cover the disturbance. They all had to hope that no one noticed various rocks spread about the floor of the tomb, which had bounced free of the adit, when they were shoved down the hole.

Early the next morning, there was a change of shift of the guards. The retiring trio, who had all slept while on duty, and who tried without success to act alert when being replaced by three other guards, related, through a haze of headaches, that they had all heard thunder in the night. The centurion who attended the changing of the guards, wondered about this, for the night had been calm and storm-free. On a hunch, he ordered the rolling back of the massive stone wheel which covered the cave mouth. The six guards accomplished this feat, then stood back. Except for a blood-stained linen shroud, the tomb was empty.

The lady mother Mary and two attendants, who had just arrived in the gardens of Gethsemane for a day of mourning at the graveside, were present when the tomb was opened. They, too, saw it was empty, and immediately left the graveyard, to spread the word, to give testimony of the fact of the resurrection of their Lord Jesus on the third day, the miracle of which the prophets had written.

CHAPTER 57

COMPOSTELA 61 A.D. LETTER FROM EPHES TO HIS COUSIN BARTHOLOMEW OF ALEXANDRIA

Dearest Cousin: I hope this finds you and yours well. I am not one to believe that my scribbles are of any import, but, now, I think, I have to ask you to preserve this text. I have a feeling, a sick and sad inner certainty that this information may be significant, and I have to ask you to be the preservitor. I hope beyond hope that this is not too onerous a request, and will not result in any hurt to you or your family. You judge. Then do what you must.

Rhus came to me and my father last night. He said that James had agreed to meet with Paul of Tarsus. James reviles the man, but he knows him to be an important proponent of the new religion which has become such a thorn in the side of the Roman aristocracy. Anything that irritates, and better yet, takes the attention of the leaders of the empire, could be a benefit to James and his cause. He and Paul agreed to meet in a day lodge in James' olive orchard, which stretches over the hillside behind and above James' villa. When the olives are in season the little stone building is used for preparation of the picking crew's midday meal, and at the end of the day, for storage of their equipment, their rakes and baskets and homespun tarpaulins which have to be kept dry, so as not to spread rot spores onto the freshly picked fruit. Olive harvesting, and the pressing of the fruit of its oil, is a technically demanding occupation.

I apologize. I digress. Rhus had requested permission to attend, but James thought that what he had to say to Paul should be kept privately between them, for the sake of Paul's reputation. Rhus had then suggested that he could attend, at a distance. James ordered him to remain at home; he had no fear of this self-serving would-be proselytizer. So of course Rhus came to my father and me. We had not promised to absent ourselves from the meeting. It was agreed that I would hide myself at the rear of the day lodge—I would be out of sight but within earshot. The following describes that meeting:

Starting without any niceties, Paul said "You must give up this idea of returning to Judaea. No one there needs you, or wants you, or even believes you are alive."

"When they see me they will have to believe I am alive." James, who was inveterately well disposed to everyone had to admit that he really did not like Paul of Tarsus, and he did not appreciate that Paul called himself a disciple, when he had, in fact, once been hired to chase the true disciples down, seeking their imprisonment or deaths, after James left Judaea. But he forced himself to remain polite.

Paul strode about the tiny stone room, then went outside. "It is too close in there." He looked about himself. "Look, you have a good life here, this orchard, your lady, your children. Why would you want to leave all of this? And for what? Another death sentence?"

James walked up behind Paul, and also looked out at his property. "I need to go, because it is written that the Messiah will come again. And my people will be set free. The prophets have said this. It is in the scriptures."

Paul snorted in disgust. "Those are ancient Hebrew scriptures. And whether or not they have been translated properly is anyone's guess. That is ancient Jewish folklore." He turned to James. "We are not dealing with Judaism anymore. We are dealing with Christianity."

"What is this....this Christianity? James asked. "If it is a cult believing in Christ, the king, then it is a sect of the Jewish church." He saw Paul's look of disgust. "Or is it something else?"

"You fool. Of course it is something else. It is a new religion. No, it is 'the' new religion. It is totally separate from Judaism, it is separate from the Roman belief in a multitude of gods. It is a combination of all, and it is sweeping the known world. We have Jews who have converted, we have gentiles by the thousands, we have Greeks and Egyptians, and Turks. Even the rabble of Gaul." He stood straighter, and seemed to emote to the sky. "We are the church of the one and only God. We know that through baptism and belief in the Christ the Son, who died so our sins will be forgiven, we can be certain that we have a place in the house of our Lord God, when death has claimed us."

James began to clap. "Too bad there is no pulpit here. That speech was too good for an audience of one." He shook his head. "I am a real man, born of a woman. I am not the son of god; I never claimed to be. But I am the Messiah. The Anointed One. The king of the Jews. I am he who must return to Judaea to claim my throne, my birthright. And free my people."

Paul angrily turned towards James, and shook him by the shoulders. "You are not listening! There is no Jewish throne in Jerusalem, or Judaea, or all of the Mediterranean world! Rome will never let Judaea go." He calmed somewhat, and released James, then took a few steps away. "Listen. No new religion can exist if the Roman population does not support it; they are the world power and their religion is the world religion. We have made Christianity acceptable to them. The birth of our Lord is now consistent with the birth of Saturn and the winter solstice. The spring festival of Circe has become the date of the resurrection. Which, by the way, coincides nicely with the Jewish Passover. We have managed to fit Christianity into the existing religions, so we are acceptable to everyone." He spoke earnestly, and seemingly, had never listened to himself, nor heard his own insincerity.

"But if this Christianity fits so neatly with the existing religions, is it a true religion? Or is it a composite of compromises? A convenient construction to allow religious people of different faiths to pretend that they can be this new thing called Christian, yet still keep their habits and holidays?" James angrily pulled an inoffensive twig from a nearby olive tree. "And, sin as much as they want, but, miraculously, get to go to heaven, anyway. Because a man was put to death for treason."

"No, no. The crucifixion was not the death of a traitor. It was the shedding, by the Son of God, of his human body, and his resurrection as one with God the Father."

James stepped away from Paul, and shook his head again. "You really should write this stuff down. It should make a fine tale around the hearth in winter, when everyone is bored with the harshness of reality. It makes no sense, none at all. Scripture does not contemplate a human being becoming god. That is blasphemy. You are a Rabbi; you were trained in the laws of Moses. You know this."

Paul sneered. "Not anymore I don't. Christianity has been good to me. I am welcomed everywhere. I am feted. I am acclaimed as an apostle of the faith, as a disciple of our Lord Jesus, and I will...."

James angrily interrupted him. "You were never a disciple."

Paul grinned. "I am now. Because I say I was. And what I say...." He tapped James on the chest with his right forefinger, for emphasis. "What I say is what Christians believe. Someone had to explain the new religion, and that is what I am doing, what I have been doing for the last twenty-five years. It is the message, not the man that is important. And as the man, you cannot return to Judaea, because if you did not die on that cross, then all of Christianity is based on nothing. Without the death of Jesus for our sins, there is no message; there is no reason to be a Christian."

James began to walk away, saying over his shoulder. "I am a Jew. I never wanted anyone to be a Christian, whatever that means. I never intended a new religion to be created from the events of my family's life. And I will return to the Galilee."

What happened next....I cannot even now, give words to what happened next. But now I know why I am here, at this most significant of times, and why my strange assortment of talents, if talents they are, have come to rest in me. I will continue this story, as I now know I have been entrusted to tell it. But I will not write to you further. I fear that further correspondence would put you and your whole family at risk. Understand that I love you, and hopefully, you will one day hear of what I must write. Writing the story of what I have seen, and know, and feel, is why I am here, I am certain.

God be with you, as I trust and believe, he is with me.

Your loving cousin,

Ephes, son of Torgas

CHAPTER 58

SANTIAGO DE COMPOSTELA

Monsignor Torres opened a tall wooden door that opened from the colonnade. "This is my office," he said, leading them through, into a short hallway between what appeared to be a generously appointed bathroom, and an equally efficient kitchen area. Then they were in his office proper, a large room of warm wood finishes and furnishings, floor-to ceiling French windows and Persian carpets on polished stone floors. No computer monitor disturbed the solid wood desktop, no snarl of electrical wires betrayed the presence of an abundance of the usual office machines. "Of course, none of my work gets done here." He laughed. "I have a computer, which I keep hidden. But most of a librarian's work—at least in a library this old—is still conducted in the Reading Rooms. Ours are now temperature and moisture controlled. Which is good for the materials. But it means I can no longer sneak anything off to my office. So," he waved his arms about inclusively, "my almost unused office."

"But there was no sign on the door? No secretary?" asked Kirby.

"They are outside, the other way, through those doors." He pointed to the far end of the room. "We came through my private entrance. Head librarians have to have some perks."

He sat them down, in large upholstered chairs around a table. "Now, what can I get for you to drink? And what is it that the most respected of all antiquarian religious scholars wants in my library?"

Kirby laughed. "You are far, far too kind. And it is not your library I need. It is you."

"Ah," said Torres.

Over coffee, with the local form of honeyed churros, Kirby asked "What can you tell me about the writings of Ephes, a first century Greco-Egyptian, who lived in Compostela?"

Torres considered. "I know of no texts authored by Ephes. Certainly there are none here." Then he amended himself. "At least, that I know of. There are references to an Ephes, regarding the inception of the Guard of the Rose Cross, in the mid to late first century. For instance, he is named as its second Grand Master, after his father. The records of that society are quite complete."

"Is that the same as the Rosicrucians?" asked Joe.

"No, but close, as far as the records show. The Rosicrucians are thought to have originated in Egypt. The Guard of the Rose Cross apparently started here, right in Compostela."

"As part of the cathedral?"

"Oh no, no. The order started, as I said in the first century. The cathedral was started in 1075 in the eleventh century, and not sanctified until 1211. The Rosicrucians, as far as can be determined, started as a sect of Christianity in Roman Egypt, in, again, the first century. Which order was first, we cannot know. Though there must have been a connection; the similarity of the names is most likely not coincidence."

"Is there a pink, or rose, or even red cross that the order could have been referencing?"

"Not as far as I know. Certainly not in the cathedral. There are stories..." here Torres hesitated, "folk tales, really, nothing that can be verified. I only know of them, because I was born here, and that sort of thing still gets spoken of, you know, as legend."

Mack leaned forward; he knew from experienced scholarship that legend is often the cradle of the truth. "What legend?"

"Well. Basically, the start of the pilgrimages. The Church," here he crossed himself, "likes to suggest that the pilgrimages to Santiago started after the cathedral was completed in the thirteenth century.

We know that is wrong, by at least eight hundred years. That takes us back to the so-called dark ages, when little historical data can be verified. But there is reason to believe the legends, of a far earlier pilgrimage to Compostela, are based in fact."

"Such as?" asked Mack quietly.

"Well, the roads. The Roman roads in most of Spain,—at that time known as Iberia, — were built in the second century B.C., to allow the movement of troops out to the far reaches of the Empire. Reportedly, the roads were in good repair when St. Paul travelled here in the first century. But the Empire 'closed' in the third century. Yet the roads were still completely passable in the thirteenth century. Someone,—no, a great many someones—were using the roads, continuously from the first to the thirteenth centuries. And then there are the scallop shells, and the fish signs, and, yes, the rose crosses."

"The rose crosses?" asked Joe.

"Yes, I am certain you have seen these. A cross with a rose centred at the intersection of the two parts of the cross. They are common here in Spain, and in the British Isles, apparently. Although I know of no connection between here and there. I am sorry." He seemed to consider, then took a sip of his coffee. "I had not connected the rose blossom with the colour rose before. That must mean something."

He continued. "The scallop shells are traced back to St. James. There is the legend that his body washed ashore here, covered in scallops, and hence the *Vieira*—the Pilgrims' Shell—which today is still used to indicate the Pilgrims' Way, or ways, leading to Compostela. But, that would have had to happen in, again, the first century. If the scallop was related to James in the first century and was, and still is, a symbol of pilgrims to his burial site, I think it is fair to surmise that the use of that symbol was continuous."

"I think you are right, Monsignor," said Mack quietly. He had already expounded to Joe his mistrust of the scallop-covered body of St. James, apparently coming all the way from Palestine, and still recognizable. But for some reason, the scallop shell had continued to be an icon of the area.

"And, of course, the sign of the fish. The two crossed arcs, which form a crude pictograph of a fish. Still used today as a symbol representing Our Lord Jesus Christ. Apparently, when early Christians met, when it was dangerous in some places to be a Christian, one person would draw an arc with his foot, in the dust of the road. An innocent enough act. If the other person was a Christian, he would know to complete the sign, with another dissecting arc, completing the body and the tail of the fish. And then the two newly met people would know it was safe to acknowledge their belief in the Christ."

"But," said Joe. "Wouldn't an anti-Christian Roman, wanting to catch a Christian out, just draw the second part of the fish?"

"Maybe," said Mack. "But then the real Christian could report on the Roman, and they would both be condemned. It wasn't a time of sophisticated evidentiary rules."

Torres poured them all more coffee from the thermos his secretary had left on the table. "And, there is also the legend of the miracles."

His audience of two leaned in.

"Yes, yes. There are stories, so many, of miracles. And they are always related to the rose cross. There are ancient Spanish folksongs with that reference. Then there are our equivalent of fairy tales. Always the rose cross plays a part. But, there is nothing of proven fact, other than the Guard of the Rose Cross, which originated here, in the latter half of the first century. But—and this is just supposition, or a leap of faith, perhaps. But I have always thought that perhaps the occurrence of miracles associated with the rose cross was the reason for the pilgrimages. If you think a miracle will be granted if you go to a certain place, — crawl on your knees up steps in Quebec City, touch the statue of the Holy Virgin of Ballykildare in Ireland, or leave a padlock with the Madonna as they do in a fifteenth century cathedral in a remote town in the mountains of Mexico—if you believe a miracle will occur, that your wish will be granted, then would that not be a reason to make a pilgrimage?

I have always thought the miracles led to the pilgrimages, not the other way around. And we know the pilgrimages, already occurring, are what caused the cathedral to be built."

"You know this?" asked Kirby.

"Oh yes. There is a report from a Cardinal Friere to the Pontifical Council in 1068. He was born in Margaux, near Navarre, in the south of Gaul, and as a child saw the throngs of pilgrims who were walking the old Roman road on their way to Compostela. It is Friere who suggested that the building of a cathedral at Compostela, in the style of the great cathedrals of northern Gaul, in Rouen, and Lourdes, and Paris, would easily be paid for, from the pilgrim traffic." He laughed. "It is amazing reading, really. He even came up with what today would be called a franchise scheme. Every inn which wanted to be known as a safe refuge for pilgrims could display the sign of the scallop, but only if the landlord paid a tithe to the church, based on his income from pilgrims. Quite brilliant, and quite frightening. He apparently was killed in a knife fight in Naples in 1092. If he had lived, who knows what money-making schemes he would have devised. He might even have had the Roman Catholic Church become the world's banker, in place of the Knights Templar. The church was certainly better positioned to do that." He seemed to consider, then said "I am researching this subject, so, I apologize, I sometimes go on about it. Friere's report is in the Vatican Library, the Secret Pontifical Library."

"Secret?" asked Joe.

"Not really secret. More private, as in private papers. Like cabinet documents in a modern day nation. The records go back to the beginning of the Roman church, to Peter. They range from bills for white wax candles to the thorough and quite disgusting records of the autos-de-fe, carried out in the Middle Ages, in Spain and France. I expect it now holds documents detailing the relationship which existed between Nazi Germany and the Holy See, during the 1940's. Although, those are still very much a secret. Apparently researchers are allowed to know the price of candles, but not yet the price of perfidy."

CHAPTER 59

SANTIAGO DE COMPOSTELA

After meeting Kirby and O'Connor over their breakfast at the Abbe, Sam Wardell returned to his suite at the Hostal dos Reis Catolicos, and made a few telephone calls on his cell phone.

"Kirby doesn't have the document, yet."

"Are you sure?"

"Yes, I am sure, or I wouldn't have said so." The man truly was an idiot, but he had to be reported to, regularly. Apparently it kept him calm. "I think they trust me though. After the downing of the Gulfstream, they need a friend. I like them. Kirby reminds me of a few of my better professors."

"Kirby is important, Wardell. Do what you have to, to make him safe. Whoever the bastards are who attacked that airplane are playing for keeps. I just hope they don't get on to you. Do you have any idea who it is?" Out of habit, Sam noted the Archreverend's poor grammar, and saccharine sincerity.

"I have my hunches. Nothing written in stone. I'll let you know when I have more."

"Thanks, Sam. And take care of yourself."

"Ditto, Archreverend."

He took a drink of ice water, then telephoned Fiona's cell number. It went immediately to voice mail. He said he needed to see her, that it was important, and ended the call. He knew it might have been a stupid thing to do, to leave a message from his number, but he really did want to see her, to explain to her what was going on. If she only knew, he thought wryly.

He made a few more calls.

Fiona felt her cell phone vibrate against her thigh, opened her soutane skirt so that she could extract the telephone, checked the call number, and smiled. Perfect. Through a little addition to her telephone, she could locate the calling cell phone. And as long as she did not erase the call, from her cell phone's memory, she could access its GPS whenever she wanted to. It was that first call that was important. She also had Uncle Mack's and Joe's cells in the memory. She checked occasionally; they were together, which was good, in the Cathedral. Even safer. Probably.

And now she could keep tabs on Sam Wardell. Fiona knew that the dopamine produced in the brain during sex was the chemical explanation for love. Apparently dopamine gave you that feeling of oneness, of desire, of missing someone when not with him or her; so called love. She thought she must have an immunity to dopamine; she felt nothing but hate for Sam Wardell. But now at least, she could tell where he was.

Celeste saw the pleased look on Fiona's face. The latex of her mask was so thin, that the movement of her facial muscles made the mask move slightly, just enough to give what could pass for expressions. The camera saw more than the average human eye, and the patented latex she used had passed the camera test many times; it was her most valuable stock in trade, and her retirement fund. She herself smiled.

"You should see yourself. A pleased old man. But do not move your hands again, for a few moments. I need the ink to dry, just so." She pulled Fiona's hands back onto her work table. "This will make you look slightly grubby, the way so many old men are, and as though you have never had a manicure in your life. If you do not scrub your nails, the ink will remain for up to a week."

"Thank you, Celeste. I'm not sure I will be able to eat a piece of toast with these hands, but, thank you."

"De nada. And remember, Fiona. Elderly curates do not take taxis. They ride the buses. I will give you some Euro coins, for this very male-looking wallet."

"Buses? Really?"

"Ah *si*. But not to worry. Young people still give up their seats for elderly *religioso*. And please, keep your telephone somewhere else about you. The lifting of your skirts and exposition of your black trousers does nothing for your old-man look." And she laughed, in a very wicked way.

CHAPTER 60

COMPOSTELA 1092

The young goat herder, Vico, almost comatose with boredom, watched as members of his herd tested the tastiness of every grass, weed, vine and bush in the area. He had driven his goats a few miles from his home farm, which lay east and north of Compostela, for he enjoyed this meadow protected by hills to the south. It provided verdant growth for the goats, but it also afforded him a view of the sea. The Bay of Biscay could just be seen to the north, beyond a forest of dark cedars and pines.

Then Vico looked back at his flock. A number of young males, their horns protruding just a few inches from their skulls, were playfully pushing against each other, near a mass of vines. The goatherd was just thinking that the clump of vines did not look quite right, when one of his charges rubbed hard against the vines, revealing the sheer side of a rock, from beneath its cover of greenery. Something about the rock did not look right, either. So, with nothing else to do, young Vico got up and wandered over to the stony mass. He pulled away some of the vetch and grasses with which it was covered, and soon saw that this was no ordinary rock. It had definitely been shaped, purposefully.

Now, with something unusual and fun to do, Vico worked hard at uncovering the whole of the stone. When he was done he stood back. It was moss covered, and roughly three feet square, and about two feet high. Vico scratched at it, and found that what he had first thought to be stone was actually a clay-like concrete, almost a plaster. This was man-made. Finally, having removed all of the moss from the sides of the monument—for that is what Vico thought it was—he saw the inscription. It was in Latin, he knew that. But he knew no more. He was not lettered, that was only for town children of the better classes. But he was a keen lad, and he paid rapt attention to the Latin writing which he saw when he was allowed to visit Compostela. He might not know the words, but he could recognize the pattern. He knew the first two groupings of letters stood for San Tiago, the same St. James the church in Compostela was named for. He knelt and crossed himself. Then he stood, surveyed the fields around him carefully, and began to cover the cement box with the vines that he had recently ripped from it.

Then he raced his herd home to his parents' farm, screaming his glee the last hundred yards or so.

Vico's father went personally to Compostela immediately, riding the big horse that usually pulled a plow, or a haywain. He shyly but proudly asked to see Father Timothy about a matter of the greatest urgency, and was soon ushered into the Father's office. No new Bishop had been appointed to the See of Compostela, since Bishop Darda's death, some four short years ago, so Father Timothy was the most senior churchman in the city. Vico's father explained the reason for his visit, and for his visible excitement. Father Timothy was transfixed by the story. Truth to tell, being head churchman in this city was really as boring as Darda had always said. Vico's discovery was the very diversion he needed.

Being a man of some organizational skills, Father Timothy immediately ordered a horse for himself, a guard of five Templars, and a dray filled with hay, with two stout wagon-horses and two equally strong men.

It was late afternoon when the group made their way into the mountain meadow that Vico had told his father of. Of course, the youngster was there; he had to be a part of this, no matter that his father had ordered him to stay away, out of fear for his young son's life, should bandits or other marauders have seen the discovery, and be planning to come back for the tomb.

"Father, father!" Vico screamed, when he saw the group of mounted men. "Over here! Here it is." Father Timothy grinned at the exuberance of the child. His father 'tsked' a few times under his breath, over the lad's disobedience.

Before sunset, the tomb of Saint James, for it was identified as such by Father Timothy, was lifted and carefully placed into the body of the cart. It was placed on a bed of hay, and hay was placed under all of the securing ropes, which were lashed in every direction possible, over the rough concrete box. This artifact was not about to be damaged while under Father Timothy's care.

When the party was ready to return to Compostela, Father Timothy looked down at Vico. He raised his right hand and made the sign of benediction. "Vico. You are a blessed young man. May you grow in the grace of God."

Vico beamed up at the churchman, but perhaps not as widely as did his father. Father and son rode together, back to their farm. Vico was not sure which was better, being blessed by Father Timothy or getting to ride home behind his father on their farm horse.

No one seemed to have noticed the regular planting of the vines around the tomb. To be fair, some of them had been ripped right out by Vico, in his exuberance at his discovery. And no one bothered to consider that the gravel under the tomb was not indigenous, and was quite patently only recently placed there. So exciting was the discovery, that no one noticed the signs—the very visible signs—that the tomb had not stood in that field for even a decade, much less the centuries they were all dreaming of.

Father Timothy had his men carry the concrete box into his church, and place it in his small private office, to the left of the altar. It might be in his way there, but it would also be in his sight. He studied the thing, then prayed, and then called in a stonemason from the cathedral grounds. The stonemason easily chiseled out a groove around the top plate of the chest, then with a few strategic prying motions, managed to lift the lid from the chest, in one piece. He and Father Timothy's assistant, a young seminarian on his Michaelmas break, helped their priest to remove the packing material from around the stone box that was finally revealed. Father Timothy ran his fingers over the incised writing; he could not decipher the lines but he did know they were writing from a far earlier time. He had also heard stories of terrible afflictions brought to those who opened an ancient funeral cris,—the Latin name for an ossuary, — without the proper incantations being read and incense spread. He stopped his eager assistants from going any further.

"I will write to Rome," he intoned, in his best Sunday service baritone.

CHAPTER 61

THE VATICAN 1092

As the Papal representative for Western Europe, Cardinal Legare received the letter from Father Timothy of Compostela.

He read it twice, then requested that one of the library's translators attend his office. Father Timothy, not knowing what the ancient script on the cris meant, had copied the chiselled lines perfectly onto a piece of vellum, which he had enclosed in his letter. The young translator had no hesitation; he identified the words as ancient Aremaic Greek, and they said 'James, brother of Jesus'.

The Cardinal thanked and dismissed his library assistant, then walked to the great windows of his office. He looked out at the roofs of the churches and musea, the convents and monasteries, of Vatican City. He was deeply troubled. He knew immediately that the cris described by Father Timothy was, in fact, the ossuary described by Bishop Darda, in his missive, of 1086. Bishop Darda had said that he had found ancient texts which stated clearly that the contents of the ossuary were the bones of Jesus Christ and his wife, Mary Magdalene. Legare had immediately written to Darda, telling him those findings were blasphemous, and to destroy the ossuary and its contents forthwith. Obviously, the young Bishop had disobeyed his Cardinal. And had somehow inscribed the stone chest to suggest that not Christ, but his brother James, was the source of the ossuary's contents. Why? Why had he tried to hide the truth? Why had he disobeyed?

Cardinal Legare asked his secretary to provide a luncheon for him, in his office. This was not a particularly strange request. The Cardinal often ate in his office, when the pressures of his duties meant he had not the time, or perhaps the predilection, to attend the full midday meal served to Cardinals in their personal dining hall. That meal, with its many courses, could take hours, and Cardinal Legare did not often have the time to spare for the robust appetites and even more robust wranglings of his fellow high churchmen. So he preferred to dine alone, with his view of the Vatican.

Over a simple tray of bread and cheese, and a bowl of steaming broth, Cardinal Legare said a simple grace. When he closed his eyes, and began to quietly intone the familiar words, he felt a jolt, not to his body, but to his mind. He knew without a doubt why Darda had done what he had done, and he felt ashamed, and then grateful.

Bishop Darda had known that the earthly remains of Jesus must be honoured, not lost or destroyed. He had understood that if the ossuary was silent as to its contents then someone, sometime would open it, and without the knowledge of the scrolls Darda had spoken of, that person would not know the unutterable value of what he was beholding. And the bones might be consigned to some Jewish burial site, as unidentifiable and uninteresting. Or, and even worse, if the ossuary was inscribed with text that spoke of its true contents, then basic human greed would make the artifacts valuable, very valuable indeed, and at some point in time, perhaps at many times, they would be stolen, moved, disseminated to a thousand churches and cathedrals which would all pay a premium to have a true relic of Jesus. Darda had known that to protect the bones of his Christ, he had to mislead everyone about them, give them another identity, not a minor identity which might cause them to be lost or destroyed as of no value. So Darda had named them as St. James' relics, St. James, the brother of Jesus.

Over his broth, Cardinal Legare worked through what he now knew, without a doubt, had been Bishop Darda's plan. And he could not fault it. Yes, the truth would surface at some time, as these things will. When Darda's scrolls were found they would reveal the truth. And if the scrolls had been destroyed when Darda's party had been attacked and killed, Legare knew Darda to have been too careful a translator, too conscientious a librarian, to have not made a copy, and perhaps that would one day be found. He truly believed that. And he did still have the letter he had received from Darda, telling him of the true significance of the ossuary and its contents. That was in his own papers, but he would see that it got into the Vatican library proper, where it belonged. It was not enough, on its own, perhaps, but it would give someone a good premise from which to begin to trace the artifacts of Jesus.

Legare was deeply ashamed of his response to Darda, telling him to destroy the evidence of Jesus' survival and marriage. He was only glad that Darda had disobeyed him. Legare might have rested more easily if he had known that Darda had never received that instruction from him, that his letter had been misappropriated by Viandicondi, all those years ago.

Legare sighed. Bishop Darda had been strong enough to do the right thing. He had to be just as strong, and just as disobedient. He left his office and walked through a myriad of hallways to the antechamber of the magnificent chapel which housed the throne of St. Peter, the office of his Pope, Urban II.

Odo of Chatillon-sur-Marne had been born to a noble French family in the Champagne region of France. He had been named as Pope Urban II in 1082, and was presently entrenched in the strife that was European politics. He was about to order troops into Jerusalem, in what would become known as the First Crusade. This was really just a plan to get the ornery Teutonic knights out of Europe, and fighting someone other than fellow Christians, but he would admit that to no one, not even his closest advisors. He was a busy man, with enough worries to confound any lesser administrator. So when his trusted senior librarian, Cardinal Legare, advised him of the discovery of the bones of St. James the Younger, in an Arcadian grave in northern Galicia, he was happy to bless his colleague with the handling of the affair.

"Your Holiness. Perhaps I might remind you," gently spoke Cardinal Legare. "We are building a cathedral in northern Iberia, not far from where the tomb of St. James was found. You will recall, the church of St. James in the town of Compostela has been a pilgrimage site for centuries, although I believe that no one really knows why. So the construction of a cathedral there, to serve the pilgrims, was approved years ago." To serve the coffers of the Vatican, if truth be known, he thought. "It is still under construction, of course, but it is said to be quite magnificent, at least in concept, based on the great churches of France. Perhaps you would consider consigning the remains of St. James to this cathedral."

Urban, who had been reading a report throughout Legare's speech, looked up, as though just seeing his Cardinal. "Of course. Then it will be a basilica. Much better for donations. Make it so. Thank you."

"Thank you, Your Holiness." Legare withdrew from the room, smiling.

Cardinal Legare wrote to Father Timothy and to Master Architect Bernard Gelduin, telling them by order of His Holiness Pope Urban II, the remains of St. James must be provided pride of place in the crypt of the new cathedral, and that henceforth the church would be known as the Basilica de Santiago de Compostela.

The cris—or ossuary as it really was—was consigned with all due pomp to the lowest level of the crypt of the rising cathedral, below what would one day be the high altar. A stone was inscribed with the date and the name of the interred, and this was placed in the floor of the new church. Breg, as foreman, was involved in the work. He alone of everyone there knew that the marble box had been placed in the nearby field only a few years previously. He also knew that its final resting place, under the altar of the ancient church, was what Bishop Darda had wanted, and he was happy to be part of his dear friend's last wishes. The cris was being placed in the undercroft of the new church, very near to the stone tomb made only years earlier for the church's first bishop, Darda of Malta. Placing the cris near to Darda's coffin made him feel the presence of Darda, as though that man was there in spirit, not only in effigy, and approving of all they did. Breg had never felt so happy to attend a funeral.

In the years remaining to him in Compostela, Breg sometimes visited the undercroft. The way there, through various levels of crypts, planned for the funerals of high churchmen and rich Compostela burghers for the next many centuries, was a way known to only a few, and not used by any but Breg. He would sit next to the tomb of Darda and near to the ossuary. Both had been placed on the granite floor beneath that strange altar, set into a wall of stone, under which the ossuary, in its cedar chest, had first been found, some decades ago. When visiting this place, Breg would occasionally rub his thumb over the strange rose cross, which had been carved into the altar wood. He would sit and let the quiet surround him, and then enter into his being. This was a holy place.

In time, the name of the little town of Compostela was subsumed into the name of the church. The name of the basilica, Santiago de Compostela, became the reference for the whole of the town. Almost as if London had become known as St. Paul's of London, or all of Paris known as Notre Dame de Paris. The name made no sense, but names do not need to make sense; they need to be heartfelt. And, as the cathedral rose, the numbers of pilgrims rose. The name change of their destination made no difference. They were on a pilgrimage to the church in Compostela, and if that church had become, in a century, a cathedral, then a basilica, so be it. The church was still the goal of every pilgrim; from Albion or England as it was now known, or Gaul, now France, or Germany, or Italy, or Portugal or other parts of Spain itself,—the goal was always the church.

CHAPTER 62

SANTIAGO DE COMPOSTELA

Monsignor Torres noted that his guests had finished their coffee and churros, and had declined further refreshments.

"If you wish, let us move to the Reading Rooms. You can review the records of the Guard of the Rose Cross for yourselves. They provide interesting reading." He stood and moved quickly to the door of his office, then turned, and grinned. "If you read Coptic Hebrew."

"Not as easily as I read Aremaic Greek, but it's not too hard."

Torres ushered them from the room, and down a short hall. "A man after my own heart. I have to admit, I still stumble over Latin."

He ushered them through what was quite obviously a recently installed air-lock. Open one door, step into the five by five foot space, close the rear door, and then open the facing door. Both doors could not both be open at the same time. When they stepped through, Torres said "The Reading Rooms and the stacks are provided with enhanced oxygen content. For the protection of the ancient texts, papyri, etc. I don't know if it helps them any; I do know it tends to keep me more alert. Even after churros."

He led his guests through. Beyond the airlock, the short hallway leading to the reading rooms was like any other older library space. Joe looked confused.

"Is that it?" he asked. "Just extra oxygen? No state-of-the-art... uh, I don't know?"

"Oh, like unbreakable glass modules, and infra-red lighting, and everything else you saw in 'The Da Vinci Code.'? It was a good movie, I always enjoy the acting of Tom Hanks. But that depiction of the Vatican Library was really quite bizarre. Impressive, yes. Authentic, no. And our little library is not on the list for upgrades. We had one once. They changed the formula of the oil used to polish the tables. Apparently it was too easily absorbed into some of the vellum documents students were spreading onto the tables outside of their protective plastic sleeves. Boys will be boys. So the oil was changed. Easier than changing the students. Not much else besides that."

Torres led them through an elegantly furnished reading room. A wall of windows flooded the space with natural light augmented by rows of green-glassed bankers' lamps placed strategically along the centres of the long wide oak tables. Upholstered chairs, each on swivels and complete with arm rests, surrounded the tables. The walls were decorated with framed oil paintings, some of which Joe recognized as the work of masters; he could identify an El Greco and a Velazquez, and thought he saw a Berroguete. If these, and all the other paintings closely spaced on the walls, and the statuettes adorning the niches of the room, were originals, he could not even guess at their value.

Torres noticed his interest. "We have five reading rooms, all furnished in much the same way. Do you enjoy fine art?"

"Yes, as we all do, I suppose. I am a rank amateur, but are some of these originals?"

"Oh, yes. Every one." He walked on, through the room. "Not to worry. The public are not invited here." Then he turned quickly and shrugged his shoulders in apology. "You and your esteemed uncle are not considered 'public', or course. You are my guests." He pushed open double doors, simply marked as 'Biblioteca', and they entered, what in every other library, would be known as the stacks.

Beyond banks of card filing cabinets, and a table holding two computer screens and keyboards, long rows of metal shelving tapered off into a warehouse-sized space. The lighting was provided by overhead metal-guarded bulbs of low wattage. Obviously, no reading was expected to be accomplished here. The shelves held modern hardcover books, unbound reports, and old leather-bound volumes, and masses of cardboard boxes filled with scrolls.

"Further to that end," pointed Torres, "are the older scrolls and papyri. We do not yet have everything catalogued into our computer system, so the card files are still in active use. But, of course, as in any library which has existed for a millennium, we are never certain if every document, book, scroll, scrap of paper, has even been recorded. There are probably thousands of documents in here which are nameless." He turned to his two companions, and shrugged. "It is embarrassing, really. But then also quite thrilling. When I feel the urge for a Eureka moment I come into the back here and dig. I always find something." He laughed. "And then I assign it to an assistant, and he has to do all the work of authentication, numbering, filing and creating a computer entry and photograph. Please feel free." He waved his hand, in a gesture of welcome.

Joe looked anxious. He liked libraries to have state-of-the-art computerized records. Mack smiled broadly, a youthful joyousness suffusing his face.

"We are looking for anything which mentions Ephes, or is perhaps authored by him. Letters to him, copies of his letters, anything."

"And his dates, again?" asked Torres. He put on a pair of half-lensed reading glasses, and peered at them over the lenses. He could not have looked more like a cathedral librarian if Central Casting had done the job, thought Joe. Somehow he had expected Europe to be a bit more modern.

"The scroll I have been reading was found in the Quhram horde. It is no doubt a copy of an earlier text, as most of those are. We think that when the Emperor Constantine called the conference at Nicaea, that most churches, monasteries, and royal libraries provided copies of documents which they had in their safe-keeping. No one would have sent an original document. So, although the materiel—the ink, and the vellum or the papyri, can be dated to the late second and early third centuries, the texts can predate that time substantially."

"Of course," agreed Torres.

"From the references in the text, I believe Ephes lived in the early to mid-first century, and wrote in the mid to late century."

Torres nodded. "That would agree with the references to him in the papers of the Guard of the Rose Cross. That material is over here." He lead them down a long row of shelving, took a right angle at a cross section in the shelving, walked on, and took a few more turns. "This area contains the oldest material we have here. It is probably quite well referenced in the catalogues, but to use the catalogues you have to know how the material would be recorded. You know the issue here." He nodded to Kirby.

Kirby did know. A librarian could well catalogue what he had read, but it was all too easy to miss the sub-references. For instance, Ephes' work could be recorded as referring to the Guard of the Rose Cross, because his name was associated with that league of warriors. His work may very well not be recorded as relevant to James and Mary, because if the one document being examined did not refer directly to them, then the librarian would have no connecting data. If he did not know of the Testament of Ephes, then he would not connect the later references to Ephes to the founding Christians of Compostela. That gap would leave huge spaces which an ardent researcher could eventually cross, but not without a great deal of work.

But this was Kirby's milieu, his claim to fame. He had found many an artifact, simply by sifting through documents, and putting numbers to the dots and then connecting them, so to speak.

Kirby looked about the shelves. "I would have bet on Ephes keeping the original of his Testament, even if he did send a copy elsewhere, and a further recopy of that ended up at Quhram. A man of his clarity of thinking, the grace of his writing...he would not have done otherwise." He looked around, as though to draw inspiration from the miles of rigid shelves and tons of slightly mouldy books.

"Finding something like that, in here...." started Joe hesitantly, "would be more difficult than finding a...a."

"A needle in a haystack?" completed Torres. English was his third language, after Spanish, of course, then Italian. But he was proud,—and totally guilt-free about that pride—of his complete command of English syntax. "At least then, the prick in your finger tells you that you have found it. Here, even with the document in hand, you might well miss its relevance."

"That is why we will start with what we know. The records of the Guard of the Rose Cross." Kirby was actually rubbing has hands together in anticipation of what he would find. "And I believe I just might have an inkling as to why a concurrent order, the Rosicrucians, began at about the same time in Egypt."

CHAPTER 63

SANTIAGO DE COMPOSTELA

Brother Martin let his Cardinal drink the better half of their bottle of *cava*. Even though he was a big man, and could hold his liquor, as they say, with the best of them, he was aware of the effects of alcohol on driving capacity. He had no desire to attempt driving in the cramped centre of Santiago de Compostela without a very clear head. The Cardinal seemed happy with the arrangement.

"No, following the trail of the communications between the Hapsburgs and the Vatican did not lead me to anything. We do know that Sauniere spent time in Paris, being wined and dined by the beautiful people, the rich, the landed, the crème of the art world. Why, we do not know. He was apparently not a particularly learned or witty man, just a simple country cure."

Brother Martin sat with his chin propped on his index fingers. "So, perhaps the money was passed to him, through those people. Or at least one of them. Perhaps his trips to Paris were a front for receipt of payments."

"That is obvious. Now that you have said it." Cardinal Contini's smile lit up his handsome face. "And all this time I was searching for telltale letters or messages in the vaults of the Vatican Library. Yes, and if the money was being passed to Sauniere through the very expensive churches of Paris—by expensive I mean receiving a lot of financial assistance from Rome—then there would be no trace.

Simple donations from various churches to their poor brethren in Carcassonne. Perhaps for the purchase of stone, or the commission of a stained glass window, or whatever. That money, although substantial in Rennes-le-Chateau, would have never been missed from the hundreds of northern French churches. And, of course, those churches were not giving away the money out of charity. Although they would have called it that. They were giving away a portion of the funds they received from the Vatican, in normal church business, in accordance with the instructions from someone at the Vatican."

"Yes, that would work. I will give you one million francs, if you give 100,000 to this poor country cure. Of course I would agree. Why turn down the gift of the 900,000 francs?" mused Brother Martin.

"*Va bene.* Okay. So if the financial trail will reveal nothing, what will?"

"That's easy." Martin paid the bill, and led the way from their street-side patio table to where he had parked their SUV, some hours ago. Of course, they had a ticket, but nothing as monstrous as the 'shoe' which stopped overdue parkers in their tracks in cities in the USA, or the even more drastic removal of the vehicle to an impound yard. Europe was really so much more civilized, thought Brother Martin; here small-business entrepreneurs tried to find ways to serve tourists, not to interfere with them.

Martin opened the passenger door of the SUV for his superior, then drove deftly into traffic. "You told me that Professor Kirby is searching for the lost scrolls? Yes?"

"Yes," agreed Contini.

"So, we find Professor Kirby, and keep him in our sights. When he finds the scrolls, we find the scrolls, if you know what I mean."

"I think I do."

Brother Martin handled the big vehicle as though it was an Italian sports car, moving in and out of lanes of traffic, using his horn, and generally driving like a true European—a continental

European. Not for the first time, Cardinal Contini wondered where Martin Froese had honed his various skills.

"And in the meantime, we can look at Bishop Darda," continued Contini, in the vehicle. "Remember I told you that Rennes-le Chateau is on the pilgrimage route which includes part of the ancient Roman highway system, known as the Via Domitia? It skirts the Pyrenees on the north east, sometimes in Spain, sometimes in France. Now, if I was a pilgrim on my way to Santiago, I doubt I would be carrying ancient scrolls. Why take them to Santiago? Whereas, someone leaving Santiago and going the reverse way, that is, from Santiago to the Mediterranean, would pass by Rennes-le-Chateau. Darda may well have been on his way to Rome, and he could be carrying the scrolls. I know from records at the Vatican that he was a very capable ancient texts translator, that he was the Papal representative in Compostela when the cathedral building was started, and that he died in 1087."

"Do you have any idea what was written in the scrolls? Or who had written them?" asked Froese.

"No to both questions. But Santiago de Compostela was a pilgrimage site way before the cathedral was built. Perhaps the scrolls say why."

Froese maneuvered their vehicle under the porte-cochere of the Parador de Santiago, the Hostal dos Reis Catolicos, commissioned by the Iberian royalty in 1499, as a hostel for pilgrims. It is a fine old building, deserving of its place on the Plaza de Obradoiro, the best address in Santiago de Compostela. He waved away the valet, opened the Cardinal's door and retrieved his luggage from the rear space of the SUV.

"I can park here for only a minute. Driving in the Plaza is reserved for special cathedral dignitaries, and guests of this hotel. But if I don't remove it quickly, our car will be 'parked' for us."

"That is fine, Martin. I have only the one bag. I can manage." The Cardinal retrieved his bag, and waved to Froese, as he got back behind the driver's wheel. "Breakfast, tomorrow?" Here?"

"Certainly, Your Eminence. After early Mass, of course."

"Mass at the Cathedral?"

"No, that is a real gong show." Then Martin grinned. "Sorry, shouldn't have said that, but it really is, reciting of the names of all the countries that have pilgrims there that morning, everyone cheering, selfie-sticks everywhere. Like I said, a gong show. No, I will enjoy Mass with my brethren at the Monastery of St. James. They are a silent order. And, Your Eminence, don't get lost in the lobby."

The Cardinal realized the significance of Brother Martin's parting words when he went through the main entrance of the Parador. The lobby stretched a few hundred feet, to a welcoming front desk. The old hospital—which really meant hostel in the fifteenth century—surrounded a number of cloistered gardens, which meant there were long and relatively narrow areas circling the cloisters. The lobby formed one whole side of the lower floor of the building.

At the desk, Cardinal Contini was informed that his room had been upgraded. He reddened slightly; he never liked to have attention centred on him because of his high churchman status, or to have that influence how he was treated. That was an important part of his camouflage.

"Yes," the desk manager smiled. "Of course, we have moved you to the Cardenal Suite." He smiled happily, and Cardinal Contini blushed fully.

CHAPTER 64

SANTIAGO DE COMPOSTELA

After breakfast Cardinal Contini and Brother Martin Froese made their way to the library of the Basilica Santiago de Compostela for their mid-morning appointment with Monsignor Torres. Of course Contini knew Monsignor Torres; he had contributed to the younger man's training as a religious artifacts librarian in the vast Vatican Library, and had surreptitiously helped to get Torres appointed to Santiago de Compostela.

The Monsignor had just left Mack Kirby and Joe O'Connor in one of the main reading rooms, with their table spread deeply with plastic-encased vellum scrolls and a myriad of the volumes which recorded the history of the Guard of the Rose Cross.

Torres was pleased to welcome his old tutor to his library, but was somewhat dismayed when he was introduced to Brother Martin. The man was obviously what he looked like—muscle, in the criminal sense of that word. When Torres had resided in Vatican City, the Cardinal had a reputation for unsavoury transactions involving written artifacts, the acquisition of them, and sometimes the disappearance of them. Torres hoped that the presence of 'muscle' in his library did not mean that the Cardinal had designs on any of his treasures. Then he chided himself. Cardinal Contini was a world-renowned expert of Vatican history and, even more telling, Torres' superior. As a senior churchman, he was deserving of trust.

Torres told himself that, and he tried to believe it, but just could not convince himself. At least both men were wearing street clothes. Difficult to stash a two thousand year old scroll in the sleeve of a sports jacket. Now if they had both been wearing soutanes, one in cardinal red and the other in Jesuitical black of course, then he would know he should be worried. It was easy to secrete documents under a skirt, and somewhat embarrassing to conduct a search. That situation had arisen before.

But Torres reverted to his usual jovial self, and was smiling with bonhomie as he conducted his two guests through the hallways of the great library, and into a vacant reading room. It too, led to a small computer and catalogue area, at the edge of the stacks.

This reading room was as elegantly furnished as was the one that had somewhat over-awed Joe O'Connor. Again the walls were covered with expensive artworks, shelves and plinths laden with sculptures and vases, the floor home to Persian rugs, and the reading table itself a fine piece of furniture. Contini did not seem to notice; Brother Martin was impressed.

"So," started Torres, "you said that you are researching an early bishop of the basilica?"

They had gone into the catalogue room attached to the reading room.

The Cardinal smiled. "The earliest. Bishop Darda of Malta was sent to oversee the start of the construction of the church, in 1070. Sadly he died while still a young, well, youngish man, in 1087. We have those records at the Vatican. What I am looking for are his private papers, his correspondence, a diary perhaps? Anything, really."

"What cross-references might you wish to explore?" asked Torres. It was a reasonable question, from a librarian. But of course, the answer would give any librarian worth his card-index a very good clue as to what his visitor was really looking for.

"Oh I thought we would just poke about, and see if anything rises up." The Cardinal smiled again, and Torres thought he now knew how Little Red Riding Hood felt when she looked into the manic grin of the wolf in old-lady's clothing.

While Torres explained where material concerning Bishop Darda would most likely be found, Mack and Joe were busy in their own reading room.

"In the first scroll, Ephes wrote that he had been born in Egypt. His mother was a younger daughter of the ruling Greek family," Mack said to Joe. He was studying a copy of a letter written by Ephes to a cousin in Alexandria. "I think that Ephes is the connection between the Compostela Guard of the Rose Cross and the Rosicrucians. The group we still hear of today originated in Egypt. Best guess, in the first century."

"Really?" asked Joe.

"Really," replied his uncle. "I don't make this stuff up, you know." He was carefully scanning the document in front of him, still encased in a protective clear plastic sleeve. "At that time, a good number of the Desposyni resided in Egypt, predominantly in Alexandria."

"Desposyni?" asked Joe. Fiona had mentioned to her Uncle Mack that Joe could be depended on to ask the obvious question, right on cue, like a comedian's straight man—Mack had to agree.

"Yes. Remember I mentioned them? Originally that word was translated to mean the descendants of Jesus Christ, but later translations suggest the word probably means all extended family members. Such as nephews, nieces, cousins, and their descendants. Members of the Desposyni met with the Christian church leaders in Rome, some years after the crucifixion. As the family of Jesus, they felt they had the right to control the church started by him. They were arguing about the direction the early church was taking. That meeting did not go well for them. The church leader, the esteemed St. Peter, proclaimed them to be heretics and they were summarily executed."

Joe grimaced.

"And the ones not actually present at the confrontation

were hunted down by the Romans and killed. Some escaped, to Alexandria."

Joe looked perplexed. "But what is the connection, between the Guard of the Rose Cross in northern Spain and the Rosicrucians in Egypt?"

"Both were founded for one purpose. To protect the family of Jesus Christ."

Cardinal Contini scanned through pages of computer lists of documents, then turned to the card index files, making careful notes the whole time. Brother Martin waited patiently.

"I have enough to begin with," said Contini. "Come. Some of these materials may be quite cumbersome. I might need your help."

He walked off into the stacks, and Brother Martin dutifully followed. The Vatican material regarding Bishop Darda was sparse; and it seemed the library of the cathedral the man had served could provide little more. The material was spread about: references to Darda were found in the reports of the master architect Bernard Gelduin to the Vatican, usually asking for further advances for the construction of the cathedral, always naming Bishop Darda as witness to the progress which was being made; there were copies of a few letters Darda wrote and originals of ones he received; there was an official record of his internment in the undercroft of the cathedral below the altar, more than a hundred years before the cathedral was consecrated in 1211, there was an inventory of his goods and chattels when he died, to which his See was entitled.

"Let's see where they buried him," he said to Froese as they made their way to the stacks which housed the records of the construction of the cathedral.

Hours later, having pored over huge vellums carefully drawn with the architectural plans of the great church, Contini mused. He was studying the dates of the drawings, then arranging them in chronological order.

"Something wrong?" asked Froese.

"I think so. At the time of the good bishop's death, there was no altar in the cathedral. That came over a century later."

"But if their planning was any good at all, they would have known where the altar would be placed, wouldn't they?" Brother Martin asked.

"Yes, of course. But there is this letter, in Master Gelduin's material. A copy of a letter he wrote to Bishop Legare, at the Vatican, in 1088. He states that the Master of the Site, one Breg of Grenoble, reported to him that the sarcophagus of Bishop Darda had been placed below the altar of the church. This Breg goes on to describe the tomb, its height, breadth, that it is fashioned from the local granite." Contini sat back, and looked at the ceiling lights. "This Breg is very exact about everything else. I cannot imagine that he would misuse a preposition."

Froese merely frowned. Most people he knew constantly misused prepositions. Hell, most people did not even know what they were.

"Please arrange for us to have a tour of the mausoleum. Now, let's get on with the Darda inventory. And letters."

As an experienced investigator of dead people's papers, Contini knew that the inventory would prove educational. What a person owns when he dies, especially when he dies suddenly and hence has no time to clear away anything he might like to keep private, can say a great deal about that person's life and interests. And of course, all of the letters had to be read, just for background. And for the fact that they might open up new areas of investigation. This was going to be slow, thought Contini, but that was nothing new to him. Voyeurs of dead people's lives learn to be patient.

"But, sir, I really should be seeing about Professor Kirby. We need to find him in order to...."

Contini was already striding back into the stacks. "That can wait, Martin. You can attend to that this evening. Right now I need you to help me."

Some two reading rooms away Mack and Joe were busy with their own research.

"So," asked Joe, "if this group, the Guard of the Rose Cross, was busy keeping Jesus' children safe, why is there no record of that? Their records talk about membership, and rules, and training schedules, and even the construction of fortifications. No mention of Christ's offspring."

"Joe, in the first century, in most of Europe, Rome was the power. If Rome wanted the Desposyni dead, would any group—especially a group of Jews, who were not all that popular either—advertise its dedication to keeping them alive? No, this was in many ways a very secret society. Yes, they kept records, but they are incredibly well edited records." As he spoke he carefully used his white cotton gloved hand to flip over pages of an old archive. The record spanned so many years that it started in ancient Coptic Greek, which he could read with facility, then switched to an old German, perhaps a third or fourth century language, then progressed to Latin. Mack would have struggled with the German, but for the simplicity of the material. This was a record of marriages, and children born of those, and on and on, through centuries. It appeared that the scions of Jesus and Mary had lived quietly, for centuries, in northern Spain. Another settlement of Jews, emigrating from a war-torn Judaea in the first century, was established in southern France, and the two groups intermarried prodigiously. The record ended in the seventh century.

"We need to find the next volume of this archive." Mack spoke slowly. "Now, we really need it now." His excitement was barely contained.

Mack and Joe went back into the stacks, to the area where they had found the first archive. They could hear footsteps, and soft voices near to them, but paid no attention. Many historians and students used the library, daily. If they had met, and compared notes with Cardinal Contini and Brother Martin, at that time, things might have gone quite differently for all of them.

Joe found the volume easily; it was where it should be, next to where they had found the first volume.

Mack could not wait, and began to leaf through the book immediately, but the lighting was too dim in the stacks for his eyes, and he had to return to the reading room. He did ask Joe to bring the next volume in the set.

After two hours of study, Mack leaned back from the table, and removed his glasses. "This is incredible. Quite incredible."

"Yes, Uncle?"

"You remember I told you about some of the theories about Jesus and Mary, and their bloodline being the Holy Grail? This was expounded in *Holy Blood, Holy Grail,* one of the best-selling religio-historic books of all time. Quite a good read, really. The authors also delved into the Rennes-le-Chateau mystery, the suddenly rich poor parish priest. What I did not tell you, is that later, recently really, *Holy Blood, Holy Grail* began to be referred to as 'pseudo-historic'. If you Google it—that really is a verb I abhor, but you know what I mean—you find it has fallen into disrepute. Seriously. The historic references the authors used have been found to be falsified documents. All part of a scheme to have the present Grand Master of the Priory of Sion, become named as the king of all Europe."

Joe looked perplexed. "But how could anyone expect that..."

"Precisely. Anyone capable of falsifying so many documents, from so many epochs, in so many languages, would know better than to think he could be king of Europe."

"Actually, what I was thinking, is that if you are that good at forgeries, forget about being king. Just print Euros, by the millions. And some Sterling, since you guys are Euro holdouts." Joe considered. "And some Swiss francs, too."

Mack 'tsked' audibly. "Naughty, Joe. But what I was about to tell you, is that this volume, well, both of these together, prove the basis of what Leigh, Baigent and Lincoln were claiming, that the Merovingians married into every royal house of Europe. Of course, in the beginning, in the fifth century or so, there were only a few true dynasties and many royal 'wannabes.' Every couple of generations a new family took over. But later, when royalty was better established, intermarriage was the universally accepted way of maintaining and strengthening royal bloodlines and alliances. Hell, by the early twentieth century, even the Kaiser of Germany was a grandson of Queen Victoria."

"That must have made World War I fun," said Joe.

"Not as much fun as the Second World War when the Nazis were openly wooing Prince David to become the puppet king of Great Britain under the auspices of a victorious Berlin."

"Prince David?"

"You know. The Duke of Windsor, with the skinny American wife. But that is another story."

He gently touched the leather cover of the archive in front of him. "This proves that *Holy Blood, Holy Grail* was, in fact, based on verifiable and reputable documentation. Not a piece of scholarly twaddle, as Wikipedia suggests. And if the thesis of that book is correct, then I can take a leap, and extrapolate that the history of the Priory of Sion is also true."

He got up and began to pace around the table.

"Which would explain why Leonardo da Vinci, who is reputed to have been one of its Grand Masters, knew the true story of Jesus Christ and Mary Magdalene, and hinted to everyone who ever saw his *Last Supper* that James was the man who died on the cross. Only an executive of the Priory, perhaps only its Grand Master, would have been privy to that knowledge. I feel that I am getting deeper into things, but it is like I have descended into a whirlpool, with strong currents, very strong currents, moving around my little bit of understanding. Who, or what, is distorting the truth? Who is publicly casting doubt on historical fact?"

Joe nodded. "And, apparently, casting that doubt in the most public, and therefore, injurious way. On the internet. That is where most people do their research these days."

His uncle looked daggers at him.

Joe responded. "Well, why not? Who has access to a library with the wherewithal to contain enough books to cover every conceivable subject? And be up to date? You yourself check out Google. You said you did."

His uncle sat back down. Joe was glad; he was getting dizzy just following the older man's peregrinations about the table.

"You are right. I think you may have seriously assisted me with my research."

"Really?" asked a surprised Joe.

"Yes. We have to find out who is 'doctoring' the web. Now, lunch is not only late, it is required."

Cardinal Contini had retrieved the inventory of Bishop Darda's effects. It was not a long document. The Cardinal was reviewing it, with disgust. "A bishop. The Papal Legate in Northern Iberia. For over a decade. And when he died, these were his belongings." He almost snorted in disgust. "He basically had nothing!"

Brother Martin was still listening, although he himself wondered why he would still be doing so. "Perhaps it is what he did not have, that would tell more of his story."

"God, you really are a Jesuit, aren't you?" said Contini. But then he considered. "You might be right."

He went through the inventory again. Pens, inks, papers of various qualities, some vellum scraps, and some reference books indicated his interests. Clothing, his bible, his vestments, his prie-dieu artifacts, were what would be expected in the rooms of a priest. It was all so ordinary. So....something was niggling at Contini's very astute brain. "Of course! If he had pens and ink and paper, where is his writing? That is what is missing." He jumped up and went to embrace Martin, but stopped short of what could have been an embarrassing gesture. "You are a genius," he said, much to Martin's disbelief. "Bishop Darda was a writer. And yet, we have nothing of that. His writings were removed from his rooms. If we find those, we might just understand what the man was about, and what he was doing when he was killed, on the way to the Vatican."

CHAPTER 65

SANTIAGO DE COMPOSTELA

Mack and Joe were enjoying a lunch of the local seafood, mussels this time, in a little bistro far down an alley off the Plaza de Obradoiro. Tourists did not usually venture this far. So the food was good, the service was perfect, and they were not disturbed.

"Uncle Mack. While you were ordering and everything....I went on line." Joe was looking at his tablet, a device he could carry in his backpack and set up anywhere. "I just thought I would check that problem with the Prieure de Sion, or as we now call it the Priory of Sion. You know. The internet suggesting that Jacques Plantard made it all up in 1964."

Mack answered quickly. "He registered it in 1964."

"Yeah, well. There was all that stuff on the internet about him using the name because it kind of joined his group up with the Sisters of Sion, an old monastic order established in Jerusalem. But, I wondered."

"Yes?" asked Mack. He knew his nephew was an intrepid researcher. Any actuary had to be. And, to his knowledge, Joe was one of the best analytical actuaries in the American university system. Why he was not in private practice, Mack did not know—he thought it must have to do with ethics.

"Well, I think this is really cool. Apparently the word 'sion' as in Prieure de Sion, in old French could mean scion. You know, the descendent or offspring, usually of a noble family. Or, in the horticultural sense, a shoot or twig, cut for grafting or planting."

"I think sometimes, in those times, a scion could be both. A son or daughter could become a tree, as in the family tree sense," said Mack, disconsolately.

Joe continued. "But if 'sion' means 'scion' then, couldn't it just be, that the Priory of Sion was really protecting the 'scion' of Jesus Christ, all these years? The reference was not to some place known as Sion in Israel. It was a direct definition of what they were doing. Protecting the offspring of Jesus. You know, for centuries spelling was sort of hit and miss. Shakespeare had about a dozen different spellings of his own name. So the French 'scion' could become 'sion' and it can have the same meaning as the English word scion. Well, Latin word I guess. It kind of makes sense."

Mackellan Kirby stared at his nephew. He knew he loved this young man, always had since his birth some thirty years ago. But now he loved him anew. "I am buying lunch," he said. "You, my boy, have earned it." He smiled and raised his glass to Joe. "And if you found that on that Wikipedia thing, then you better print it off fast. You never know when the mysterious Dark Writers of the internet will get around to changing it."

When they had finished lunch, Mack suggested a walk around the Plaza. He said he needed to clear his head. "Not clear it, really, just give it a chance to catch up to the information I have been feeding it. It seems my brain is like my stomach, it needs time to digest what has been put into it. If I do not allow it some peaceful introspection I can easily miss something important."

They strolled over the ancient paving stones of the plaza towards the very baroque fountain which occupied the centre of the square. Comely young cherubs appeared to play in the mists of the fountain's upper levels, and great stone dolphins leapt happily in the heavier sprays of the two lower basins. They stopped to admire the vast and complicated piece.

"Apparently the required aquatic species for fountains is the dolphin. Sometimes a large-scaled fish, like a grouper or mullet, makes an appearance. But dolphins take it, ten to one. Have you ever noticed, Joe?"

Joe, who had not been exposed to many European fountains at all, certainly not enough to have developed a criticism of their sculptures, just nodded. He knew his uncle needed to think about mundane things, in order to let the more important thoughts, half-formed but milling about in his head, come to the fore, as fully functioning and well-reasoned conclusions.

As they continued to walk, Mack said, as though to himself "The Guard of the Rose Cross and the modern-day Rosicrucians. I know the term Rosicrucian is used to describe or name some of the rites in Free Masonry. And some of the degrees. So those are interrelated. And the Masons have long suggested they are in some way related to the Templars. They like to think that their symbols, the trowel, the apron, and the square and compasses, show they are descendants of the builders of the castles and keeps that the Templars were famous for."

"The guys in white tunics with the big red cross on their chests?"

"Exactly. The Poor Fellow-soldiers of Christ and the Temple of Solomon was their real name. Mostly Teutonic knights going to the Holy Land to rescue Jerusalem from the so-called infidels. In the eleventh century. The Middle Ages, when Europe was in disarray, with civil wars in most countries as brother fought against brother for kingship, and with the Pope managing to stir up..... Wait. That was what was bothering me! Again, Joe, I am in your debt."

"What did I do?" asked a perplexed Joe.

"It is not what you did, but what you just said. 'White tunics with the big red cross.' Of course you know that from childhood adventure stories, television series, even movies. And a goodly number of family portraits—not our family, of course—mostly dating from the Renaissance. That big red cross is how you know the armoured knight is a Templar."

"Yes?"

But that rich beautiful bright red was not available then. That is derived from the cochineal plant—native to Mexico. And not available to Europe until after the Spanish conquest, in the sixteenth century."

"But they must have had red before that? I can't imagine a king, or a cardinal, without red."

His uncle nodded, and kept walking slowly, his hands clasped behind his back, the personification of a thinking man. "Oh yes. They had red. But it was a dull thing. Derived from some insect bodies, hence rare and expensive. The more common, and less expensive Madder Lake was the dye available at the time of the Crusades, when it was introduced into Italy from the Middle East. But madder produced a muddy pinkish brown. Or rose, if you will." He looked at Joe to see if he had caught the suggestion.

"You mean, the red cross of crusading Templars would have been rose, not red as we know it? That the painters of the Renaissance painted Templars with their red crosses as they had come to know the then modern colour, the colour as we know it today?"

"Precisely," smiled Kirby. "And what does that suggest?"

"That the Guard of the Rose Cross, the Templars, and even our modern day Rosicrucians and Masons, are all related. Not through blood, of course, but through their arcane organizations. Every one of them uses the rose cross symbol."

Mackellan Kirby clapped his open hand to Joe's shoulder, and directed him towards the library entrance of the Basilica. "I will make a religious studies scholar of you yet, lad. It is not a boring life, even if jumping to conclusions is sometimes the most vigorous exercise we get."

They walked off, side by side, unknowingly the attention of a number of pairs of eyes.

CHAPTER 66

SANTIAGO DE COMPOSTELA

Brother Martin and Cardinal Contini left the cathedral library soon after Kirby and his nephew, also headed for lunch. They opted for a café with tables and chairs on the verge of the Plaza de Obradoiro, basking in pleasant autumn sunshine. They ordered the local version of paella and a bottle of an old vine Godello. Froese opted for sparkling water. Froese's cell phone pinged, and he excused himself, walking some distance from their table. The Cardinal could see he was having an unpleasant conversation. Froese returned to their table and sat.

"Trouble?" asked Contini.

"None of our people can locate Professor Kirby and his nephew and niece. We have been watching the airport. They are probably still here. Or they could be on their way to Rennes-le-Chateau. That would be by vehicle. We cannot watch every auto route out of the city. I really should get to our HQ and oversee our....."

He was interrupted by his Cardinal. "I think if you look over there, towards the fountain. Those two men, one in tweed. Good heavens, tweed in Spain. What next?" He harrumphed. "You might recognize our good Professor."

Brother Martin looked to where his Cardinal indicated. Sure enough, Professor Kirby and his nephew, Joe O'Connor, were strolling through the Plaza de Obradoiro.

"Really?" breathed Froese. "They are here. Right in front of us. Gracias Deiu!" He repalmed his cell phone. "I will let our people know." He dialled, spoke softly for a few seconds, and then hung up. "They are on it."

The Cardinal continued to look about the square. "They might also be on that man sitting alone at the café with yellow sunshades. The handsome man, American is my guess. He was watching Kirby and his nephew." He indicated with a nod of his head the man he meant. "Ah yes. He is getting up, paying his bill quickly, and, I do believe, is following Kirby." The Cardinal smiled. "Yes, I think our people should be on to him, also."

"Of course, Your Excellency," said Martin. He did feel somewhat embarrassed, but covered that up by taking a surreptitious photograph of the American. He sent it to his people for identification.

Meanwhile, a thin elderly priest, in an old-fashioned soutane, watched from his place in the sunlight at the base of the Basilica. Fiona had seen Mack and Joe, and had had a hard time not running up to them and hugging them. But training kicked in. She also saw Sam Wardell get up from his table and follow her relatives.

What she did not notice were the two well-dressed large men at lunch across the plaza. While watching Wardell, they had been having coffee. No food. It meant leaving quickly was easier. They dropped some Euro notes on their table, stood, and began to follow Wardell. They maintained a good distance, but never let that distance increase.

The plaza was a busy place, as usual. Thousands of tourists packed its every corner, and thronged about the doors of the Basilica. It was easy to miss a cue.

Mack and his nephew walked back to the side door of the cathedral, the entrance to the library. They knocked, and were granted immediate entry; a word from Monsignor Torres was an important word, indeed.

"Now, we have to concentrate on Ephes. We already know there is a relationship—a significant relationship—amongst the Guard of the Rose Cross, the Rosicrucians, the Templars, and even the Masons. But Ephes wrote five scrolls. The world has had access to two, through the Cure Sauniere, which are now, reportedly, lodged in the Vatican Library. By way of the Hapsburgs, apparently."

"It all seems a bit up in the air, if I can put it that way," said Joe, somewhat apologetically.

"Up in the air, lad?" said Mack. "This is about as good as it gets in ancient theological texts. We have to presume a lot, guess at some more, and then enjoy the end result. If we are right, of course." He grinned his irrepressible grin, and ushered Joe back into the stacks of the library of the Basilica de Santiago de Compostela.

"Now, I was allowed to read the texts of Ephes, the copy that exists in the Quhram hoard. There were a lot of deletions, ink-overs so to speak, because they did not know how to delete in any other way back then. Which means that someone was redacting the testimony before the hoard was hidden. So we are talking about the second or third centuries."

"How would anyone know, at that time, that the text should be edited, in such a way? And who would presume to have the authority to make such amendments?"

"The texts to be examined and equivocated about, to gain entry into the bible, were being collected from all over. In the year 385 there were Christian sects all over the known world. And there were hundreds of texts to be considered for inclusion. But even then, I think, there were some things that just could not be said; things that would immediately bring the source of the information into disrepute, or worse."

"Worse? What is worse for a document than disbelief?"

"Immediate immolation," quickly responded his uncle.

CHAPTER 67

SANTIAGO DE COMPOSTELA

Fiona limped slowly but manfully, the truly operative word, after Sam Wardell. Her slight frame was jostled constantly by the throng of tourists, pilgrims and otherwise, in the Plaza de Obradoiro, and Wardell began to outdistance her. She was passed on either side by two large men wearing suits. So, neither tourists nor pilgrims. The men moved adroitly, almost weaving through the crowd, and Fiona remembered they had not bumped her when they had passed around her. They had training, and Fiona's own training came to the fore. Without paying any apparent attention, she noticed that they kept pace with Wardell. When he stopped to let a large family party cross in front of him, they stopped to look at a vendor selling lemonade; when he hurried to keep Kirby in sight, they picked up their pace. Interesting, she thought. Anyone following Wardell so surreptitiously could not be his back-up, and any enemy of her enemy could be her friend, as they say.

Fiona was close enough to see Wardell enter a door to the left tower of the cathedral. She then saw the two men in suits—the Suits she had mentally named them—follow him in, then immediately return to the side street. They spoke together for a minute, then moved further along the side of the cathedral, past the door she could now see was marked with the word 'Officios'. Clearly something about the Officios was not to their liking, so they had returned to the street and now appeared to be waiting, no doubt for Wardell.

Sam Wardell smiled at the attendant behind her glass cage. "*Buenos dias, Senorita*." He said pleasantly. "*Hablas tu ingles*?"

"Yes," she said, unsmiling. He had used the familiar of the word 'you', and she did not appreciate that.

"Good. I am certain your English is better than my Spanish." His smile was still not being returned. This did not usually happen. "I am looking for my friends, Professor Mackellan Kirby and Joe O'Connor. I believe they just came in here."

"What is your name, sir?"

"Sam Wardell."

He heard the street door open behind him, then close almost immediately. He did not look around; he did not want to break his eye contact with the secretary. He could feel that no one else had entered the small space.

She scanned her computer screen, as she flicked her fingers over her keypad. "I do not see your name on the visitors' list. You need an appointment to enter the offices of the Basilica."

"But I just saw them come in here. I just need to talk to them for a minute." He kept smiling as he said "They will want to see me."

"Then perhaps you should arrange to meet them. Elsewhere."

"Look, Miss. I need to see them, just for a min..."

He felt his right elbow sandwiched in a meaty fist. The uniformed guard had responded immediately to a nod from the secretary.

Before the guard could frog-march him to the door, the secretary passed a printed paper under the grill of her cage. "This is a list of the telephone numbers for the departments of the Basilica. Any department can grant you access." Then she smiled.

"*Buenos dias, Senora*." He bowed, pulled his arm from the grip of the guard, and left. Somewhat embarrassed that his usually dependable charm had so flatly failed, he could at least be pleased about something. "I managed to age her ten years, by calling her missus," he told himself.

Once in the side street, Wardell returned to the Plaza, using his cell phone the whole way. The Suits looked the other way, then discreetly followed him. Fiona blended into the background, an elderly priest enjoying the Spanish afternoon sunshine. When the men were all out of sight, she too, used her cell phone. Joe answered on the second vibration. Kirby heard his nephew quietly ask a few questions, then end the call.

"Fiona. She says Sam Wardell is following us, and two goon types are following him. Just thought we should know." Joe looked worried. "Are they your goons?"

"No. No goons." answered Mack. "But I don't like the idea of being the head of a parade. Maybe Manuel can help us."

Mack found his way to Monsignor Torres' office.

"We have a slight problem, Manuel," he started. "It seems that Joe and I were followed here, this afternoon, by two parties."

Torres poured a rich dark coffee into three small cups, the demitasses so beloved by Europeans for their afternoon coffee. The coffee is usually so strong that three ounces are enough for most people. Mack smiled appreciatively after his first steaming sip.

"They would not have got through the Office." The Monsignor looked grim.

"No, I am sure your security stopped them, at the gate, so to speak. But I am wondering if there is a way...um....a way out that might not draw any unwanted attention?" Mack asked, hesitantly.

Manuel Torres smiled his big, beaming grin. "Ah. You said you are staying at the Abbe?"

"Yes."

"Then I believe I can help you, help you very well indeed. When you wish to leave today, come back here, and I will show you. This will be fun."

Some hours later, after more research into the history of the Guard of the Rose Cross, Mack and Joe returned to the Monsignor's office. Torres was ready for them, with a small silver tray holding a decanter of sherry, three small glasses, and a plate of cheese filled pastries.

"With unwanted company hovering about, you will not want to enjoy five o'clock in the bar of the Abbe. So we can enjoy it here."

The sherry was a *fino* of rare vintage. Even Joe could tell that. And the cheese puffs were light and airy, filled with a buttery but strong cows' milk cheese.

"The cheese is *queso Nata de Cantabria*, a specialty produced here in Galicia. These pastries are why I have to exercise so much," laughed Torres. "I actually carry some of the books back to the shelves, myself, sometimes." His good mood might have been catching, if Mack and Joe were not so worried about the men who had been following them. But after a few more of the pastries and another glass each of the sherry, and given the Monsignor's obvious lack of angst, Joe and Mack began to relax. The three men discussed the research that had been started that day, Mack sharing with the Monsignor that he thought that the Guard of the Rose Cross might have been a group dedicated to the preservation of the family of Jesus and Mary Magdalene. Joe was somewhat surprised that the Monsignor accepted too easily what would have been condemned as blasphemy only a few years earlier.

"So, that would explain the Merovingians. Their names were Jewish, but their religion appeared to be firmly Christian. And they really did marry into every royal or ruling house in Europe. Just as you found in the records of the Guard. It makes sense." He nodded, considering the import of what the professor had just told him.

"It also explains who looked after the royal blood line until the Knights Templar came on the scene. There is a gap of a thousand years there," said Kirby.

"And it might even explain why there was such antipathy between the Vatican and the Templars, later." The Monsignor said this quietly, as though to himself, but Kirby stiffened. A thought had crossed his very keen mind.

"Joe?" he said.

"Yes, Uncle. I will remind you of the Monsignor's comment, tomorrow."

"Good lad. Now, there are two pastries left. I hate to say this, but I think age should take precedence." He offered the plate to Torres, who shook his head. "You are in luck, Joe. I need only one more."

The impromptu cocktail party over, Monsignor Torres led his guests from his office and out into the myriad of hallways. He did not take them back to the *Officios*, but led them ever further towards the centre of the cathedral proper. He pushed through a massive wooden door, into a stairwell. Stairs appeared to ascend forever, as far as Joe could see, but they were conducted by their guide downwards.

"We are going into the crypts of the church," explained Torres. "Not the lowest ones. Just to the level of the cellars which were still in use in the fifteenth and sixteenth centuries. They were used then as passageways for the orders housed here, for storage, even for stabling, we think. It was later that this level began to be used for the internment of church officials, noted citizens and members of our orders."

He led them ever downward, until the staircases became narrower, made of stone, and spiral, as though they had been confined within a tower or a circular shaft of the cathedral. That would make sense, thought Joe; the thick stone walls which surrounded the staircases would give strength to the overall structure, like an internal brace.

At what Joe thought must be at least three stories below street level, Torres stopped at a door opening off of one stair, in what seemed a never-ending staircase. He led them through the narrow wooden door, into a vast low space, stretching off into the gloom in every direction. Joe could see columns of rock set at regular intervals, some of them appeared to be one massive carved stone, others made of rocks concreted into the form of a column. He had been right: the staircase column was a support, one of many, in the vast under structure of the huge building above them. Torres touched a switch on the wall of the staircase column and dim electric lights lit the space.

"The first cellar level," said Torres. "Now, we walk this way."

He led them over the stone floor, past some columns, towards what appeared to be a perimeter wall. He moved along the wall, through an ancient wooden door, and into a short square hall. The room had four doors, the one which they had come through, the other three set squarely in each of the other three walls of the tiny chamber.

"This one," said their guide. He opened the door on the west wall of the room—Joe is one of those people who have an internal compass, so they always know their direction of travel—and they entered a corridor. Torres pressed another switch and a long line of electric lights lit the space, not well, but sufficiently enough to allow for safe walking.

"This is great," enthused Torres. "I haven't been here for years. Housekeeping has really improved. Someone must be keeping out the cobwebs. Or maybe the spiders gave up." He sounded almost giddy, thought Mack. But even he had to admit, this was rather exciting.

They walked for what Joe calculated to be a hundred yards at a slight upward grade, to where their corridor was blocked by an imposing and rusty iron door.

"Welcome to the Abbe de Soeurs Noir, your hotel," a grinning Monsignor Torres announced. "This was the way the sisters of the order went, to and fro, to the cathedral, when they were in charge of its housekeeping, laundry, cooking, etc. Everything women were expected to do, and which of course, could not be accomplished by the men of the Benedictine Order who resided in the cathedral proper."

He turned the handle of the door, and it opened stiffly with a groan of disuse. But open it did. "This is kept functional," he said, "in case of emergency. Bombing was a very real threat during the Basque issue. And, of course, the preeminent cathedral in Galicia could easily have been a target. So, our escape route. Or, one of them, at least. We also connect to the Dos Reis. But we are not sure they know that." He grinned and laughed.

"Up one flight of stairs. Then through the door on your right.

The only door actually. That takes you into an unused anteroom at the parkade level. The parking garage used to be the storerooms of the Abbe. It got structurally enhanced for automobile parking some sixty years ago. But the anteroom was left alone, through a bit of government suggestion." As he spoke Torres led them up the staircase which Mack and Joe noted extended far above them, into the upper levels of the Abbe. Torres stopped at the first level and opened the staircase door to the anteroom. "Here," he said. He reached into an aperture cut into the wall to the left of the door, and pulled out a large iron key. "Just in case you have to return this way. This opens this door, directly off the parkade, and it opens the door we came through at the end of the corridor, beneath the Basilica. There are others here, so take one with you."

Kirby picked up a key, held it in the fingers of his right hand, and palmed a second one. "Thank you, Manuel. I appreciate your trust."

"Just be careful when entering the parkade. We don't think anyone at the Abbe actually knows of this entrance. You don't want to be surprising some parking attendant. Explanations could become formidable."

Joe was astounded. Did all of Europe have secret passages? Mack looked grateful.

"Manuel. Thank you so much. For everything."

The Monsignor bowed slightly. "It is my pleasure, Professor. And if you should feel the need of research at midnight, my office, and my library are now open to you," smiled Torres, as he slid through the passageway door of the anteroom back onto the dimly lit staircase.

Mack gently opened the door, and sure enough, the parkade of the Abbe spread out before them. The elevator shaft of the Abbe had had to be based at the lowest level of the basement, so when it was installed, also in the 1950's, it extended to the parkade. They looked uncertainly about, in the usual dimness of a parking garage, saw no one, exited from the anteroom into the garage, and locked the door behind them. They were at the eastern wall of the Abbe, and now strode unselfconsciously towards the centre of the parking area to the elevator. Within two minutes they were in Kirby's suite, unseen by anyone.

Joe was shaking his head. "I can't believe the Monsignor would just give you a key to the library. All of those art works. To say nothing of the books. Worth millions."

"Although I am certain that the cathedral's insurer would not appreciate the gesture, I certainly do. And I do have some standing as a religious scholar. Enough to be considered trustworthy, I should hope."

"Of course, Uncle," said Joe contritely. He knew his uncle had been an important religious historian, he just had no idea how well-known and respected he really was.

Sam Wardell waited at a café table in the Plaza de Obradoiro, where he could watch the alleyway that led to the cathedral's *officios,* for as long as he thought he could stretch out a half litre of wine and an appetizer of squid. When a pigeon landed on his table, he realized his lack of movement might be becoming noteworthy, so he gave up and returned to his suite at the Dos Reis. The suited men followed him at a distance. Fiona followed at an even greater distance. Wardell she knew. Now she wanted to know about the other two. When Wardell strode through the main door of the Hostal dos Reis Catolicas, the two followers walked past the door a short way, then one used his cell phone. They walked through one of the alleyways that connected the Plaza to the main street grid of the city, and within minutes were picked up by a private vehicle, an expensive looking grey sedan. Fiona mentally noted the make, colour, and license plate number, and as back up, surreptitiously photographed the vehicle with her phone. She then called a number she had hoped she would not have to call while on this holiday trip with her family, transmitted her photos of the two men and their vehicle, and spoke quietly for a bare minute. As she limped back to the Abbe—why let her room go to waste, even if a country cure was probably a rare sight at the upscale hotel—her cell phone rang. She retrieved it from her manly looking shoulder satchel, a suggestion from Celeste, and was relieved to see Joe's number appear on the screen.

"We are back at the Abbe, Fiona. Where are you?" her cousin asked, somewhat anxiously.

"I am just about there, too," she said, happily. It was good to know that Mack and Joe were safe, and nearby.

Room service at the Abbe provided as elegant a meal as the main restaurant, and was a lot safer. Fiona had changed out of her soutane and latex mask, but her hands were still short-nailed and dingy. Joe noticed, of course, but said nothing.

"So," said Fiona, "how did you two get away from Wardell? And his groupies?"

"You will never believe it," said Joe, excitedly. "There is a tunnel which connects the Abbe to the cathedral. The nuns who lived here, centuries ago, used it to go to the cathedral, for their chores. In the unenlightened Dark Ages apparently the sisters did all the housekeeping, cooking, etc. for the Benedictines."

"It was the Middle Ages, actually," corrected Mack. "And I think that perhaps the traffic was in both directions. A lot of children were born of priests and nuns in those days. One can usually find an infant graveyard, somewhere on the grounds of an abbey, especially when it is located so conveniently near to a monastery."

"Gross! Why not just pretend that the baby was left at the gate?" Fiona delicately, with very indelicate looking fingers, raised a raw oyster to her lips, and sucked it back. "At least the parents would be able to agree on the child's religion."

Joe laughed; Mack looked stern, then grinned. He was secretly very pleased, and relieved, to have Fiona and Joe both safely with him.

Having demolished three courses, and now enjoying true Spanish coffees, not the American variety as Mack reminded them, they relaxed in the living room between Mack's and Joe's bedrooms. The coffee was deliciously dark-roasted, augmented with a brandy, and a hint of toffee, and frothy with real whipped cream. Dessert in itself, thought Joe.

"So what has been happening?" asked Fiona, in her chirpiest voice.

"Well, Sonia had to fight off a bad guy, but she did it, perfectly of course, with the help of a blond FBI agent, and she and Marsha are safe. We found the records of the Guard of the Rose Cross, which prove that Jesus survived the crucifixion and his children now rule most of Europe, and Uncle Mack has free range of the Basilica de Santiago de Compostela library, which, by the way, houses millions of dollars worth of art treasures. And I like sherry. That about describes our day."

"Sonia and Marsha?" asked Fiona. She was clearly upset.

Mack and Joe explained what had happened.

"Do they know yet, who the perpetrator was working for?"

"No," said Mack, as he silently noted that Fiona was less concerned about the thug's name, than she was about his allegiances.

"He is in custody, of course," said Mack. "And the authorities should be able to track him and his associates."

"Who has him?" asked Fiona.

"Mostly the FBI. But some of my people know some of their people, so I will be told immediately of any break-through information."

Uncle and niece looked at each other, squarely. For some reason, they wanted to protect Joe from what they knew, or suspected, or did for a living. Fiona nodded.

"Your other news sounds interesting," she said, trying to feign interest in her uncle's research.

"Interesting?" Joe's voice was raised. "I just told you that Jesus Christ was alive and well, and fathering children, after his well-advertised crucifixion! This is news!"

Fiona leaned back, and sipped her coffee. "But Uncle Mack already told us that. Or at least that he suspected that. And I always believe what Uncle Mack tells me, whether he has an idea, a theory, or actual proof." She gently licked whipped cream from her lips. "Because if he needs proof, he always finds it. That is what he does. Didn't you know that?"

"Thank you, Fiona. But something is niggling at my brain. What was it I asked you to remind me of, Joe? Something Manuel said today?"

"You said that the Templars were probably the group that watched over the scions of Jesus, taking that duty over from the Guard of the Rose Cross. The Monsignor suggested that that may have been an integral reason for the Vatican's denouncement of the Templars, and their eventual extermination by Papal order." Joe's mathematical and professorial mind was working perfectly.

"What is the Guard of the Rose Cross?" asked Fiona.

"You know I was reading the Testament of Ephes? The part that was recovered as part of the Quhram hoard, the Dead Sea Scrolls?" Fiona nodded. "And that I thought Ephes might once have been in Santiago de Compostela, Compostela as it known then?" She nodded again. "Well, he was here, and after his father, one Torgas, he became the Grand Master of the Guard of the Rose Cross. As I explained before, Ephes is too rare a Greek name for coincidence to kick in. I am certain there was only one Ephes, the writer of the testament was the Grand Master. He knew Jesus and Mary. And I believe that the missing scrolls of his testament will explain what happened to them and their children. The Guard itself seems to have been originated to ensure the safety of the Blood Royal, the descendants of Jesus."

"The Holy Grail you spoke of, when we were flying here," said Fiona.

"Exactly. The Order of the Poor Fellow-soldiers of Christ and the Temple of Solomon, the Templars as we call them, was granted the status of a Papal Order, when the Holy See, the Vatican, needed soldiers to free Jerusalem from the control of the Muslims. Infidels as they were termed, although I am sure they thought of the Christian knights as infidels, in return. That was the First Crusade. I think it is not only possible, but highly likely, that the men, or at least some of them, who made up the Guard of the Rose Cross, simply continued to be employed under that symbol, and became known as Templars.

Fiona frowned. "But Templars were famous for the red crosses on their white tunics. Rose to red?"

"Uncle Mack says that good red dyes did not exist in the eleventh century, so the red crosses of the Templars were most likely a dark muddy rose," added Joe.

"Cochineal came from the Americas, so it was not available until after Columbus," Fiona mused. "So, yes, I think you could be right."

Joe looked strangely at her. "How do you know about cochineal?"

Fiona shook back her hair. "Fashion correspondents have to learn something." She then looked at her uncle. "But how did the Templars get the Pope so mad?"

"The Templars were famous for introducing international banking. Anyone, but mostly traders, of course, could deposit gold with one Temple keep, retrieve a note or chit to that effect, and be able to change the note for the gold at any other Templar castle. So the trader did not have to travel with his gold about his person, which in those times was not particularly safe."

"Why not just steal the note? If you were a bad guy?"

"There was an identification process, similar in ways to our modern day PIN code and signature rigmarole. Anyway the system worked. And many historians have postulated that the Catholic church was quite envious of the Templars' monopoly of banking. Personally, I have never thought the banking prowess of the Order would have been sufficient to make its members *personas non gratis*. But in 1312 the Order was disbanded, their lands, castles, keeps, and gold all confiscated by the Vatican. Except their possessions in France, which were confiscated by the French king. The knights were named as outlaws, and their leaders were put to death. Significantly, they were charged with heresy."

"Ooh," said Fiona.

"Precisely," said Kirby. He poured himself more coffee, plain, this time. "Monsignor Torres suggested that the duties of the Templars, regarding the scions of Jesus, may have been the reason for their disbandment and the death sentences of their members, pronounced and carried out by the church. The Vatican of the fourteenth century would have done anything to scotch any suggestion that Jesus had not died on the cross; it would have fought tooth and nail to maintain the truth—the absolute word for word truth—of the Bible, as reported by Christian writers of the second and third centuries. The church was under attack from all sides, from its point of view. The Roman Catholic Church had fought the Crusades against Muslims, who openly believe that, while Jesus was an important prophet, he was not the son of god, and did not die on the cross. The Muslims under Saladin had won back the Holy Land which had to suggest that perhaps theirs was the true god. The Eastern Orthodox Christian church had its own ideas, contrary to the tenets of the Vatican. And the thinkers of the early Renaissance were casting scientific doubt on everything. The Vatican had to maintain control of Christians, through their belief in the forgiveness of sins. If Jesus did not die so that the sins of every other Christian can be forgiven, then why be Christian?"

"That was its big selling point," agreed Fiona.

"Still is," added Joe.

"So..." said Mack, obviously paying more attention to his thoughts than his speech, "What happened in the early fourteenth century to turn the holy order of Templars into a threat?"

"Perhaps they had been a threat for some time, but now with that Frenchman's help, the Vatican decided to act," said Fiona. "Just taking advantage of the politics of the day."

Mack looked off into the distance. "Philip the Fair was an ambitious man. He married a princess of the House of Navarre, consolidating the northern kingdoms of France, centred about Paris, and Navarre in the south. The king of England held lands in modern-day France as his vassal, which was causing wars on that front, and he was fighting the Flemish. Add to this, he wanted to mount another crusade, so that he could become King of Jerusalem."

"He was nothing if not politically ambitious."

"Yes, he was, Fiona." Mack was still visibly thinking of something else. "Joe, we have to get back to the library. We need to check that bloodline again. I am wondering if Philip didn't see himself as the king of the world, because of his bloodline. And if he thought that, then the Grand Master of the Priory of Sion must have told him some Priory secrets, out of school, so to speak.

CHAPTER 68

SANTIAGO DE COMPOSTELA

Sam Wardell was frustrated, but not defeated. He called the Abbe switchboard, and asked to be connected to Professor Kirby. The call went through, but was not answered. By putting the call through, the desk clerk was unknowingly acknowledging that Kirby had retrieved his room key, hence he,—and now Sam— knew Kirby was in the hotel. But not answering. So, Wardell walked over to the Abbe, went to the desk, and explained that he wanted to leave a message for Professor Mackellan Kirby. He handed the folded paper message to the desk attendant, then walked away. In the miniscule mirror attached to his plain glass eye-glasses, skillfully disguised as the hinge between the frame and the left ear piece, he saw the desk staffer place the message in box 413. Life was wonderful when hotels were so old fashioned as to still have boxes for letters and messages for their guests. He then noted the clerk dialling, three numbers only, so in house. He appeared to leave a message. All good, thought Sam.

Minutes later Sam Wardell was outside room 413. He knocked.

"*Excusa. Uno mensage para el Professorio,*" he said in his best Spanish accent, which was very good indeed.

Kirby had just received a call from the front desk saying there was a message for him, so Joe opened the door immediately, and Sam took the opportunity to push his way into the suite. If Joe had not been taken off guard, the entry might have been a lot more difficult, Sam knew, this being the first time he had seen Joe in shirtsleeves. His obvious upper body strength was very well displayed in his cotton dress shirt.

"Hi, guys," Sam gushed, with just a touch of his Southern accent. "Too long, no see."

Mackellan and Fiona stared at him. Joe closed the door and moved over to stand between Sam and his uncle and cousin.

Sam continued. "Hey, I thought we all agreed to work together. I would provide protection and you would provide the scholarly research? But you keep disappearing. Makes protection difficult."

Kirby cleared his throat. "Ahem. Mr. Wardell. On reconsideration, we do not think we need protection from you." He seemed to realize how his words could be interpreted. "That is, there seems to be no danger to us here."

Sam walked around their dining table and sampled bits of the remaining food. "Ooh. You didn't wait dinner for me. Do you mind if I deal with your leftovers? I had squid, while waiting outside the cathedral for you, by the way. It was good, but not that filling." He sat down, and began to eat bits of everything left on the table, but, to be fair, he did employ good manners, using an unused salad fork and dessert knife properly, Mackellan noticed.

"And before you decide that you do not need protection, you might consider the two thugs who followed me home today," Sam said, between mouthfuls.

Fiona spoke up. "So you knew they were following you?"

"Of course. How could I miss two suits in a city of tourists and pilgrims? Obviously, by their choice of clothing, they meant to be noticed. And feared." He bit delicately into a piece of lemon-sauced baked hake. "Well, they succeeded with one out of two."

He continued to nosh happily away, then looked up at Fiona. "So you were there, too? Let me guess. The pretty blond with good legs and even better....uh, hiking sandals?"

Fiona felt irritated that he had noticed a good looking woman, then felt annoyed with herself. "No, not me."

"But you must have been there. You knew I was being followed, so Q.E.D., you were there."

Fiona desperately wanted him to get off that subject; if he reviewed the street scene with his famed photographic memory, he might just remember the old priest, and be able to see through her disguise. She hid her short and dirty fingernails in closed fists.

Mack noticed his niece's consternation. "Your syllogistic reasoning aside," he said, in his best professorial tones, "If 'thugs', as you say, were following you, why would that have any bearing on us, or any one of us?"

Sam dabbed at his lips with an unused napkin. "Look people," he said, "You are in danger, whether you accept that or not. I want to prevent you from succumbing to that danger. And I want the scroll that you, Professor, are trying to find. So let's cut the crap, and we all get on with the job. Okay?"

His audience looked unhappy.

"Well, I mean, you get the bragging rights for having found it, but I have to get that scroll back to my people."

Kirby smiled. He knew he could fob off any Coptic parchment on anyone. Very few people in the world would know the difference between a verse from Genesis and a grocery list, if that list was written in Aremaic Greek. He thought that just might be the answer. And in the meanwhile, this Yank could be of assistance, even if he just kept the 'suits' occupied. "On reconsideration, I think you just might be right. I hate to think of my niece or nephew being placed in a dangerous situation."

Fiona and Joe simultaneously started to say something, but were shushed by their uncle's upraised hand. "I have felt bad about involving both of you, in something that could be beyond any of us."

Fiona immediately picked up on her uncle's careful words. She knew nothing was beyond either herself of her uncle, and she was beginning to think that maybe Joe was no slouch either. So Uncle Mack was talking in code.

Kirby continued. "I think we could do with your assistance, Sam. And thank you for offering." He poured more coffee. "But I am here to look at some volumes in the cathedral's library. I don't know where you get the idea that I am looking for a....scroll, did you say?"

CHAPTER 69

SANTIAGO DE COMPOSTELLA

In his room at their private hostel, the big man, more comfortable now that he had discarded his suit jacket, was still sweating. It was not the heat; it was the telephone call he had to make.

The telephone was answered after one ring.

"Yes?" asked the carefully unaccented voice.

"Sir, it is Blais. We followed Wardell today. He appeared to be tailing the Professor and O'Connor. But they never met up. The Professor and his nephew were in the Cathedral and Wardell couldn't get in. Neither can we, by the way."

"I will make a call. Expect to hear from my office."

"Yes sir. I think Wardell made us. I mean, we stick out, wearing suits and ties, so my guess is he is aware of our presence." He listened. "No, no reason for him to know who we are, just that someone is following him. And, we have not seen Fiona Kirby. She was not with her uncle or cousin, today. Or with Wardell." He listened then said, "Of course. You told us of her....ah....abilities. We will look at everyone, with care."

He ended the call, and found his hand was shaking. There was something about that man that just scared the hell out of him.

Within half an hour he received a call.

"I am calling from the office. Your contact at the cathedral is Father Mezzoni, the choir master. You want to provide him with a computer application which will let every choir member know if he is tonally perfect." The big man said something in response. "Yeah, well, who knows if choir members check their I-phones while singing hymns. Whatever. Your names are on the visitors' list, and business cards will be delivered tomorrow, before 9:00 a.m. local. You're welcome. Ciao."

The next morning a package arrived at the hostel. It contained business cards for two Italian electronics engineers, apparently working for an IT company based in Naples. That just might explain our accents, thought the big man.

He and his confederate dressed, slightly more casually today, looking like businessmen, but not in the office. Open shirts, black sports jackets, expensive black jeans. They practised their names as they were driven to the Plaza de Obradoiro.

Sam Wardell had left Kirby's suite at about eleven p.m., having been invited to breakfast at the Abbe the next morning. Mack had decided that the easiest way to deal with Wardell was to get him into the library, as his guest, palm off a scroll on him, and let him deal with the issue of smuggling it out. That should keep him busy.

The next morning, Fiona was again not answering her room telephone or her cell, and did not respond to their knock, so Mack and Joe went down to their appointed breakfast.

"But why would you give him the scroll?" asked Joe, as they walked towards the elevator.

"Well, because it isn't the real one, to begin with," said Mack.

"No, what I mean is, why would you give him the scroll?" He emphasized the word 'would'. "From his point of view, what is your motivation? Isn't he winning too easily? Won't that make him suspicious?"

"I hope it makes us look as though we are afraid for our lives. The Gulfstream was brought down. Sonia and Marsha were almost abducted. Besides Wardell's Congregation of the Holy Baptism, whoever wants the testament, or wants it destroyed, is playing for keeps. So it makes sense that when Wardell gets the scroll back to the USA, the other group will stop going after us. If they go after the Congregation for the scroll, so be it. Not our problem. Wardell appears capable of handling himself."

"I hope so. I kind of like the guy," said Joe, "and Fiona seems pretty smitten."

"Yes, she did try too hard to appear disinterested. I noticed that, too."

Wardell was waiting for them, at a table on the terrace.

Over their very western breakfast, Mack advised Wardell that he would photograph the scroll, then give Sam the original.

"I hate to do that. The first two parts of the testament were worth a fortune to someone. Who knows the value of the remaining parts. And, as an historian, I hate to see any museum piece disappear into a private collection somewhere."

Sam Wardell studied the older man, then said "Aren't we ignoring the elephant in the room?"

"What?" asked Joe.

"What we aren't talking about. Who else wants the scroll? Or wants you killed so you can't locate it? You've been shot at, you said. That plane was bombed, presumably in the expectation that you would be aboard. There are two big thugs lurking around the cathedral."

"Yes," said Mack quietly. "Who, or what, is so afraid of what the scroll might contain, that keeping it hidden is worth murdering for? Because you are right, whoever shot at me knew I had not discovered a long lost scroll—I hadn't even left Innescarrig. And the aircraft was bombed before I had had a chance to get into the cathedral here. So, it is not the scroll that someone wants. It is to keep it hidden, a secret forever."

An hour later, back in their reading room in the cathedral library, Mack had been looking, but in an unfocused way into the middle distance for some time, when Joe noisily said "Ahem" in order to get his uncle's attention.

"Yes?" asked Mack, quietly.

"I was just wondering where you were?"

"Ah. I have been around and about. Let's go see Manuel." Then he raised his voice, so Wardell could hear him. "Mr. Wardell, please stay here. I am not certain our host would appreciate me having an uninvited guest, so to speak."

Wardell remained seated, and nodded.

Kirby and his nephew wandered through the hallways towards the Monsignor's private office. "I have been thinking," said Mack. "We know the men of the Guard of the Rose Cross were dedicated to the preservation of the children of Jesus. Because they knew he was a king on earth, perhaps a king in heaven. So would they not have also been careful to preserve his earthly remains? In the Jewish tradition his body would be enshrouded for a year, then the remains placed in an ossuary, a stone box for the preservation of bones. It was a good system; an ossuary is less than a quarter the size of a western coffin, so family tombs didn't get too crowded too quickly."

Joe was always amazed at his uncle's ability to morph from the pedantic religious scholar to the profane pragmatist, who with one sentence could make the arcane and mysterious simply practical.

His uncle continued. "I think they would have accorded the relics of Jesus pride of place, so to speak. Apparently there was an early Christian church here in Compostela, dating back to the first century. We need to know where that was exactly."

Sam Wardell sat at the table in the reading room, apparently engrossed in a book of particularly gory woodcuts showing how witches were treated in medieval Spain. He waited until he could barely hear Kirby's and O'Connor's footsteps echoing in the stone corridor, then he followed after them. His high-top running shoes, not proper footwear with a sports jacket, to Sam's way of thinking, but apparently made acceptable the world over by the popularity of American hipster rappers, allowed him to move silently through the normally echoing halls.

Over demitasses of coffee, Monsignor Torres was happy to oblige their query.

"The church was here," he smiled.

Mack looked concerned. "But that means, it was razed, in order for the cathedral to be built?"

"Almost," their jovial host smiled. "We have the collection of letters from Master Gelduin, the head architect of the cathedral. He was always complaining about workmen, or supplies, or money. But in one of his early letters to his Cardinal in Rome, the off-site official who was overseeing the construction of the cathedral, he did complain about Bishop Darda and how he had ordered that the pre-existing Christian church, reportedly from the first century, be salvaged. Or at least all that was still here when Darda arrived on the scene. Apparently, not much. The ground level church had been destroyed totally, to make room for the cathedral. Remember, that earlier church would have been far too meagre to allow for renovations. It could simply never become a cathedral." The Monsignor poured more coffee, and passed a plate of macaroons.

"But, we know from Gelduin's complaints to his paymaster Cardinal in Rome that Darda did insist that a stone wall in the cellars of the original church be retained. Some months later, when they were checking the stone wall for stability, the wall was found to contain a cedar chest, cached beneath a wooden beam. Apparently the space beneath the beam had been covered with a thin wall of stone and concrete, and the chest was secreted behind that wall. All quite exciting; Gelduin wrote about it extensively. Mostly, he demanded that his Cardinal give him access to the chest, which this Bishop Darda was keeping to himself. It seems that the Cardinal, who was clearly an enlightened leader of men, set aside Master Gelduin's wishes, and let the Bishop free rein with the chest. Apparently it kept the bishop happy, and that made the Cardinal's world happier. Bishop Darda's job was not one to envy; he was the man in charge of the construction of a cathedral, one in which he himself would never officiate at a service, within which he would never even bend his head in prayer because he was too old to kneel. No, the cathedral would be constructed over more than a century, finally being consecrated in 1211. So Darda was in charge of a monument he would never see. I can only imagine the hopelessness of that."

Mackellan's eyes shone. "Where is that chest now? The chest that Bishop Darda kept?"

Torres wagged his right forefinger at Mack. "Oh, now. That would be too easy, even you have to agree." He drank the last drop of his coffee. "That would be too easy. When we have such a celebrated religious artifacts scholar in our midst, why would we make things easy as pie?"

He laughed, then frowned, and said "Seriously, there is no record of the chest, or its contents. The eleventh century was a long time ago. The house where Darda lived, even the church in which he celebrated Mass, have long since disappeared. We know where they were, from ancient plats drawn by Master Gelduin's assistant, one Robertus Galperinus. Apparently the Chief Architect did not like to share the designing of the cathedral with his assistant, so he set him about surveying the town. His plats are quite beautifully detailed. He even drew in the *de riguer* red light at the site of a local tavern, so we now have irrefutable evidence that that sign of female availability predates the eleventh century. Do you know when that started?"

"Well, yes, I do, actually," said Mack. "But, back to the cathedral. There is no record of that chest?"

"Perhaps because of the way in which Bishop Darda was taken from his congregation," said Torres quietly. "It was a sad affair, a local disaster, really." He told Mack and Joe of Darda's last journey, as recounted by the squire Henri of Rouen in his diaries, which, in fact, were housed in the cathedral library. "The town would have been in disarray. Its bishop dead. Many of its Templar knights and their squires murdered. Henri was the only survivor, and the body of Bishop Darda was the only one returned here for burial. The knights were interred at Castle Rennes, honoured as Templars who had fallen in service. Their squires were laid beside them." Then, almost as an afterthought, he said "Their internment room is really worth seeing. But it is a bit of a drive, from here."

Joe looked queasy, again, Mack noticed. "We might do that, sometime. But you said Castle Rennes? Were they in France, then, near Chateau-le-Rennes, perhaps?"

"Spot on. Henri of Rouen even wrote that his uncle, Captain Amsted, who was the officer in charge of the knights travelling with Darda, was found dead from various wounds, just at the door of the Church of the Magdalene, an ancient church in the town of Chateau-le-Rennes. It is also worth seeing, by the way," he added. "Apparently Henri discovered the body of his uncle. Must have been shocking for a teenager. They tend to believe that death will never strike, don't they?"

"So Bishop Darda was buried here in Compostela?" asked Mack. "In a churchyard? Is there any record?"

"Oh, ye of little faith," smiled Torres. Joe was getting a little tired of the Monsignor's out-of-date English expressions, although he had to admit to being rather impressed that someone who had learned English as a second—or perhaps even third—language, should have such knowledge of its rarer idioms.

"Bishop Darda was interred, not buried, here, in the cathedral. He famously got in just ahead of Saint James himself." Torres smiled. "Darda was the first person to be interred here."

Joe spoke up. "Is there a difference between 'buried' and 'interred'? You have used that word twice now, Monsignor, and I have noticed that you speak English very well. So?"

The Monsignor beamed his appreciation of Joe's compliment then answered. "Buried means placed under ground, of course. Interred can mean that, but it also means entombed. Bishop Darda's remains were placed in a tomb, in the lowest level of the cellars of the cathedral, placed there even before the cathedral had a functioning catacombs, which was in the next level up, of course."

"Did this lad, Henri you said, write of the tomb of Darda?" Mack tried to keep the excitement from his voice, but knew that he had failed miserably, when he noticed Joe leaning closer, not wanting to miss anything.

"He was a prodigious diarist. He wrote that the body of the bishop, after arriving from near Navarre, had to be kept, on ice, so to speak, for a period of two more days, while the superintendent of the cathedral construction, one Breg from Grenoble, had his men construct the tomb. It was granite, so you can imagine that completing the job in just a few days meant that a lot of men worked night and day. Apparently, Darda and Breg were great friends. And Breg wanted to honour his dear friend with a fitting memorial. Perhaps the short amount of time they had explains why the stone sarcophagus has such outlandish dimensions. It is at least two and a half metres long."

Mack was so out of practice that he could not keep the grin of triumph from suffusing his face. He used to be so good at hiding his emotions. Must be old age, he thought.

"May we see the tomb of Bishop Darda?"

"Of course. Of course. Strangely enough a visiting Cardinal from Rome has also asked to be taken to the lowest crypt, in order to view the cris of St. James. Only a few years after the death of Bishop Darda, the cris was unearthed in a field only a few kilometres from Santiago de Compostela. The remains were certified by Pope Urban II as those of St. James, the younger brother of Jesus, a disciple in his own right. If you do not mind, I will conduct you and His Excellency Cardinal Contini to the cellar, at the same time. We do like to keep visitations to that area to a minimum. Who knows what damage can be wreaked by a change in the air flow, or even the inadvertent spreading of contaminants. Those reliquaries have been there for nearly a millennium. We don't want to damage them now."

CHAPTER 70

SANTIAGO DE COMPOSTELA

Fiona was again costumed as an elderly country priest, in long soutane and, new this morning, a broad-brimmed straw hat which would easily place her in the nineteenth century. She had been in the sunshine too long yesterday, for the longevity of her latex mask, so the hat was a requisite. She was again positioned in the Plaza De Obradoiro, at a tiny terrace just outside the Parador dos Reis. She did not want to be too near the Abbe where one of her relatives, or Sam, could spot her.

Her cell phone was at the ready, in the outside pocket of her satchel. People would call her when the silver sedan was spotted. Other people would call her about the identity of the 'suits' she had photographed yesterday afternoon. Now she had only to wait. Not easy for Fiona. Every twenty minutes she checked the GPS signal of both Mack's and Joe's cell phones. They were safely ensconced in the cathedral library. With Sam Wardell. Uncle Mack had told her he would be taking Sam into the library today, both for safety for himself and Joe, and to divert Sam from any other activity which could possibly prove interfering at the best, and dangerous at the worst.

Her coffee grew cold. Then hot when a kindly waiter replaced her old cup with a new one filled with steaming *café au lait*. Fiona knew that cafes in Europe served only one cup per customer with no refills. She felt slightly guilty that her costume was providing her with perks.

Then her cell phone pinged.

"Yes?"

"The vehicle is two blocks away, so here, that means two minutes." The English voice sounded less than sanguine about the traffic in the city centre. "Both targets are aboard. Dressed as hipster business-types today. Bit different, but we will stick with them and keep you up to date."

"Thanks."

Just as she was ending that call, she heard her incoming call signal.

"Hello?"

"Fiona Kirby?"

"Yes."

"Please hold for Air Marshall Patterson."

"Sir?" she said.

"Now don't you 'sir' me, young miss! You promised to call me Neil. Or have I slipped your memory?"

Fiona smiled, then remembered her mask, and curtailed the spontaneous muscle movements. "Of course not, Neil. That was the only time I beat Uncle Mack at billiards, and it was all thanks to you," she said warmly.

"We were good partners," Patterson responded, with a hint of a sigh. "But to business. Because I was already here dealing with that aircraft incident, I was given point on this operation. Your uncle—that is, your American uncle—was not that happy, but we do have our secret little deals, so my people are in."

Fiona sighed with relief. She knew she was being 'assisted' through Santiago de Compostella, but the assistance was faceless, as usual. It was comforting to be able to have a familiar face at the head of her team.

"The photos you sent to us of those two men following your Mr. Wardell. They have been identified as hired muscle for some

American church, the Congregation of the Holy Baptism. Haven't heard of that group operating here before, but apparently they are pretty big in the USA. And the man who attempted to kidnap Ms. Pratek and her daughter is also a known associate of the same group. Not a coincidence, we are certain."

"Oh. Oh no."

"What is wrong, Fiona?" The voice was sharp with anxiety.

"Sam Wardell. He also works for the Congregation. And he is with Mack and Joe."

"Where are they?"

"I just checked their GPS's. They are in the cathedral. Mack was taking Sam there so that they could give him some fake scroll, to get him off their backs." She thought quickly. "I can get you in there, into the cathedral. Can you meet me at the Abbe?"

"In a minute, my dear girl. What?" Patterson was obviously listening to someone else. "They are there, in the Plaza. Don't look around, Fiona, just believe me."

She lowered her head to take a sip of her coffee, and surreptitiously looked towards the cathedral. No vehicle was allowed to approach its entrance, unless carrying the Pope, of course. But there was a silver BMW just parking under the *porte cochere* of the Parador Dos Reis. She was within spitting distance of the two men who exited from its rear doors. The one on the right hand side of the car stared at her, his attention drawn to her cell phone.

Crap, thought Fiona. Nice old cures probably do not carry this year's I-phone. She laid it down on the table, hit the speaker phone button, and from behind her coffee cup, said "I think they just made me."

"Shit! Okay. We are at the Abbe. Can you get here?" Patterson asked.

Fiona looked across the square at the Abbe, some eighty metres away. And noticed, with thanks, the number of tourists already strolling through the plaza, gossiping and gathering before the morning mass at the cathedral.

"I think so," she said, her lips barely moving. She gently placed Euro coins onto her table, picked up her cell phone, stood quickly and began to stride though the crowd, towards the Abbe. This was no time for an old man limp. As she moved she noticed the man from the car, move to the front passenger window and bend down. Then she could no longer watch, just avoid tourists, and keep her eye on the plaza entrance of the Abbe hotel.

The silver sedan began to move slowly, because that was the only way it could navigate the crowded Plaza, towards the Abbe's entrance. The two men who had exited it watched, then began to walk to the side street that led to the offices of the cathedral.

Fiona's heart was pounding; it did not matter how trained you were, how prepared for danger; if the brain said you were frightened, the limbic responses took over, reflexes of the body kicked in, adrenalin pumped, and muscles became hard to control. Every synapse in her brain urged her to run or alternatively fall down and play dead. Fiona stayed to the middle course, walking quickly towards her goal.

She got to the entrance before the silver BMW, and darted through the double doors. Immediately a strong arm grabbed her elbow and led her off to the side of the doors, out of sight of the men in the car, then her guide conducted her through to an anteroom off the main foyer.

"We need your hat and mask. Fast," demanded a clipped English voice. "And the priest jacket."

Now that the flight was over, Fiona's fight instincts took over. "What the hell! Who are you, and don't touch my face." She removed herself from the man's grasp and was backing away, when she heard:

"Fiona. Play nice." It was Neil Patterson, in full uniform, at the vanguard of a group of uniformed men and one slim man in a black shirt with a Roman collar, who had just come into the anteroom, from a side door. "Jim here really does need your mask."

Fiona dropped her wide straw hat to the floor, and gently removed the latex mask from her head and neck, and handed them to the man identified as Jim. She quickly unbuttoned her black coat and handed it to the man next to Jim, who had already recovered the hat. Jim, dressed in Fiona's soutane moved quickly to place the mask over his head, adjusted the eye-holes and mouth area, then placed the straw hat on his head. He was very slim for a man, and just an inch taller than Fiona. Now their resemblance was downright scary, thought Fiona. He had, within a minute, become the elderly country cure that she had been playing. She looked questioningly at Patterson.

"We were lucky to have Corporal Kershaw with us. Hopefully, he will divert your company," said Patterson. His telephone alerted him and he listened for a few seconds. "The car stopped at the Abbe entrance, the passenger is in the hotel." He listened again. "The driver is taking the car around to the rear entrance, as we thought he would." He spoke to the man in the soutane. "Corporal. Are you ready?"

The mask partially hid his expression but Kershaw was grinning. "Aye, sir. Ready to roll."

"Move out then, lad," said Patterson.

"Wait," said Fiona, as she ran up to the corporal and passed him her satchel, which he quickly draped over his shoulder, the way Fiona had been carrying it. She kept her I-phone.

The corporal strode back to the door of the anteroom which Fiona had been manhandled through, just minutes before. Then he slowed his pace, developed a limp, and pushed through the door, back into the plaza end of the hotel lobby. He looked dazedly about, as though somewhat confused, closed the door, then made his unsteady way through the length of the lobby, towards the rear entrance of the hotel.

Every man in the room, and Fiona, wanted to watch, but of course could not. They had to rely on Air Marshall Patterson's telephone contacts.

Corporal Kershaw limped slowly through the lobby of the Abbe, looking about as though he expected to meet someone. He did see the big man who had just come in through the plaza entrance stop when he saw him, feign a telephone call, then continue on behind him. Kershaw steadily advanced towards the rear entrance, which was the main entrance for guests arriving or leaving by automobile. He stepped outside and walked behind the silver BMW which was parked imperiously by the door; he did not trust his disguise enough to walk right in front of the driver. The man tailing him made a hand signal to the driver and continued on foot after the corporal. Kershaw kept his hands tucked into the opposite sleeves of his robe; he knew his hands could give him away. They were much larger than Fiona's, and nothing could disguise that.

So, the elderly priest walked out and across the narrow roadway, his head bent under his wide-brimmed straw hat, for all the world as though he was remembering a long forgotten prayer. He turned down one of the tiny side streets, this one so narrow that traffic was one-way, in the opposite direction. The big man tailing him entered the street; the silver BMW drove past, as it had to. Once in amongst the closely placed buildings of the street, Kershaw turned down an alley, grabbed a bicycle from its place against a street sign, and peddled for all he was worth for the end of the alley. The big man pounded along behind him, then grinned maliciously when he saw that the alley ended in a narrow staircase, leading downwards. Kershaw stood on the pedals, pushed strongly downwards on both tires, then pulled up on the handlebars, lifting the bike onto the narrow stone balustrade that formed the side of the staircase. He sped downwards, leaving his follower dumbfounded and far behind. Air bound momentarily at the end of the balustrade, the corporal easily kept his balance and flashed on at high speed through twisting and narrow walkways and alleyways, ducking under laden clotheslines, avoiding baby carriages and pedestrians, and generally having a high old time.

The man who had been following him, checked the street names, and while still moving made a telephone call. Within a block he was picked up by the BMW, and then the search was on. The two men in the vehicle occasionally caught glimpses of the speeding priest, but could never seem to follow, as the bicyclist took every advantage of one-way traffic and narrow walkways. And then, as they were about to give up, the speeding bicyclist would appear again, and the chase continued.

The man positioned to watch the bicycle by the street sign—so no one else took it—called Patterson.

"Kershaw is a go, sir. I just watched him go down a staircase, on the bloody balustrade! Excuse me, sir. But he really is good."

"Thanks, Sergeant. You can move on to your rendezvous point. Tell Kershaw thanks." He turned to his waiting men and Fiona, still in the anteroom in the Abbe.

"What happened?" asked Fiona. She felt totally responsible for young Kershaw's predicament, and hoped he was okay.

Patterson grinned. "Last year Kershaw was the first runner-up in the Scottish mountain bike championships. It was just coincidental, and we were lucky, that he was with us today. Of course, having him here gave us the idea. And sometimes fresh ideas are the best." He took Fiona's elbow and turned her towards the door. "We are also lucky that the Corporal isn't built like a bri..." He cut himself off. "Like most of us. Now, Fiona dear, lead us to the Cathedral, please."

CHAPTER 71

SANTIAGO DE COMPOSTELA

The two men who had exited the BMW, the 'suits' as Fiona had dubbed them, each carrying a slim metal attaché case, walked briskly into the Cathedral's *Officios.* They presented their business cards to the receptionist. She checked her ever-present visitors' list, telephoned Father Mezzoni, then nodded to the uniformed guard. He looked pointedly at their cases, but just then Father Mezzoni, the cathedral's choir master strode into the little foyer, grasped the arm of the older man with his left hand as he heartily shook the man's hand with his right.

"It is all right, Giorgio. These gentlemen will be demonstrating a computer program for me. They have their laptop computers with them. And I can vouch for them both." He smiled. The guard nodded. Mezzoni and his two charges exited through the doorway into the cathedral proper, into the visitors' waiting room that Joe had so admired just yesterday.

Mezzoni immediately dropped his hand from the older visitor's arm, and marched stalwartly through the room. He did not look happy. He led them through some hallways to a staircase.

"The library is on level three. If anyone asks, you went to the washroom and got lost. Ask the way back to the choir practice hall. I will be there." He turned and abruptly walked away. He did not enjoy having his past, or at least certain regretful but apparently everlasting parts of it, used against him in this way. But he was powerless to stop the blackmail. He could only hope that however the two strangers had got here, and whatever their business was in the library, the theft, for that was what Mezzoni thought it must be, would not be noticed. At least for some time, so that, hopefully, it could not be traced back to these visitors.

The older man, the leader Mezzoni presumed, called tauntingly after his retreating back. "*Ciao, Padre. Grazie mille.*" Clearly not Italians with that accent, Mezzoni thought, so I wonder who they really are? Then he thought, I don't care who or what they are. I just do not want to see them ever again.

Behind Mezzoni's retreating back, the two visitors stopped and pulled white plastic collars from their jacket pockets, and expertly adjusted them to the necks of their shirts, now buttoned up and very credible as priest's habits. They checked each other, nodded, and walked on, now secure in their identity as visiting Roman Catholic priests, certainly a common enough sight in the cathedral. They took the stairs to level three.

In Monsignor Torres' office, he was introducing Mackellan Kirby and Joe to Cardinal Contini and Brother Thomas. Kirby kept the smile on his face as he shook Thomas' hand, although he knew, instinctively, that this was the birdwatcher who Jim Grady had alerted him to. What was happening, he wondered.

The Cardinal spoke. "Professor Kirby, of course I know you by reputation. The world of religious art history owes you a debt of gratitude." He beamed as he shook Kirby's hand. "I myself was particularly engrossed when you identified the nails in Magalenus' *Cristos en Morsus* as the actual nails used to bind Our Lord to the cross."

"*Christ in Pain,*" Kirby said in an aside to Joe.

"So, not only is it a beautiful sculpture, but it has historic significance. I was happy to see that the proposed removal of the nails for preservation was determined to be unnecessary," the Cardinal smiled.

Again to Joe, Kirby said "The sculpture is in the Hermitage in St. Petersburg. The Vatican threw a bit of a hissy fit about the nails. Wanted them back." Kirby then looked up at the Cardinal. "It is a shame that the statue was ever removed from Split, but given what happened later, I suppose we must be thankful." Kirby was referring to the civil war in Yugoslavia in the nineties which had caused the destruction of so many early Christian churches. "The nails need no better preservation than they have enjoyed for centuries. I am glad the decision met with your approval."

The Cardinal looked at him steadily, as though trying to decide whether Kirby was being heartfelt or sardonic. He could not determine which; Kirby's poker face had returned.

The ever pleasant Monsignor, sensing latent enmity between his two esteemed visitors, quickly stepped in. "Gentlemen, it is so wonderful that you know....." he paused, then continued, "and respect, each other."

He clapped them both on the back, bringing them into a near embrace. "We will each need a light, in case we get separated." He handed each of his guests a modern LED flashlight. "Now, are we all prepared for our descent into the netherworld?" He laughed but both Joe and Brother Martin looked slightly ashy. Come," he said, and ushered them from his office.

Torres led them to the staircase tower he had used the night before. This time, the descent continued further. Joe recognized the door the Monsignor had led them through, just last evening, but they continued downward. Now that he knew what to look for, Joe noticed other doors, at regular intervals down the flight of stone steps; obviously access doors to every level of the crypts. Finally, at what Joe estimated to be some four floors below the entrance off the square, the staircase ended, and they were in a narrow stone hallway.

Sam Wardell, a safe distance from the Monsignor's party, followed silently. When he saw Torres' light lead them from the staircase into what seemed to be a level tunnel, he checked his cell phone. There was no reception, due to the thick stone walls of the cathedral, he thought, so he made his way back up the staircase, in complete darkness, his right hand against the wall, guiding him in the narrow space. Occasionally he checked his cell phone, shading its light with his hands. When enough bars showed, he made a call.

"The upper crypts are approximately the width and breadth of the main structure of the cathedral," said Torres, leading them down the passageway. "This hallway circles around a much smaller undercroft, or cellar, far below but centred under the Cathedral. We think it was to allow access for inspection, for leakage of any sort, for stability of the concrete, for replacement of any wooden members, that sort of thing. Those architects knew they were building for a millennium." He carried on, into the gloom now lit only by his flashlight.

The main altar of the cathedral is in the central block between the two towers. Joe thought that they were probably very close to that area of the church, when an opening appeared on the right hand side of their tunnel. That would lead towards the altar, Joe knew. Torres led them through the opening and shone his light about, showing them a quasi-circular area of perhaps thirty feet in width. For a deep cellar room, that was seldom accessed, the air was strangely fresh, with no hint of mold or staleness. The four guests walked into the room, turned on their flashlights, and looked about the space, every one awed in his own way. Kirby was drawn to the granite sarcophagus, on a dais, set at right angles and in front of what appeared to be a wooden beam mounted into a wall of stone. Joe rested his hand on the wooden beam, waiting for direction from his uncle. Then he turned his light full on the beam. He had felt indentations in the wood, and now looked more closely, at what appeared to be a leaf motif; the stems of the leaves formed a cross, and even in the harsh LED light, Joe thought he saw a tinge of discolouration.

"Shine your light here, will you Joe?" Kirby flashed his light over the stone sepulcher and Joe moved to stand beside him, and add his own flashlight to the stone. They both frowned at the coffin's strange outline. The tomb was nearly eight feet long, and appeared to have two lids, one just over six feet long, the other about eighteen inches in length. A crude effigy, still recognizable as that of a bishop decorated the longer lid. At the base of the effigy's feet the smaller lid was undecorated except for a small incised cross.

"That is the tomb of Bishop Darda, first bishop of the Cathedral of Santiago de Compostela," said Torres, quietly, as he stood beside them, and played his own light over the stonework. "When he died the cathedral was under construction. None of the current crypts were finished or in use, so he was interred here. This was apparently the cellar, or crypt if you will, of the church which was razed so the cathedral could be built."

Kirby said quietly. "And that church was built upon the site of the earlier church, the one from the first century. This room would have been part of that earlier church, perhaps all of it." He looked about the room and spoke solemnly, out of respect for the age of the space he was within and for its sanctity.

Cardinal Contini shone his light on the wooden beam, still solid after two thousand years, and knelt below it. There, in the niche in which it had been found, was the marble cris which had been identified as the ossuary of St. James, brother of Jesus. He gently touched the inscribed marks on its side, the ancient Arimaec script from which it had been identified.

Monsignor Torres stood just behind him. "The remains of Saint James the Younger, brother of Jesus. The remains disappeared for some time, when someone thought Sir Francis Drake would plunder them. He plundered a lot of other things, but not bones. And the fellow who had moved them forgot to tell anyone where they were." He went on cheerfully, obviously reciting a favourite story. "When the Portico da Gloria was being restored the architect found the cris, and happily it has been here ever since."

"It has never been opened?" asked Contini.

"Not they we know. The remains were certified by Pope Urban II, as those of St. James, in 1092. From the inscription on the cris, I presume. There is no record of any other evidence. At least not here, as far as I know."

Contini knew what evidence the Pope had received from his trusted Cardinal Legare. And he also knew what information the Cardinal had—the letter from Bishop Darda, detailing the truth about the cris. A student had found the letter in a miscellany of unrecorded documents in the Vatican Library, was thrilled at his momentous discovery, and had immediately told his superior, Contini. The Cardinal had dashed the student's hopes by telling him that such claims arose from time to time, made by some bishop or other trying to come up with important bones, in order to sell them to unsuspecting churches and cathedrals all over Christendom. The Middle Ages' trade in relics was the main financial support of some poorer parishes, he told his student. And then he had taken the letter aside, saying that he would see that it got properly catalogued. Of course, it never had. To his knowledge, Contini was the only person who knew whose remains were in that ossuary.

"Strange though," continued the Monsignor. "In 1884 Pope Leo XIII reauthenticated the bones, with a Papal Bull, then requisitioned, and paid for, a huge statue honouring Pope Urban. Urban was French, so perhaps Leo was simply thanking him for so generously allowing the relics of St James to remain here, in Spain. That certainly helped with the popularity of the pilgrimages, to this day."

I should think it did," agreed the Cardinal. He stood, and gently stroked the marble of the ossuary lid.

"Monsignor," said Kirby, "may we open the tomb? I have reason to believe that within that smaller part, at the feet of Bishop Darda, we will find his missing chest." He paused, having difficulty with his words. "I believe that what is within that chest is....important."

Monsignor Torres could not believe his luck. Professor Emeritus Mackellan Kirby, the famous discoverer of religious artifacts, thought there was something of importance, right here, in his cathedral. Oh my God, he thought, then crossed himself for his near blasphemy.

"Of course, Professor. Of course." He bustled over, and placed his light upright on the effigy of Darda, so that it shone on the lid at the effigy's feet. "Perhaps Brother Martin and young Joe here could lift the lid?" He organized the men, and they rather easily lifted the square of granite, some two inches thick and eighteen inches square. They slid it gently onto the carved work of the longer lid, so as to cause no damage. The sarcophagus had been constructed with an internal wall between the tomb itself and the smaller square space. Within that space was, not the hoped-for cedar chest, but what appeared to be a wooden-bound book.

Monsignor Torres removed a crumpled mess from his pants' pocket and handed it to Kirby; it was a pair of thin latex gloves, always near and dear to every conservator in the world.

"Thank you, Manuel," Kirby said quietly. "May I touch it?"

"Of course, my friend. Who else should have the honour?"

Kirby gently lifted the book out, placed it on the recently removed lid, and very, very gently lifted the wooden cover. The leather that had bound it to the bottom cover was rotted through, and fell away. But the vellum of the first page was intact, unstained, and still quite readable.

Kirby bent over the text of the first page. Even in the poor light he could recognize the word 'Ephes' in the Latin text.

"I believe this is Bishop Darda's translation of the Testament of Ephes." He bent closer over the work, noticed the marginal notations, and circled numbers, which would suggest the author was creating an appendix or what the modern scholar might know as footnotes. The translator was providing himself with options, for some of the words, to be certain not to overlook the nuances of the text.

"This was his workbook," breathed Kirby, "and what a careful translator he was." He continued to read, silenced by his awe of the scholarly bishop.

"Uncle?" said Joe. "Should I photograph it?" He had spent hours photographing texts for his uncle, during their time in the library high above them. The Cathedral of Santiago de Compostela did not extend borrowing privileges to anyone, even a scholar of Professor Kirby's renown, so cell phone photos were now the accepted standard for researchers.

Mack looked at Torres, and the Monsignor nodded. It was impossible to know how stable the old book was. Moving it further might destroy some of the fragile vellum sheets. It would be safer to photograph it here, with as little disturbance as possible.

Joe aimed his cell phone directly above the title page, and clicked. Then Mack gently moved the top page to the wooden cover. He did not turn it over, as one normally would when collating pages. That turning could prove destructive, and Kirby knew from experience that vellum was only inscribed on one side. Even in an age when vellum was a rare and expensive commodity it was never written on the obverse. The skin was tanned so thin that inks bled through, and to use it thus would make both sides of the skin unreadable.

Kirby meticulously moved page by page, waiting for Joe to photograph the uppermost, and continuing on. There were only about thirty pages, so the job was quickly done. Kirby gently placed the bottom wooden cover onto the neat stack of vellum sheets; that would provide some protection when the document was moved. Joe put his cell phone back in his jacket pocket.

The Cardinal had watched the whole process, intently. "We know there was a Testament of Ephes considered for inclusion in the bible, at the Nicaean conference of bishops. But no copy exists in the Vatican library. And I understand that the copy unearthed in Palestine as part of the Quhram hoard is heavily redacted." Contini looked straight at Kirby. "Accordingly, I would appreciate receiving a copy of those photographs."

Kirby, who had maintained a hunched protective stance over the book, while it was being photographed, now straightened himself to his full height. He looked evenly at the Cardinal. "But you already have half of it, if I am not mistaken, Your Eminence."

Joe looked between the two men, and irreverently thought that this was how it must have been in the Wild West when the sheriff and the bad guy waited for the other to go for his six-shooter.

The two cathedral visitors, left to their own devices by Mezzoni, wandered rather aimlessly through the library, until the leader's cell phone pinged. He looked at it, and curtly told his companion "This way. And we need to find that staircase, the one in the plans. The one leading to the crypt."

Air Marshall Patterson's second-in-command, a burly captain, handed Fiona a jacket which was, in fact, a bullet-proof vest with sleeves.

"The modern flak-jacket," said Patterson. "And for god's sake, get rid of that pebble in your shoe. We don't need you limping."

Fiona put on the jacket, it was a bit roomy and heavy but secure feeling. She removed her boot and shook out the little stone she had placed there. How Patterson had guessed that, she did not know. She felt rather ridiculous leading a group of uniformed and armed men through the lobby of the Abbe, past the elevators, because Patterson did not want to use them, down the stairs to the parking garage. Patterson assured her that the hotel staff thought they were practising a bomb scare drill, and would take no particular notice of them. Once in the garage she led them unerringly to the door that Uncle Mack had described to her, used the key her uncle had given her and led them into the anteroom. She looked about, then opened the only other door, onto the staircase. Fiona had remembered her uncle's description, perfectly.

The captain went ahead of Fiona, down the narrow stone staircase; he had no idea where they were going but as a gentleman, he felt he had to protect Fiona from whatever might be up ahead. For her part, Fiona was fine with that; she knew the odds were against the person in the vanguard of an attack force, and that was what this felt like.

The group of seven men, plus Fiona, found the tunnel, and its light switch, and went forward.

"Joe said the tunnel is about one hundred yards long," she said quietly to Patterson, who was walking beside her, again protectively, she thought.

"Thanks. Men, easy for some fifty metres, then silence," he said.

Sam Wardell had finished his call, and was making his way back down the spiral staircase. He knew, from the recurrence of wooden doors at about every twenty steps, that he had ascended four levels above where he had last seen the Monsignor leading his visitors off through that level tunnel. He slowly descended, by touch again. Down thirty steps, a flight and a half, he saw a light shine into the stairwell. One of the doors below him had been opened. His view was obscured by the turns of the stairs, but he felt that two people, probably men, were now descending the staircase, some twenty feet or so below him. He could hear their footsteps, ringing on the stone. Wardell waited, until the men were so far ahead of him that they would not hear his nearly silent footsteps, then followed slowly after them.

When the two men ahead of him reached the lower tunnel, they stopped, and looked about them. Sam was now close enough that he could see, by the light of their own flashlights, that they were armed with what he thought were small automatic machine guns. They doused their lights, and by the light of the night vision scopes affixed to their rifles, continued down the tunnel. But in the dim light Sam was able to recognize them.

God help me, he thought to himself, then called out "Fellahs." The two men turned as one, and quickly came towards Sam, their rifles cradled, but not aimed. "Mathieux instructed me to call you off. I have everything in hand." He was bluffing. "I'll have the scroll soon. Kirby has agreed." He smiled, but his mind was racing. These two thugs worked for the Congregation of the Holy Baptism, or more specifically Archreverend Mathieux, from time to time, when muscle, stupid muscle, Sam amended to himself, was needed. Had they been behind the bomb on the Gulfstream? They would have needed a bomb expert, but maybe they had been the conduit for the payment to the bomber. That was within their pay grade. Both men knew Wardell, had assisted him on some activities. Sam hoped that familiarity would give substance to what he was so blandly claiming. It did not.

"We don't take orders from you, Wardell. Not this time." The leader of the two, the bigger man, was speaking. "Maybe never again. Mathieux isn't all that happy with you. Seems things have been leaking, a bit, you know what I mean?" He grinned. "Too many witnesses been left round about. You been getting sloppy."

Sam's mind raced. He could not let these two follow Kirby and Joe; he was afraid he knew what was intended. The plane crash had failed, submachine guns would not. He thought quickly: for some reason these hoods had not killed their intended victims out in the Plaza, or even in their rooms. There must be something in the cellar, something Kirby was about to unearth, that was a part of the equation. So, Sam computed, he had to stop these two from getting further into the crypt. Or he had to get there first, to give Kirby a chance.

"I just talked to Claud," Sam continued to bluff, but now he was frowning. His voice harshened. "He told me to call you off. You can call him if you want to confirm that. But I can't allow you to go on with your plans." He gazed evenly at the leader's eyes. "You will ruin everything if you proceed now."

"How do we know that?" asked the second and smaller man. His voice quavered a bit; Sam knew he was winning.

"Phone him," said Sam. He knew their cell phones could not work this far beneath the stonework of the cathedral.

"No," said the larger of the two gunmen. "This is what Mathieux warned us about. That you would try to talk us around. It ain't gonna work, not on us."

"But what do we do?" asked his comrade.

The leader seemed to think, then grinned. "Who's to say we even met up with Mr. Wardell, here? Maybe he missed us. So we never got no new instructions. Not our fault." He walked toward Sam, and Sam knew it was now or never. If he could just get the safety off on one of the rifles, he could count on jangled nerves to fire the hair-trigger gun. A blast of machine gun fire, in the confines of the cellar, would alert Kirby. Sam sidestepped, to get past the big man, but as he moved he heard something behind him, far back but approaching, down stairs, he thought. Fiona? In that moment of distraction the bigger of the two men slammed the butt of his rifle into Wardell's jawbone, just below his left ear. The impact was forward and upward, from the corner of the mandible. Wardell dropped like a stone, unconscious.

His assailant grinned. "The Bertuzzi spot. Who knew watching hockey could be so educational."

He and his helper left Wardell on the floor, and moved off into the passage.

"Bertuzzi spot?" questioned the second man.

"Yeah, you know? Hockey. This Bertuzzi guy slammed another guy, right there. It knocks you out, but good. Now let's boogie. He might come to." He grinned again. "Sometime."

Kirby had placed himself between the workbook and the Cardinal. "I believe that at least two scrolls of the Testament of Ephes were received by the Vatican within a few years of their discovery in 1891. I don't know if they were the first two scrolls of the Testament, or installments one and three, or two and five. I don't know, but I believe you do."

The Cardinal tried to stare down Kirby, then shrugged. "I don't think it matters now. Yes, the Vatican did receive parts of the writings of Ephes. We may have received them all, but only two are still extant in the Secret Library. From the text, and the numbering thereof, I believe they are the first and last scrolls written by Ephes. I have dedicated my life," he snarled as though to emphasize his point, "my whole professional life, to tracking down those three other scrolls. If those pages you have just photographed contain the translated text of the scrolls, then I will be taking that book, or whatever it is, back to Rome with me."

"But you seemed more interested in that cris?" said Kirby gently. "I headed straight for the tomb, not you. What do you know of the cris?"

Contini smiled thinly. "What we all know. That it is the ossuary of our Saint James, brother of Jesus Christ, a most beloved disciple."

"How were his remains identified?" snapped Kirby. Joe did not think this was either the time or place, but his uncle continued. "By the scallop shells attached to his body? That is the story isn't it? Is there some description of that, in a letter perhaps, in the Library of the Vatican? Just how do we know those are St. James' bones within that box?"

"The remains were authenticated by Pope Urban II, as our illustrious Monsignor explained. And because this cathedral was under construction at the time of their discovery, it was determined that the relics would rest here, and this became the Basilica of Santiago de Compostela. But you know this," the Cardinal said smoothly. He appeared unruffled but Brother Thomas noticed the twitching of the fingers of his left hand.

Before the two historians could continue their strangely unfriendly discussion, they all heard heavy footsteps, and then saw a strange green glow which Kirby recognized as the light from night-vision scopes, scopes usually mounted on weapons. He grabbed for the manuscript; he wanted to get it back into the space at the end of the coffin, when a harsh voice stopped him.

"Back away from the book, Professor. Now."

Kirby did as ordered, but managed, while moving, to 'accidentally' swing up the beam of his flashlight right to the front of the green-lighted scope, and the man holding what Kirby now recognized as an AK 47 assault rifle. Kirby stepped even further back without being told again.

The man holding the rifle swore. "That puts paid to the night light, you asshole." He moved menacingly towards Kirby, but was stopped by his companion. "Let's just do what we came to do," he growled, then turned his own gun towards the notebook, and began firing on full automatic. Slugs tore into the book at a rate exceeding four hundred per minute. One short burst blew the book to pulp, miniscule pieces of wood and papyrus floating in the still air of the chamber. Kirby felt sour bile rise in his throat.

"You were never supposed to do that!" shouted Cardinal Contini. He stepped toward the shooter and shone his own LED light full onto that man's face, but the first man waved his weapon, a silent suggestion to the Cardinal to back off.

"We have other orders," said the shooter, the obvious leader. "And now that you people have seen our faces, we need to extend those orders."

He raised his rifle in the direction of Kirby, when Joe screamed. His agonized "No!" echoed throughout the room. The armed man turned his gun on Joe, and opened fire.

Everything happened at once; at once and in slow motion. Kirby leapt towards the leader of the thugs, but was smashed in the face with the rifle butt of the second man. Kirby grabbed at his legs and brought him down. Joe ran at the leader, the man whose rifle had just jammed. He took two fast steps then launched himself at the armed man, in a full-out rugby tackle. His head smashed into the man's jaw, and Joe heard the unmistakable—and very satisfying sound—of his opponent's lower mandible breaking. The impetus of his tackle still propelling him, Joe slid his head up the man's face, and heard the crunch of the man's occipital orb, the bony circle of bone which protects the eye socket. The sound of cracking bone was like manna, a gift from heaven. He knew he had badly torn the skin from his own skull; the forehead skin is too thin and tender to take that much friction without shearing in a wide gash. But the adrenalin in his system kept him from feeling the pain. He did have to wipe blood from his eyes, and that was when he knew he was injured. Bad, but not as bad as his adversary, who had dropped his weapon, was on his knees, and gurgling in pain. And not as bad as his cell phone, which he had inadvertently smashed against his opponent's AK47. The rifle had won, the cell phone was in pieces.

Kirby's target was on his knees but still armed. His finger pressed on the trigger of his assault rifle and bullets flew randomly. The rifle swung wildly around, and some bullets smashed into the corner of the St. James ossuary. Contini screamed "No!" and moved towards the ossuary, only to have a slug, ricochet from the thick marble, and slam into his torso. He sank to the floor, blood gushing from his abdomen.

Brother Martin Froese moved quickly, keeping his body behind the shooter, away from the gunfire. He neatly pressed his forearm across the man's throat, and pulled hard. The gun fired spasmodically for a few rounds, then, as the man's fingers relaxed on the trigger, there was silence. Relative silence. Kirby was swearing audibly, Contini was moaning quietly, Joe's victim was now shrieking in pain, and Joe was breathing heavily. Brother Martin's man was silent, as was Brother Martin, who was moving quickly to the Cardinal.

Then Kirby said, jokingly but with tears in his eyes, "I never really understood the rules of rugby, but my guess is that was an illegal tackle."

Fiona burst into the room, closely followed by the burly captain, and the rest of Patterson's cadre. Minutes before they had found Sam Wardell, still groggy and down. Fiona had bent down and touched him gently, then moved on, knowing that the medic in their group would be of more service to Sam. The team was already in the circular passageway which surrounded the undercroft when they had heard the gunfire. She had run ahead of her armed guard, and they were vainly trying to catch and pass her, when they entered the room. The captain took in the situation immediately, and began ordering his men. First, the incapacitation of the two gunmen, then securement of their weapons, and finally attention to the injured.

Fiona had eyes only for her Uncle Mack and Joe. Mack was standing, a bit unsteadily if truth be told, but he looked fine. Joe was bleeding copiously from a ragged-looking gash on his forehead. She ran to him.

"Sit down, Joe. Before you faint." She knew her cousin was slightly haemophobic, especially when the blood was his own.

"I'm okay," he said. His voice was steady.

One of Patterson's men came over to him, and gently touched a moistened medical towelette to Joe's forehead. The cloth came away blood soaked, but the skin beneath the cloth was whole. No gash, no scar, showed on Joe's forehead.

Fiona shook her head in disbelief. Then looked towards her uncle. Mack was kneeling near the cris. It had been damaged by the gunfire, but was still basically intact. One top corner had been blasted off, leaving a small hole. Kirby was shining his LED light into the hole, and peering closely at what he could see of the contents. He then signalled for one of the soldiers to help him. Fiona watched, as she saw the two men pull the cris from under the wooden beam, turn it one hundred and eighty degrees, and then push it back into its hiding spot. The shattered corner was now out of sight, at the back wall of the space, directly under the beam.

The Cardinal, prone but still aware, also saw Kirby at the ossuary. He was being given first aid by the medic in Patterson's cadre, involving the application of pressure and a wad of bandages to his abdomen. Through a grimace of pain he said quietly "What did you see?" He gasped a bit, then continued. "In the cris?"

Kirby got up from in front of the cedar beam, and looked down at the Cardinal. "What you expected that I would see, I think."

CHAPTER 72

SANTIAGO DE COMPOSTELA

Air Marshall Patterson sent one of his patrol with Monsignor Torres, up to Torres' office, so he could telephone for police and ambulance support. The Monsignor was visibly shaken, but unharmed. He even remembered to tell the emergency services that they would need a stretcher which could detach from its carriage for the Cardinal; the twists of the ancient staircases were too tight for the usual trolley-type stretcher. The assailant taken on by Brother Martin did not need a stretcher; his remains needed a body bag; his neck had been snapped. The undercroft was cleared out quickly, after the arrival of the Guardia Civil and their medical counterparts.

Sam refused to go to the hospital; he knew he was concussed and that there was nothing that could be medically done for that. So he found himself in Kirby's suite at the Abbe, with Kirby, Joe and Fiona. He wisely, but regretfully, refused the single malt that Kirby offered all around, and drank some Perrier water instead. He had to hydrate to stave off any further swelling of his brain.

Joe, enjoying a fine Spanish beer in lieu of the liquor, gingerly pulled his cell phone from his top jacket pocket. The screen was cracked, the innards were spilling from the obliterated case. He dropped it on the coffee table, with a sigh of disgust.

Kirby stared at it, as though at a fully hooded cobra within striking distance. "It's okay, right?" He looked around, unsteadily. "I mean, you can recover the photographs? Right?"

"Not from this puppy," said Joe dismissively. "This is garbage. Through and through."

Kirby sank lower into his armchair, his shoulders drooped, and for the first time ever in their lives, his niece and nephew thought he looked his age.

He sighed. "So that means the photographs you took are also...." He hesitated. "Garbage? Unrecoverable?"

Joe had opened up his I-pad, and looked over at Fiona. "Not unless Fiona's phone is on the blink, and my I-pad too. When I took the photographs I was also transmitting to both devices." He grinned. "It's the nerd in me."

"But you couldn't have," said Sam. "The rock in the cathedral crypt made transmission impossible. My phone didn't work. That's why I had to go up four stories, just to be able to contact Fiona. And even then the call was spotty."

Fiona checked her cell phone. Sure enough, she had received thirty-two photographs from Joe's cell phone. She flicked through a few. At this magnification they were totally incomprehensible, but recognizable as text. When enhanced in size and lighting, they would be easily readable, at least by any scholar of Latin.

"Yeah. I have it all. Maybe I should send this to your home computer, Uncle Mack, just to be safe?"

"Thank you, Fiona darling." Uncle Mack's stricken look was immediately replaced with a beaming smile. "I was afraid that that madman had destroyed any chance I had of ever reading the testament." Then he shook his head. "Of course, he did destroy the original. So there will be an uphill battle just to get people to accept the evidence we have as the truth, and not a made-up rendition of the words of Ephes."

Sam, the inveterate pragmatist, spoke slowly. "But how could your cell work? And from what Fiona has told me, apparently a great gaping hole in your forehead mended itself, virtually instantaneously?"

He looked questioningly at Joe.

"And then there was the matter of the MK47, which was aimed right at you, jamming," said Mack.

Joe shrugged. "I got lucky, I guess." He took a long drink of beer; he too, was wondering what had happened in that undercroft.

Kirby thought, then asked, "Joe, before you began the photographing, you went over to that beam, the wood set in the short stone pillars. Right?" Joe nodded. His uncle went on. "Did you touch it? Did you feel something?"

"Sure," said Joe. "I was just leaning against the beam when I felt what might have been a bit of carving. Under my flashlight it looked...." He paused, went pale, and then continued. "It looked like a cross, stained a dull reddish colour." Then he got it. "Oh my God, the Rose Cross!"

Kirby and Fiona looked stunned; Sam looked confused. Then Fiona went over to Joe, and kissed him lightly on his perfect forehead.

"Thank you for using a miracle to save Uncle Mack," she said.

"And the Testament of Ephes," said Kirby.

"And your gorgeous good-looks," added Fiona. "Sonia would never have forgiven us. But that is three, already. So don't go jumping in front of buses, okay?"

"Right," agreed Joe. Sam still looked confused.

"I'll explain this to you, Sam," said Fiona. "After I walk you home. You look as though you could still do with a helping hand under your elbow." She smiled, a broad open smile, but with a hint of devilry in her eyes. "Don't wait breakfast on me," she called over her shoulder, as she and Sam left the suite.

CHAPTER 73

INNESCARRIG, IRELAND

Air Marshall Patterson had got them to Hatton Royal Air Force Base on an RAF transport, then it was a short flight in his four-seater Cessna, home to Cork.

Kirby had spent their last few days in Spain attending to business as he put it. He visited the hospital where Cardinal Contini was recovering from his abdominal surgery. He would have liked to have questioned His Eminence a second time, but before he could visit the hospital again, Brother Martin had managed to spirit him and a full medical staff away to Rome, on no less than Vatican One, the private jet usually reserved for transporting the Pope and his immediate entourage. Kirby met with Monsignor Torres, mostly to calm that man's rather shaken nerves, and to quietly suggest that no more visitors should be allowed to enter the undercroft of the basilica. That was quickly and vehemently agreed; the Monsignor was not aware of all of the whys and wherefores of what had happened in the church cellar, and truth be told he did not want to know. He was just happy to be healthy and able to again putter about his beloved library. He did say a prayer for His Eminence Cardinal Contini. Kirby made and took phone calls from the USA, some from Sam Wardell. And, he had managed to spend some time translating the enlarged photographs of Bishop Darda's workbook. He had been busy.

Now, safely ensconced in Cliffside House, he was enjoying a

full Irish supper of pot roast with vegetables, served over potatoes mashed with turnips, and all sopped up with hunks of fresh soda bread.

Joe had just finished his plateful, then reached for another serving of the potatoes.

"What do you call this again, Uncle Mack?"

"Clapshot."

"No need to swear," said Fiona with a grin.

"No, really," said Kirby. "It is called clapshot. Glad you like it, Joe. But you should save room for Mary's trifle." He pushed away from the table. "Spanish food is so....so sophisticated. I couldn't wait to get back to real 'grub'." He raised his wine glass, and saluted his two young guests. "Here is to a successful conclusion to our pilgrimage to Santiago de Compostela."

Fiona and Joe raised their glasses, but Fiona looked pensive. "Was it a success? Really?" She was thinking about the RAF crew, and Sam's concussion, which was still bothering him at times, and the shocking attack that Joe and Mack had been put through. "You never did find the scrolls of Ephes. And the original translation was destroyed."

"What was really going on, Uncle Mack? Have you figured it all out?" asked Joe.

Kirby nodded. "Yes, I think so. Now let's clear away dinner, and I will tell all, as they say."

Later, with coffee and the remains of plates of trifle, that delightful sherry-soaked cake with fruit and custard and cream, they sat in Mack's den. With its wood fire, and slightly shabby old leather armchairs, it was cozier than his rather formal living room.

"First the good news," started Kirby. "I have been able to translate some of the Testament of Ephes. It is rather shattering to certain precepts. And that explains why we were all nearly killed. But I will get to that later. You know I saw Cardinal Contini in the hospital. I think he might have been somewhat drugged at the time, which could explain his uncharacteristic forthrightness."

Fiona and Joe both sat forward.

"He has enjoyed virtually full access to the libraries of the Vatican for years. And, from time to time, a student of his would discover a so-far unrecorded document. No surprise there; there must be many thousands of such documents, papyri, scrolls, whatever. One such discovery was a letter, written by Bishop Darda. You remember, the first bishop of the cathedral in Santiago, the man whose tomb we opened. Bishop Darda wrote to his cardinal in Rome, saying that he had discovered some old scrolls in the church which was razed for the construction of the cathedral. He believed the scrolls dated from the original Christian church on the site, dating from the first century. He claimed that the scrolls said that the remains of both Jesus Christ and Mary Magdalene were encased in a marble ossuary, which had been found with the scrolls. He also said he had the ossuary, safe in the cedar chest in which it had been found."

"The cardinal, one Cardinal Legare, was furious, and frightened. He ordered Darda to destroy the ossuary, or cris really. An ossuary is Jewish, and clearly this marble box was Christian, even if Jesus and Mary may not have used that term to describe themselves. Now it gets complicated. And I will skip a lot of those complications; you can ask me later, if you want to."

"It seems Cardinal Legare was very concerned that it would come out that Jesus Christ had married Mary Magdalene, and fathered children in that union. You remember, the early—and even the modern day Catholic church, has been very male-centric. Woman are forbidden to become officiants; certainly not cardinals or bishops, but not even priests. That has been a main stay of the Roman Catholic Church for two millennia. I think things are easing a bit now, but at the time of Cardinal Legare, it would have been blasphemous to suggest that a woman—and the Magdalene at that—had been an important and powerful disciple and the mother of the Christ's children."

"Legare managed to hush things up about the ossuary. It was discovered in a tomb some ten years or so after Bishop Darda's death, and because that man had had the foresight to mark the ossuary as that of Saint James, it was easy for Legare to get the ossuary certified, by the Pope no less, as the reliquary of the bones of St. James. And so it has been since the end of the eleventh century."

"By now, there has been a lot of supposition, perhaps even findings of fact that hold that Jesus the Nazarene did not die on the cross. Contrary to what the four main gospels of the Bible say. The Koran has always stated this. And now, so to do some of the newly-translated Dead Sea scrolls. The son of God not dying for the forgiveness of our sins could be a major stumbling block for Christianity. And for Christianity, read Roman Catholic Church. Christians may not outnumber eastern faiths, but they certainly control the vast majority of the wealth of the western world. And that wealth is what supports the Roman Catholic Church."

He paused. "And, the Congregation of the Holy Baptism."

Joe looked confused. Fiona recognized the name.

Kirby continued. "I will get back to the Congregation. But, back to the Roman Catholics. You have heard me talk about the Order of the Rose Cross, i.e. Templars, i.e. the Priore de Scion, the members of which purportedly protected the seed of Jesus and Mary in their Jewish enclave in Iberia. Those Jews, or early Christians, really, morphed, over centuries, into the Merovingians. The Merovingians married into every royal house in Europe, through strategic planning, and obviously, very attractive young people."

Neither Joe nor Fiona smiled, so Kirby continued. Clearly his young relations were less interested in his humour than in understanding the history of the Christian church. Their loss, he thought, but continued.

"Contini works in a rather secretive branch of the Vatican. He is not a librarian, but has full access there. He is not a diplomat, but devises instructions for the Holy See's worldwide leaders. He is a PR man, but on steroids, as you young people say. He has to produce immediate answers to immediate problems, such as dealing with sexually deviant churchmen, or the poor treatment of indigenous peoples the world over. But, his major task: he has to foreplan the next millennium of the church. He knows things will change, but he is tasked with being ahead of changes, of taking advantage of them. Hence, his interest in the Priory of Scion, and the scrolls that Father Sauniere found, in Rennes-le-Chateau, in 1891. Apparently, the Cardinal thinks, that even if Christ did not die on the cross, — which is certain to be proved beyond doubt very soon— that the fact that his descendants include the members of most of the royal houses of Europe, will mean that all of those nationalities will continue to be Christians, that knowing their prince or princess, or whatever, is a direct descendant of Jesus, will keep those populations forever Christian, and proud to be so. Makes sense, in a weird way."

Fiona and Joe nodded. It did make sense.

"Through his library contacts, Contini knew that the Rennes-le-Chateau scrolls had most probably been lost there by Bishop Darda, who was carrying them to Rome when he was waylaid and killed. The Roman Catholic bishops and lower churchmen were forever writing to the Vatican, and Contini has recovered letters from Darda, showing that he was planning that fateful trip. So, then I became interested in Santiago de Compostela, for a completely different reason—remember, I came here because I had translated a heavily redacted version of part of the Testament of Ephes, and I knew that an Ephes had been in Santiago in the first century. Anyway, Contini became interested in me. He wanted me to come here. He thought I might have more luck uncovering the ancient scrolls. I do have a reputation for such things. I think he thought I would find the three lost original scrolls. Not that I would discover a Latin translation of all of them."

"So he set Brother Martin on you?" asked Fiona. "The faked shots in your woods, the hacking of your computer?"

"The first yes. The second maybe not. But Brother Martin was definitely sent to Ireland to get me moving. How could I stay here, when I was under an attack, subtle perhaps, but an attack none the less?"

"So, the Vatican, or at least its PR man, Contini, wanted to get you to find the original Testament of Ephes. Then what?"

Kirby continued. "The Vatican already has two of Ephes' scrolls, purchased by the Hapsburgs, in 1891. Contini wanted the other three. The first two had to be pretty explosive, for him to go to such lengths. And that is where the two armed men who met us in the crypt come in. Brother Martin is good, but he is one man. Contini thought he needed extra help so he hired those goons." Here he paused for effect. "Who were actually working for the Congregation of the Holy Baptism, the whole time."

"What?" echoed from both of his guests. Then Fiona continued, "But Sam wasn't working with them, was he?"

"No. No he wasn't. He did suspect that the Congregation had other people working here. Remember, how he warned us about the plane crash, how someone was after the price on our heads? He did recognize them when he saw them, as muscle who had worked for him, on Congregation jobs."

Joe nodded. "But how did they get Contini to hire Congregation heavies?"

Kirby sighed. "The old-guard American heavies are not that distanced from Italy, if you know what I mean. Once the Congregation knew that Contini wanted me to find the scrolls, and that looked like a real possibility, its head council decided it was time to terminate me. And you."

"But how did they know, about Contini and you?"

"The Congregation of the Holy Baptism is not only the most powerful church in America. It is the most powerful user, manipulator and hacker of the internet, in the world. Apparently some genius, years ago, realized what a tool the internet could be; they got in early and have stayed ahead of everyone. Remember when I said I sensed a "presence" in my computer, when I was accessing the Quhram scrolls? On a supposedly secure site? That was the Congregation."

"Are they also the ones behind the misinformation on the net? All the trashing of those books you told us about?"

"Absolutely. Even before the internet, they would hire so-called experts to debunk any publication which attacked the premises of their church. There have been some fine and scholarly works which have simply gone out of print because of such 'impartial' reviews."

"And, no doubt, pressure on the publishers," added Joe.

"And now it is even easier for them. They simply manipulate all web information. You might be able to see a documentary saying, for instance, that the Jesus story is an amalgam of the main gods of earlier sun-worshipping religions. Next week, you won't find that film, anywhere. Gone. And when its producers put it out there again, again it is taken down. The Congregation has huge resources. And, it seems, it does not embrace change. It does not want one word of the Bible altered. It has preached, for over a century now, that the bible, as published today, is the word of God. Period. No room for interpretation or allegory."

"Yeah," said Fiona thoughtfully. "At a party once I asked a Baptist how God could write in English, when that language hadn't been invented yet. I was asked to leave. Didn't even get to finish my mushroom cap. It was stuffed with cheap cheese anyway." She shrugged.

Kirby continued. "Anyway, Contini led his goons to the crypt, thinking they would help him take the scrolls from me. Contini did not want us harmed, but the Congregationists' plan all along was to have them destroy the scrolls, and us."

"But you never found the scrolls. Or did you?" Joe asked.

"No, I never did. And I doubt I will." He looked pensive, then nodded slightly, as though to himself. "But who knows? Contini has been paying treasure hunters, for years, to search around Rennes-le-Chateau. And he sends his minions into the unrecorded documents section of the Vatican libraries. He has had no luck. But I do have Bishop Darda's translation of the testament. All five scrolls are deciphered in his workbook."

"That has been confusing me. Sometimes you refer to four scrolls, and now five. How many are there?"

"I know there were five, because of Darda's translation. But I believe he took only four with him, on his trip to Rome. The fifth was too much, even for him. He knew it would never be accepted by his church, and that even the mere possession of it could mean his death."

"At the hands of his own church fathers?"

"Especially by them," confirmed Kirby gravely.

"So what now?" asked Fiona.

"Now you two can go home, safely, to the States. You might want to stop off in Charleston, Fiona." He grinned, and she blushed. "Seriously, Sam has been assisting. He is not the man he pretends to be. He does work for the Congregation, but under the aegis of his real employer. He might even commit murder, from time to time, but the victim is always quite deserving of a hastened demise. Very deserving." He muttered the last remark under his breath. He was still unable to fathom that a reverend of the Congregation, or of any church, could do such things to innocent children. Wardell had told Kirby a lot in the last week.

"What will you do, Uncle Mack?"

"I will plod about my garden, generally annoy Mary, age gracefully and write the first draft of the Testament of Ephes, with footnotes, copious footnotes."

"Will you include the fifth scroll" asked Joe.

Kirby looked into the flames of their fire. "Yes. Yes of course. It would not be right to omit anything. Not scholarly." He looked up at Joe and Fiona and smiled reassuringly. "Sam has neutralized the Congregation of the Holy Baptism. Seems he has 'stuff' on its Archreverend and the Council. As does Neil Patterson, come to that. The Congregationists are not happy, but their claws are sheathed for now. Contini might raise his head again, when he recovers from his gunshot wound. But as a group we scholarly types do not take well to violence. He is not a bad man; just made a bad staffing choice. I think he will keep himself busy devising ways to keep my text from causing any fire alarms in the Roman Catholic Church."

"And will it? Cause alarm?"

"Yes it will."

Fiona leaned forward. "So the testament goes beyond saying that Jesus and Mary Magdalene raised a family in Spain?"

"Far beyond. Far, far beyond." He stood and walked to a sideboard. "Now, who would like a drink? I still have a smidgen of a very fine single malt. Or perhaps, champagne, this evening?"

THE END

Printed in the United States
By Bookmasters